Oddly ★ Normal

WRITTEN & ILLUSTRATED
by OTIS FRAMPTON

IMAGE COMICS, INC.

TODD MCFARLANE ★ PRESIDENT
JIM VALENTINO ★ VICE PRESIDENT
MARC SILVESTRI ★ CHIEF EXECUTIVE OFFICER
ERIK LARSEN ★ CHIEF FINANCIAL OFFICER
ROBERT KIRKMAN ★ CHIEF OPERATING OFFICER

ERIC STEPHENSON ★ PUBLISHER / CHIEF CREATIVE OFFICER
NICOLE LAPALME ★ CONTROLLER
LEANNA CAUNTER ★ ACCOUNTING ANALYST
SUE KORPELA ★ ACCOUNTING & HR MANAGER
MARLA EIZIK ★ TALENT LIAISON
JEFF BOISON ★ DIRECTOR OF SALES & PUBLISHING PLANNING
DIRK WOOD ★ DIRECTOR OF INTERNATIONAL SALES & LICENSING
ALEX COX ★ DIRECTOR OF DIRECT MARKET SALES
CHLOE RAMOS ★ BOOK MARKET & LIBRARY SALES MANAGER
EMILIO BAUTISTA ★ DIGITAL SALES COORDINATOR
JON SCHLAFFMAN ★ SPECIALTY SALES COORDINATOR
KAT SALAZAR ★ DIRECTOR OF PR & MARKETING
DREW FITZGERALD ★ MARKETING CONTENT ASSOCIATE
HEATHER DOORNINK ★ PRODUCTION DIRECTOR
DREW GILL ★ ART DIRECTOR
HILARY DILORETO ★ PRINT MANAGER
TRICIA RAMOS ★ TRAFFIC MANAGER
MELISSA GIFFORD ★ CONTENT MANAGER
ERIKA SCHNATZ ★ SENIOR PRODUCTION ARTIST
RYAN BREWER ★ PRODUCTION ARTIST
DEANNA PHELPS ★ PRODUCTION ARTIST
IMAGECOMICS.COM

Chapter 16

Idle Tears & Banana Lures

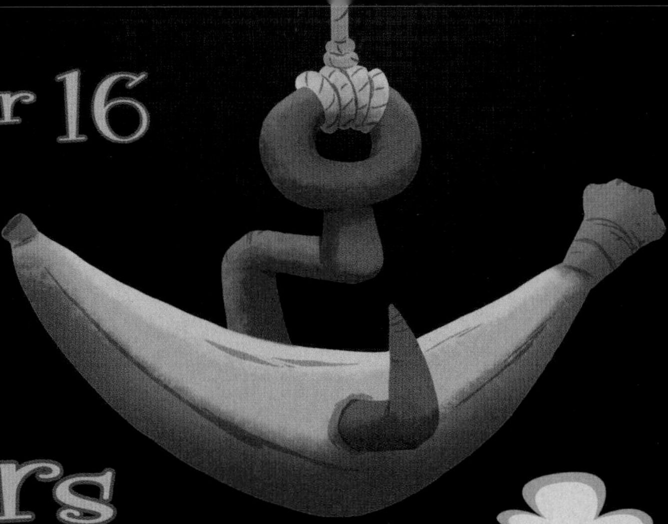

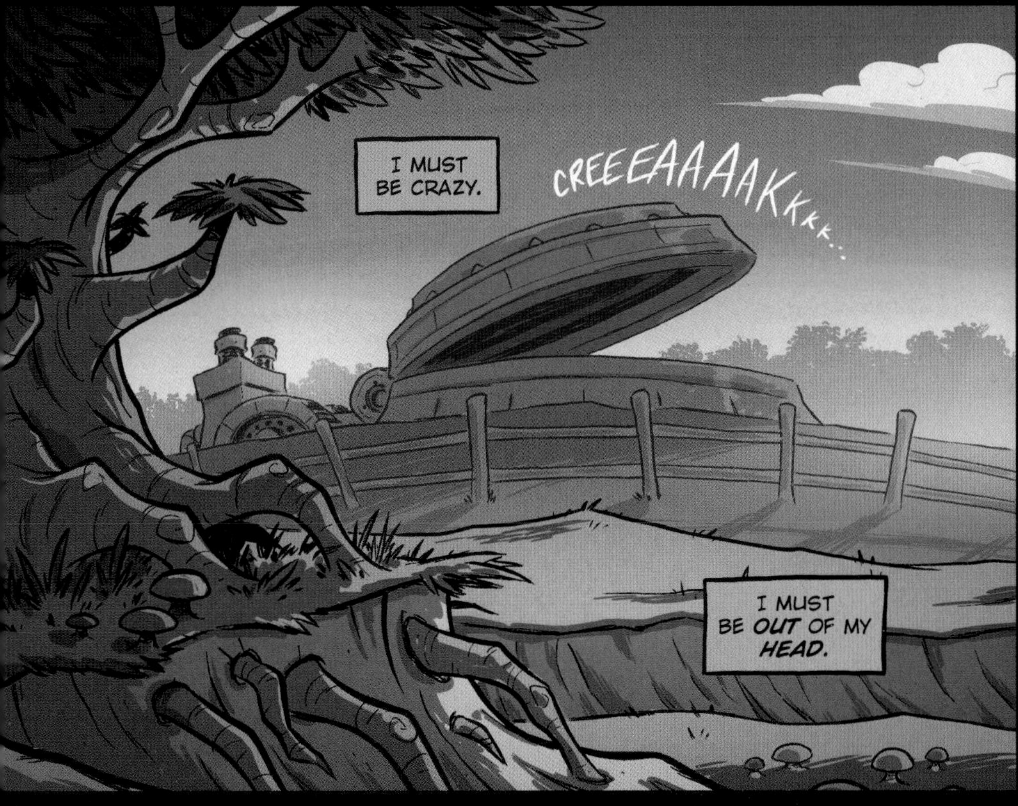
I MUST BE CRAZY.
CREEEAAAAAKKKK...
I MUST BE OUT OF MY HEAD.

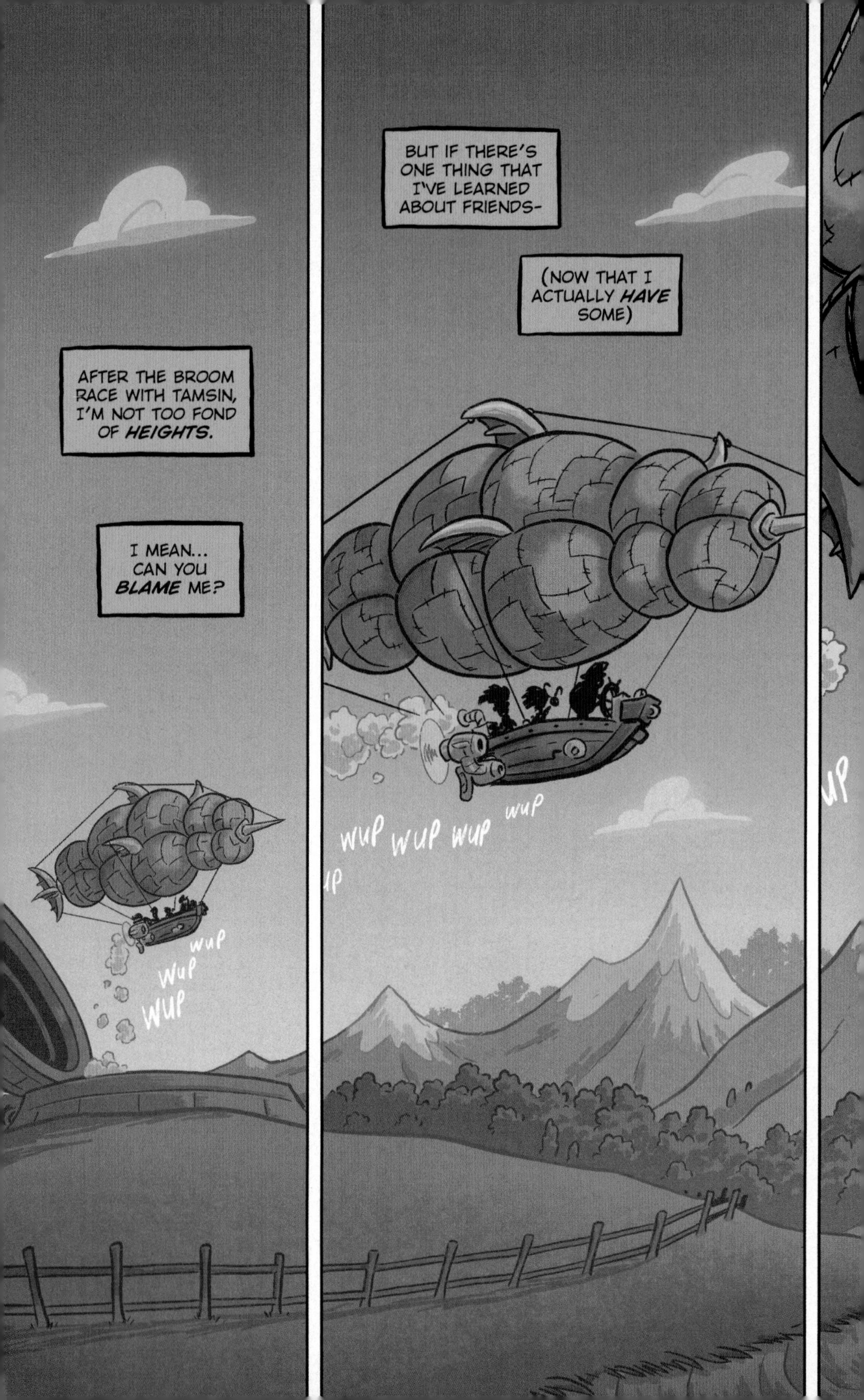
AFTER THE BROOM RACE WITH TAMSIN, I'M NOT TOO FOND OF HEIGHTS.
I MEAN... CAN YOU BLAME ME?
WUP
WUP
WUP
BUT IF THERE'S ONE THING THAT I'VE LEARNED ABOUT FRIENDS-
(NOW THAT I ACTUALLY HAVE SOME)
WUP WUP WUP WUP

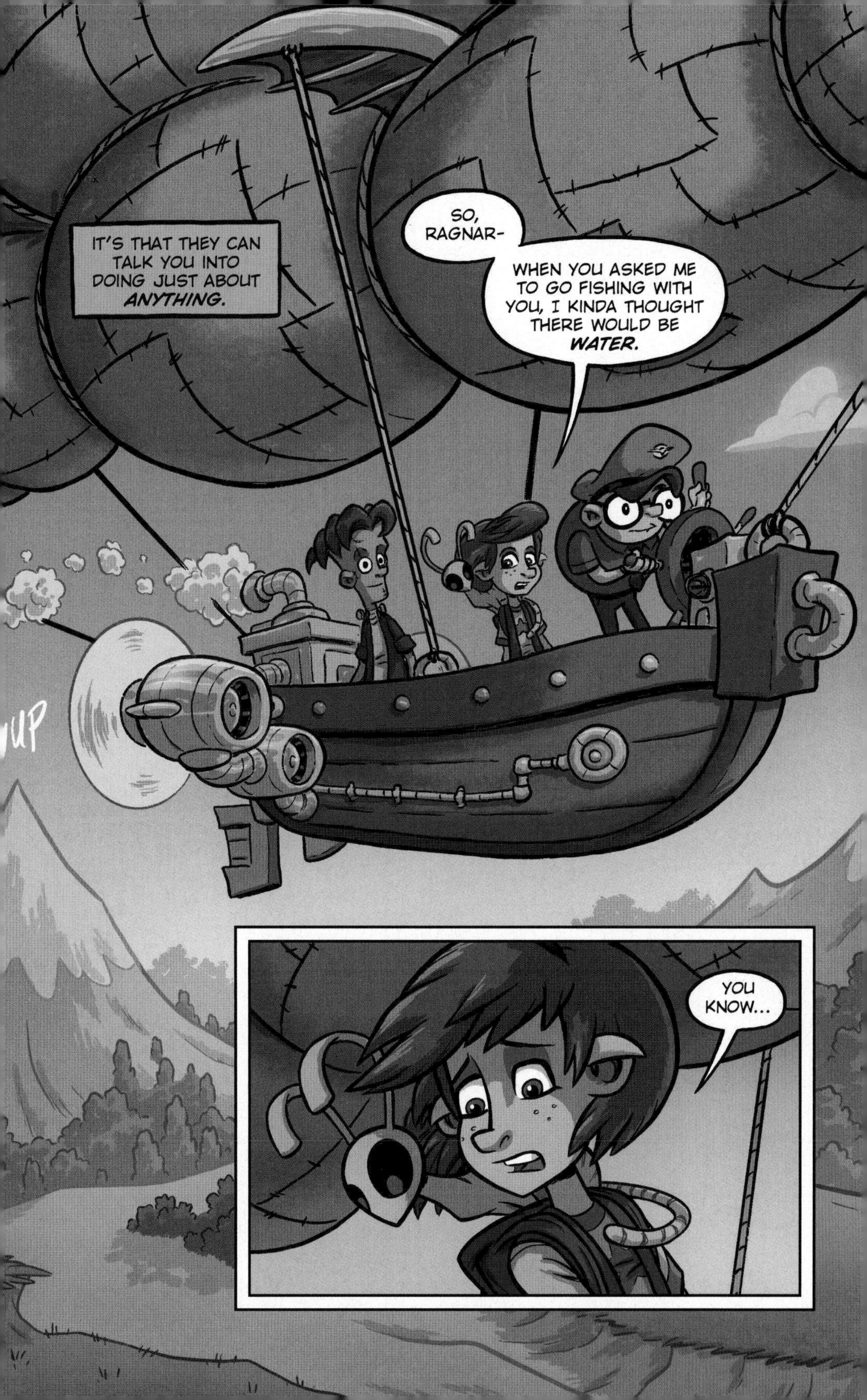
IT'S THAT THEY CAN TALK YOU INTO DOING JUST ABOUT *ANYTHING*.
SO, RAGNAR-
WHEN YOU ASKED ME TO GO FISHING WITH YOU, I KINDA THOUGHT THERE WOULD BE *WATER*.
YOU KNOW...

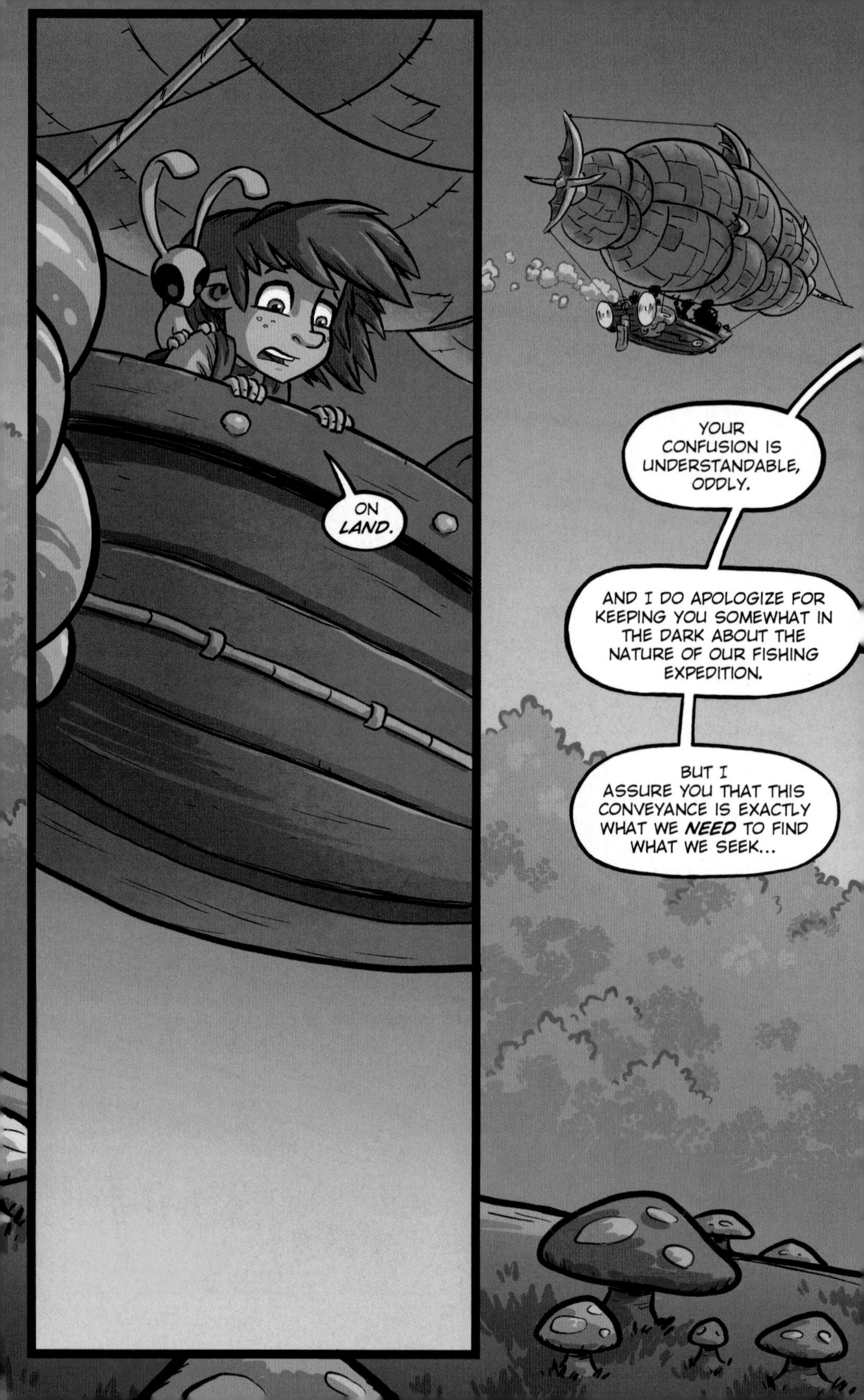
ON *LAND.*
YOUR CONFUSION IS UNDERSTANDABLE, ODDLY.
AND I DO APOLOGIZE FOR KEEPING YOU SOMEWHAT IN THE DARK ABOUT THE NATURE OF OUR FISHING EXPEDITION.
BUT I ASSURE YOU THAT THIS CONVEYANCE IS EXACTLY WHAT WE *NEED* TO FIND WHAT WE SEEK...

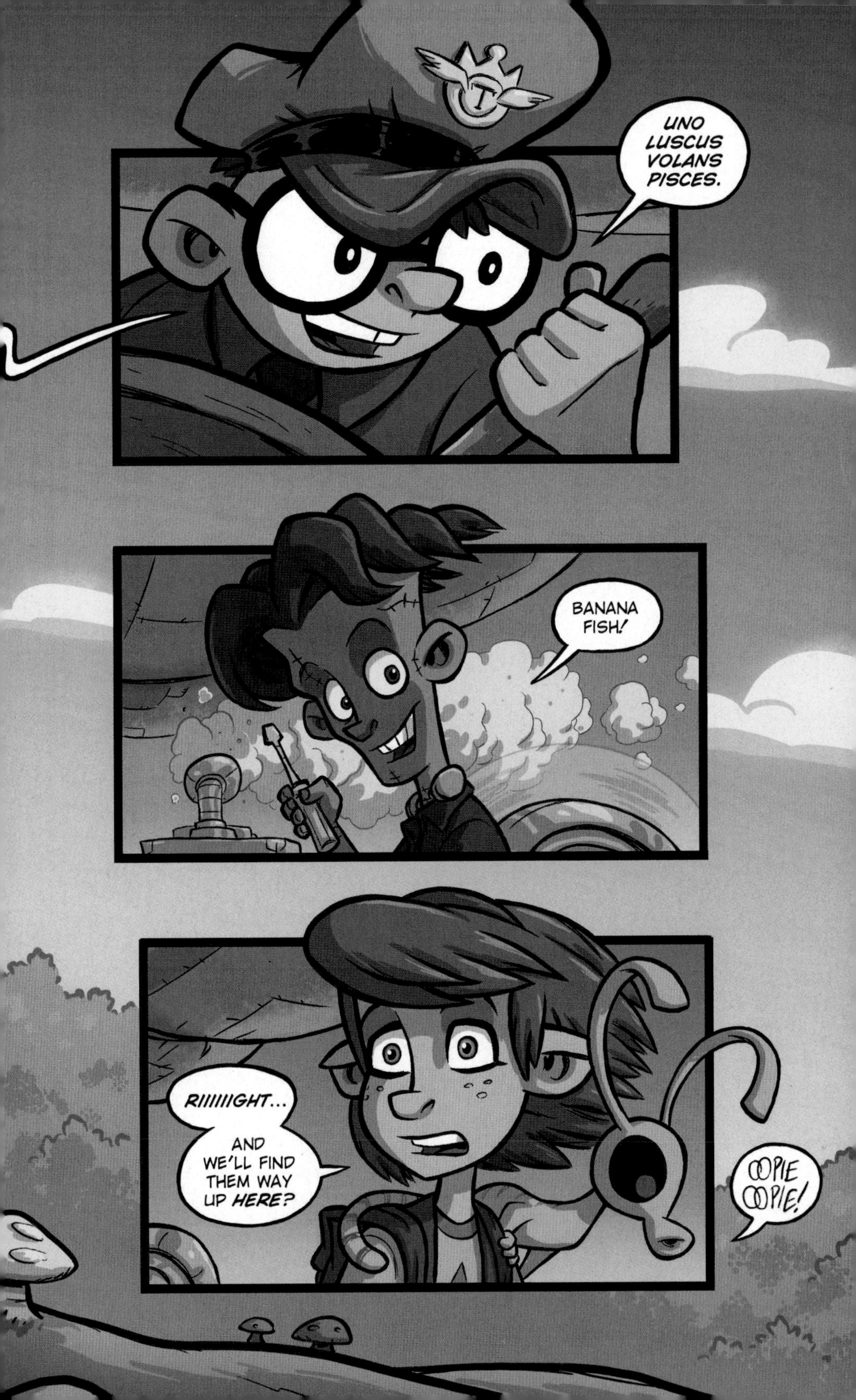
UNO LUSCUS VOLANS PISCES.
BANANA FISH!
RIIIIIIGHT...
AND WE'LL FIND THEM WAY UP HERE?
OOPIE OOPIE!

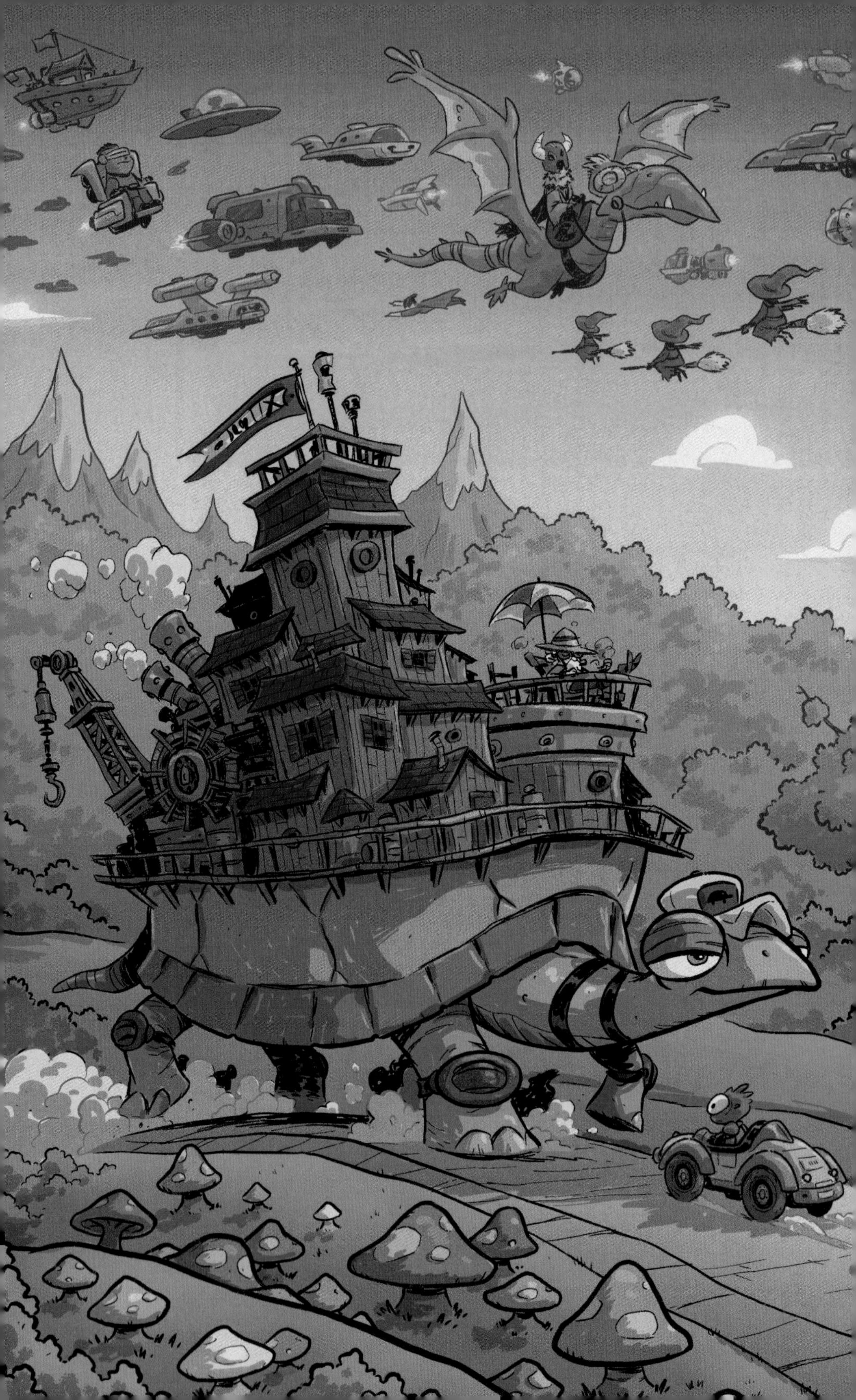

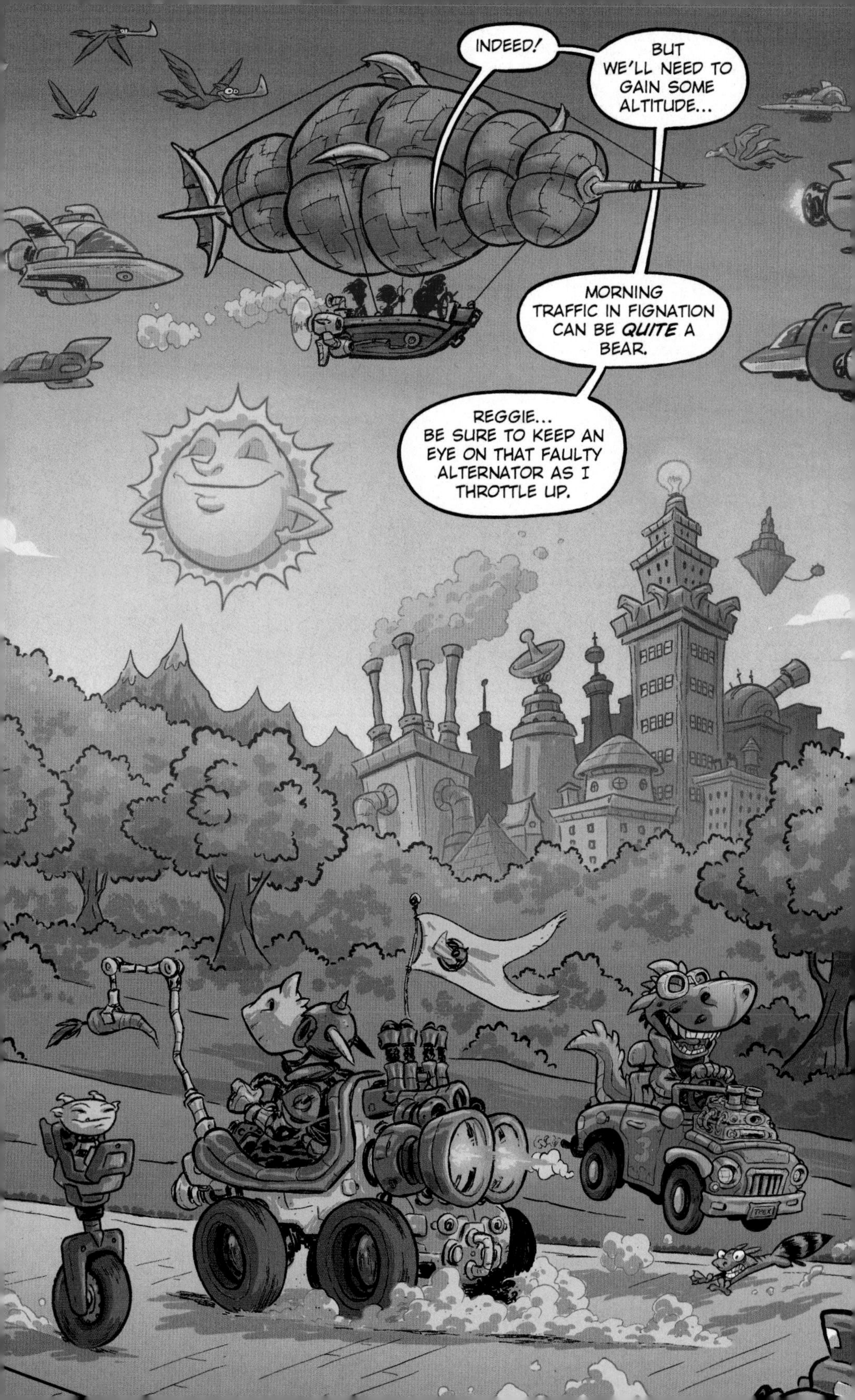
INDEED!
BUT WE'LL NEED TO GAIN SOME ALTITUDE...
MORNING TRAFFIC IN FIGNATION CAN BE *QUITE* A BEAR.
REGGIE... BE SURE TO KEEP AN EYE ON THAT FAULTY ALTERNATOR AS I THROTTLE UP.

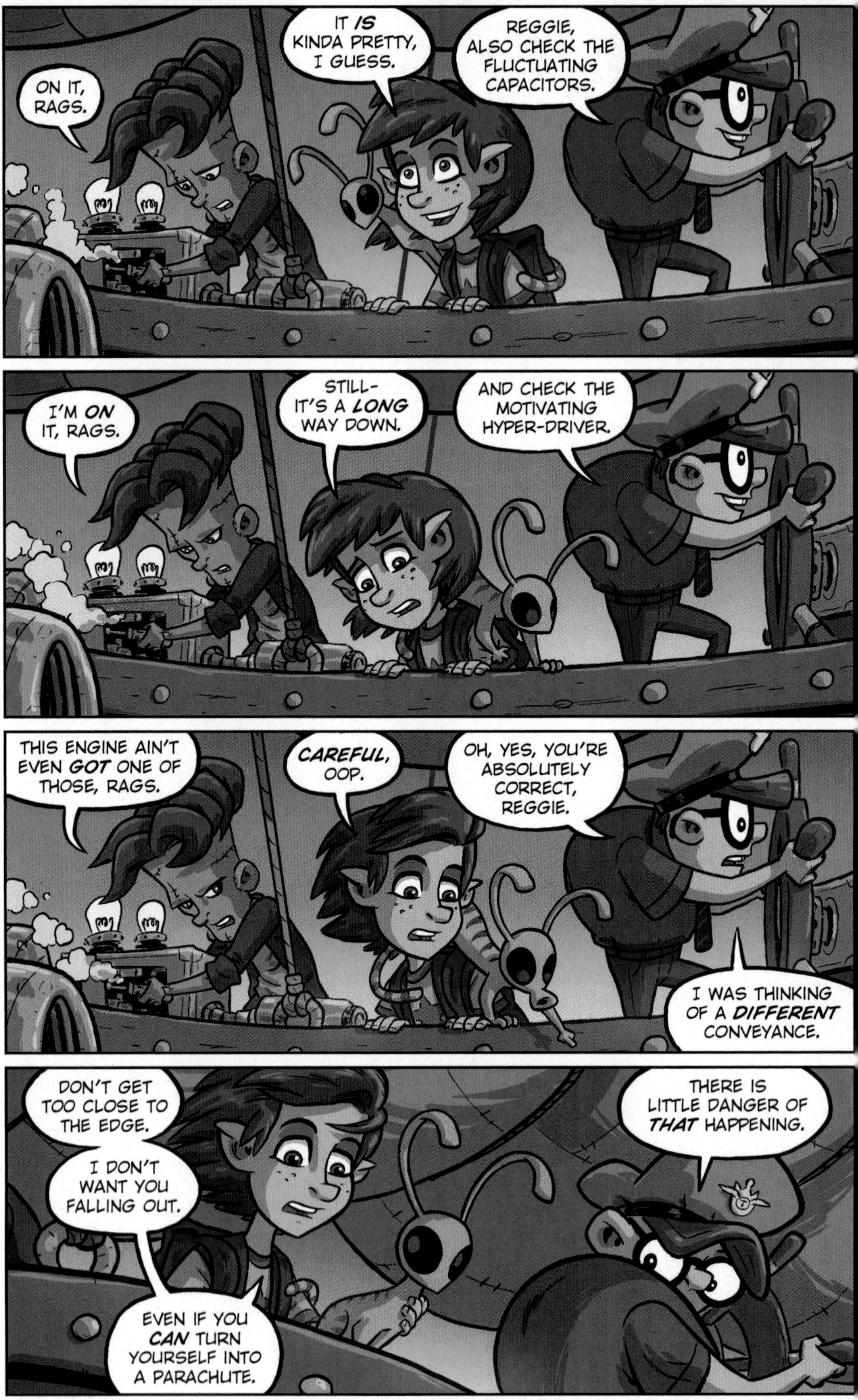
ON IT, RAGS.
IT IS KINDA PRETTY, I GUESS.
REGGIE, ALSO CHECK THE FLUCTUATING CAPACITORS.
I'M ON IT, RAGS.
STILL- IT'S A LONG WAY DOWN.
AND CHECK THE MOTIVATING HYPER-DRIVER.
THIS ENGINE AIN'T EVEN GOT ONE OF THOSE, RAGS.
CAREFUL, OOP.
OH, YES, YOU'RE ABSOLUTELY CORRECT, REGGIE.
I WAS THINKING OF A DIFFERENT CONVEYANCE.
DON'T GET TOO CLOSE TO THE EDGE.
I DON'T WANT YOU FALLING OUT.
EVEN IF YOU CAN TURN YOURSELF INTO A PARACHUTE.
THERE IS LITTLE DANGER OF THAT HAPPENING.

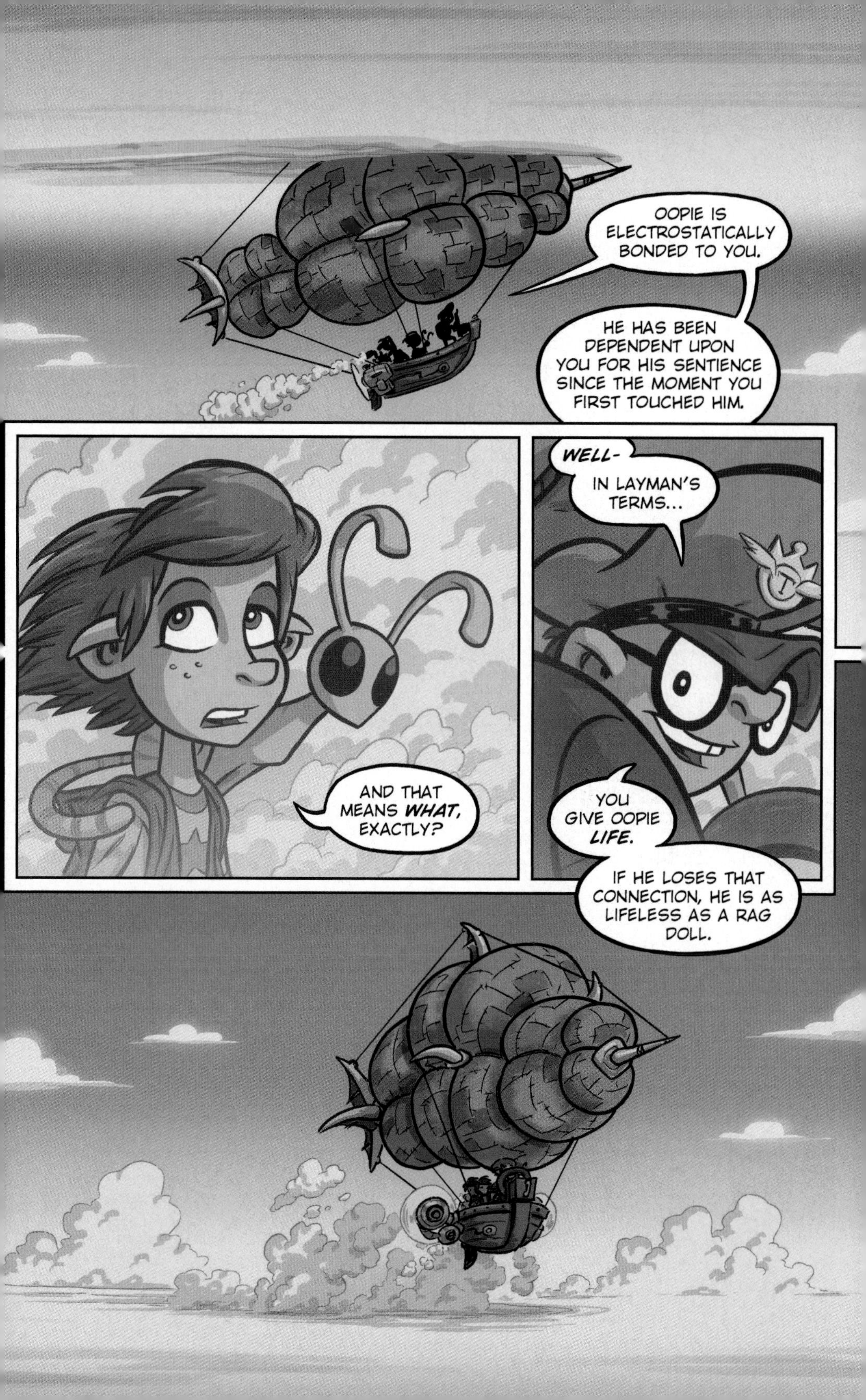
OOPIE IS ELECTROSTATICALLY BONDED TO YOU.
HE HAS BEEN DEPENDENT UPON YOU FOR HIS SENTIENCE SINCE THE MOMENT YOU FIRST TOUCHED HIM.
AND THAT MEANS *WHAT,* EXACTLY?
WELL-
IN LAYMAN'S TERMS...
YOU GIVE OOPIE *LIFE.*
IF HE LOSES THAT CONNECTION, HE IS AS LIFELESS AS A RAG DOLL.

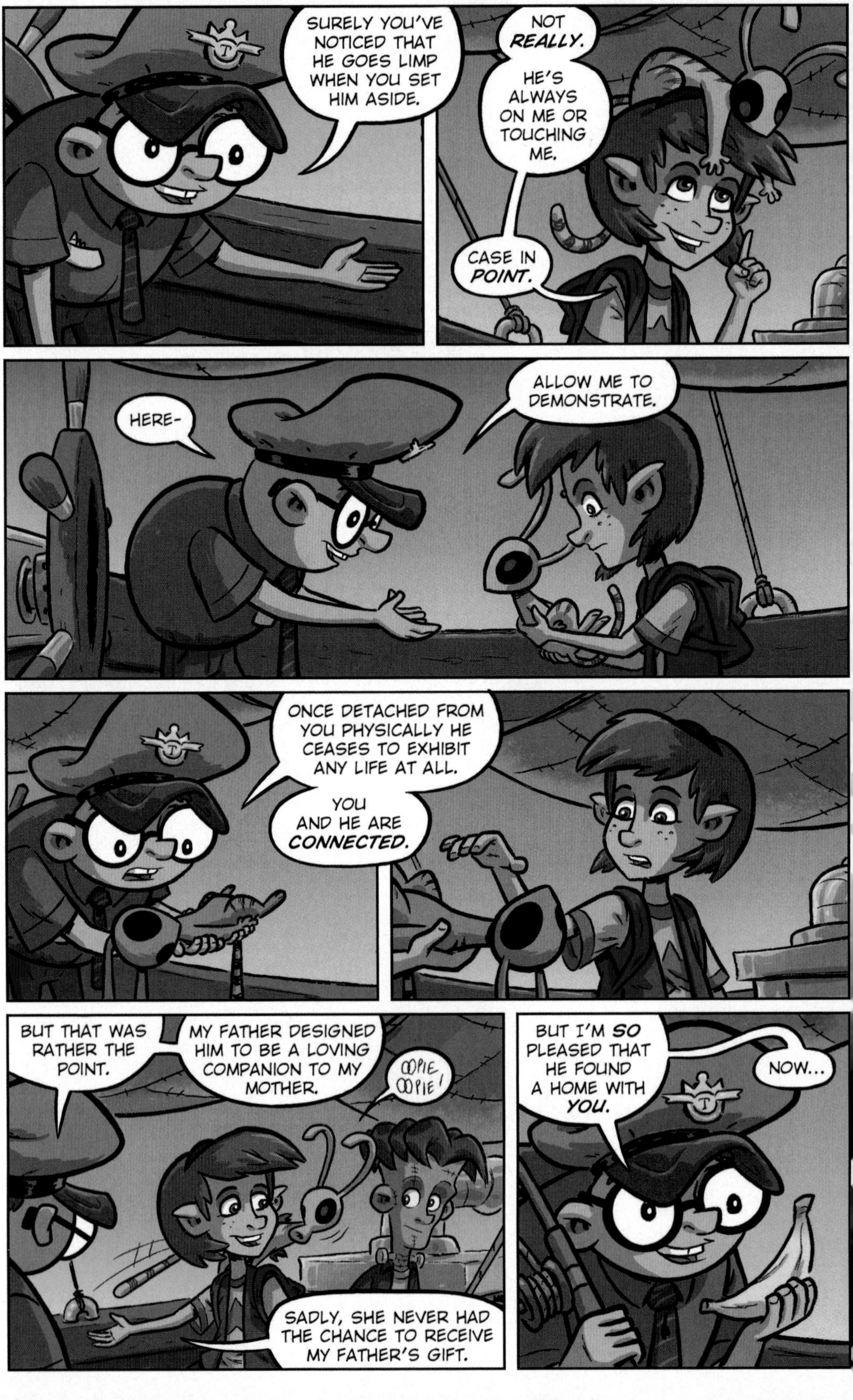
SURELY YOU'VE NOTICED THAT HE GOES LIMP WHEN YOU SET HIM ASIDE.
NOT *REALLY.*
HE'S ALWAYS ON ME OR TOUCHING ME.
CASE IN *POINT.*
HERE-
ALLOW ME TO DEMONSTRATE.
ONCE DETACHED FROM YOU PHYSICALLY HE CEASES TO EXHIBIT ANY LIFE AT ALL.
YOU AND HE ARE *CONNECTED.*
BUT THAT WAS RATHER THE POINT.
MY FATHER DESIGNED HIM TO BE A LOVING COMPANION TO MY MOTHER.
OOPIE OOPIE!
SADLY, SHE NEVER HAD THE CHANCE TO RECEIVE MY FATHER'S GIFT.
BUT I'M *SO* PLEASED THAT HE FOUND A HOME WITH *YOU.*
NOW...

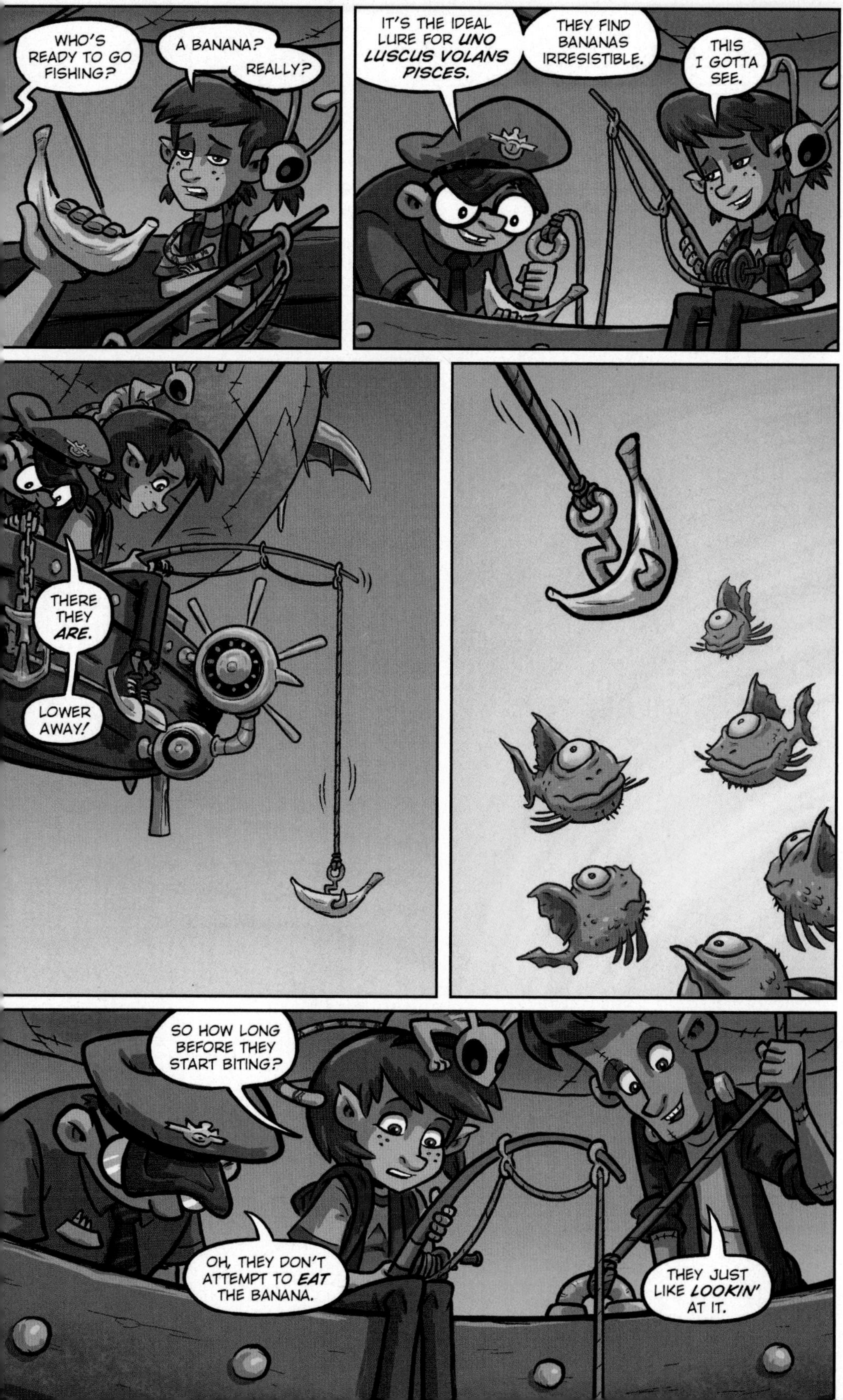
WHO'S READY TO GO FISHING?
A BANANA?
REALLY?
IT'S THE IDEAL LURE FOR *UNO LUSCUS VOLANS PISCES.*
THEY FIND BANANAS IRRESISTIBLE.
THIS I GOTTA SEE.
THERE THEY *ARE.*
LOWER AWAY!
SO HOW LONG BEFORE THEY START BITING?
OH, THEY DON'T ATTEMPT TO *EAT* THE BANANA.
THEY JUST LIKE *LOOKIN'* AT IT.

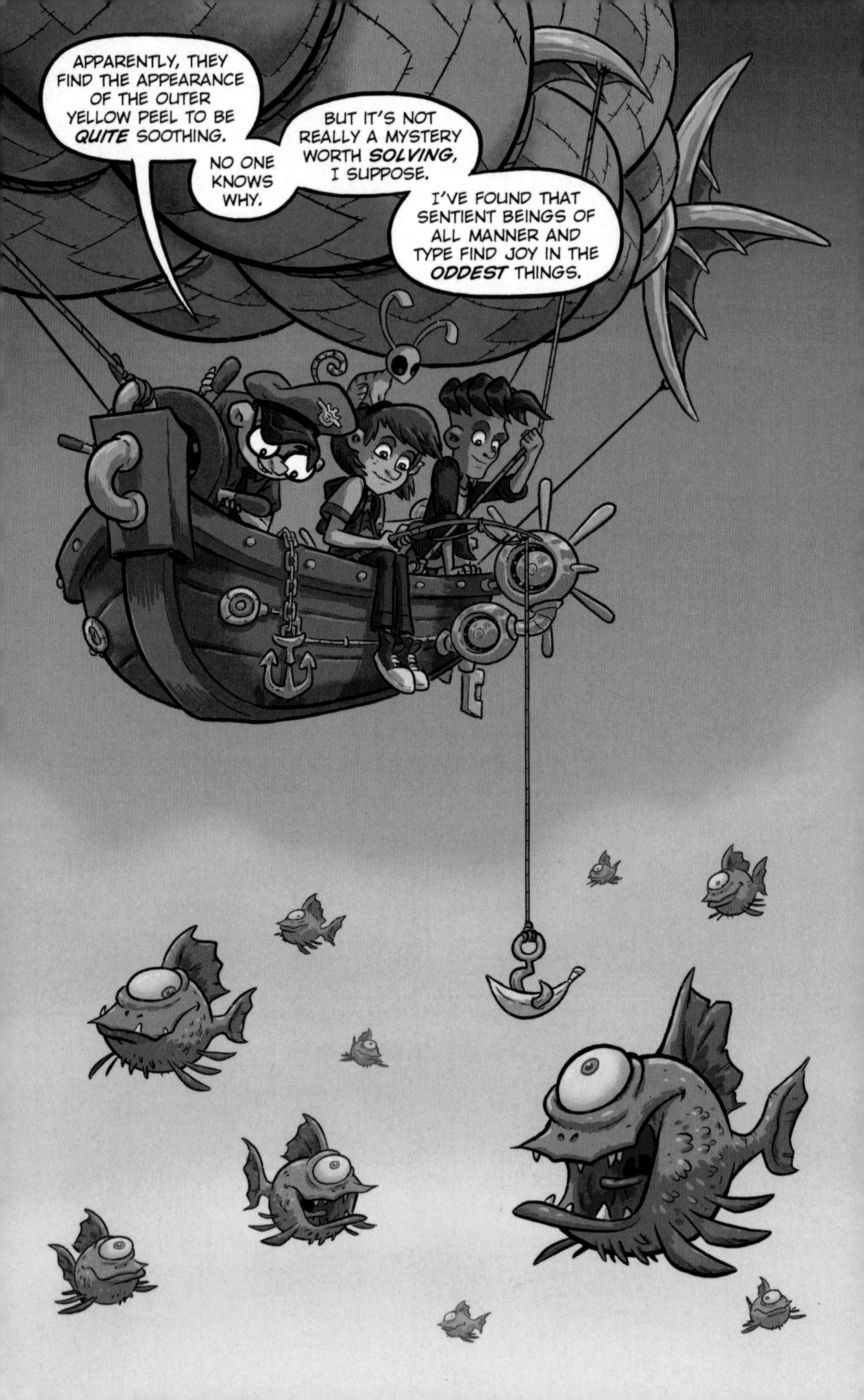
APPARENTLY, THEY FIND THE APPEARANCE OF THE OUTER YELLOW PEEL TO BE *QUITE* SOOTHING.
NO ONE KNOWS WHY.
BUT IT'S NOT REALLY A MYSTERY WORTH *SOLVING,* I SUPPOSE.
I'VE FOUND THAT SENTIENT BEINGS OF ALL MANNER AND TYPE FIND JOY IN THE *ODDEST* THINGS.

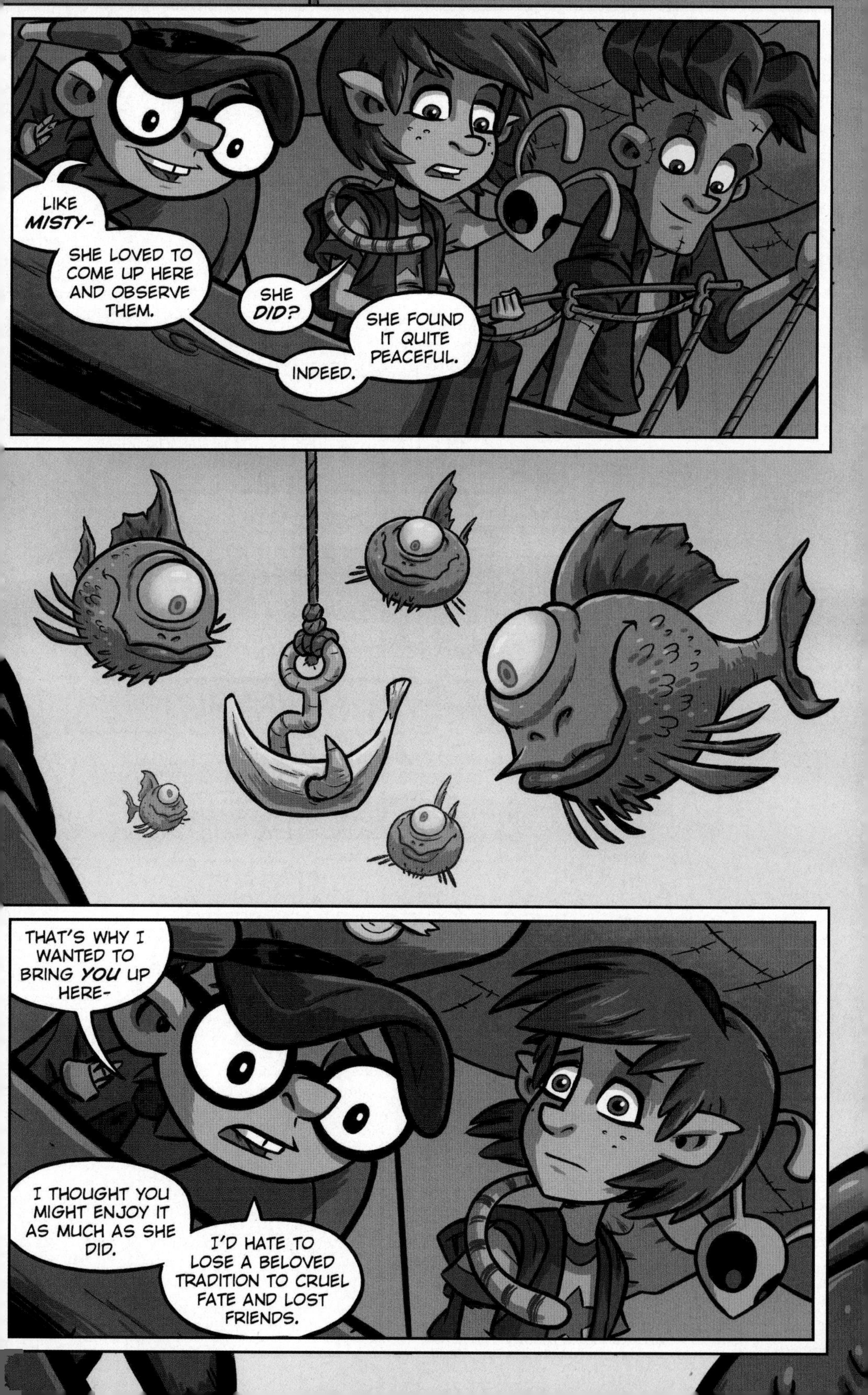
LIKE *MISTY*-
SHE LOVED TO COME UP HERE AND OBSERVE THEM.
SHE *DID*?
INDEED.
SHE FOUND IT QUITE PEACEFUL.
THAT'S WHY I WANTED TO BRING *YOU* UP HERE-
I THOUGHT YOU MIGHT ENJOY IT AS MUCH AS SHE DID.
I'D HATE TO LOSE A BELOVED TRADITION TO CRUEL FATE AND LOST FRIENDS.

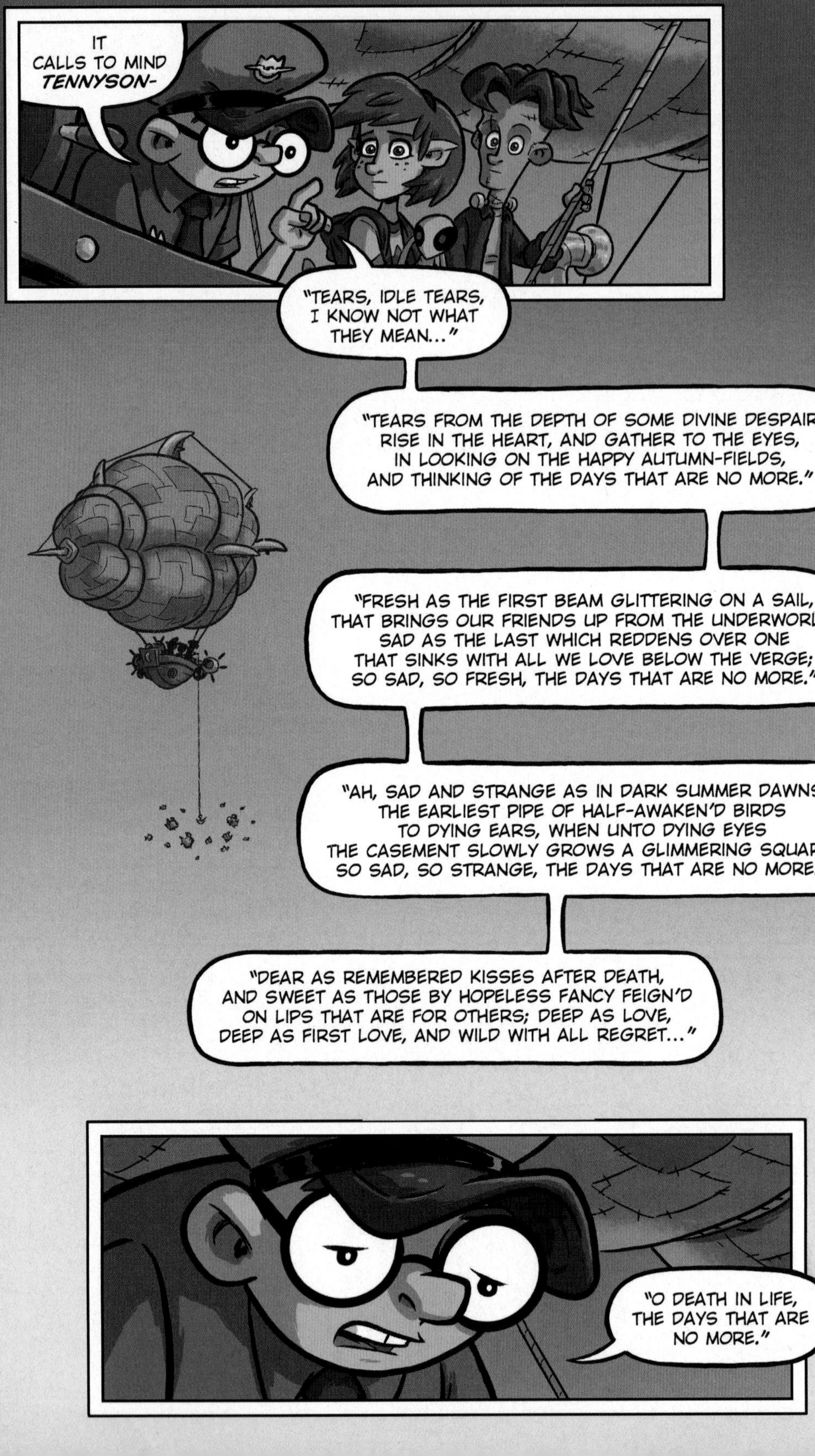
IT CALLS TO MIND *TENNYSON*-
"TEARS, IDLE TEARS, I KNOW NOT WHAT THEY MEAN..."
"TEARS FROM THE DEPTH OF SOME DIVINE DESPAIR RISE IN THE HEART, AND GATHER TO THE EYES, IN LOOKING ON THE HAPPY AUTUMN-FIELDS, AND THINKING OF THE DAYS THAT ARE NO MORE."
"FRESH AS THE FIRST BEAM GLITTERING ON A SAIL, THAT BRINGS OUR FRIENDS UP FROM THE UNDERWORLD, SAD AS THE LAST WHICH REDDENS OVER ONE THAT SINKS WITH ALL WE LOVE BELOW THE VERGE; SO SAD, SO FRESH, THE DAYS THAT ARE NO MORE."
"AH, SAD AND STRANGE AS IN DARK SUMMER DAWNS THE EARLIEST PIPE OF HALF-AWAKEN'D BIRDS TO DYING EARS, WHEN UNTO DYING EYES THE CASEMENT SLOWLY GROWS A GLIMMERING SQUARE; SO SAD, SO STRANGE, THE DAYS THAT ARE NO MORE."
"DEAR AS REMEMBERED KISSES AFTER DEATH, AND SWEET AS THOSE BY HOPELESS FANCY FEIGN'D ON LIPS THAT ARE FOR OTHERS; DEEP AS LOVE, DEEP AS FIRST LOVE, AND WILD WITH ALL REGRET..."
"O DEATH IN LIFE, THE DAYS THAT ARE NO MORE."

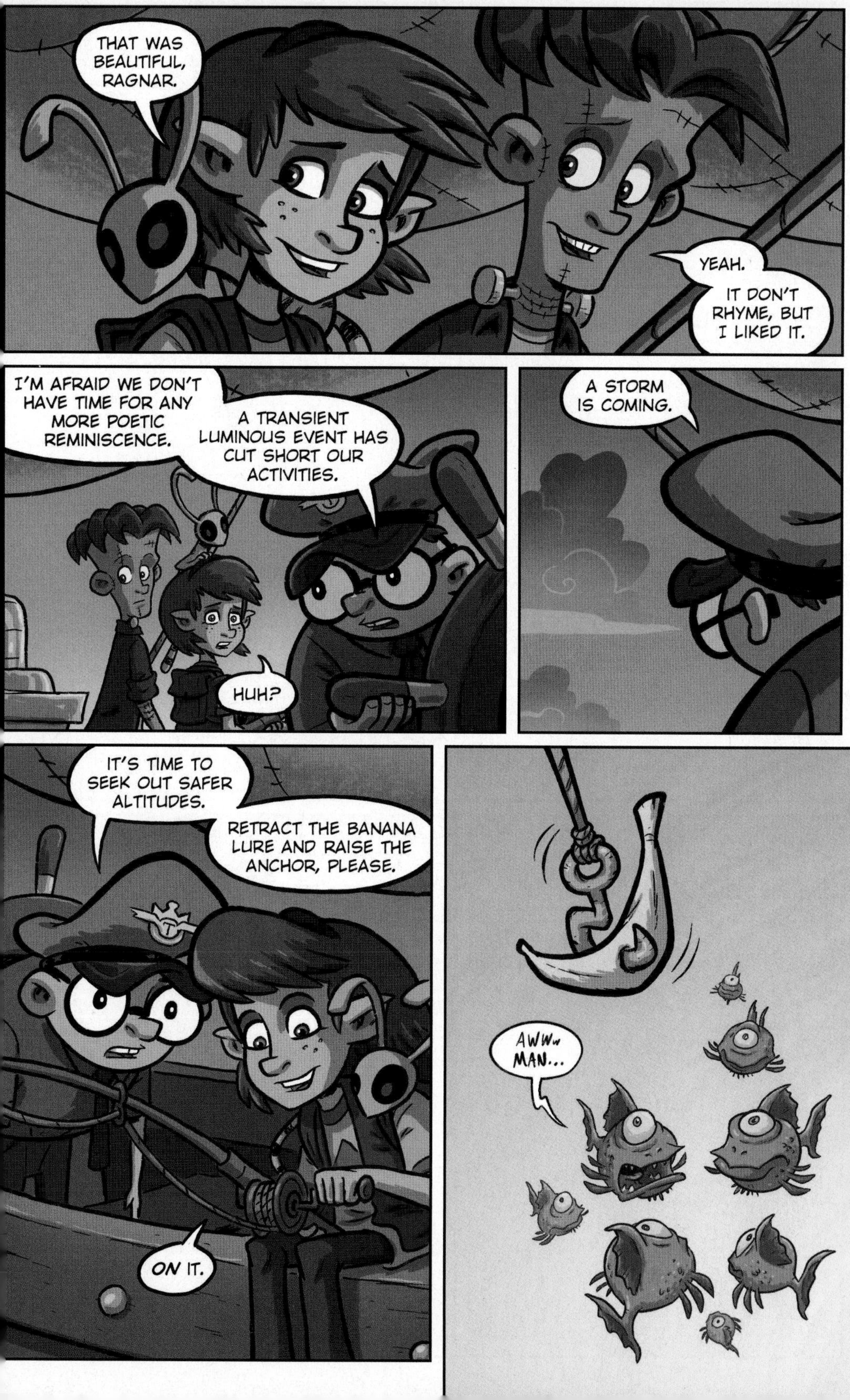
THAT WAS BEAUTIFUL, RAGNAR.
YEAH.
IT DON'T RHYME, BUT I LIKED IT.
I'M AFRAID WE DON'T HAVE TIME FOR ANY MORE POETIC REMINISCENCE.
A TRANSIENT LUMINOUS EVENT HAS CUT SHORT OUR ACTIVITIES.
HUH?
A STORM IS COMING.
IT'S TIME TO SEEK OUT SAFER ALTITUDES.
RETRACT THE BANANA LURE AND RAISE THE ANCHOR, PLEASE.
ON IT.
AWWw MAN...

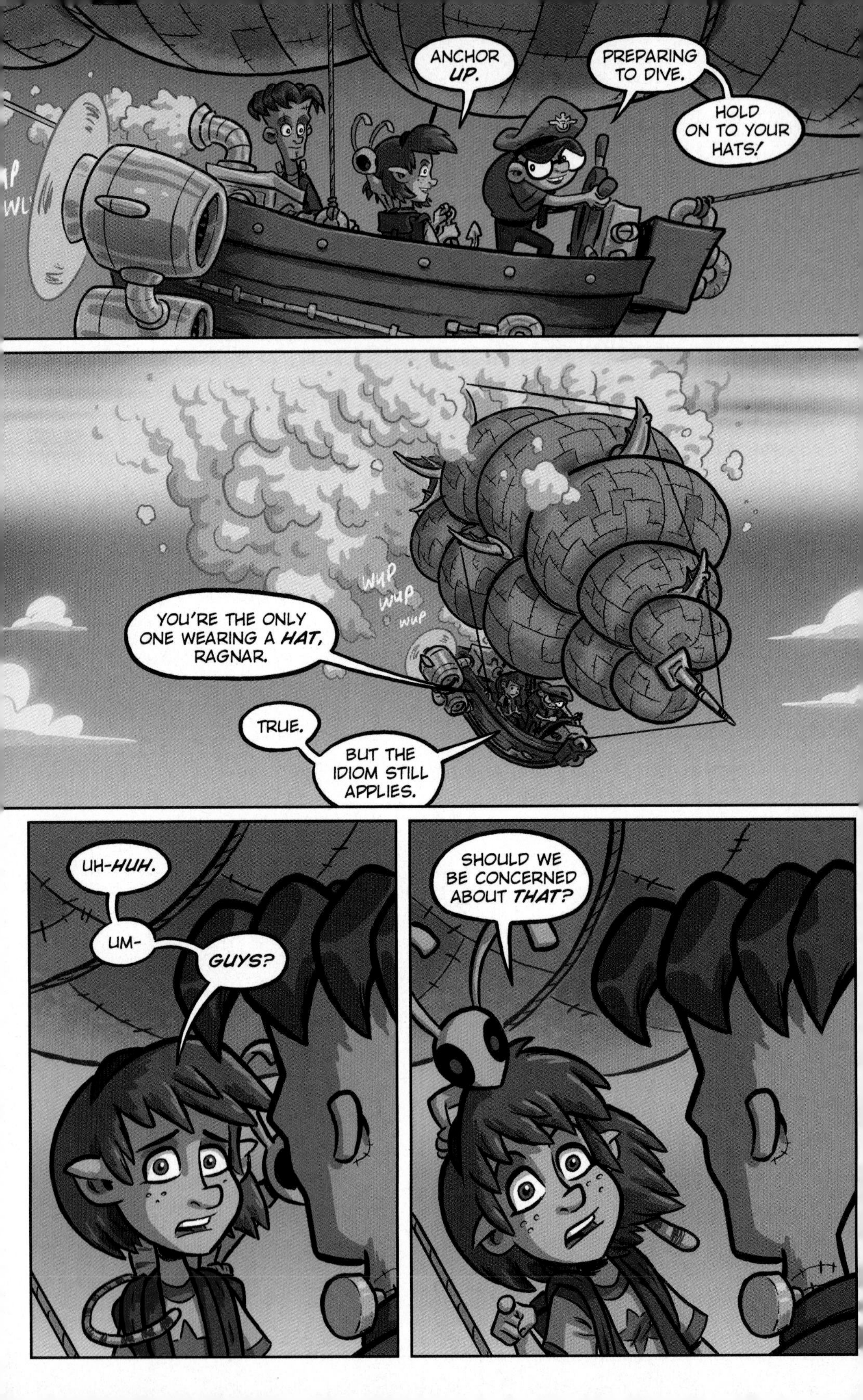
ANCHOR *UP*.
PREPARING TO DIVE.
HOLD ON TO YOUR HATS!
WUP
WUP
WUP
YOU'RE THE ONLY ONE WEARING A *HAT*, RAGNAR.
TRUE.
BUT THE IDIOM STILL APPLIES.
UH-*HUH*.
UM-
GUYS?
SHOULD WE BE CONCERNED ABOUT *THAT?*

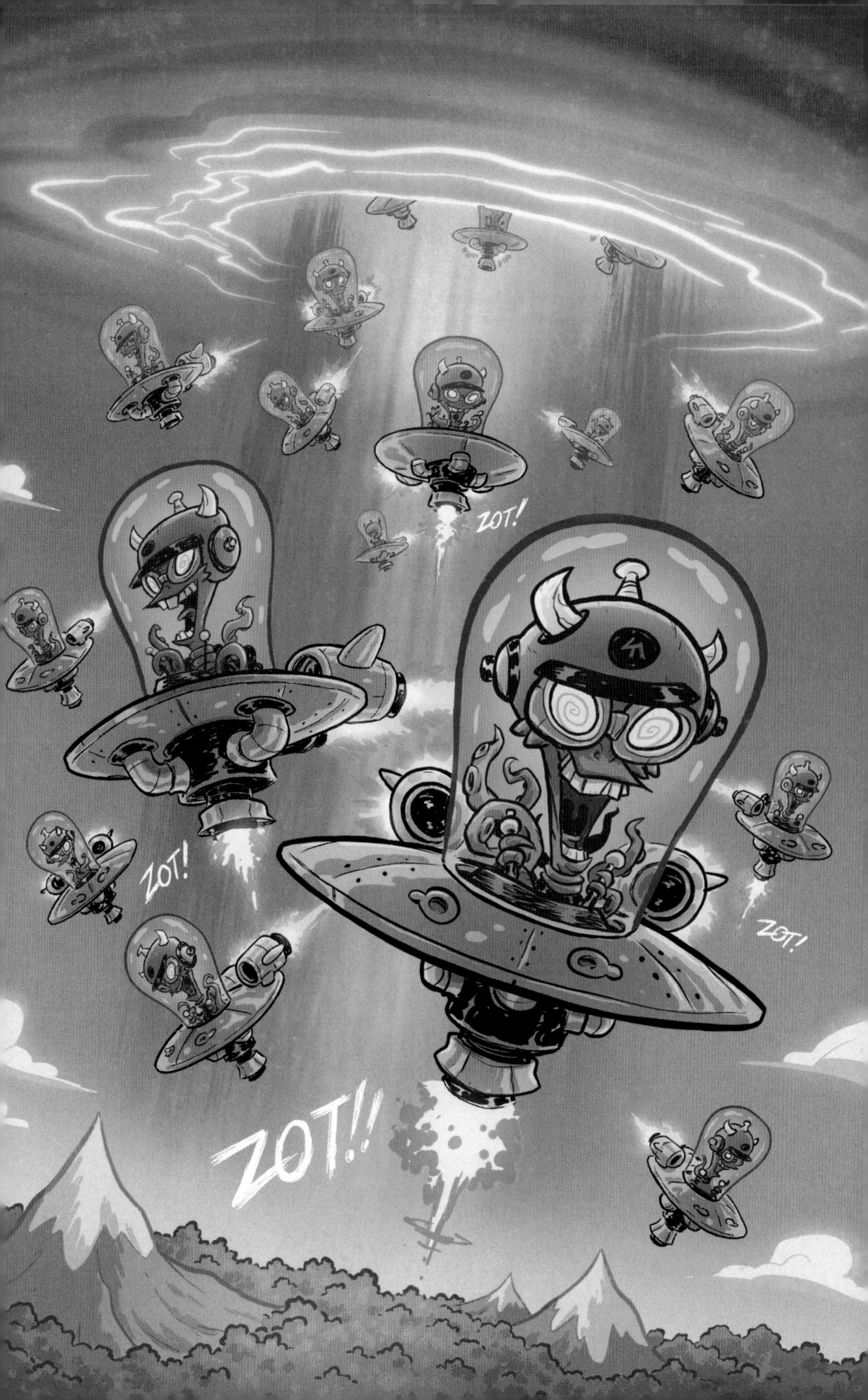
ZOT!
ZOT!
ZOT!
ZOT!!

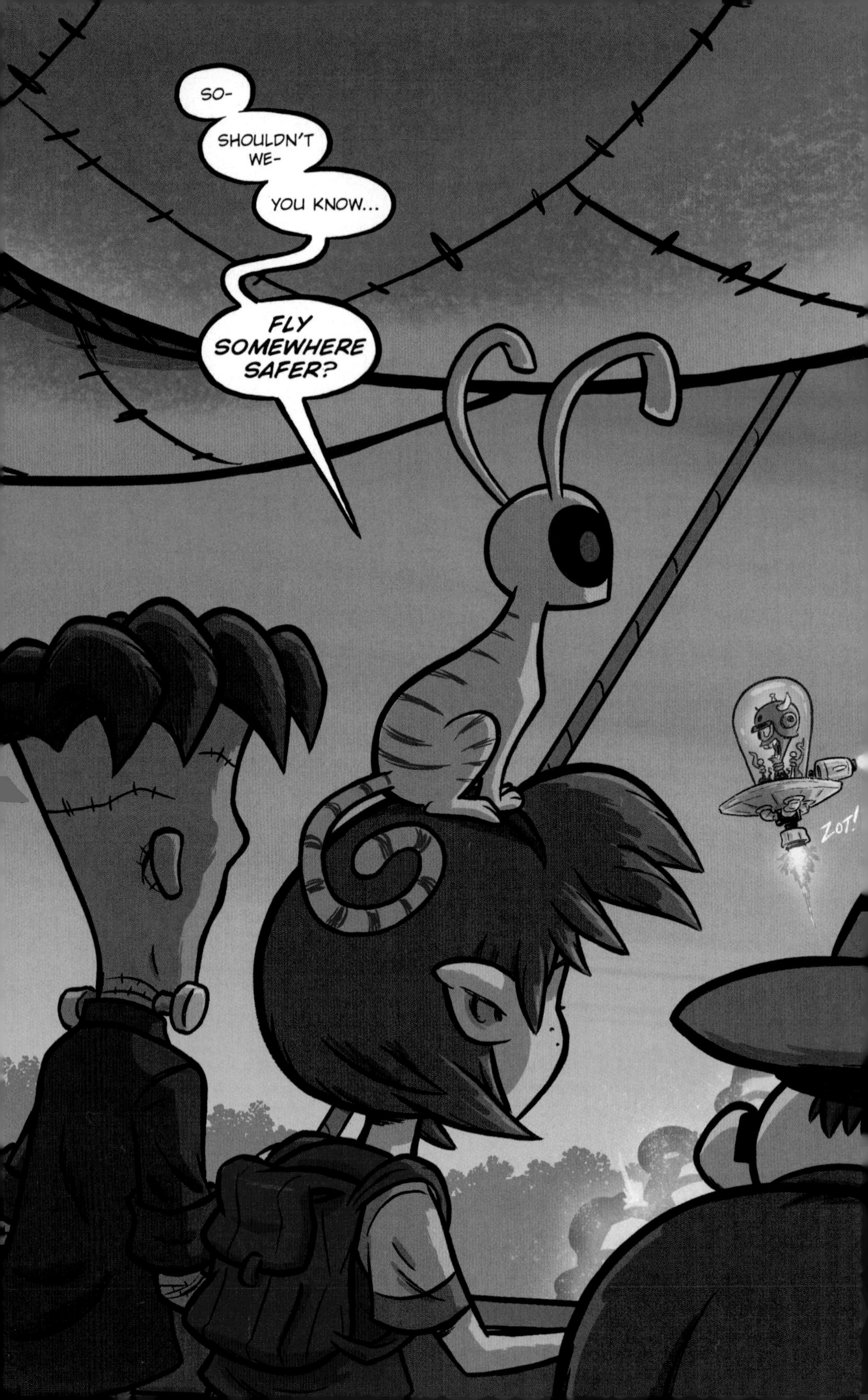
SO-
SHOULDN'T WE-
YOU KNOW...
FLY SOMEWHERE SAFER?
ZOT!

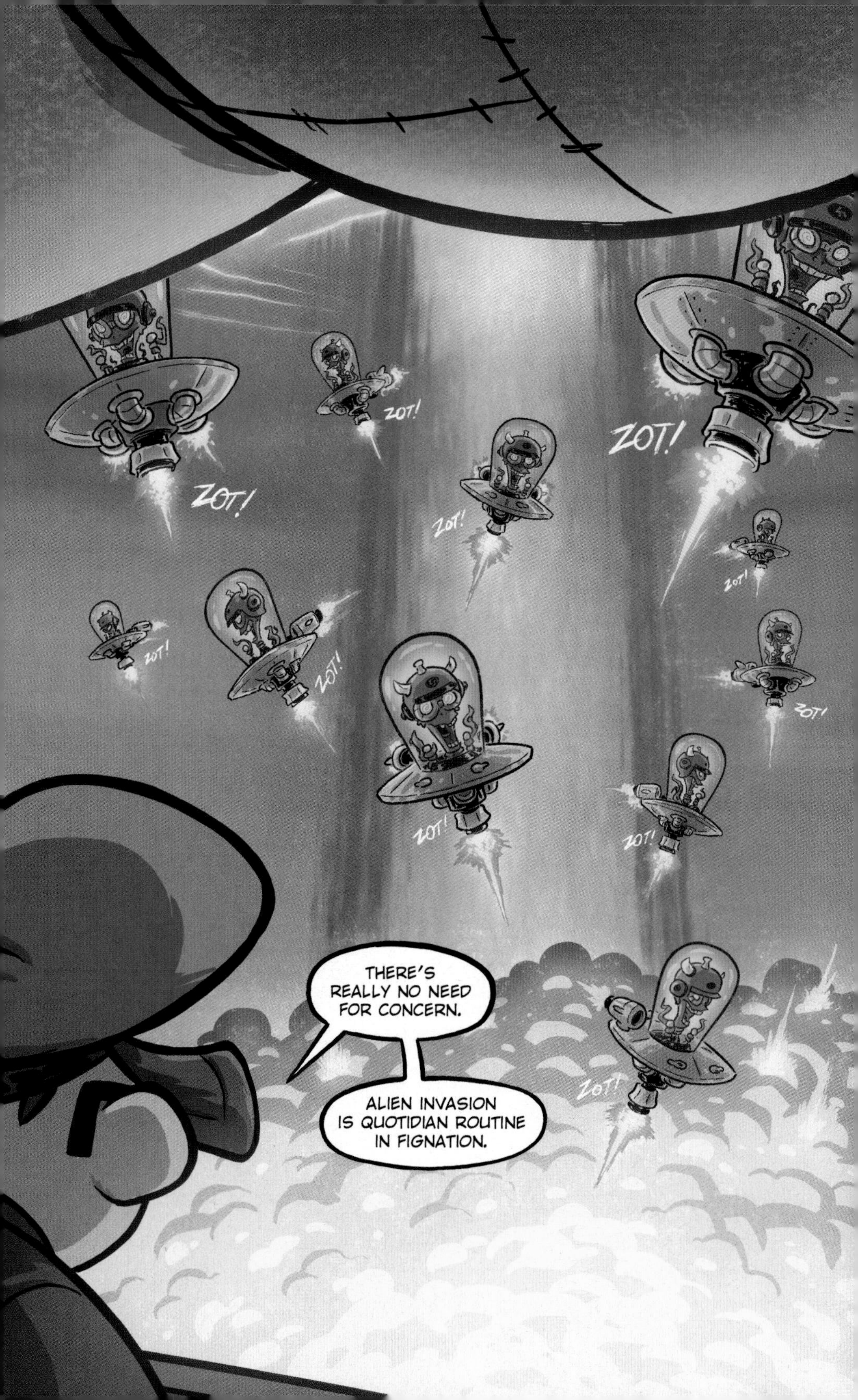
ZOT!
ZOT!
ZOT!
ZOT!
ZOT!
ZOT!
ZOT!
ZOT!
ZOT!
ZOT!
ZOT!
THERE'S REALLY NO NEED FOR CONCERN.
ALIEN INVASION IS QUOTIDIAN ROUTINE IN FIGNATION.

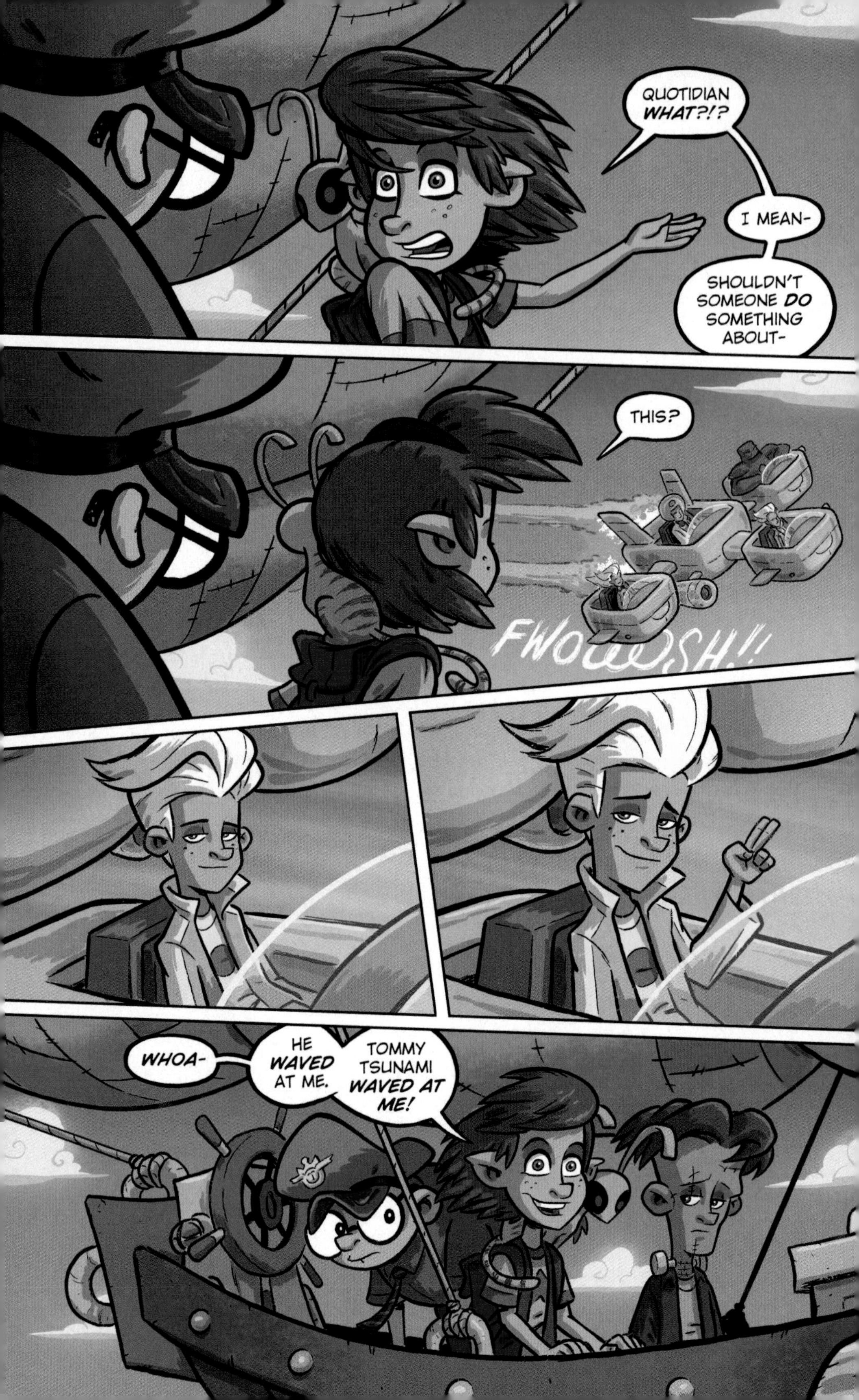
QUOTIDIAN WHAT?!?
I MEAN-
SHOULDN'T SOMEONE DO SOMETHING ABOUT-
THIS?
FWOOOSH!!
WHOA-
HE WAVED AT ME.
TOMMY TSUNAMI WAVED AT ME!

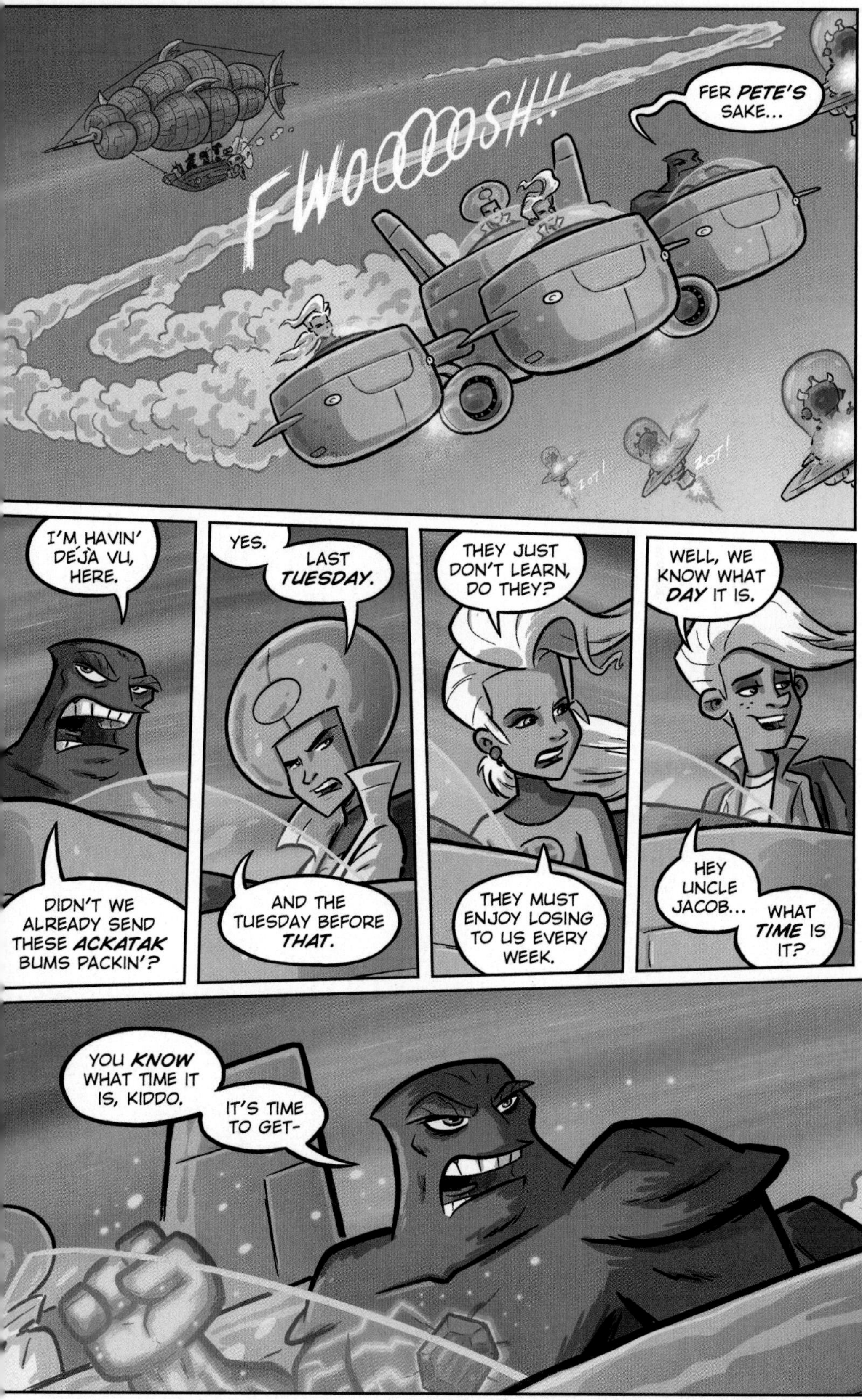
FWOOOOOSH!!
FER PETE'S SAKE...
ZOT!
ZOT!
I'M HAVIN' DÉJÀ VU, HERE.
DIDN'T WE ALREADY SEND THESE ACKATAK BUMS PACKIN'?
YES.
LAST TUESDAY.
AND THE TUESDAY BEFORE THAT.
THEY JUST DON'T LEARN, DO THEY?
THEY MUST ENJOY LOSING TO US EVERY WEEK.
WELL, WE KNOW WHAT DAY IT IS.
HEY UNCLE JACOB...
WHAT TIME IS IT?
YOU KNOW WHAT TIME IT IS, KIDDO.
IT'S TIME TO GET-

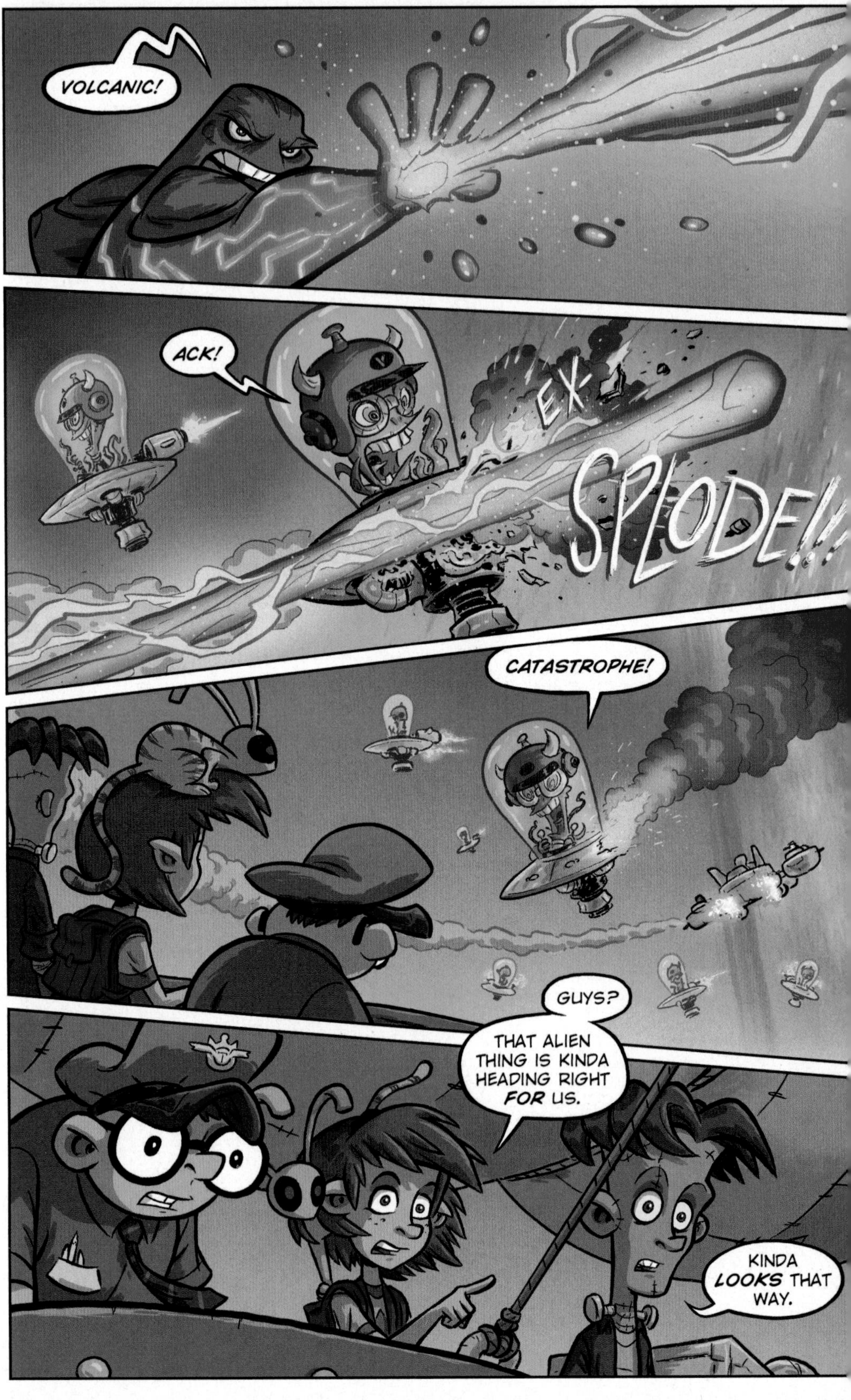
VOLCANIC!
ACK!
EX-
SPLODE!!!
CATASTROPHE!
GUYS?
THAT ALIEN THING IS KINDA HEADING RIGHT FOR US.
KINDA LOOKS THAT WAY.

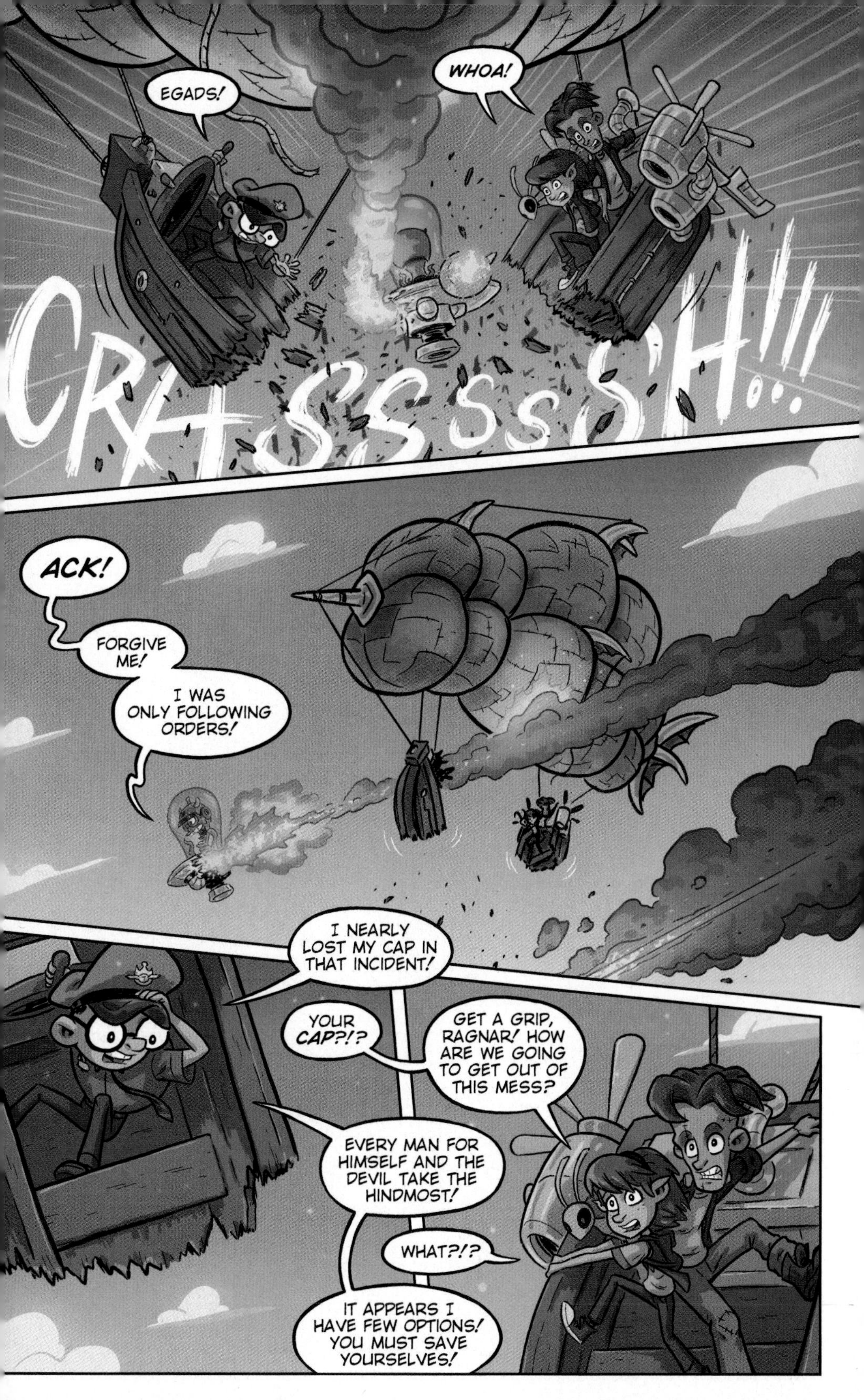

EGADS!
WHOA!
CRASSSSSH!!!
ACK!
FORGIVE ME!
I WAS ONLY FOLLOWING ORDERS!
I NEARLY LOST MY CAP IN THAT INCIDENT!
YOUR CAP?!?
GET A GRIP, RAGNAR! HOW ARE WE GOING TO GET OUT OF THIS MESS?
EVERY MAN FOR HIMSELF AND THE DEVIL TAKE THE HINDMOST!
WHAT?!?
IT APPEARS I HAVE FEW OPTIONS! YOU MUST SAVE YOURSELVES!

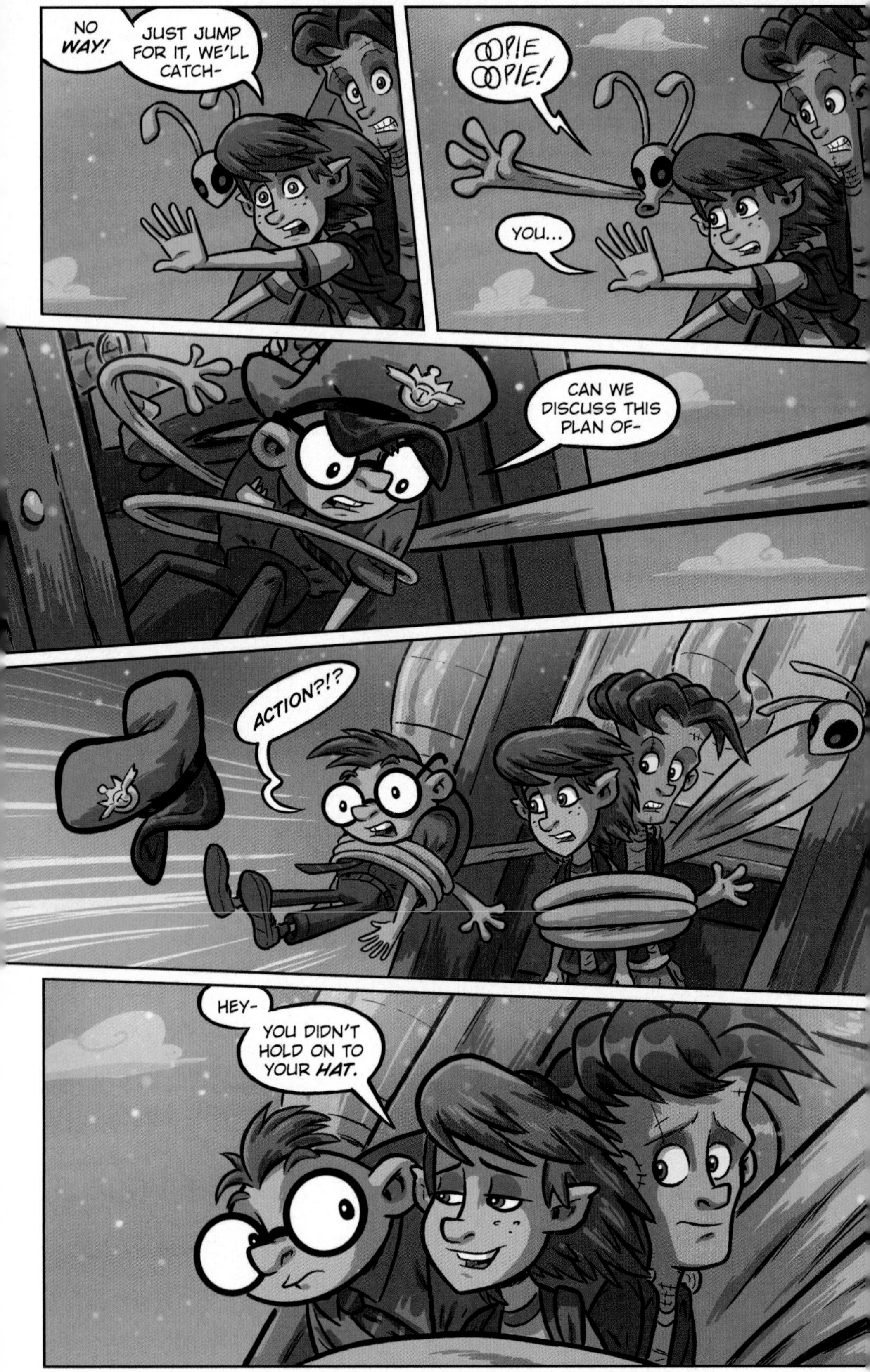
NO WAY!
JUST JUMP FOR IT, WE'LL CATCH-
OOPIE OOPIE!
YOU...
CAN WE DISCUSS THIS PLAN OF-
ACTION?!?
HEY-
YOU DIDN'T HOLD ON TO YOUR HAT.

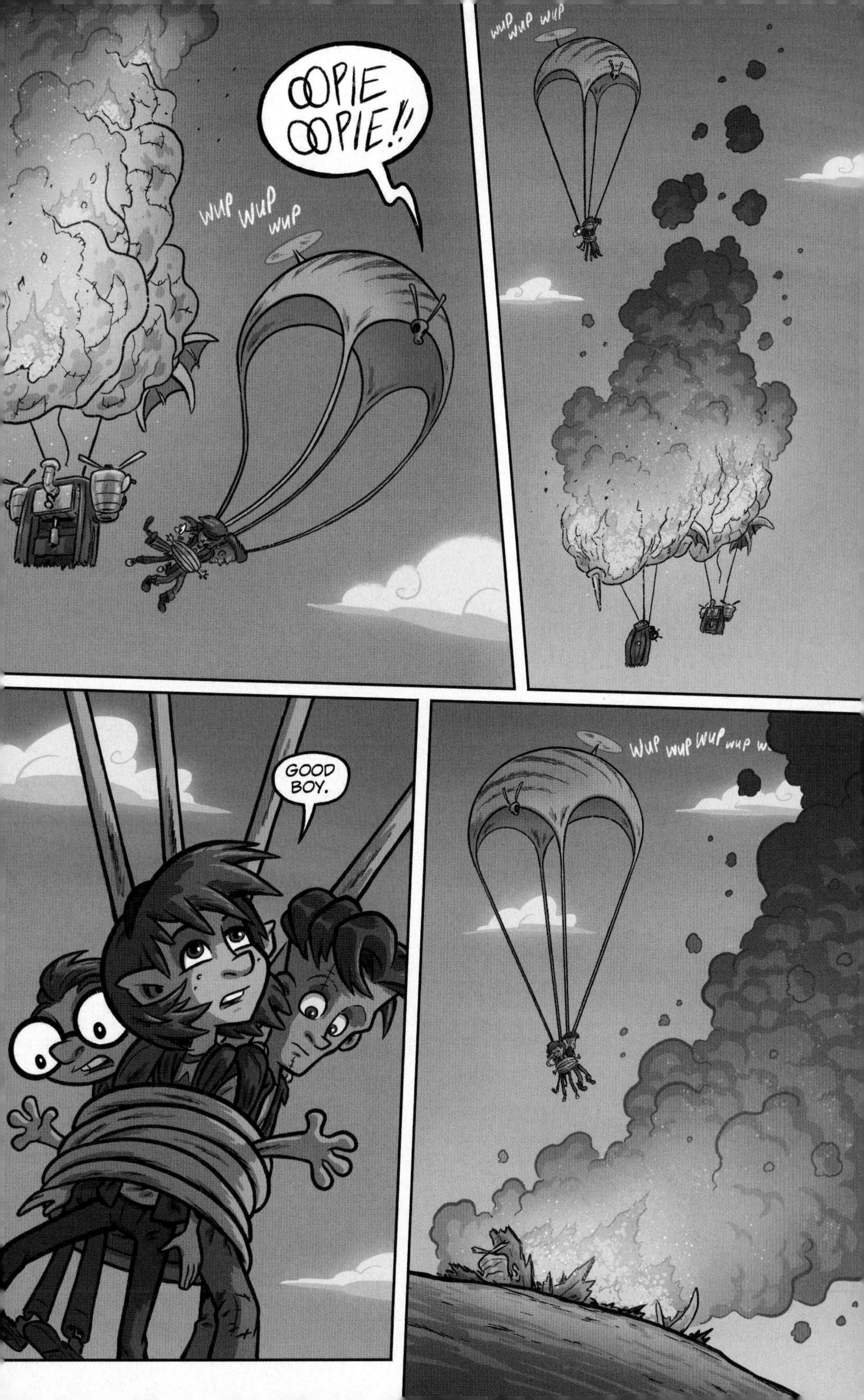
OOPIE OOPIE!!
WUP WUP WUP
WUP WUP WUP
GOOD BOY.
WUP WUP WUP WUP

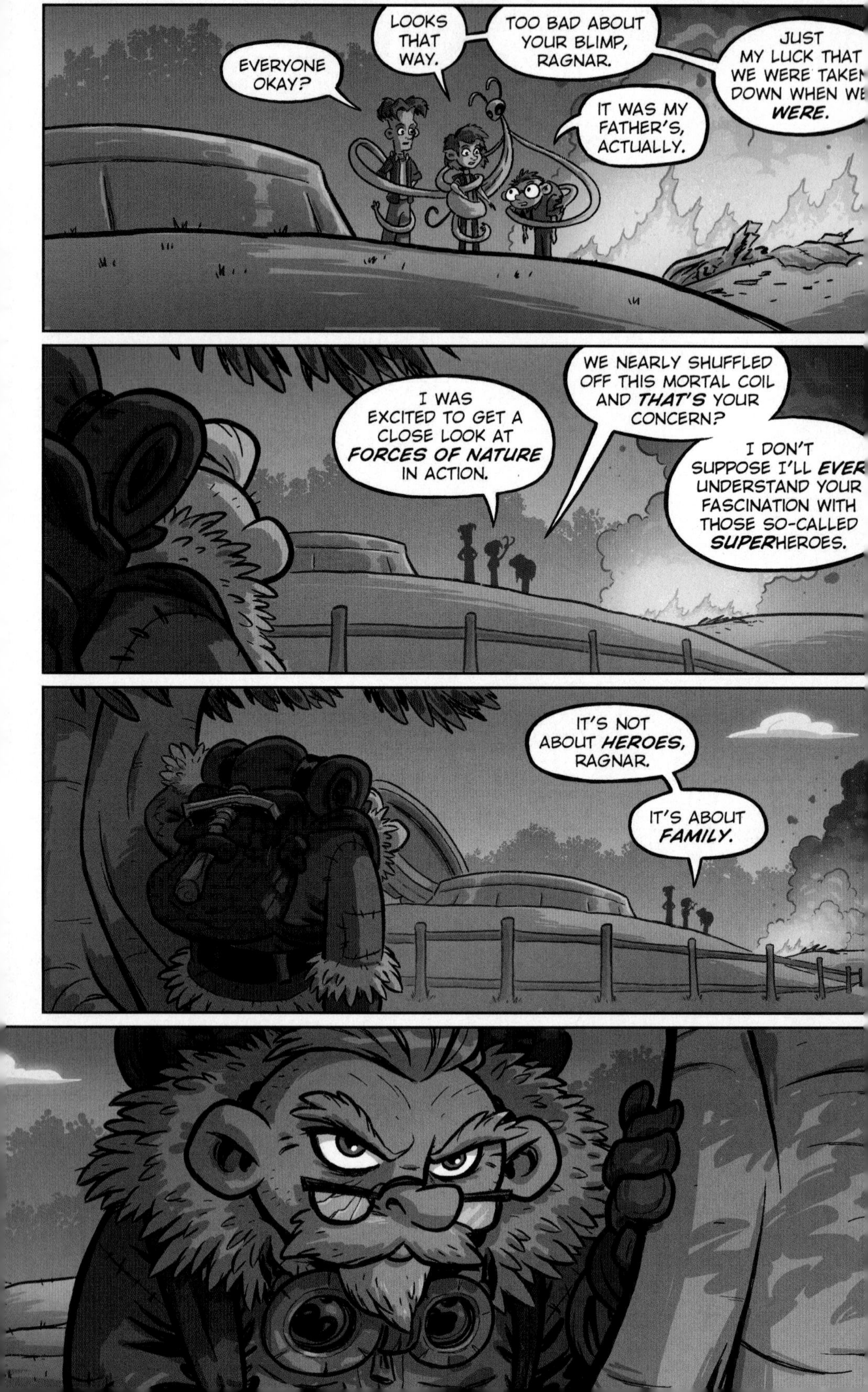
EVERYONE OKAY?
LOOKS THAT WAY.
TOO BAD ABOUT YOUR BLIMP, RAGNAR.
IT WAS MY FATHER'S, ACTUALLY.
JUST MY LUCK THAT WE WERE TAKEN DOWN WHEN WE WERE.
I WAS EXCITED TO GET A CLOSE LOOK AT FORCES OF NATURE IN ACTION.
WE NEARLY SHUFFLED OFF THIS MORTAL COIL AND THAT'S YOUR CONCERN?
I DON'T SUPPOSE I'LL EVER UNDERSTAND YOUR FASCINATION WITH THOSE SO-CALLED SUPERHEROES.
IT'S NOT ABOUT HEROES, RAGNAR.
IT'S ABOUT FAMILY.

Chapter 17

Origin(al) Sin

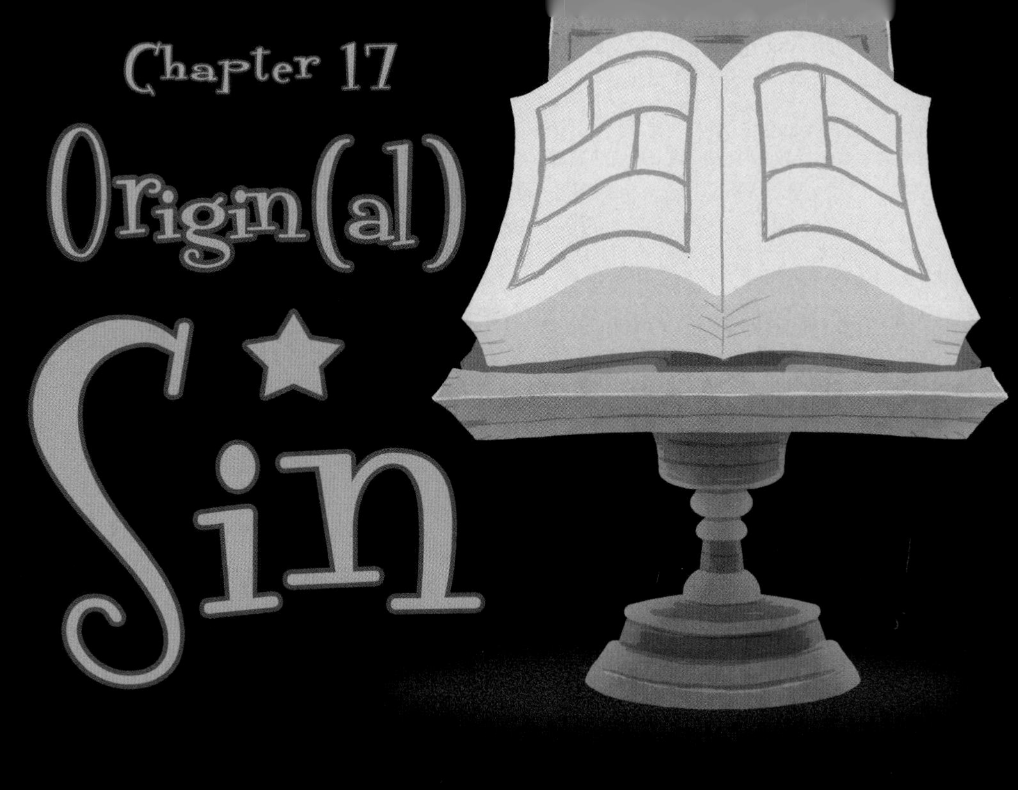

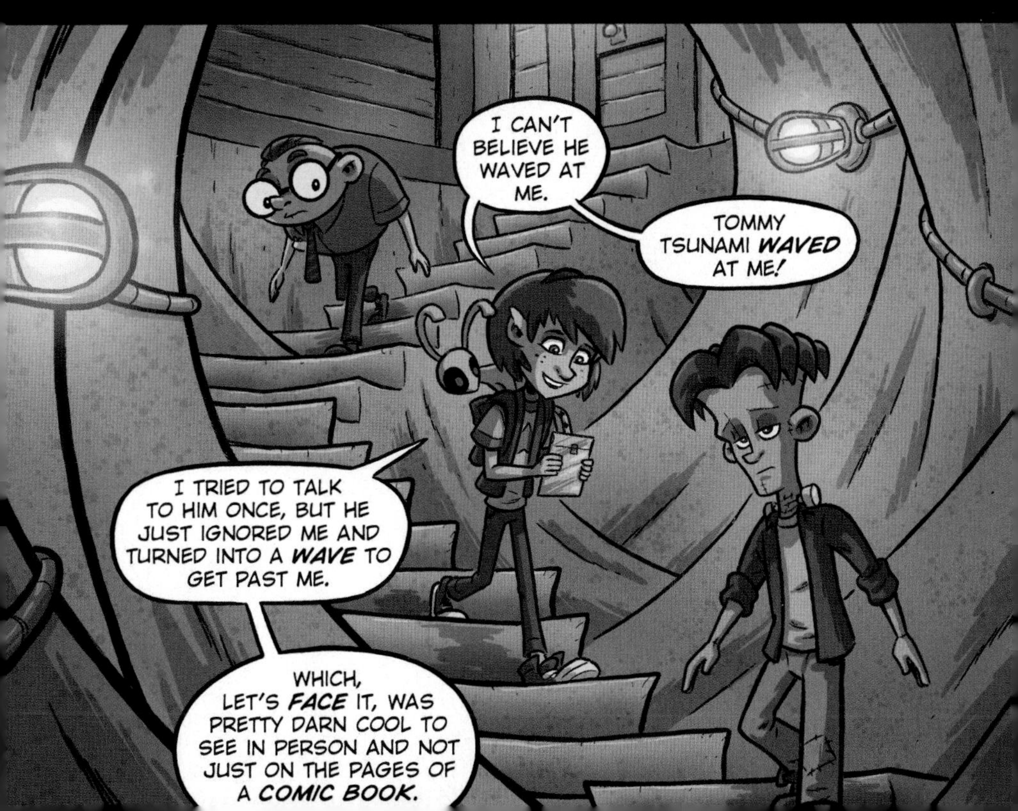

I CAN'T BELIEVE HE WAVED AT ME.
TOMMY TSUNAMI **WAVED** AT ME!
I TRIED TO TALK TO HIM ONCE, BUT HE JUST IGNORED ME AND TURNED INTO A **WAVE** TO GET PAST ME.
WHICH, LET'S **FACE** IT, WAS PRETTY DARN COOL TO SEE IN PERSON AND NOT JUST ON THE PAGES OF A **COMIC BOOK**.

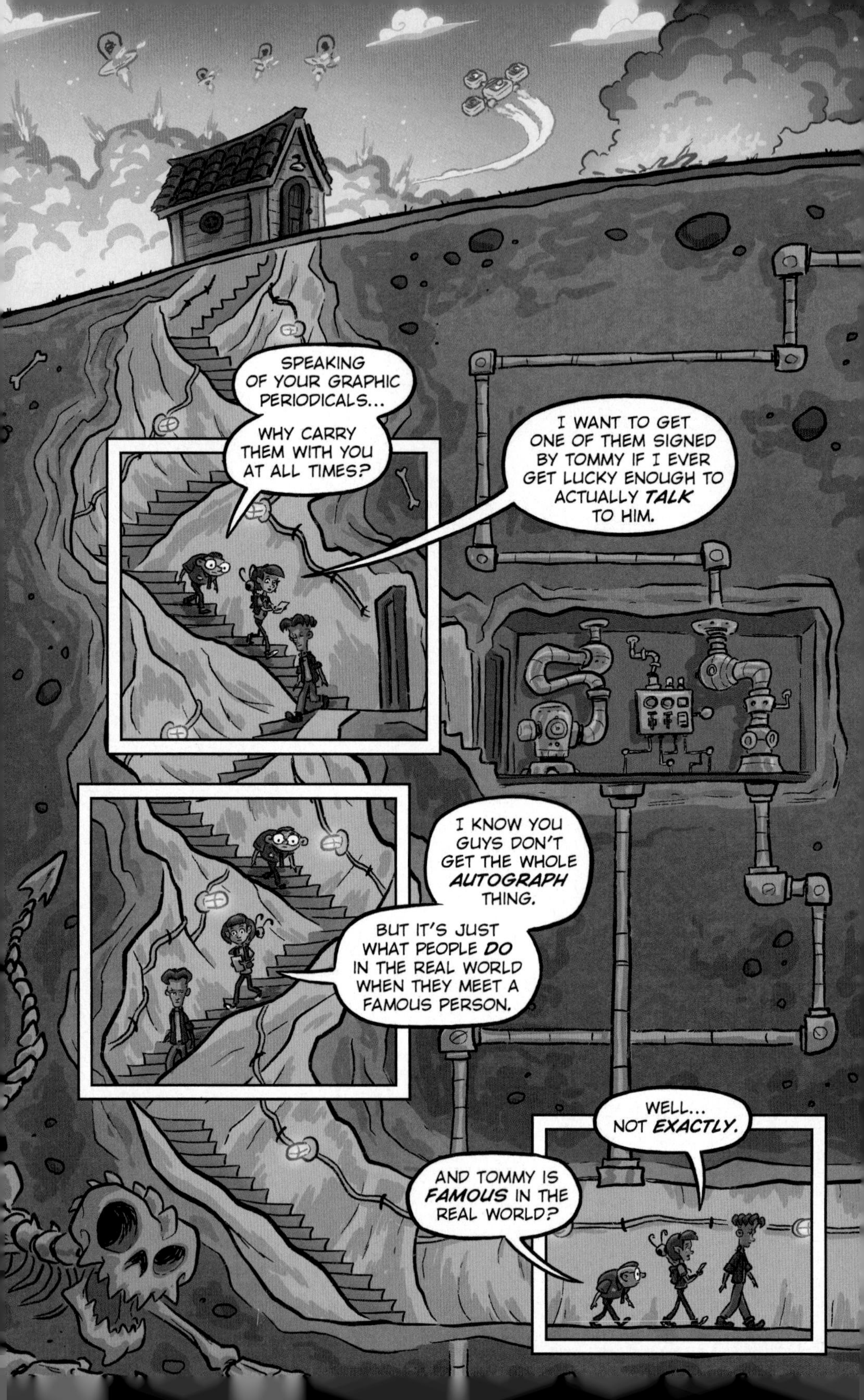
SPEAKING OF YOUR GRAPHIC PERIODICALS...
WHY CARRY THEM WITH YOU AT ALL TIMES?
I WANT TO GET ONE OF THEM SIGNED BY TOMMY IF I EVER GET LUCKY ENOUGH TO ACTUALLY *TALK* TO HIM.
I KNOW YOU GUYS DON'T GET THE WHOLE *AUTOGRAPH* THING.
BUT IT'S JUST WHAT PEOPLE *DO* IN THE REAL WORLD WHEN THEY MEET A FAMOUS PERSON.
AND TOMMY IS *FAMOUS* IN THE REAL WORLD?
WELL... NOT *EXACTLY*.

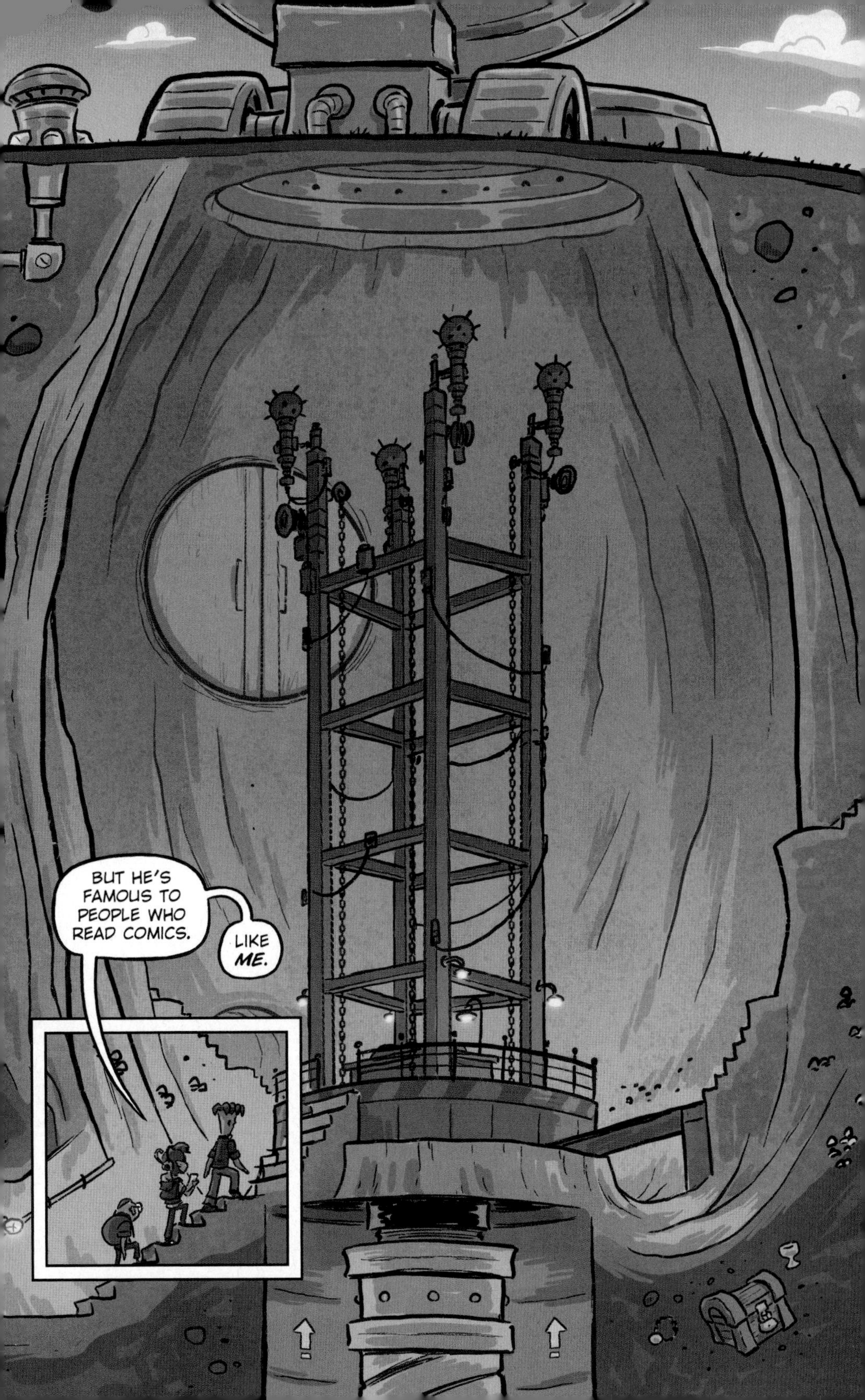
BUT HE'S FAMOUS TO PEOPLE WHO READ COMICS.
LIKE *ME*.

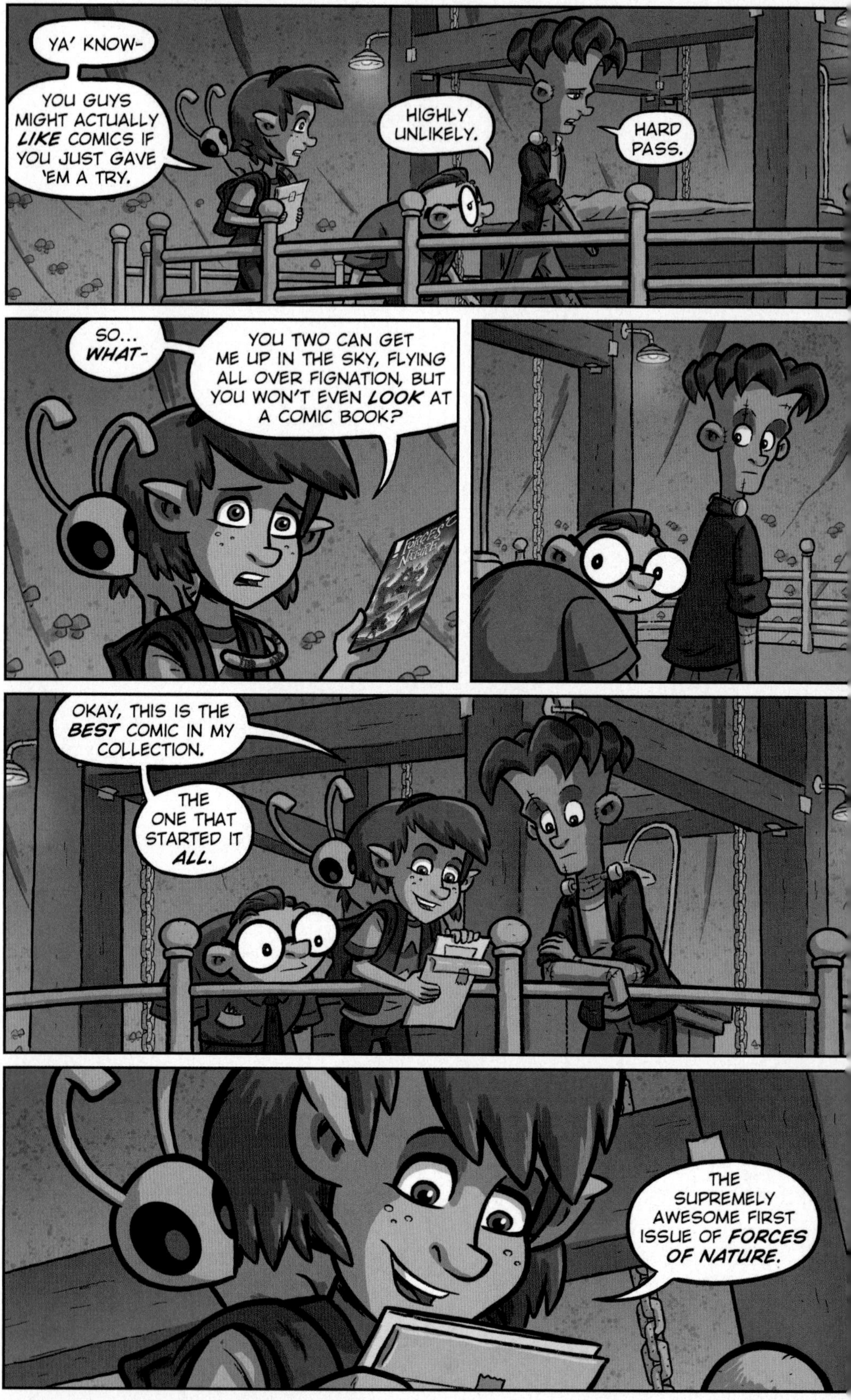

YA' KNOW-
YOU GUYS MIGHT ACTUALLY *LIKE* COMICS IF YOU JUST GAVE 'EM A TRY.
HIGHLY UNLIKELY.
HARD PASS.
SO... *WHAT*-
YOU TWO CAN GET ME UP IN THE SKY, FLYING ALL OVER FIGNATION, BUT YOU WON'T EVEN *LOOK* AT A COMIC BOOK?
OKAY, THIS IS THE *BEST* COMIC IN MY COLLECTION.
THE ONE THAT STARTED IT *ALL*.
THE SUPREMELY AWESOME FIRST ISSUE OF *FORCES OF NATURE*.

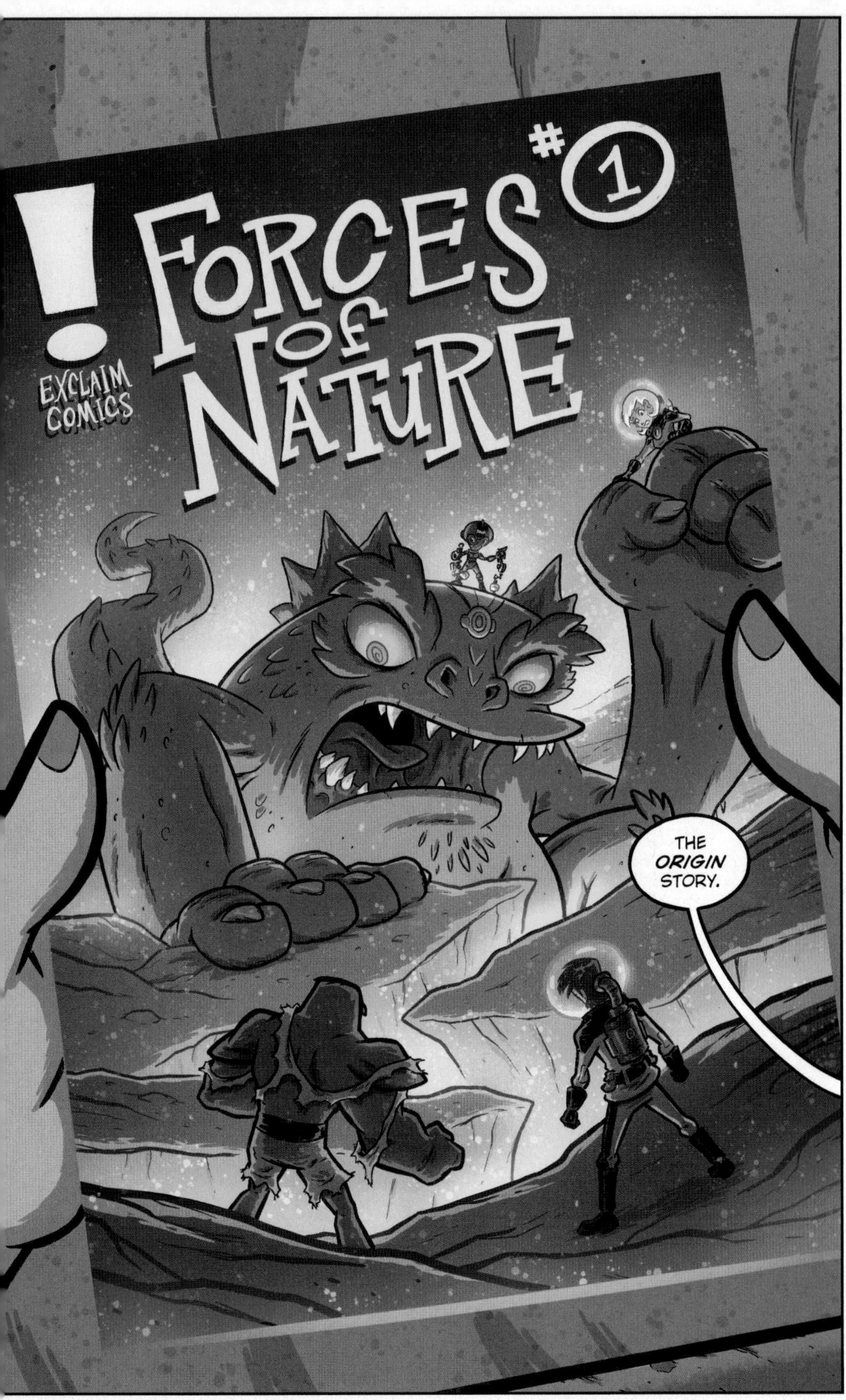
!
EXCLAIM
COMICS
FORCES of NATURE
#1
THE
ORIGIN
STORY.

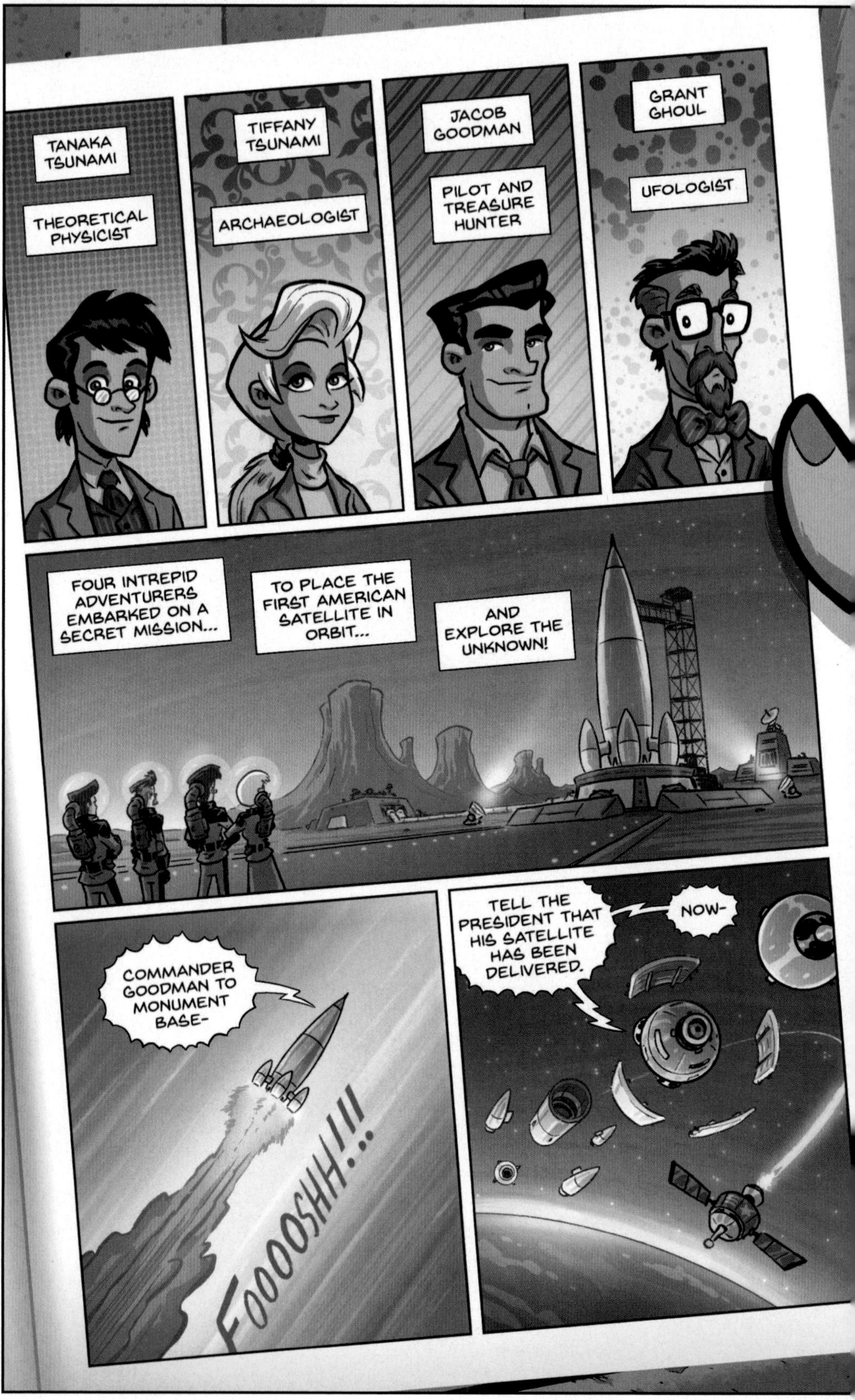
TANAKA TSUNAMI
THEORETICAL PHYSICIST
TIFFANY TSUNAMI
ARCHAEOLOGIST
JACOB GOODMAN
PILOT AND TREASURE HUNTER
GRANT GHOUL
UFOLOGIST
FOUR INTREPID ADVENTURERS EMBARKED ON A SECRET MISSION...
TO PLACE THE FIRST AMERICAN SATELLITE IN ORBIT...
AND EXPLORE THE UNKNOWN!
COMMANDER GOODMAN TO MONUMENT BASE-
FOOOOSHH!!!
TELL THE PRESIDENT THAT HIS SATELLITE HAS BEEN DELIVERED.
NOW-

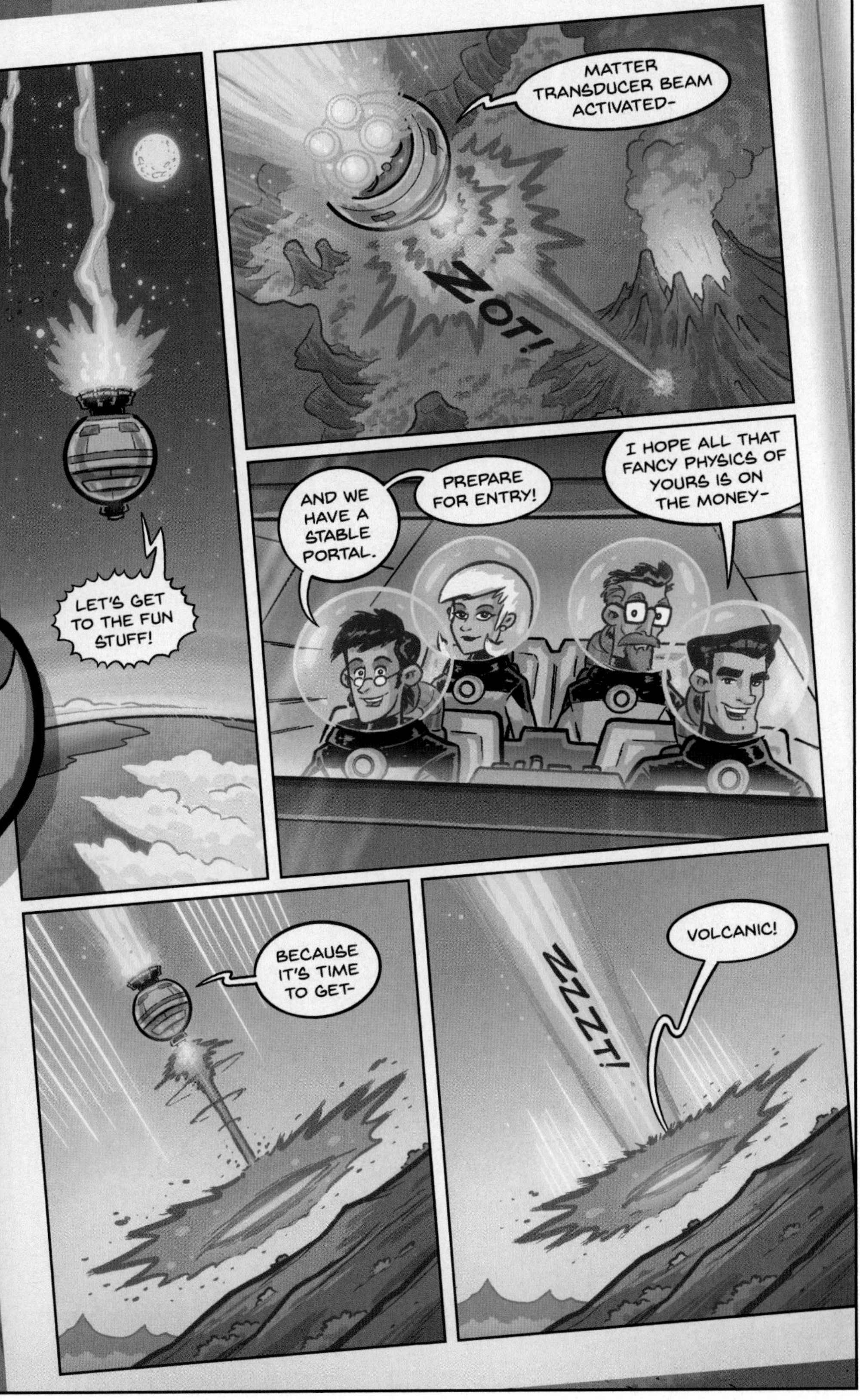

LET'S GET TO THE FUN STUFF!
MATTER TRANSDUCER BEAM ACTIVATED-
ZOT!
AND WE HAVE A STABLE PORTAL.
PREPARE FOR ENTRY!
I HOPE ALL THAT FANCY PHYSICS OF YOURS IS ON THE MONEY-
BECAUSE IT'S TIME TO GET-
ZZZT!
VOLCANIC!

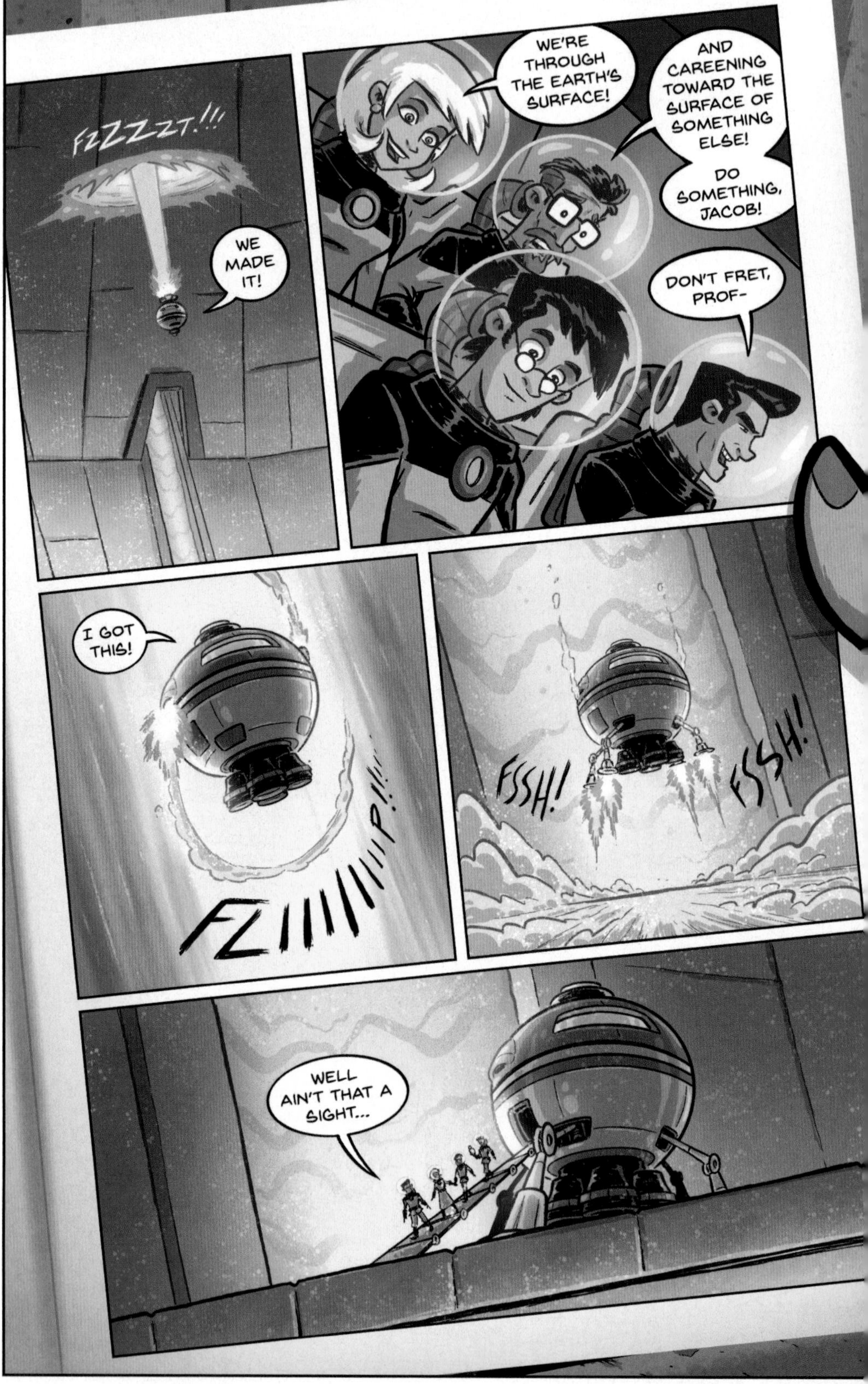
FZZZZT!!!
WE MADE IT!
WE'RE THROUGH THE EARTH'S SURFACE!
AND CAREENING TOWARD THE SURFACE OF SOMETHING ELSE!
DO SOMETHING, JACOB!
DON'T FRET, PROF-
I GOT THIS!
FZIIIIIIIP!!!
FSSH!
FSSH!
WELL AIN'T THAT A SIGHT...

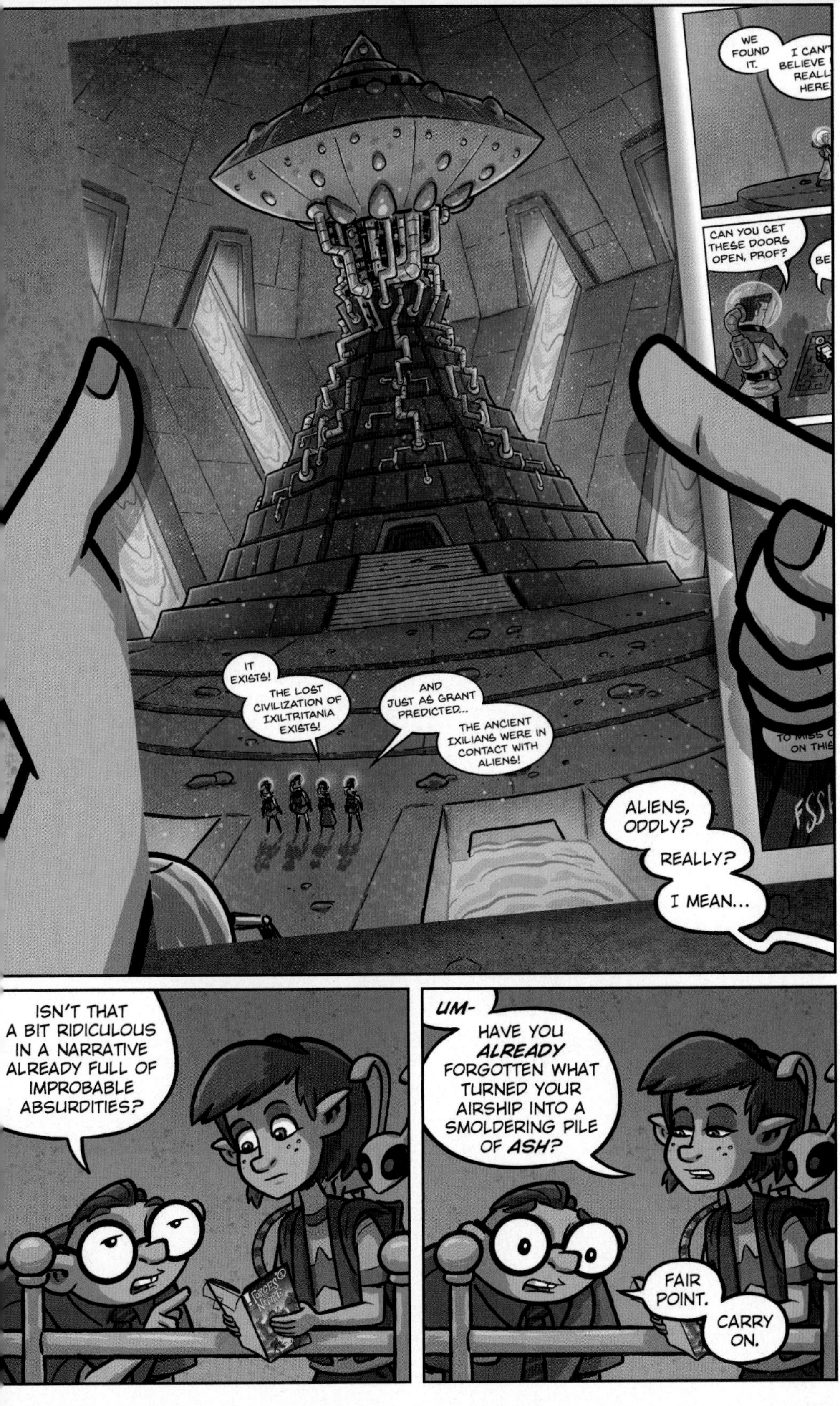
WE FOUND IT.
CAN YOU GET THESE DOORS OPEN, PROF?
IT EXISTS!
THE LOST CIVILIZATION OF IXILTRITANIA EXISTS!
AND JUST AS GRANT PREDICTED...
THE ANCIENT IXILIANS WERE IN CONTACT WITH ALIENS!
ALIENS, ODDLY?
REALLY?
I MEAN...
ISN'T THAT A BIT RIDICULOUS IN A NARRATIVE ALREADY FULL OF IMPROBABLE ABSURDITIES?
UM-
HAVE YOU ALREADY FORGOTTEN WHAT TURNED YOUR AIRSHIP INTO A SMOLDERING PILE OF ASH?
FAIR POINT.
CARRY ON.

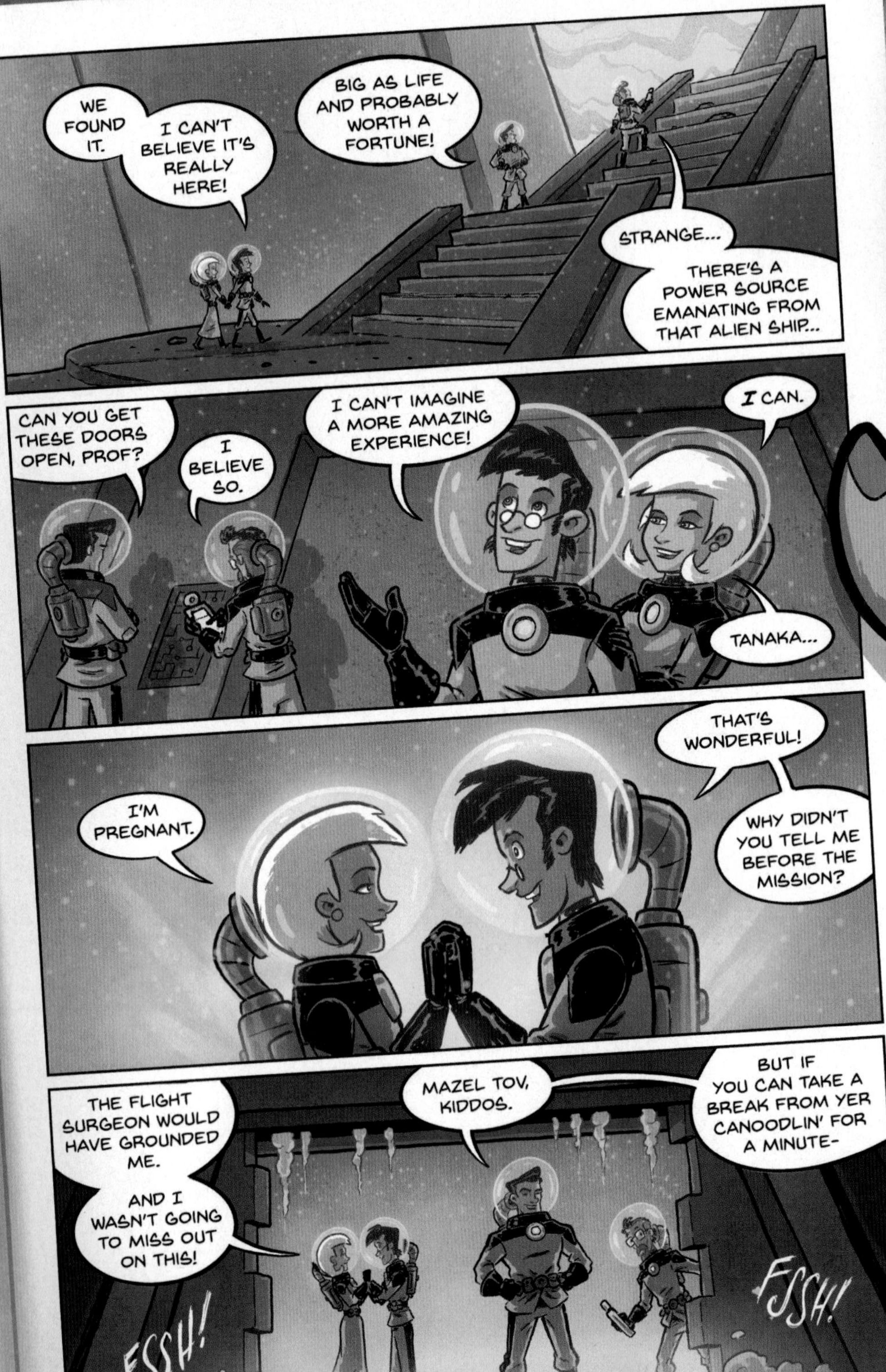
WE FOUND IT.
I CAN'T BELIEVE IT'S REALLY HERE!
BIG AS LIFE AND PROBABLY WORTH A FORTUNE!
STRANGE...
THERE'S A POWER SOURCE EMANATING FROM THAT ALIEN SHIP...
CAN YOU GET THESE DOORS OPEN, PROF?
I BELIEVE SO.
I CAN'T IMAGINE A MORE AMAZING EXPERIENCE!
I CAN.
TANAKA...
I'M PREGNANT.
THAT'S WONDERFUL!
WHY DIDN'T YOU TELL ME BEFORE THE MISSION?
THE FLIGHT SURGEON WOULD HAVE GROUNDED ME.
AND I WASN'T GOING TO MISS OUT ON THIS!
MAZEL TOV, KIDDOS.
BUT IF YOU CAN TAKE A BREAK FROM YER CANOODLIN' FOR A MINUTE-
FSSH!
FSSH!

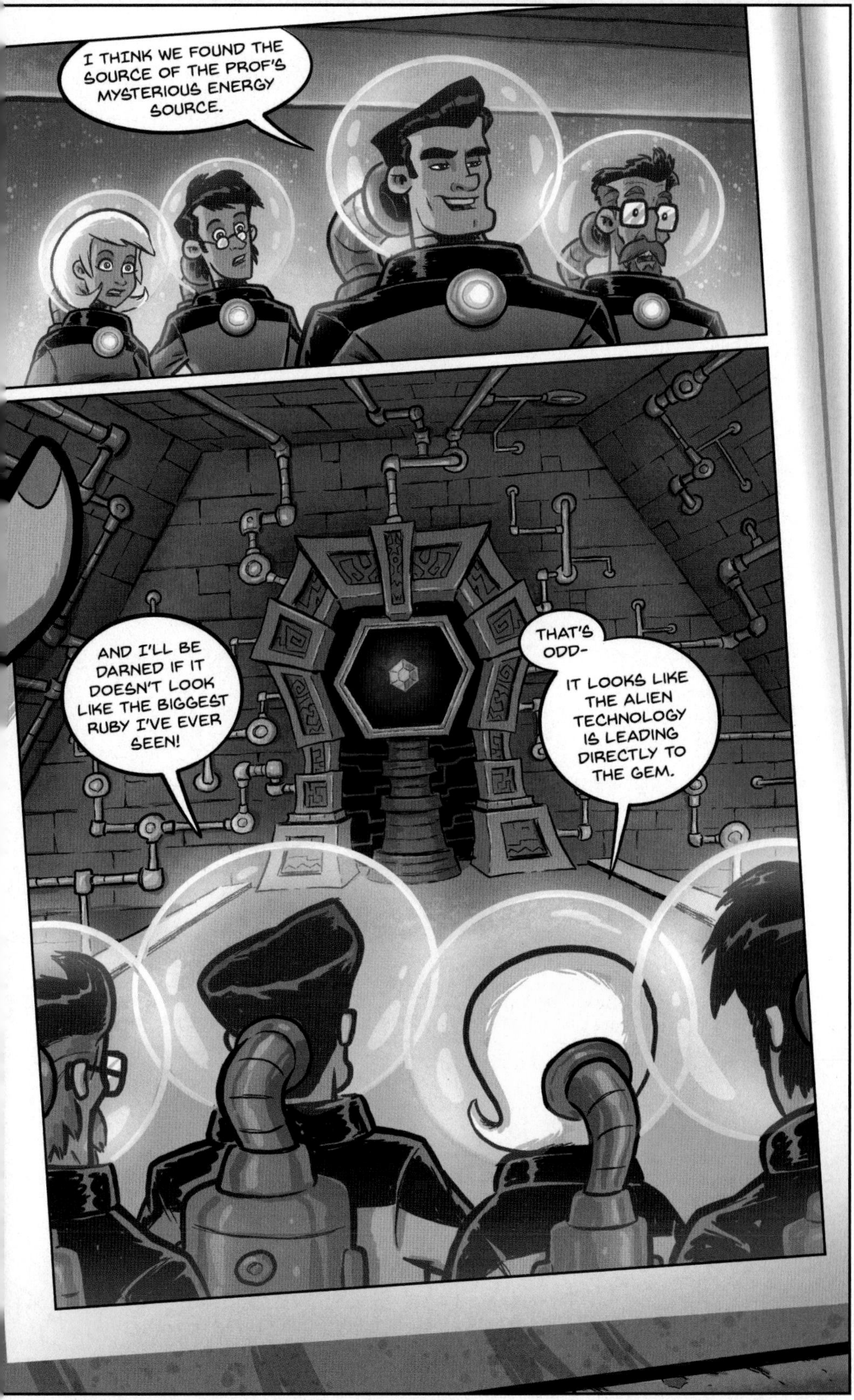
I THINK WE FOUND THE SOURCE OF THE PROF'S MYSTERIOUS ENERGY SOURCE.
AND I'LL BE DARNED IF IT DOESN'T LOOK LIKE THE BIGGEST RUBY I'VE EVER SEEN!
THAT'S ODD-
IT LOOKS LIKE THE ALIEN TECHNOLOGY IS LEADING DIRECTLY TO THE GEM.

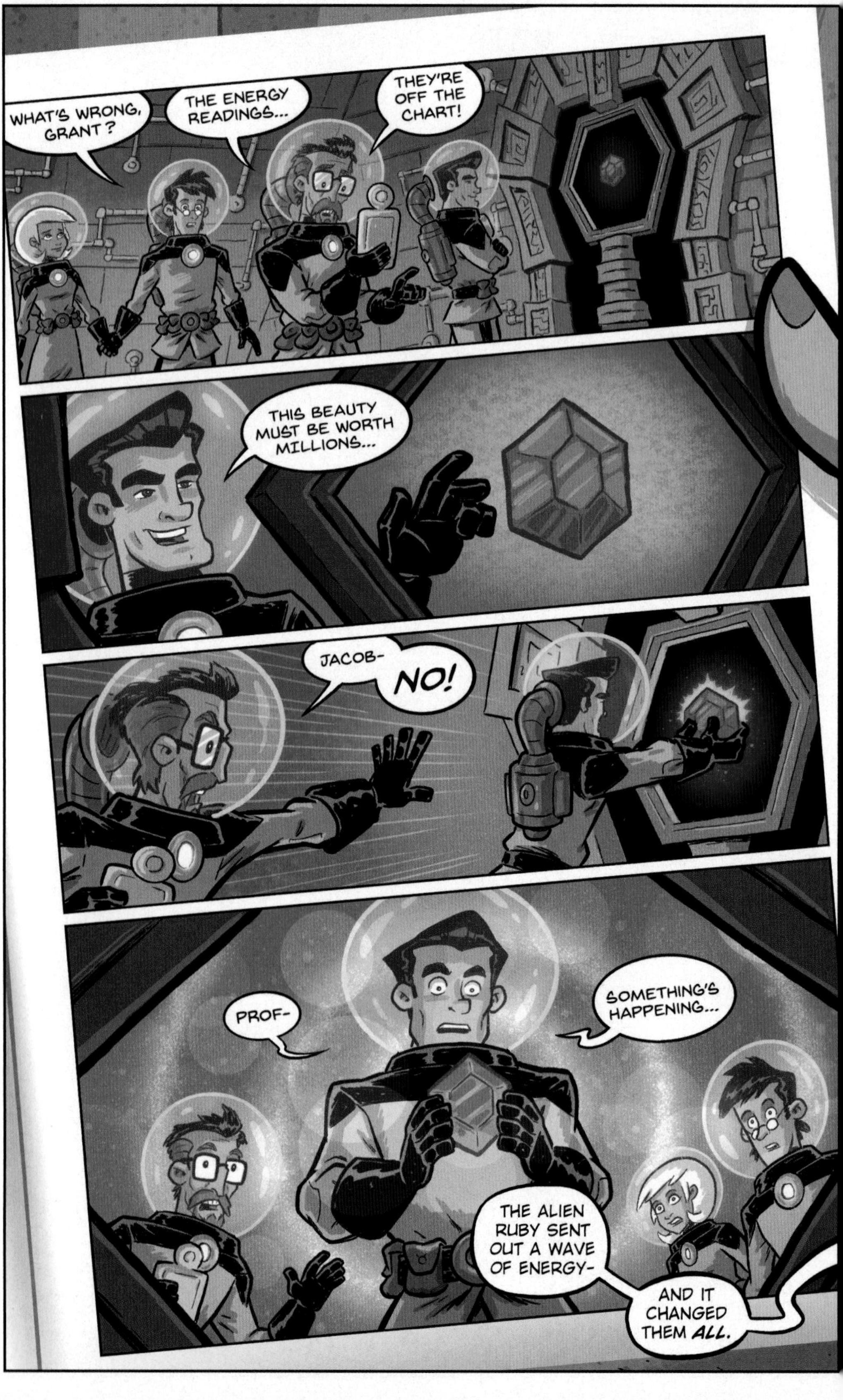
WHAT'S WRONG, GRANT?
THE ENERGY READINGS...
THEY'RE OFF THE CHART!
THIS BEAUTY MUST BE WORTH MILLIONS...
JACOB-
NO!
PROF-
SOMETHING'S HAPPENING...
THE ALIEN RUBY SENT OUT A WAVE OF ENERGY-
AND IT CHANGED THEM ALL.

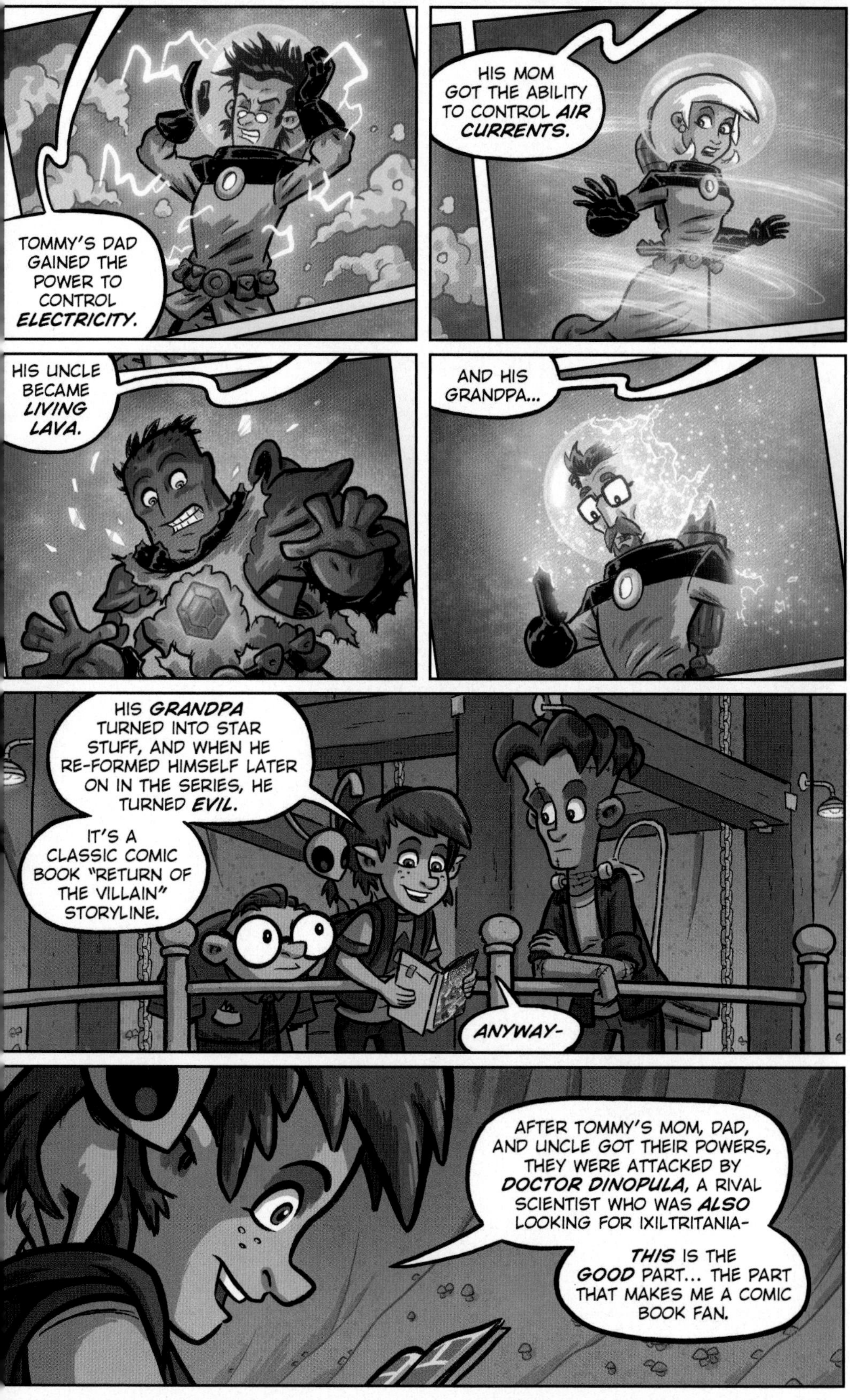
TOMMY'S DAD GAINED THE POWER TO CONTROL ELECTRICITY.
HIS MOM GOT THE ABILITY TO CONTROL AIR CURRENTS.
HIS UNCLE BECAME LIVING LAVA.
AND HIS GRANDPA...
HIS GRANDPA TURNED INTO STAR STUFF, AND WHEN HE RE-FORMED HIMSELF LATER ON IN THE SERIES, HE TURNED EVIL.
IT'S A CLASSIC COMIC BOOK "RETURN OF THE VILLAIN" STORYLINE.
ANYWAY-
AFTER TOMMY'S MOM, DAD, AND UNCLE GOT THEIR POWERS, THEY WERE ATTACKED BY DOCTOR DINOPULA, A RIVAL SCIENTIST WHO WAS ALSO LOOKING FOR IXILTRITANIA-
THIS IS THE GOOD PART... THE PART THAT MAKES ME A COMIC BOOK FAN.

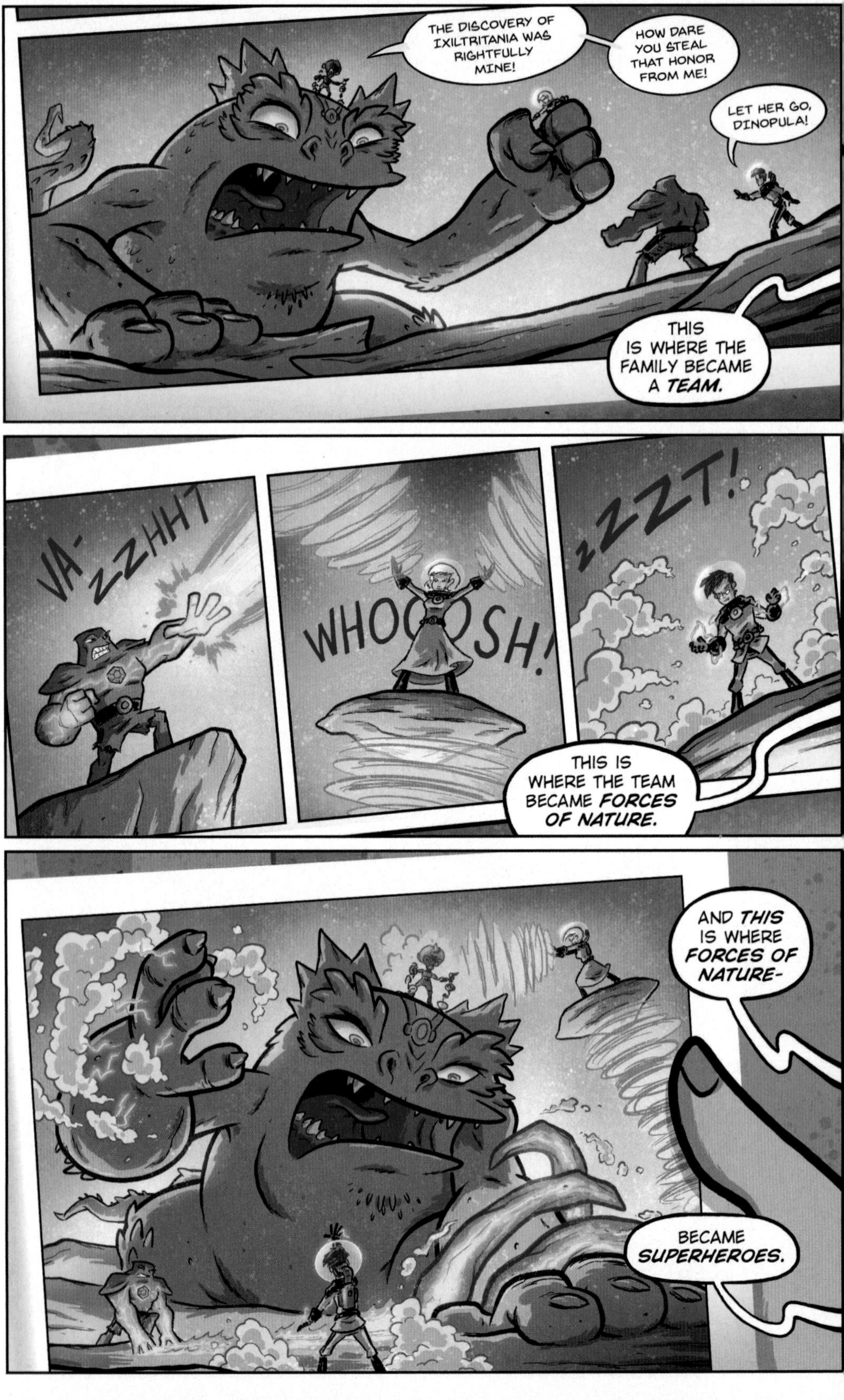
THE DISCOVERY OF IXILTRITANIA WAS RIGHTFULLY MINE!
HOW DARE YOU STEAL THAT HONOR FROM ME!
LET HER GO, DINOPULA!
THIS IS WHERE THE FAMILY BECAME A *TEAM.*
VA-ZZHHT
WHOOOSH!
ZZZT!
THIS IS WHERE THE TEAM BECAME *FORCES OF NATURE.*
AND *THIS* IS WHERE *FORCES OF NATURE-*
BECAME *SUPERHEROES.*

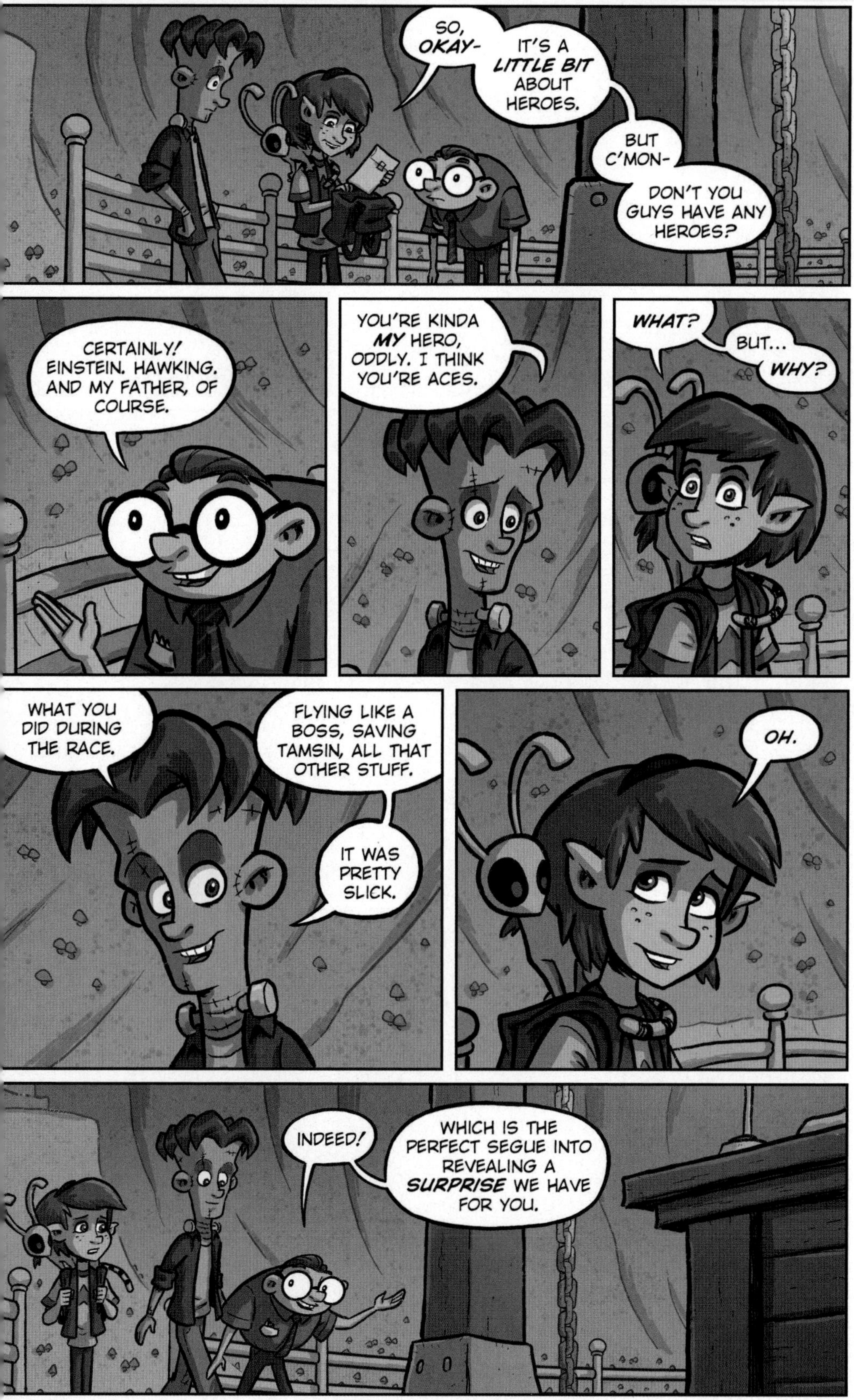
SO, OKAY-
IT'S A LITTLE BIT ABOUT HEROES.
BUT C'MON-
DON'T YOU GUYS HAVE ANY HEROES?
CERTAINLY! EINSTEIN. HAWKING. AND MY FATHER, OF COURSE.
YOU'RE KINDA MY HERO, ODDLY. I THINK YOU'RE ACES.
WHAT?
BUT... WHY?
WHAT YOU DID DURING THE RACE.
FLYING LIKE A BOSS, SAVING TAMSIN, ALL THAT OTHER STUFF.
IT WAS PRETTY SLICK.
OH.
INDEED!
WHICH IS THE PERFECT SEGUE INTO REVEALING A SURPRISE WE HAVE FOR YOU.

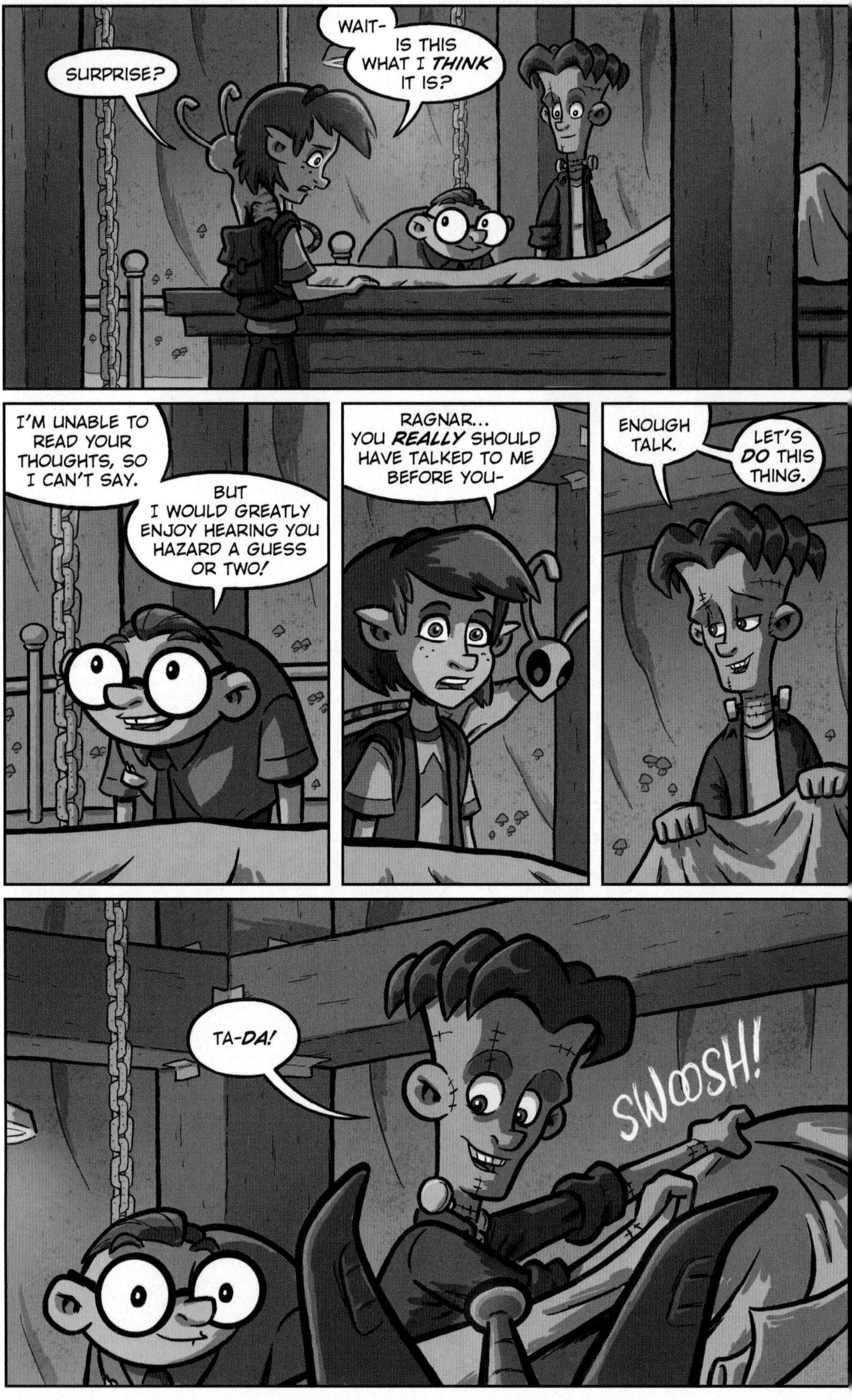
SURPRISE?
WAIT-
IS THIS WHAT I THINK IT IS?
I'M UNABLE TO READ YOUR THOUGHTS, SO I CAN'T SAY.
BUT I WOULD GREATLY ENJOY HEARING YOU HAZARD A GUESS OR TWO!
RAGNAR... YOU REALLY SHOULD HAVE TALKED TO ME BEFORE YOU-
ENOUGH TALK.
LET'S DO THIS THING.
TA-DA!
SWOOSH!

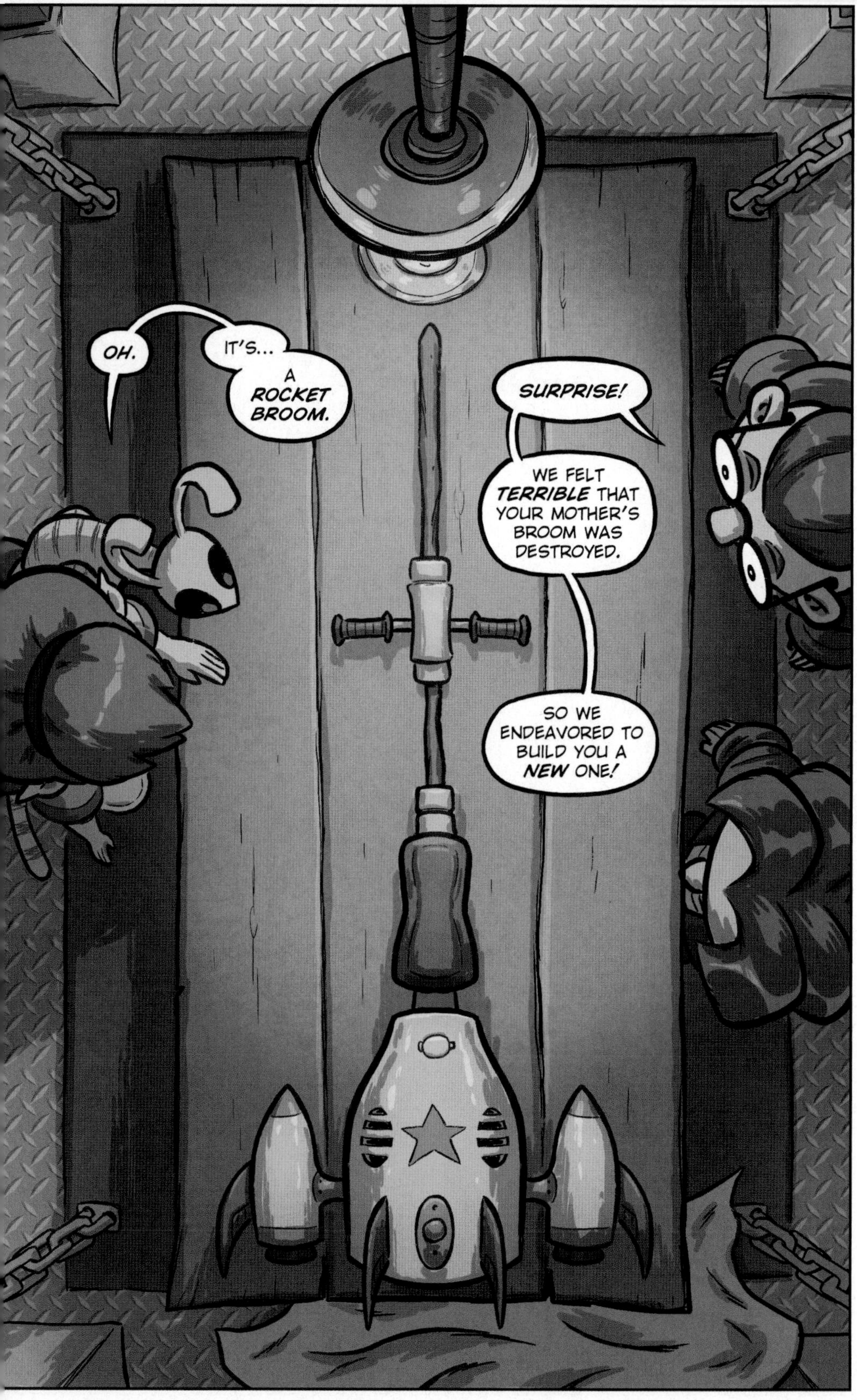
OH.
IT'S... A *ROCKET BROOM.*
SURPRISE!
WE FELT *TERRIBLE* THAT YOUR MOTHER'S BROOM WAS DESTROYED.
SO WE ENDEAVORED TO BUILD YOU A *NEW* ONE!

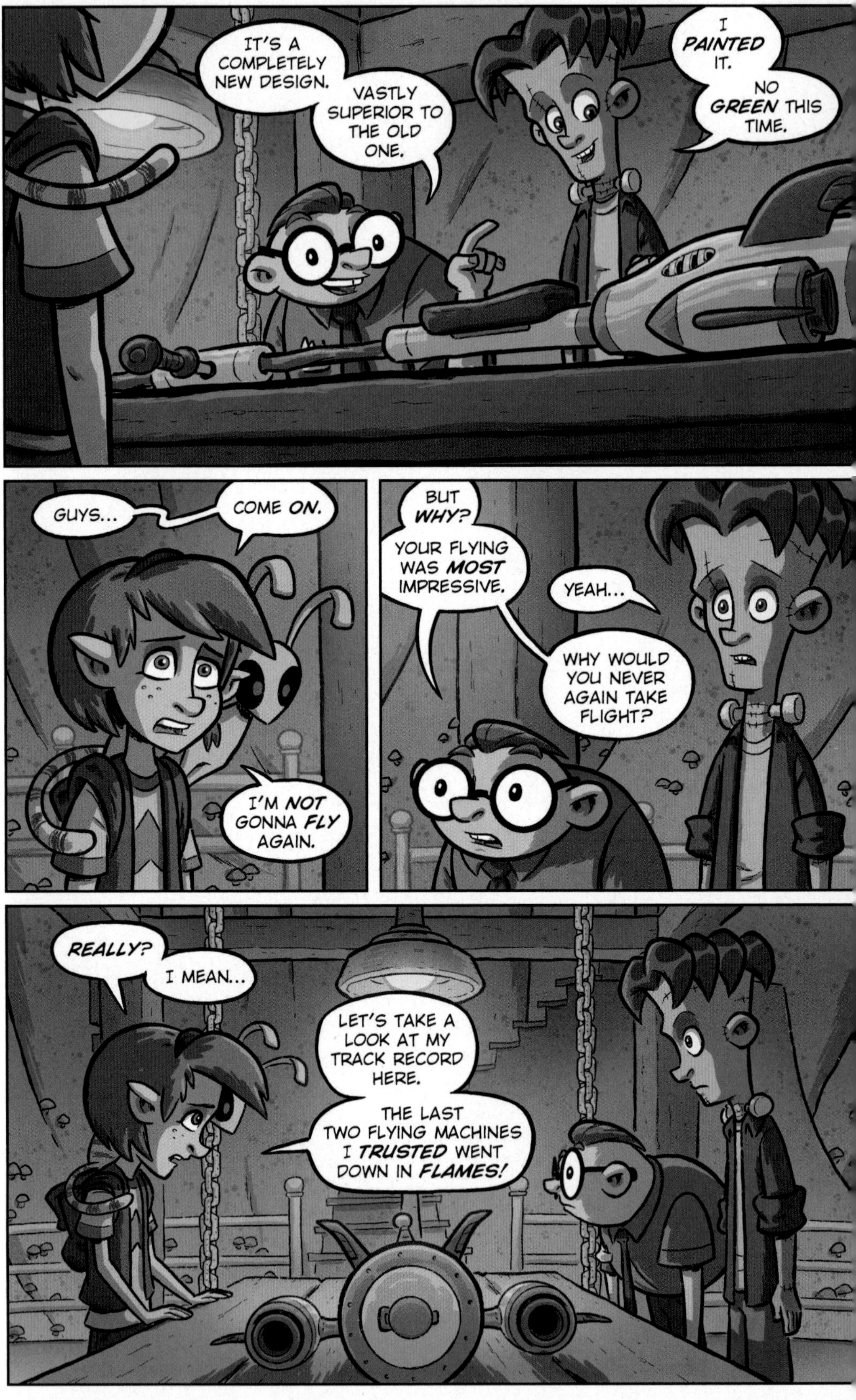
IT'S A COMPLETELY NEW DESIGN.
VASTLY SUPERIOR TO THE OLD ONE.
I *PAINTED* IT.
NO *GREEN* THIS TIME.
GUYS...
COME *ON.*
I'M *NOT* GONNA *FLY* AGAIN.
BUT *WHY?*
YOUR FLYING WAS *MOST* IMPRESSIVE.
YEAH...
WHY WOULD YOU NEVER AGAIN TAKE FLIGHT?
REALLY?
I MEAN...
LET'S TAKE A LOOK AT MY TRACK RECORD HERE.
THE LAST TWO FLYING MACHINES I *TRUSTED* WENT DOWN IN *FLAMES!*

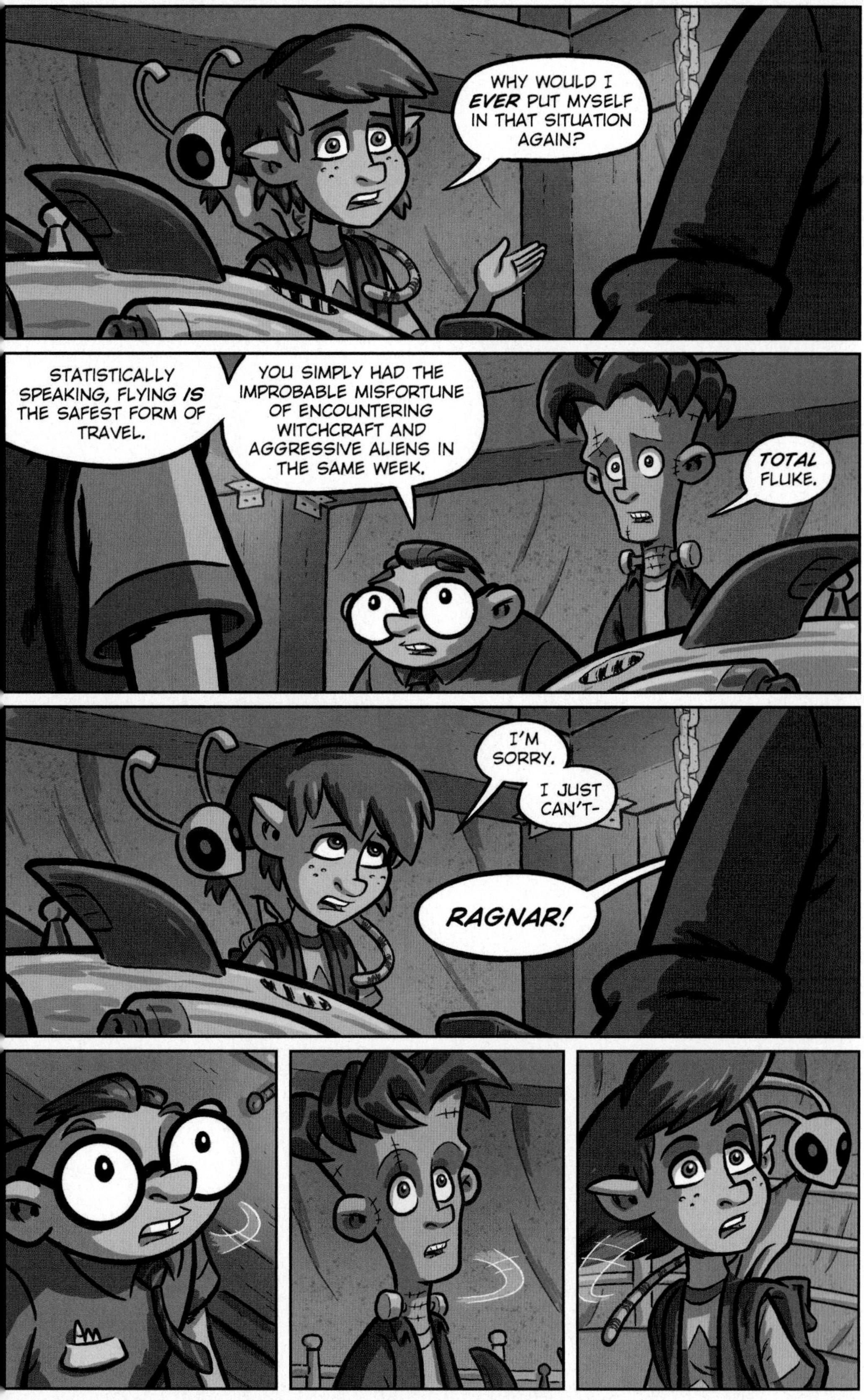
WHY WOULD I EVER PUT MYSELF IN THAT SITUATION AGAIN?
STATISTICALLY SPEAKING, FLYING IS THE SAFEST FORM OF TRAVEL.
YOU SIMPLY HAD THE IMPROBABLE MISFORTUNE OF ENCOUNTERING WITCHCRAFT AND AGGRESSIVE ALIENS IN THE SAME WEEK.
TOTAL FLUKE.
I'M SORRY.
I JUST CAN'T-
RAGNAR!

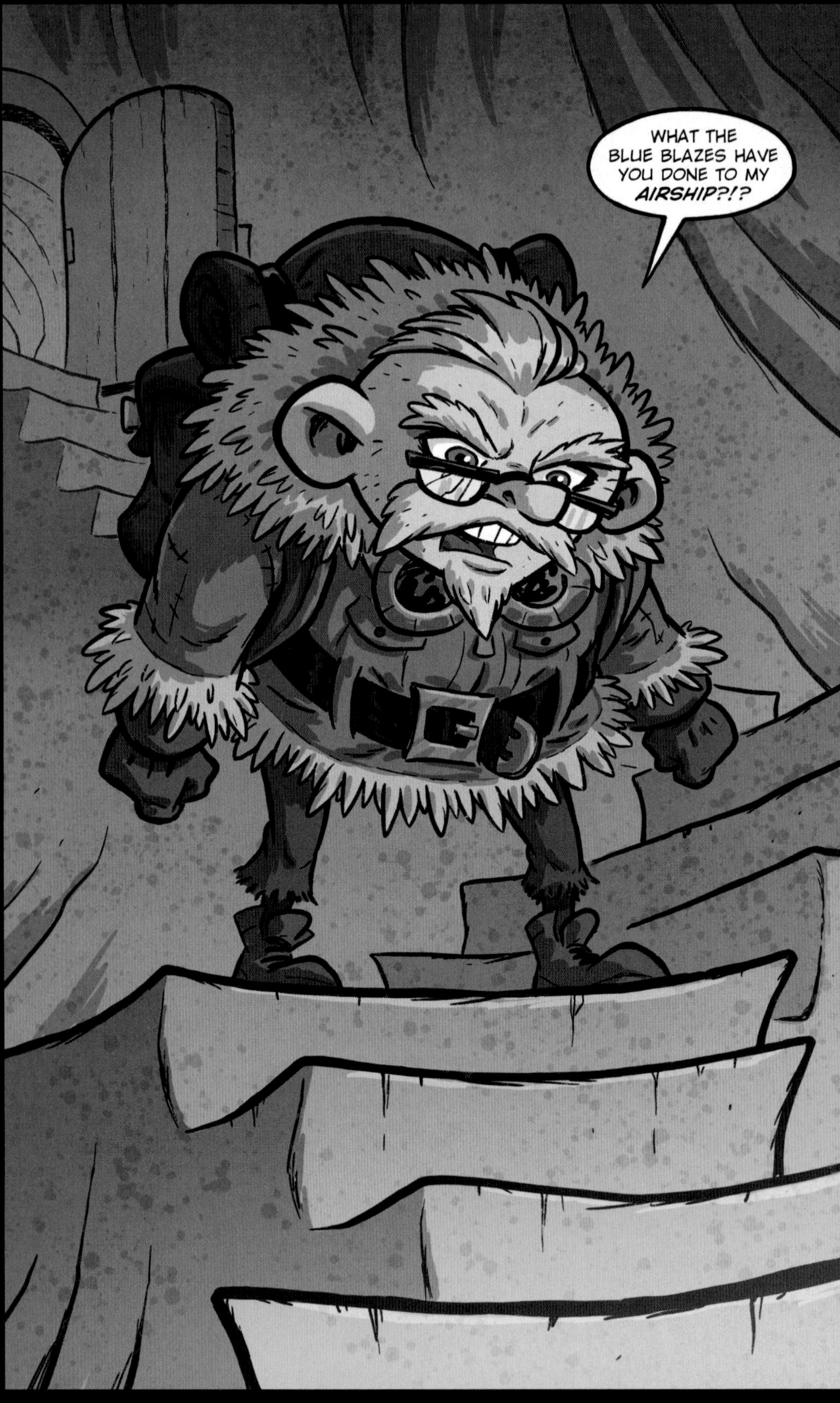
WHAT THE BLUE BLAZES HAVE YOU DONE TO MY *AIRSHIP*?!?

Chapter 18
A Change In The Weather

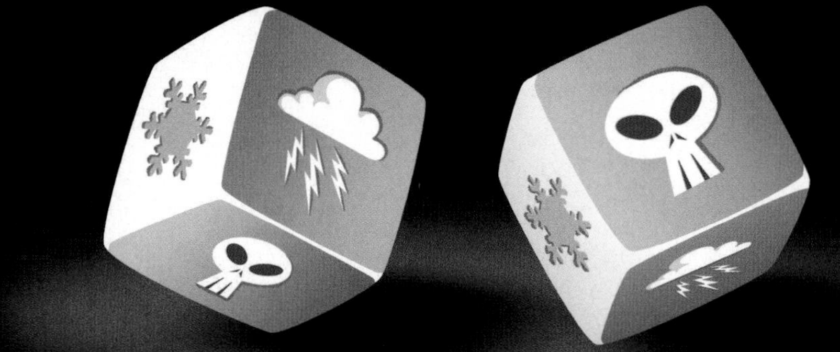

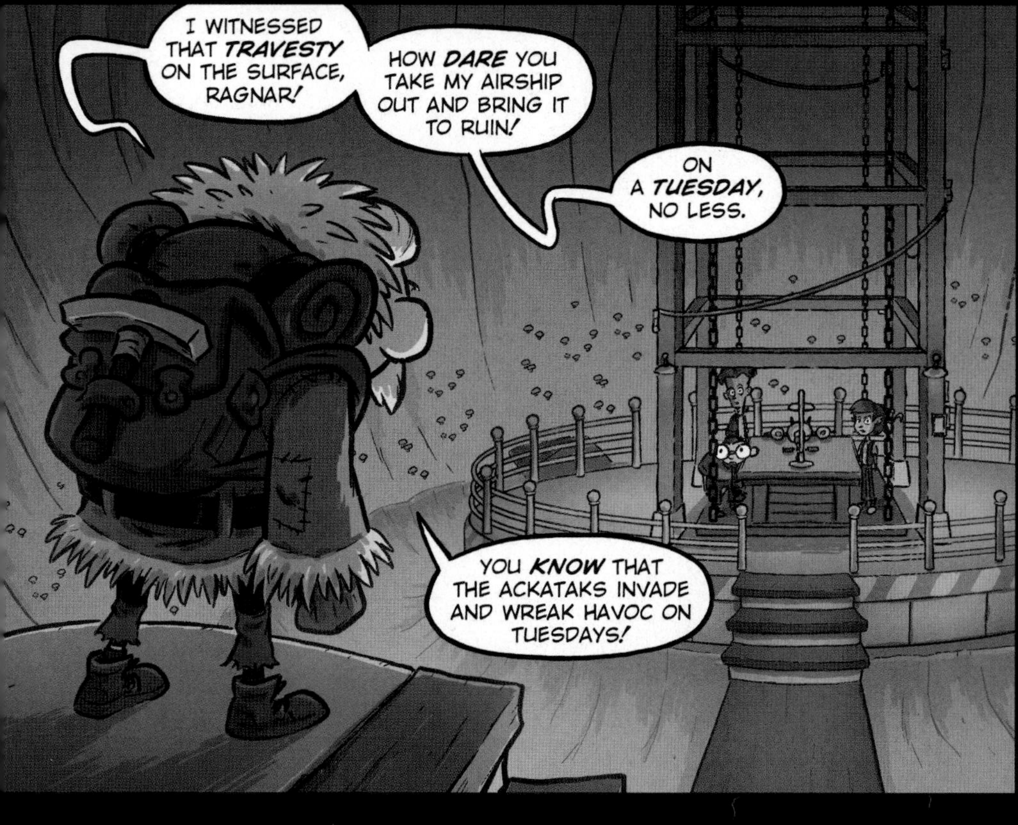
I WITNESSED THAT TRAVESTY ON THE SURFACE, RAGNAR!
HOW DARE YOU TAKE MY AIRSHIP OUT AND BRING IT TO RUIN!
ON A TUESDAY, NO LESS.
YOU KNOW THAT THE ACKATAKS INVADE AND WREAK HAVOC ON TUESDAYS!

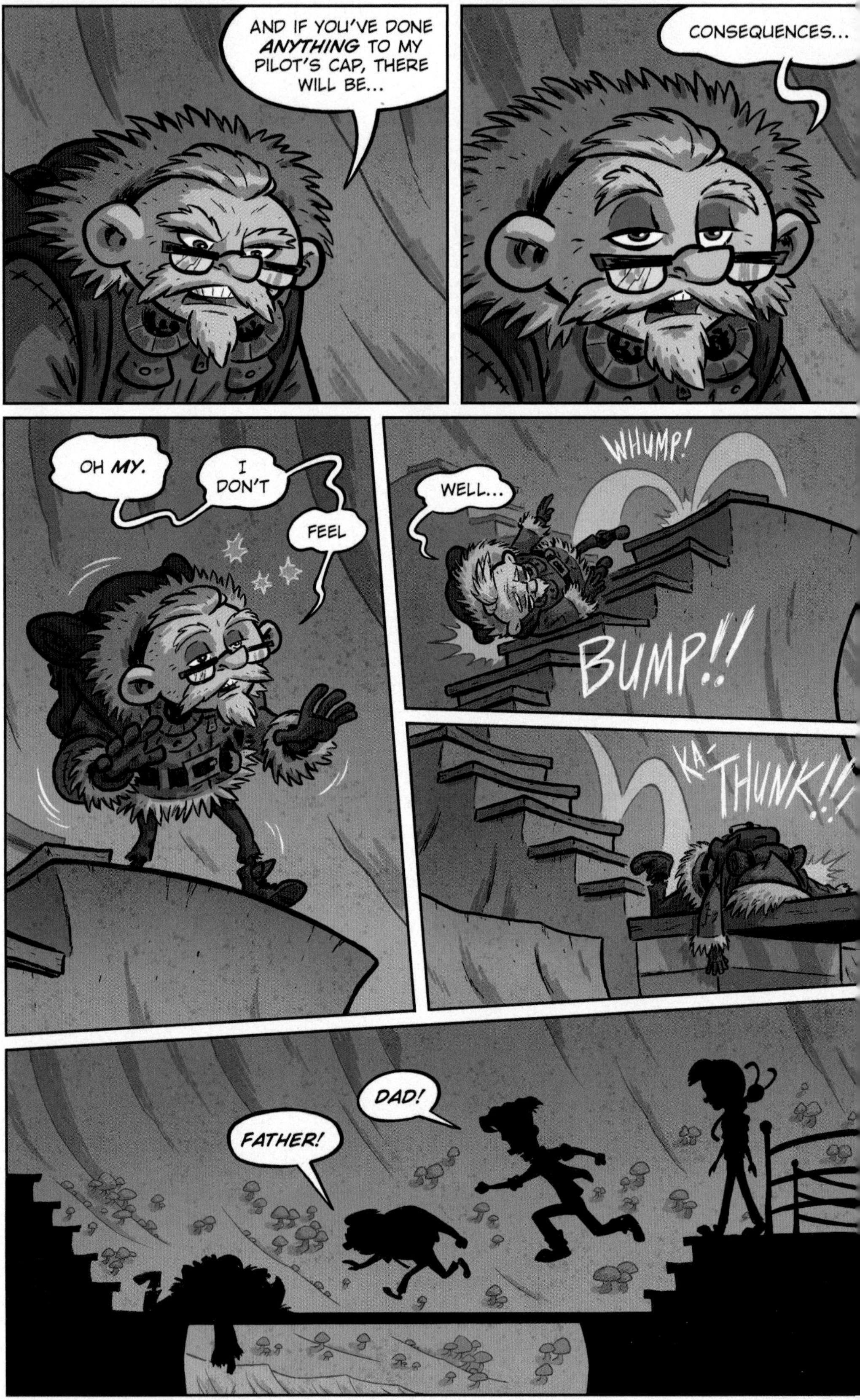
AND IF YOU'VE DONE ANYTHING TO MY PILOT'S CAP, THERE WILL BE...
CONSEQUENCES...
OH MY.
I DON'T
FEEL
WELL...
WHUMP!
BUMP!!
KA-THUNK!!!
DAD!
FATHER!

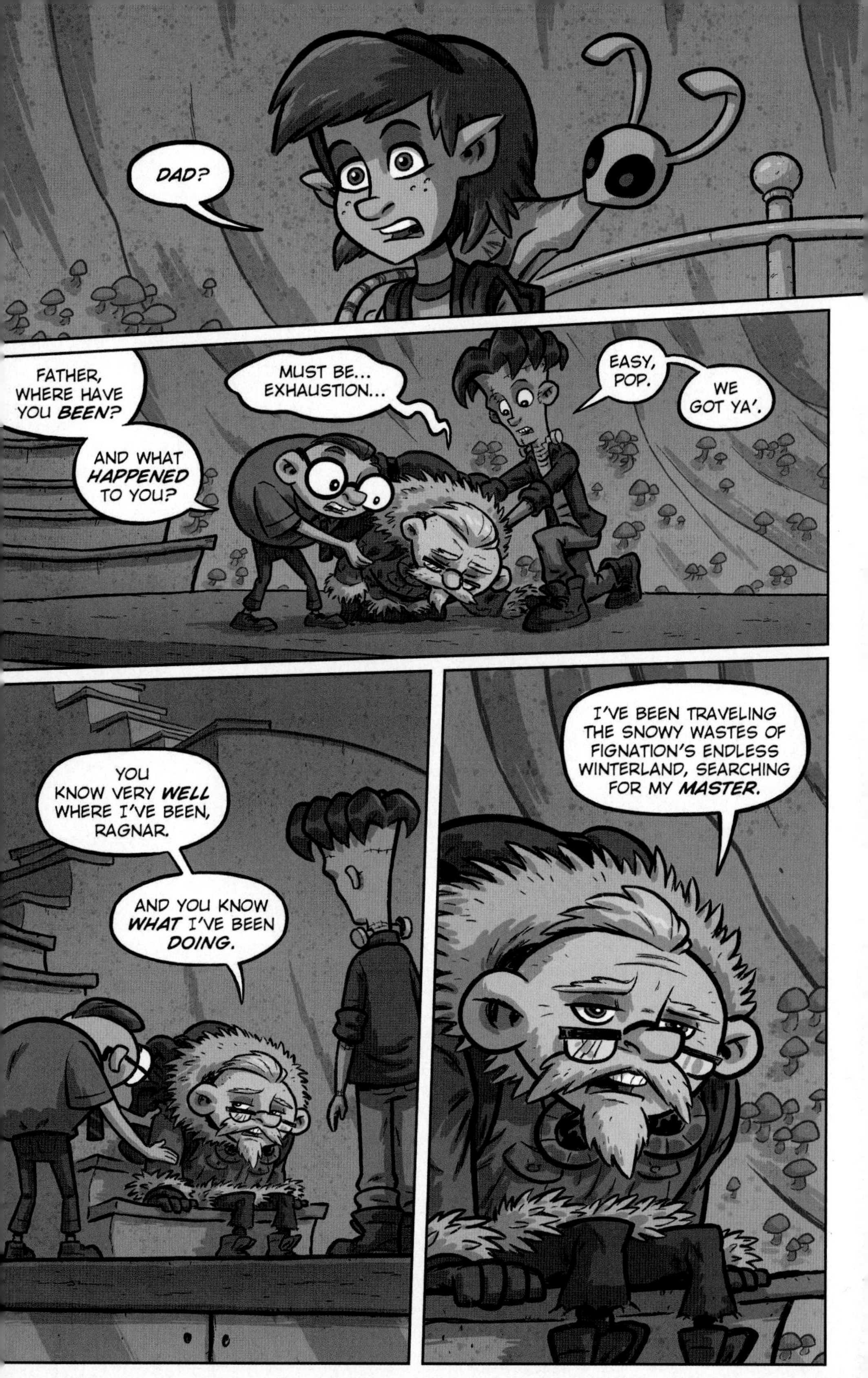
DAD?
FATHER, WHERE HAVE YOU BEEN?
AND WHAT HAPPENED TO YOU?
MUST BE... EXHAUSTION...
EASY, POP.
WE GOT YA'.
YOU KNOW VERY WELL WHERE I'VE BEEN, RAGNAR.
AND YOU KNOW WHAT I'VE BEEN DOING.
I'VE BEEN TRAVELING THE SNOWY WASTES OF FIGNATION'S ENDLESS WINTERLAND, SEARCHING FOR MY MASTER.

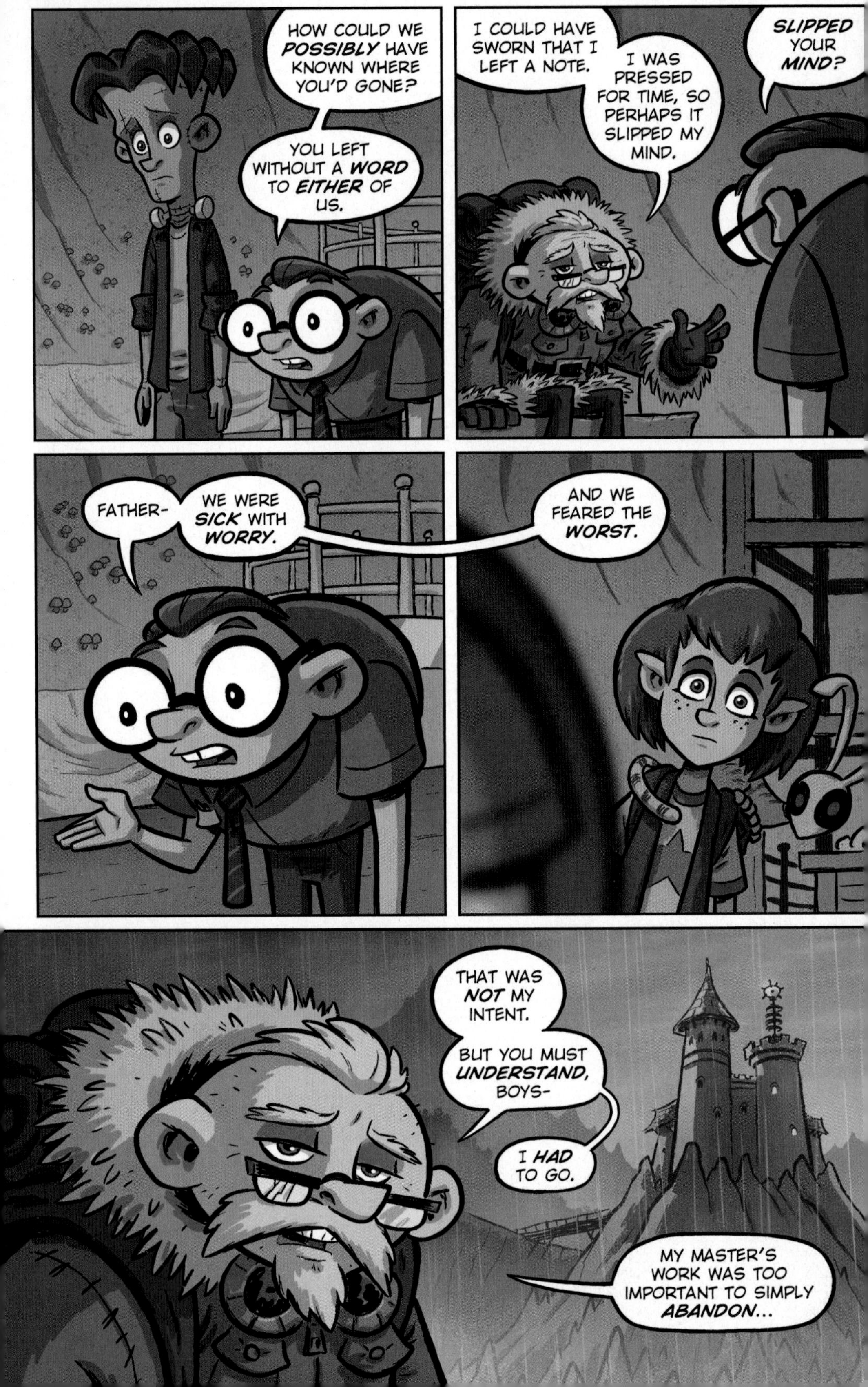
HOW COULD WE POSSIBLY HAVE KNOWN WHERE YOU'D GONE?
YOU LEFT WITHOUT A WORD TO EITHER OF US.
I COULD HAVE SWORN THAT I LEFT A NOTE.
I WAS PRESSED FOR TIME, SO PERHAPS IT SLIPPED MY MIND.
SLIPPED YOUR MIND?
FATHER-
WE WERE SICK WITH WORRY.
AND WE FEARED THE WORST.
THAT WAS NOT MY INTENT.
BUT YOU MUST UNDERSTAND, BOYS-
I HAD TO GO.
MY MASTER'S WORK WAS TOO IMPORTANT TO SIMPLY ABANDON...

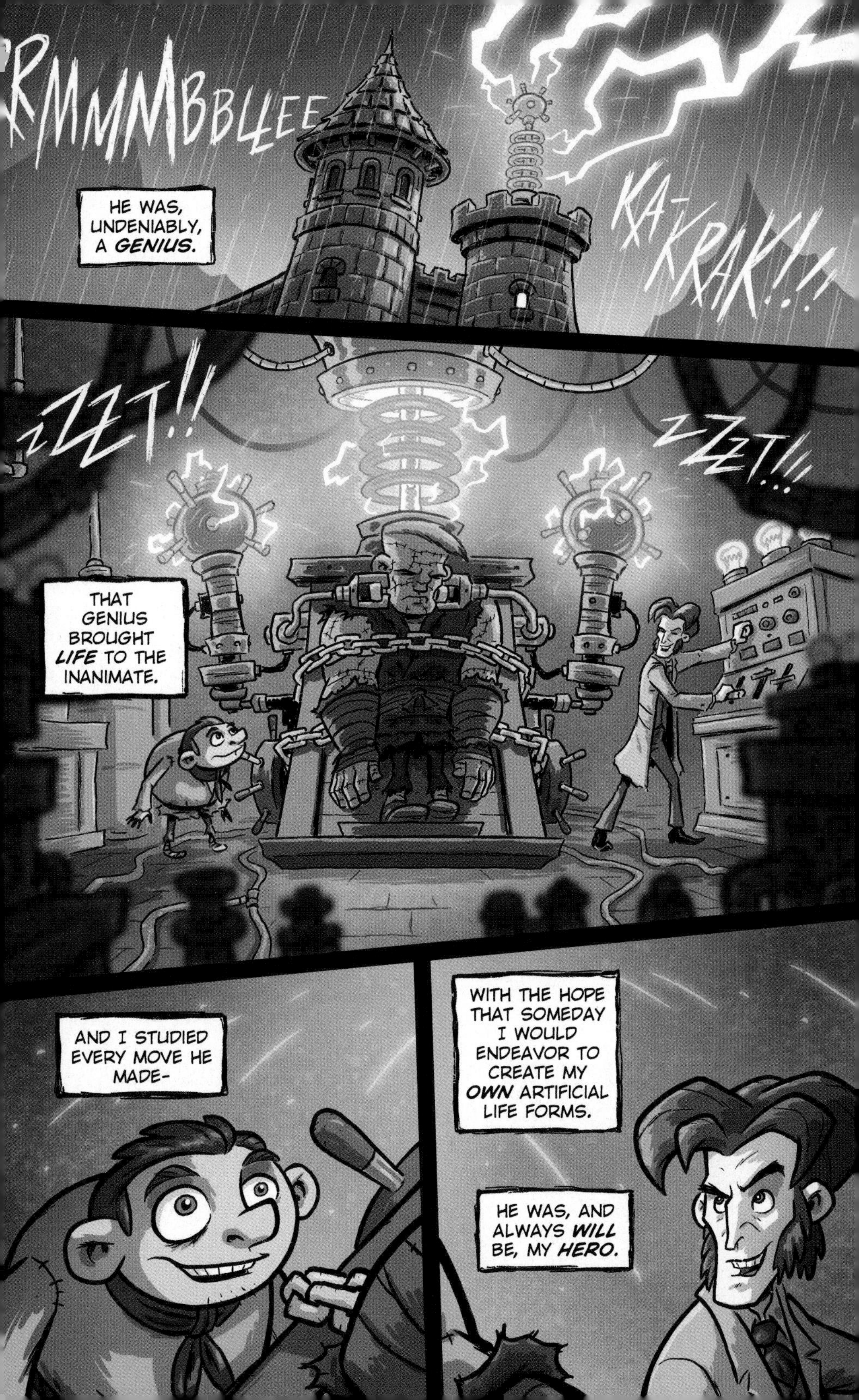
RMMMBBLLEEE
HE WAS, UNDENIABLY, A ***GENIUS.***
KA-KRAK!!!
ZZZT!!
ZZZT!!!
THAT GENIUS BROUGHT ***LIFE*** TO THE INANIMATE.
AND I STUDIED EVERY MOVE HE MADE-
WITH THE HOPE THAT SOMEDAY I WOULD ENDEAVOR TO CREATE MY ***OWN*** ARTIFICIAL LIFE FORMS.
HE WAS, AND ALWAYS ***WILL*** BE, MY ***HERO.***

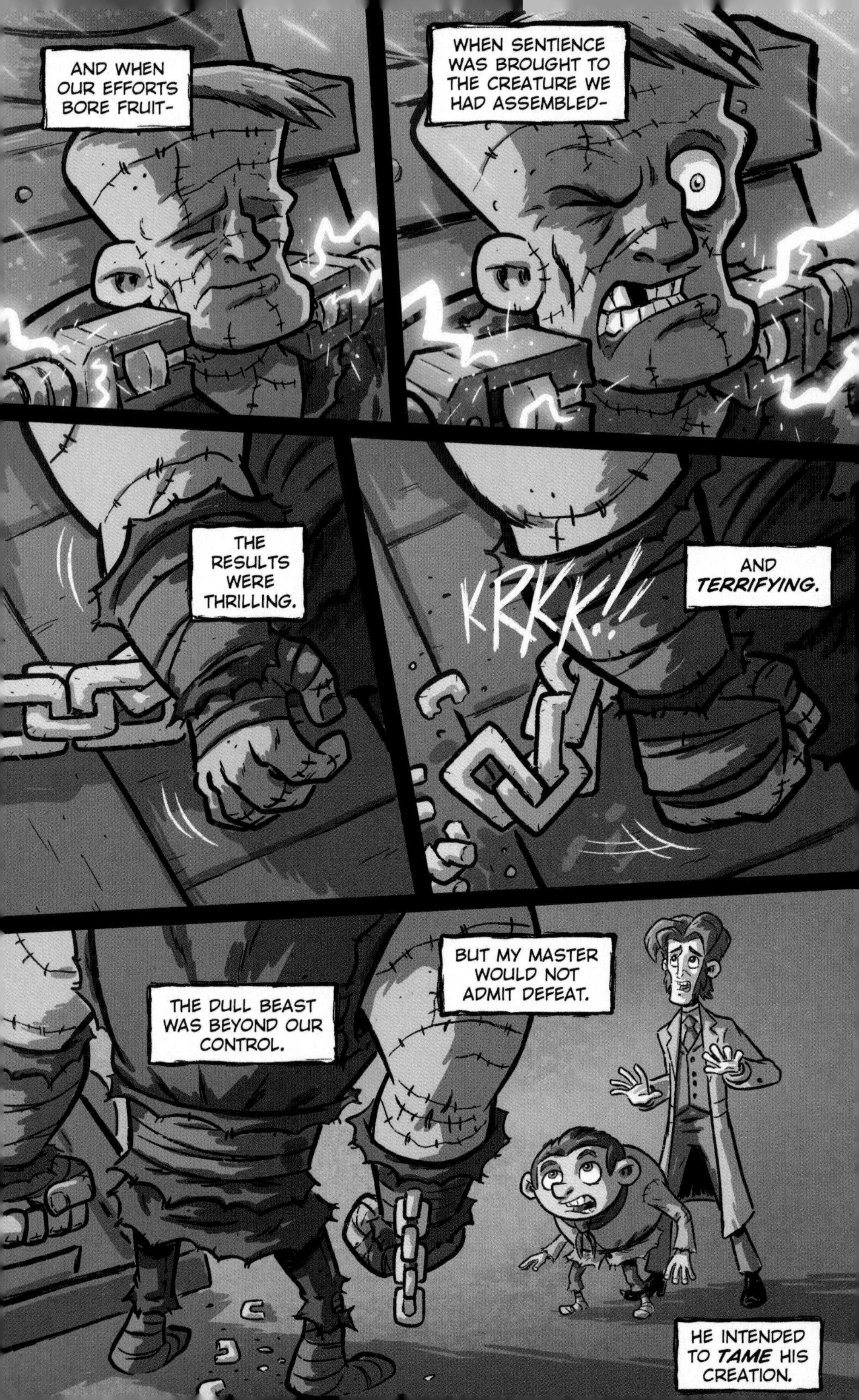
AND WHEN OUR EFFORTS BORE FRUIT-
WHEN SENTIENCE WAS BROUGHT TO THE CREATURE WE HAD ASSEMBLED-
THE RESULTS WERE THRILLING.
KRKK!!
AND *TERRIFYING.*
THE DULL BEAST WAS BEYOND OUR CONTROL.
BUT MY MASTER WOULD NOT ADMIT DEFEAT.
HE INTENDED TO *TAME* HIS CREATION.

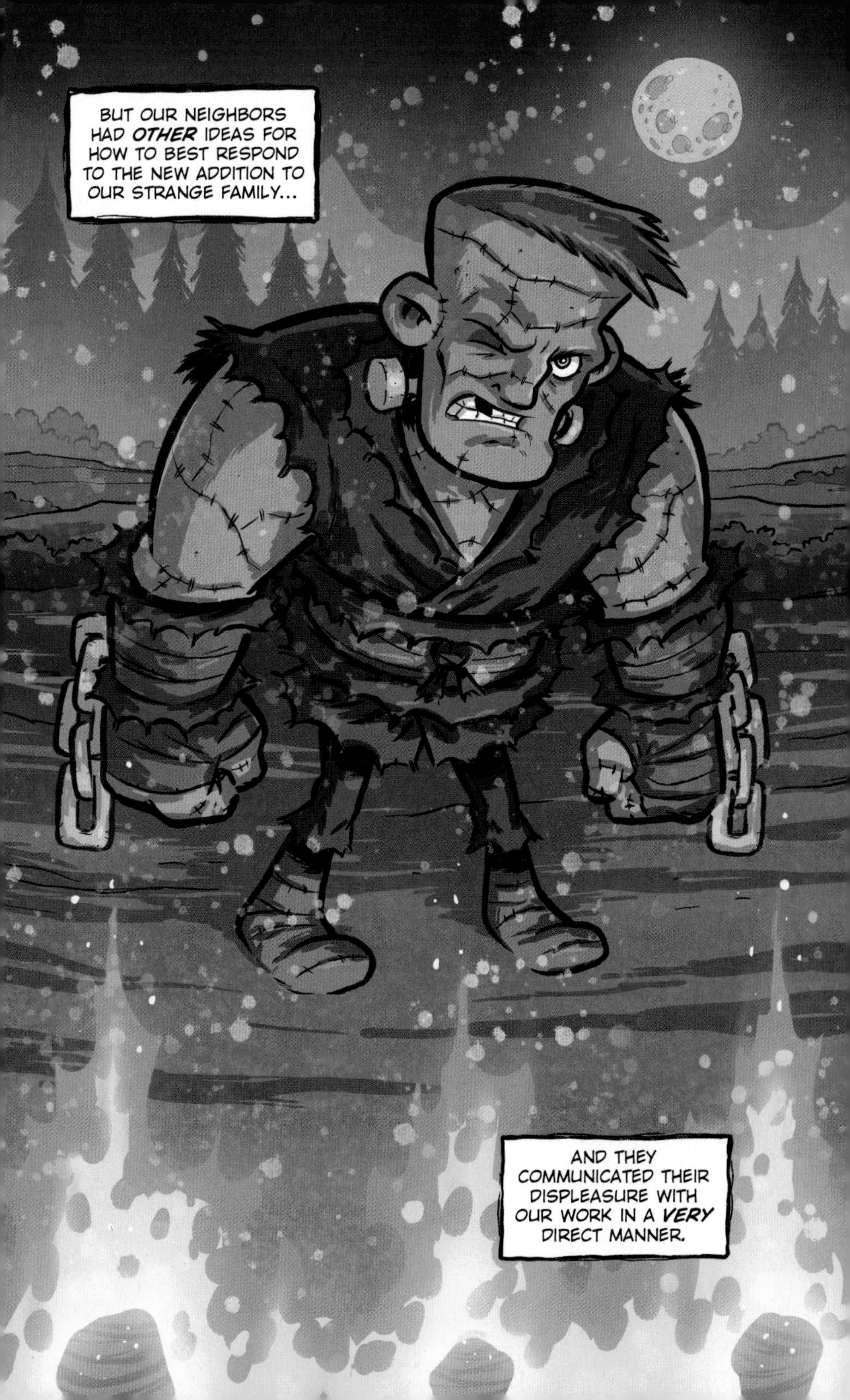
BUT OUR NEIGHBORS HAD *OTHER* IDEAS FOR HOW TO BEST RESPOND TO THE NEW ADDITION TO OUR STRANGE FAMILY...
AND THEY COMMUNICATED THEIR DISPLEASURE WITH OUR WORK IN A *VERY* DIRECT MANNER.

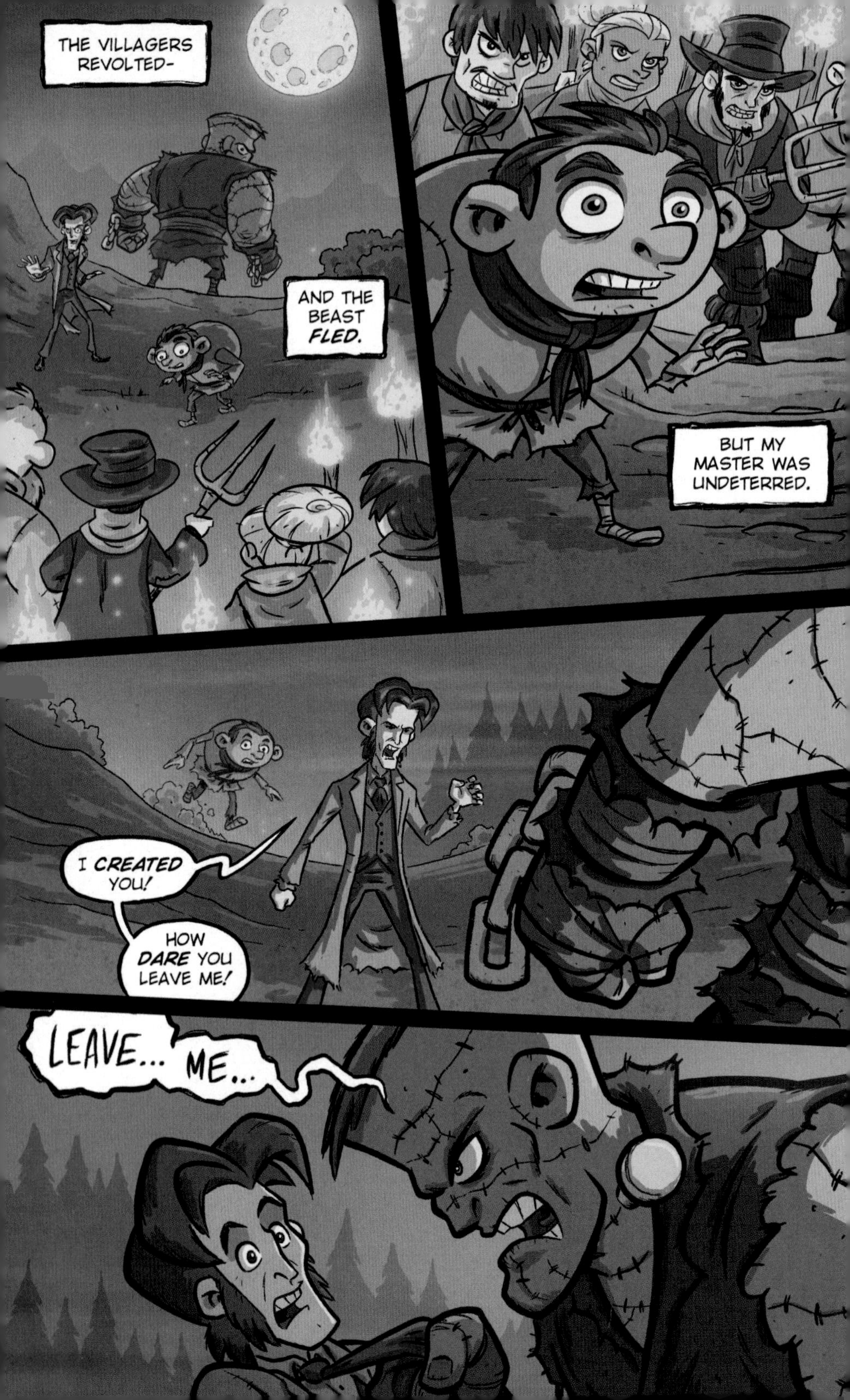
THE VILLAGERS REVOLTED-
AND THE BEAST FLED.
BUT MY MASTER WAS UNDETERRED.
I CREATED YOU!
HOW DARE YOU LEAVE ME!
LEAVE... ME...

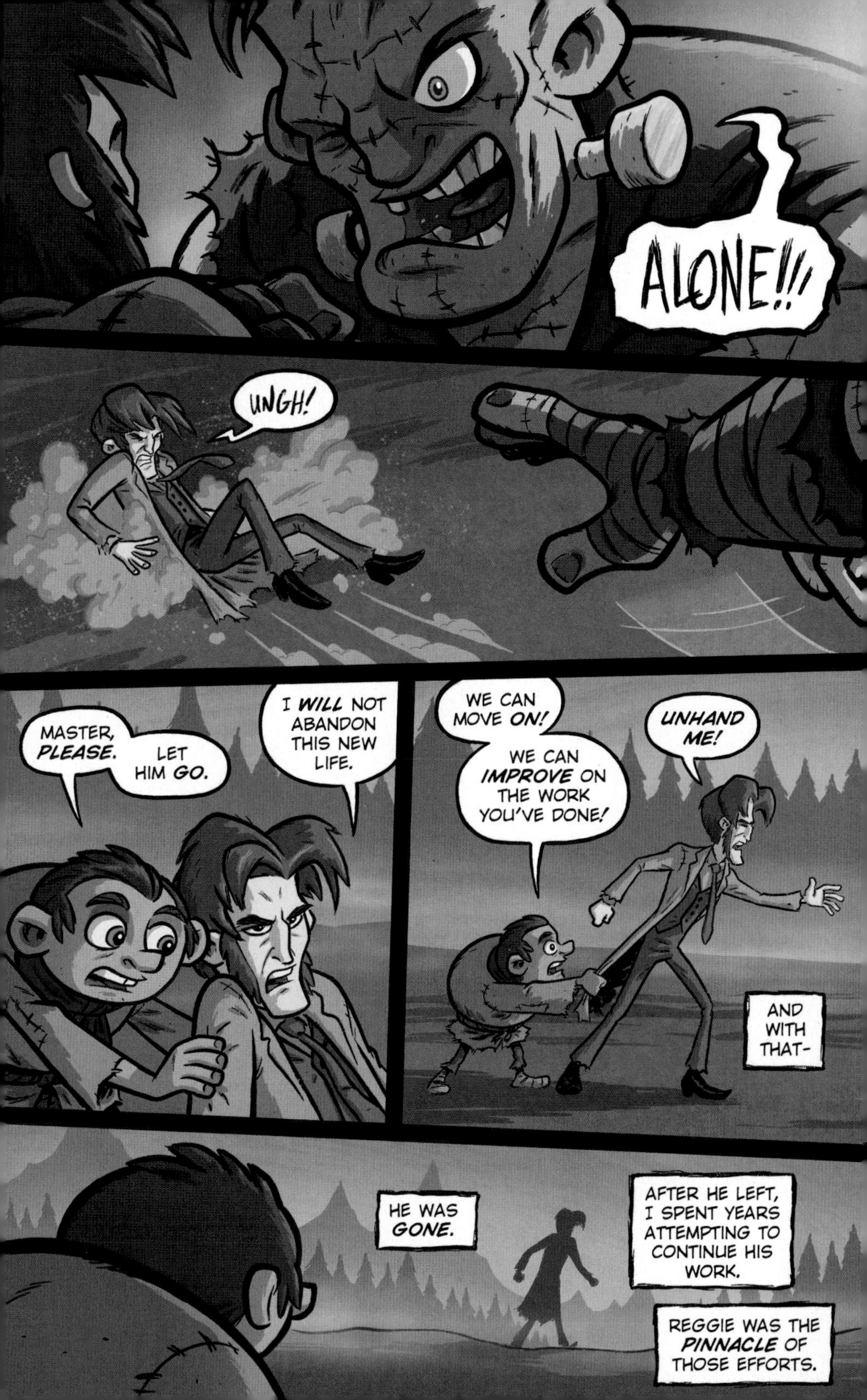
ALONE!!!
UNGH!
MASTER, PLEASE.
LET HIM GO.
I WILL NOT ABANDON THIS NEW LIFE.
WE CAN MOVE ON!
WE CAN IMPROVE ON THE WORK YOU'VE DONE!
UNHAND ME!
AND WITH THAT-
HE WAS GONE.
AFTER HE LEFT, I SPENT YEARS ATTEMPTING TO CONTINUE HIS WORK.
REGGIE WAS THE PINNACLE OF THOSE EFFORTS.

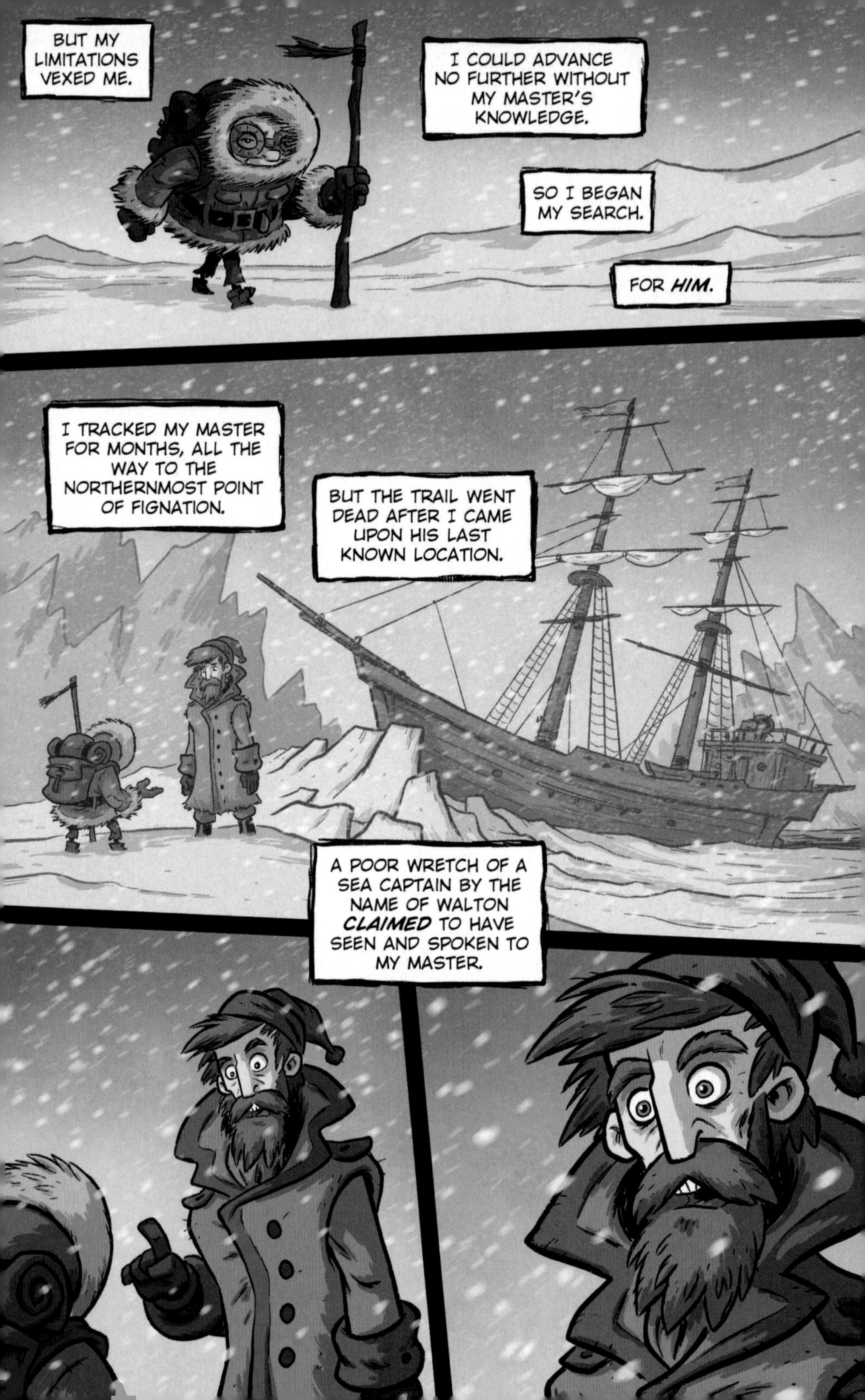
BUT MY LIMITATIONS VEXED ME.
I COULD ADVANCE NO FURTHER WITHOUT MY MASTER'S KNOWLEDGE.
SO I BEGAN MY SEARCH.
FOR *HIM*.
I TRACKED MY MASTER FOR MONTHS, ALL THE WAY TO THE NORTHERNMOST POINT OF FIGNATION.
BUT THE TRAIL WENT DEAD AFTER I CAME UPON HIS LAST KNOWN LOCATION.
A POOR WRETCH OF A SEA CAPTAIN BY THE NAME OF WALTON ***CLAIMED*** TO HAVE SEEN AND SPOKEN TO MY MASTER.

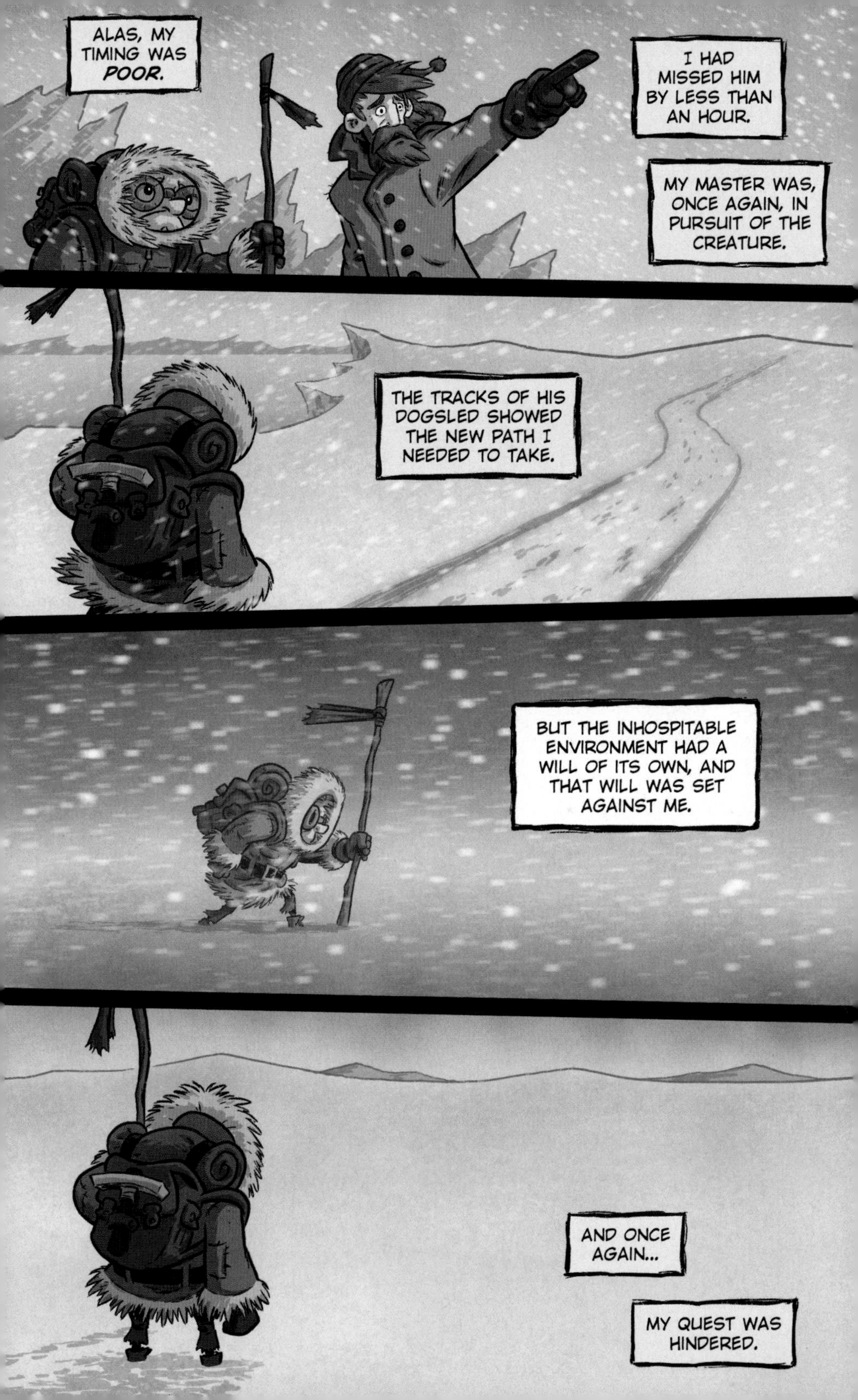
ALAS, MY TIMING WAS POOR.
I HAD MISSED HIM BY LESS THAN AN HOUR.
MY MASTER WAS, ONCE AGAIN, IN PURSUIT OF THE CREATURE.
THE TRACKS OF HIS DOGSLED SHOWED THE NEW PATH I NEEDED TO TAKE.
BUT THE INHOSPITABLE ENVIRONMENT HAD A WILL OF ITS OWN, AND THAT WILL WAS SET AGAINST ME.
AND ONCE AGAIN...
MY QUEST WAS HINDERED.

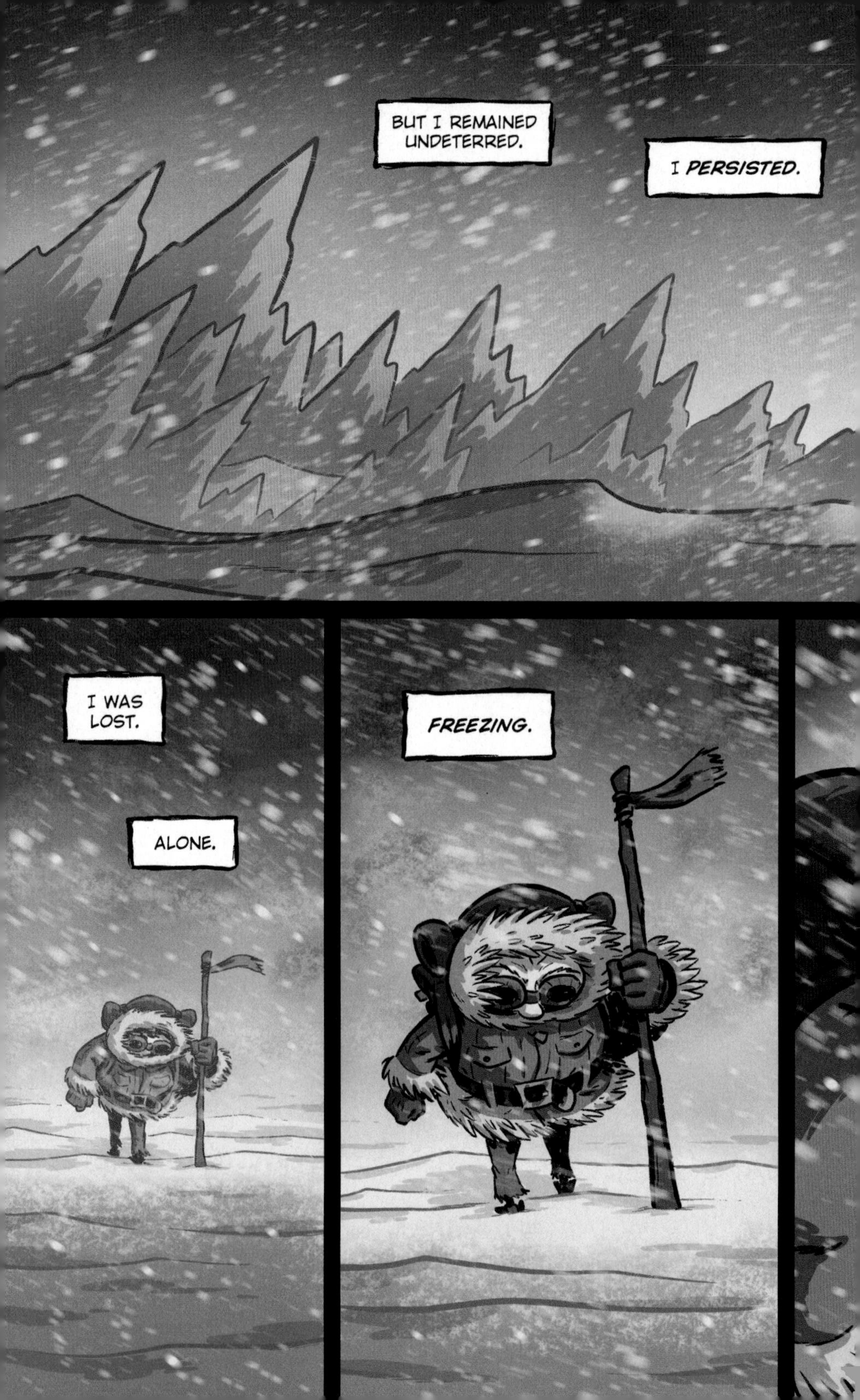
BUT I REMAINED UNDETERRED.
I PERSISTED.
I WAS LOST.
ALONE.
FREEZING.

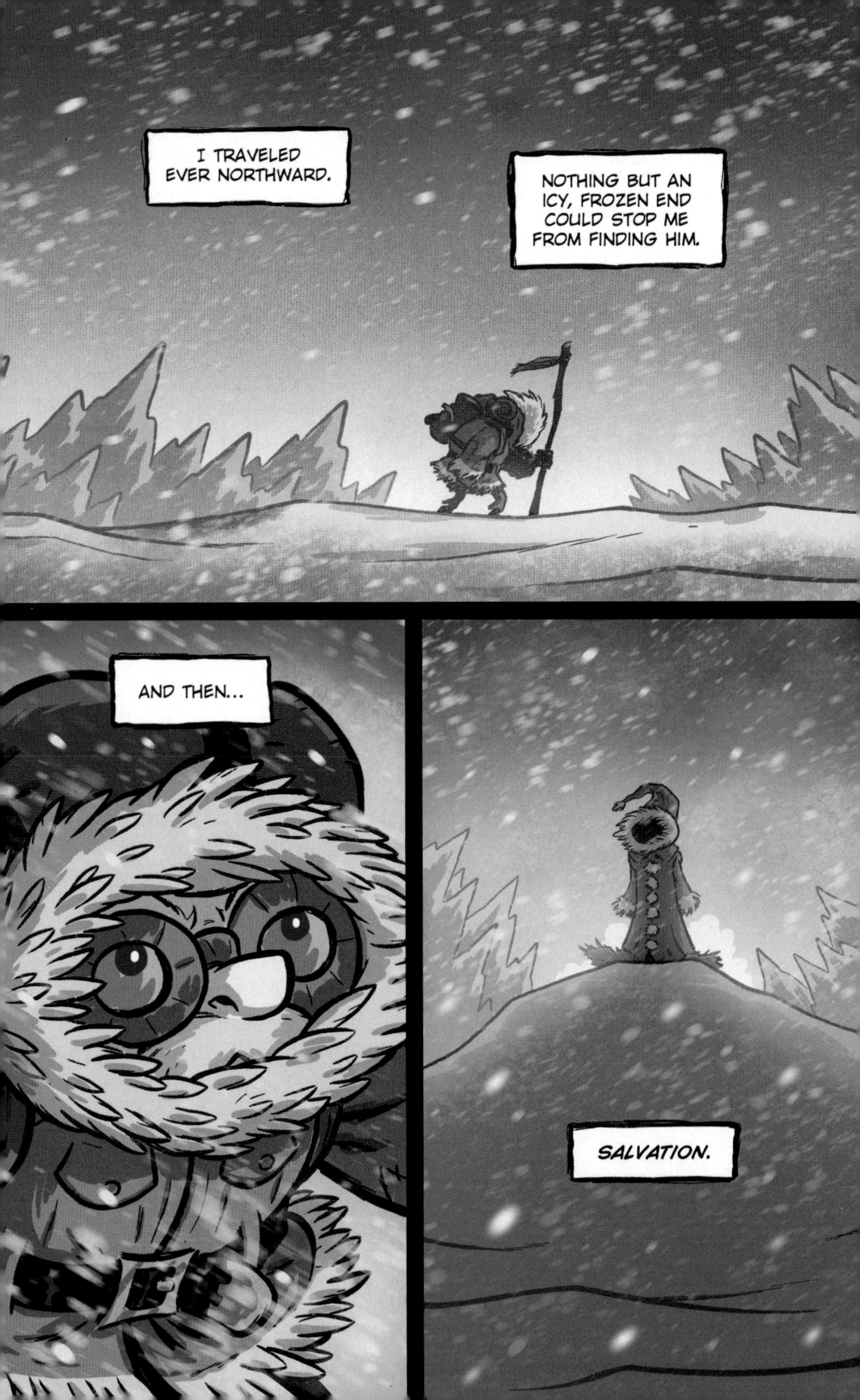
I TRAVELED EVER NORTHWARD.
NOTHING BUT AN ICY, FROZEN END COULD STOP ME FROM FINDING HIM.
AND THEN...
SALVATION.

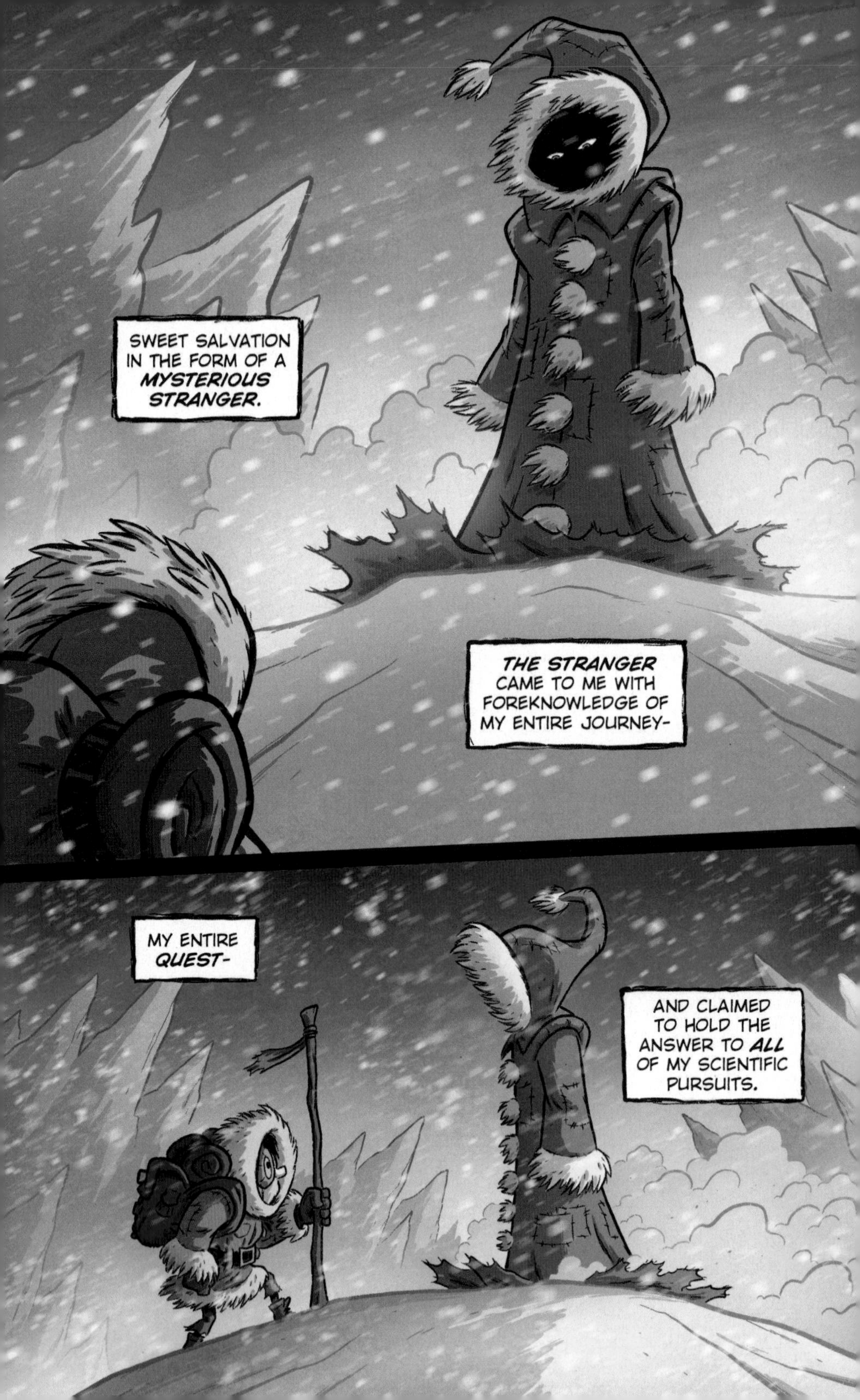
SWEET SALVATION IN THE FORM OF A *MYSTERIOUS STRANGER.*
THE STRANGER CAME TO ME WITH FOREKNOWLEDGE OF MY ENTIRE JOURNEY-
MY ENTIRE *QUEST-*
AND CLAIMED TO HOLD THE ANSWER TO *ALL* OF MY SCIENTIFIC PURSUITS.

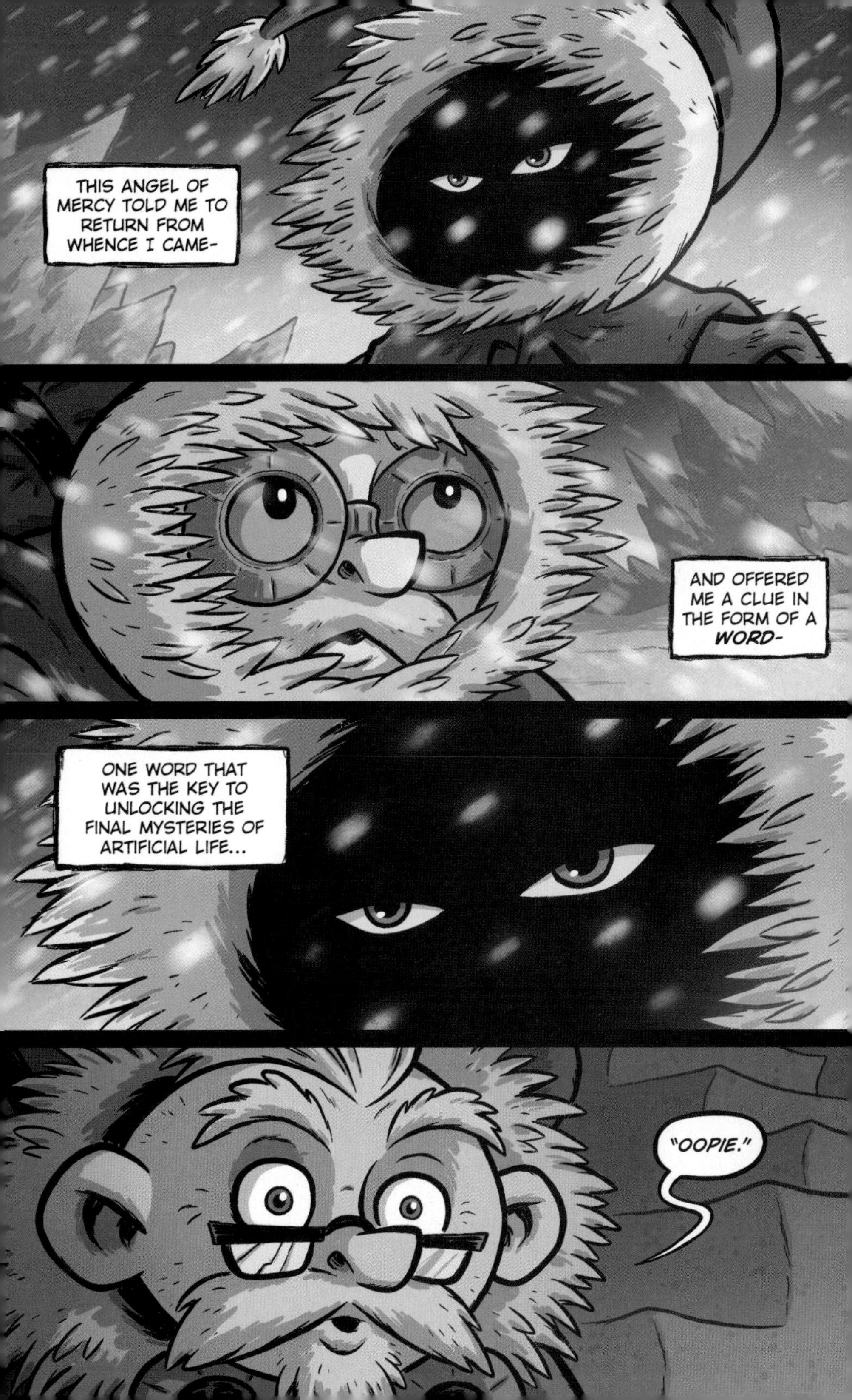
THIS ANGEL OF MERCY TOLD ME TO RETURN FROM WHENCE I CAME-
AND OFFERED ME A CLUE IN THE FORM OF A *WORD*-
ONE WORD THAT WAS THE KEY TO UNLOCKING THE FINAL MYSTERIES OF ARTIFICIAL LIFE...
"OOPIE."

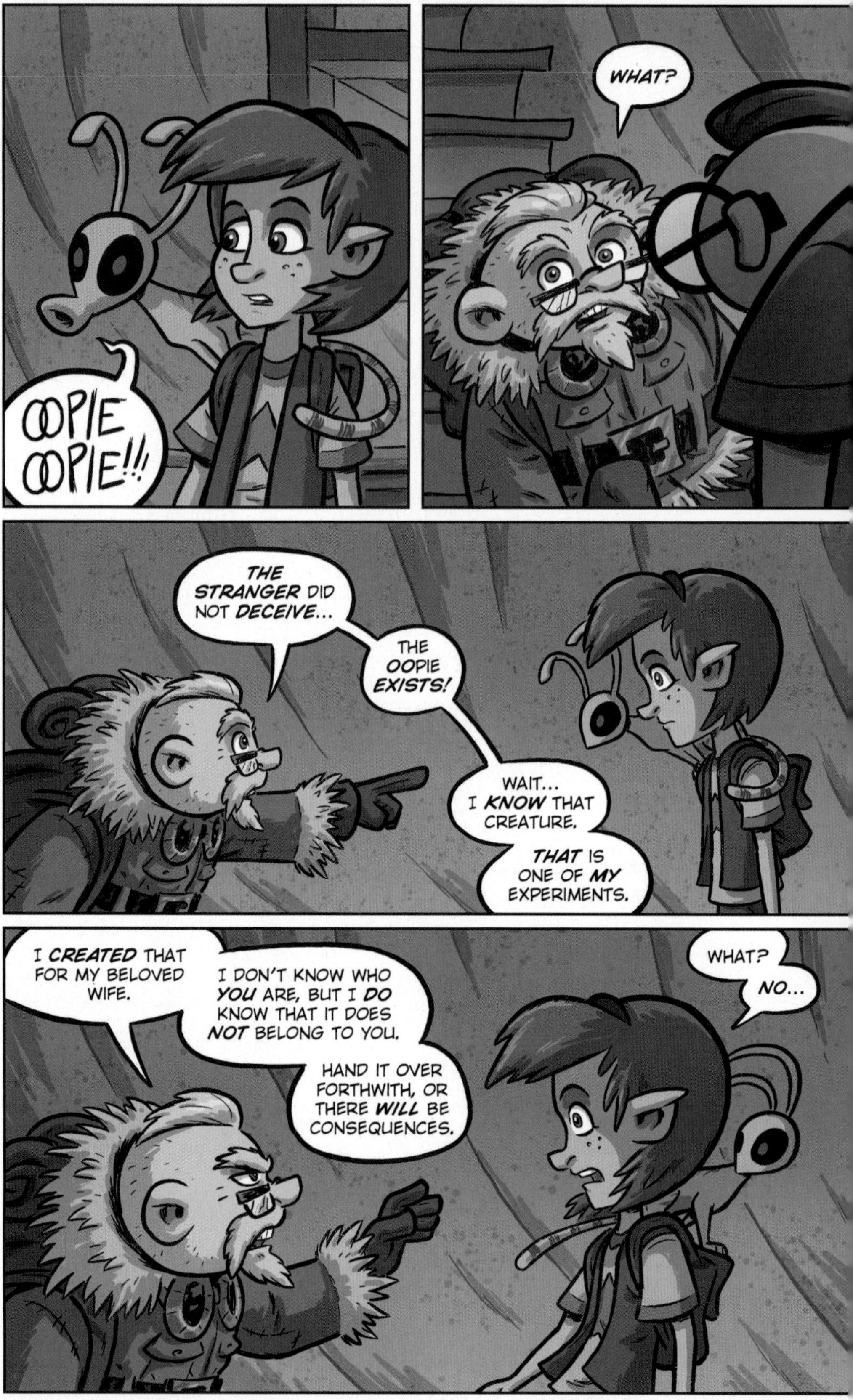
OOPIE OOPIE!!!
WHAT?
THE STRANGER DID NOT DECEIVE...
THE OOPIE EXISTS!
WAIT... I KNOW THAT CREATURE.
THAT IS ONE OF MY EXPERIMENTS.
I CREATED THAT FOR MY BELOVED WIFE.
I DON'T KNOW WHO YOU ARE, BUT I DO KNOW THAT IT DOES NOT BELONG TO YOU.
HAND IT OVER FORTHWITH, OR THERE WILL BE CONSEQUENCES.
WHAT?
NO...

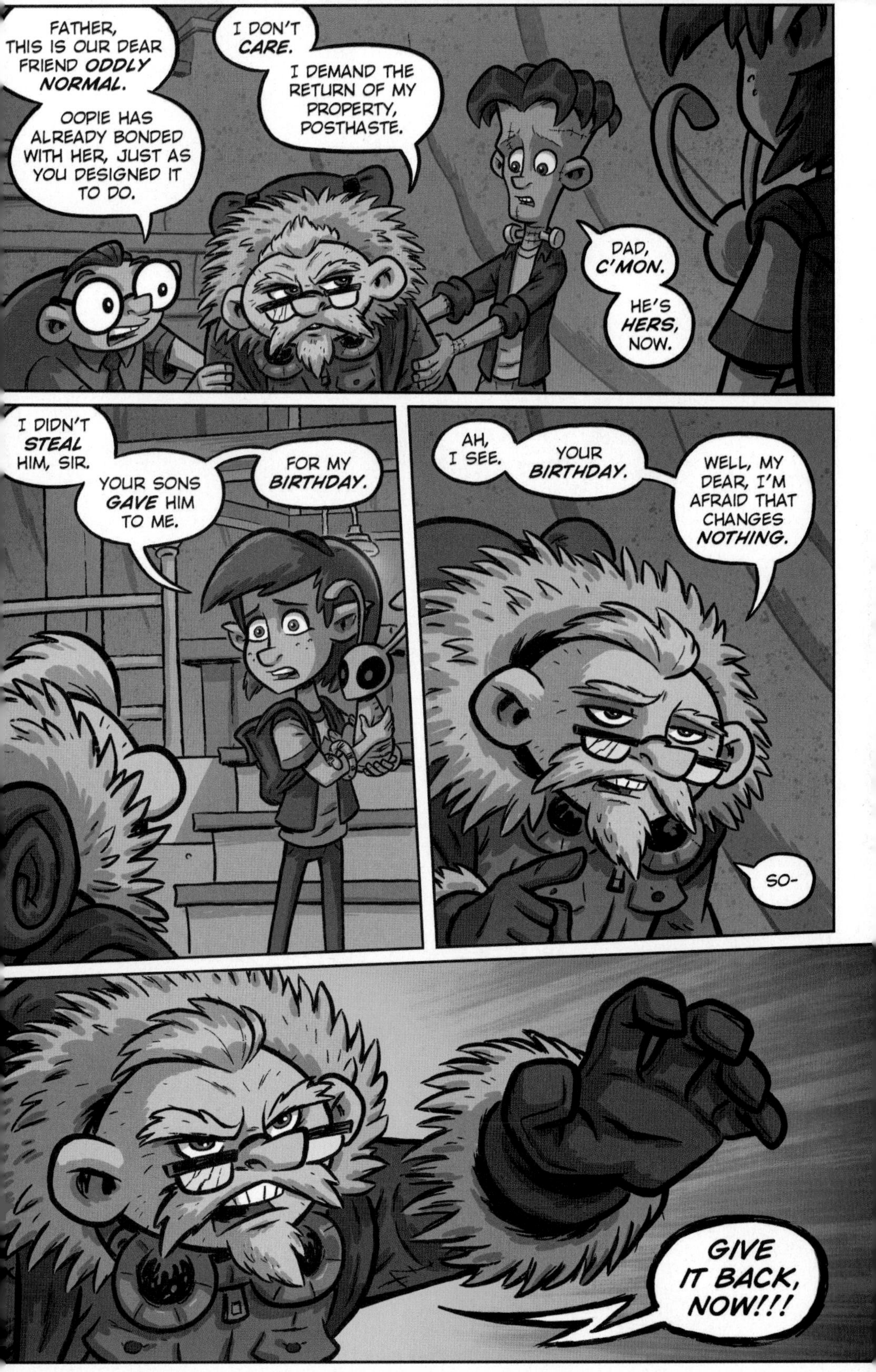
FATHER, THIS IS OUR DEAR FRIEND ODDLY NORMAL.
OOPIE HAS ALREADY BONDED WITH HER, JUST AS YOU DESIGNED IT TO DO.
I DON'T CARE.
I DEMAND THE RETURN OF MY PROPERTY, POSTHASTE.
DAD, C'MON.
HE'S HERS, NOW.
I DIDN'T STEAL HIM, SIR.
YOUR SONS GAVE HIM TO ME.
FOR MY BIRTHDAY.
AH, I SEE.
YOUR BIRTHDAY.
WELL, MY DEAR, I'M AFRAID THAT CHANGES NOTHING.
SO-
GIVE IT BACK, NOW!!!

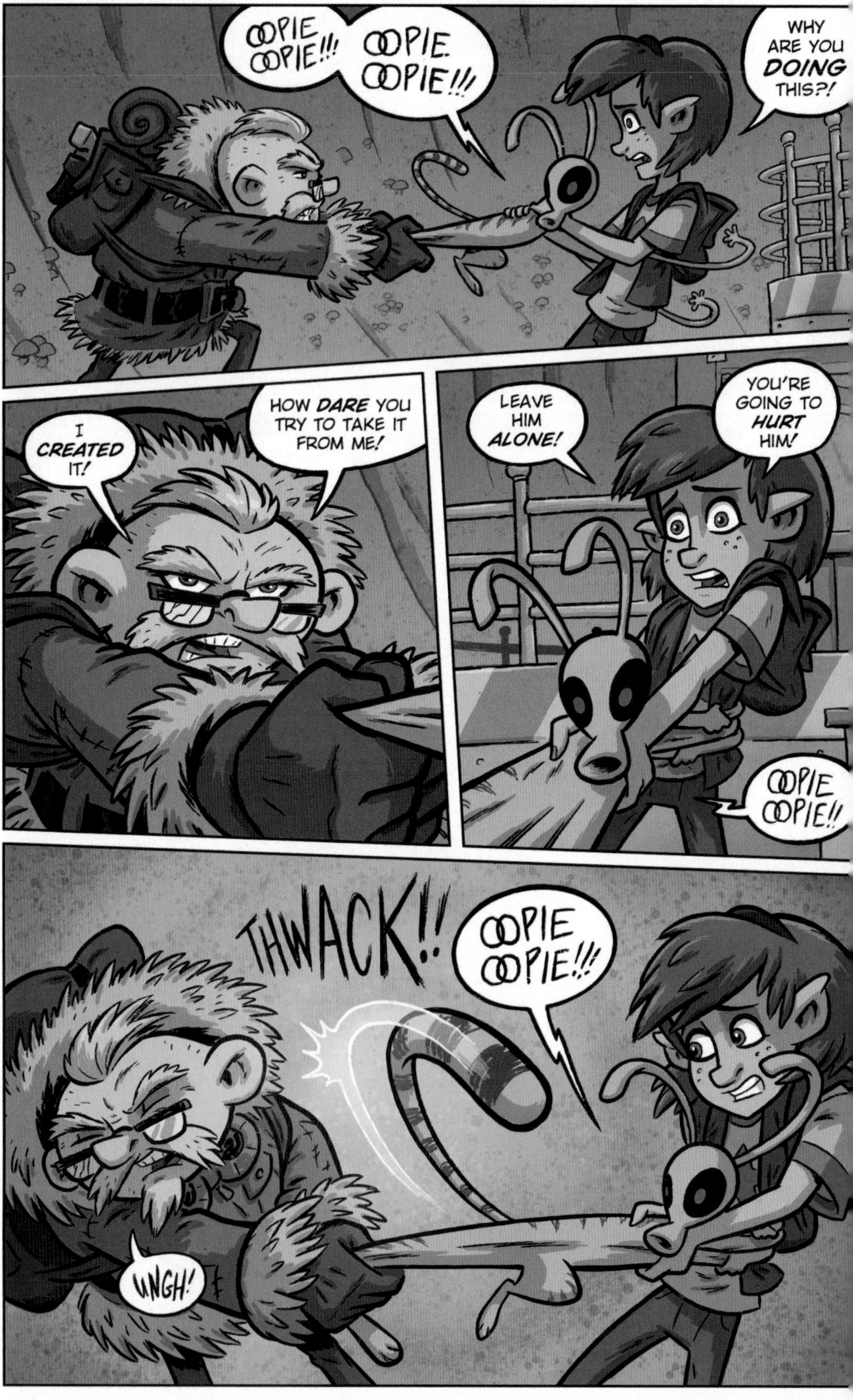
OOPIE OOPIE!!!
OOPIE OOPIE!!!
WHY ARE YOU DOING THIS?!
I CREATED IT!
HOW DARE YOU TRY TO TAKE IT FROM ME!
LEAVE HIM ALONE!
YOU'RE GOING TO HURT HIM!
OOPIE OOPIE!!
THWACK!!
OOPIE OOPIE!!!
UNGH!

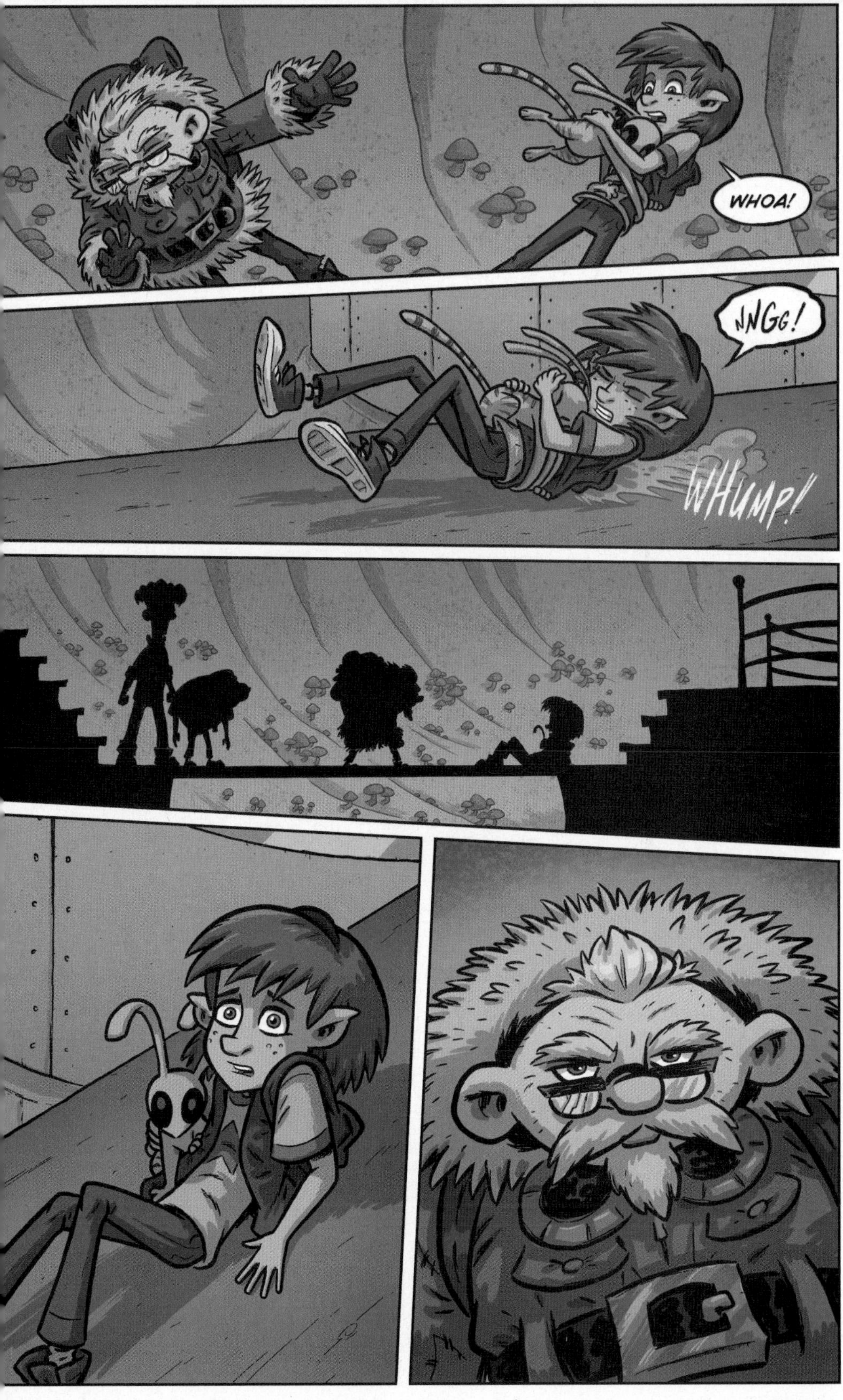
WHOA!
NNGG!
WHUMP!

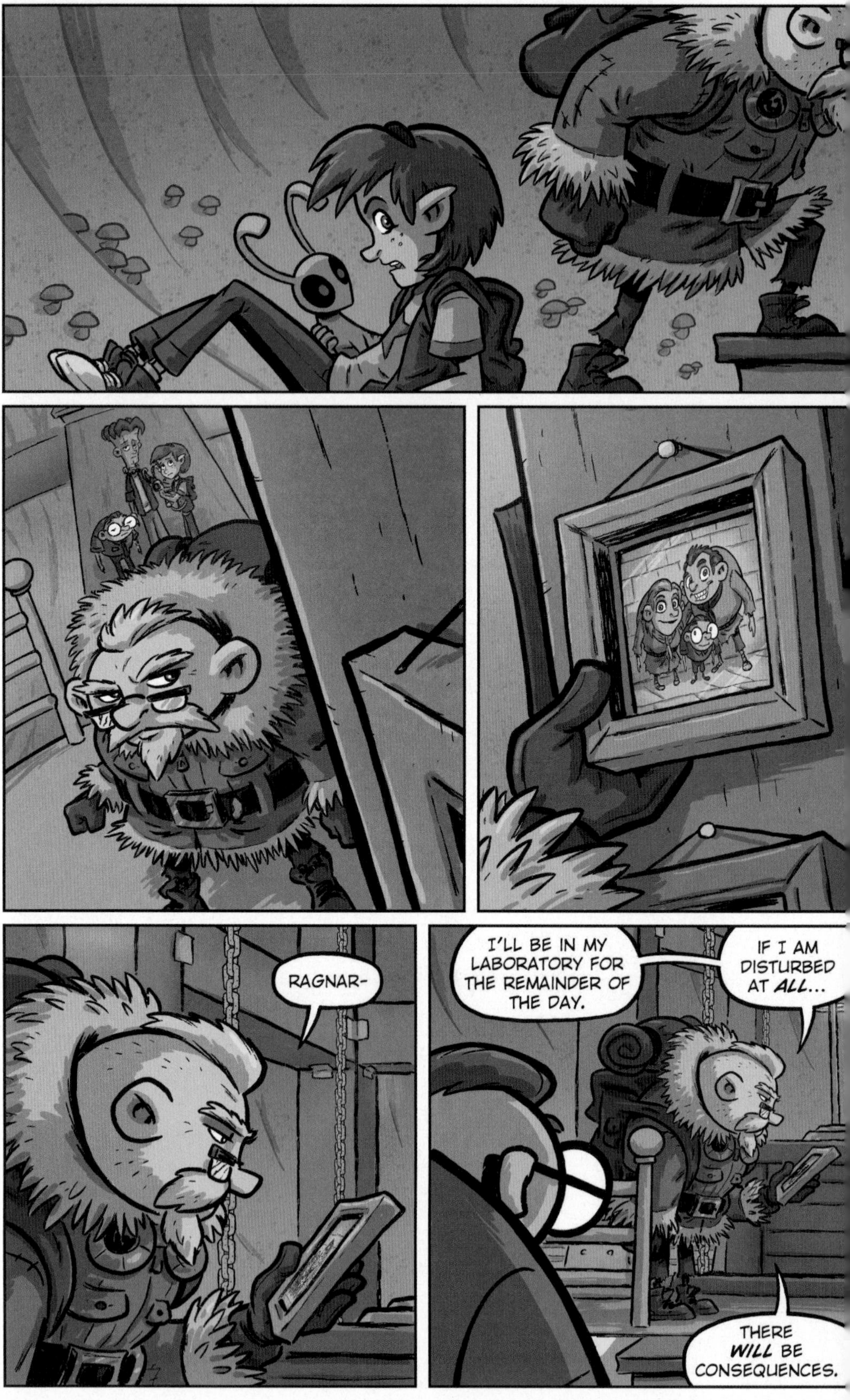
RAGNAR-
I'LL BE IN MY LABORATORY FOR THE REMAINDER OF THE DAY.
IF I AM DISTURBED AT *ALL*...
THERE *WILL* BE CONSEQUENCES.

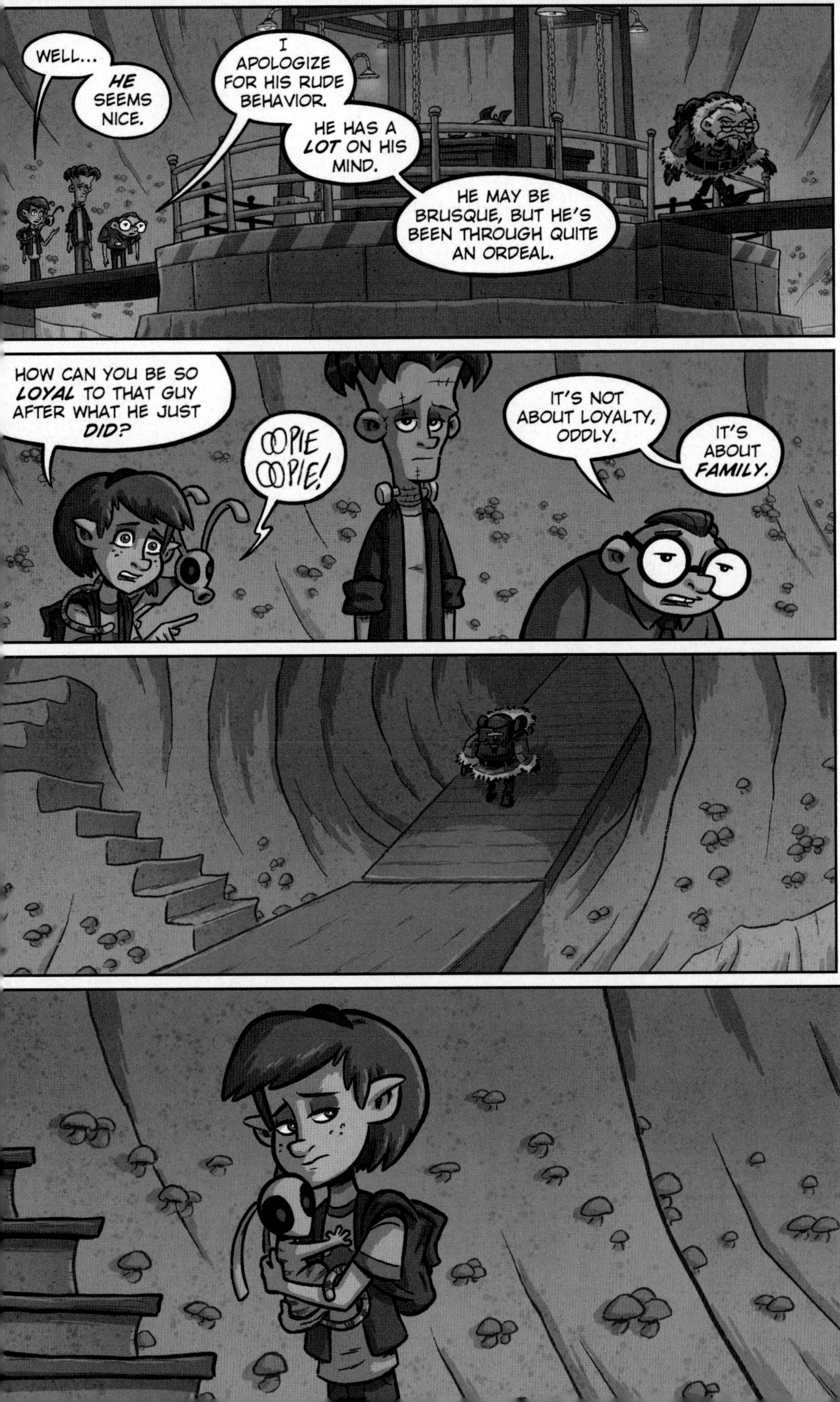
WELL... HE SEEMS NICE.
I APOLOGIZE FOR HIS RUDE BEHAVIOR.
HE HAS A LOT ON HIS MIND.
HE MAY BE BRUSQUE, BUT HE'S BEEN THROUGH QUITE AN ORDEAL.
HOW CAN YOU BE SO LOYAL TO THAT GUY AFTER WHAT HE JUST DID?
OOPIE OOPIE!
IT'S NOT ABOUT LOYALTY, ODDLY.
IT'S ABOUT FAMILY.

Chapter 19
Familiar Faces

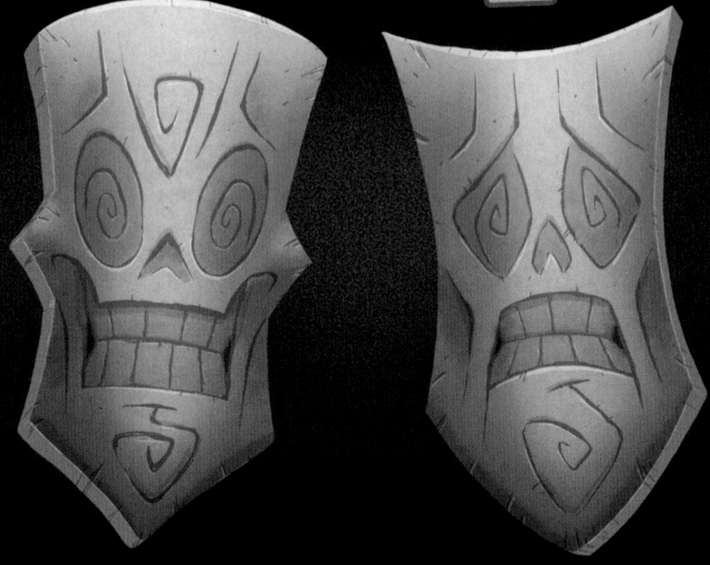

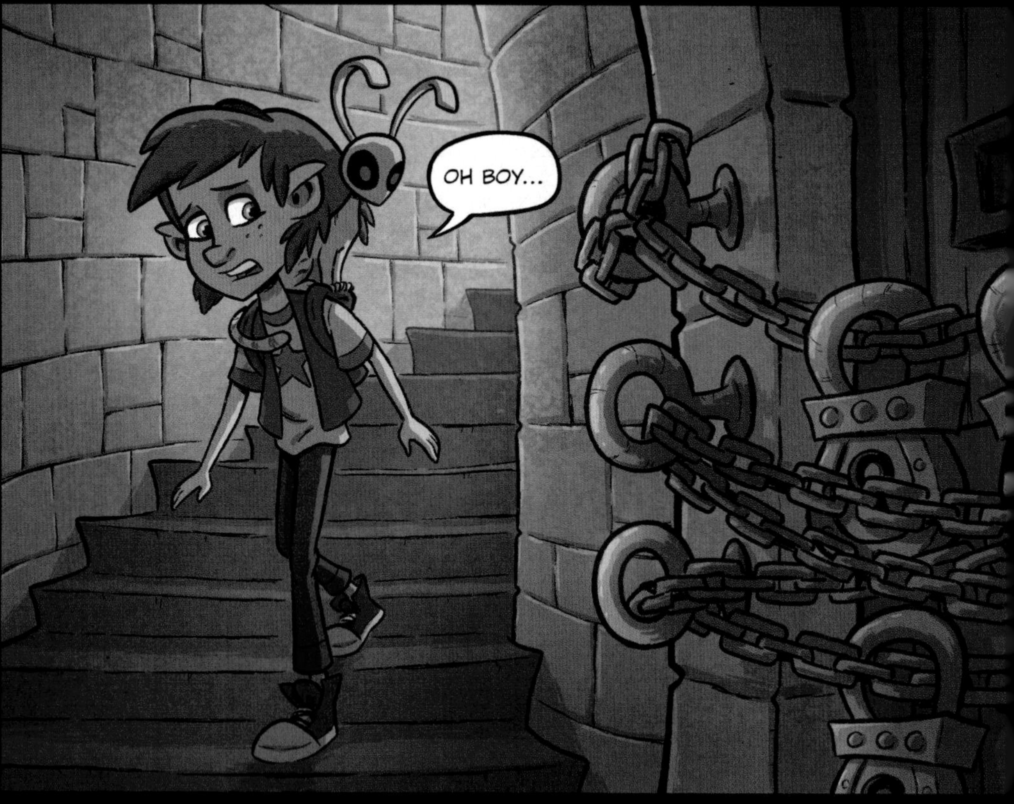
OH BOY...

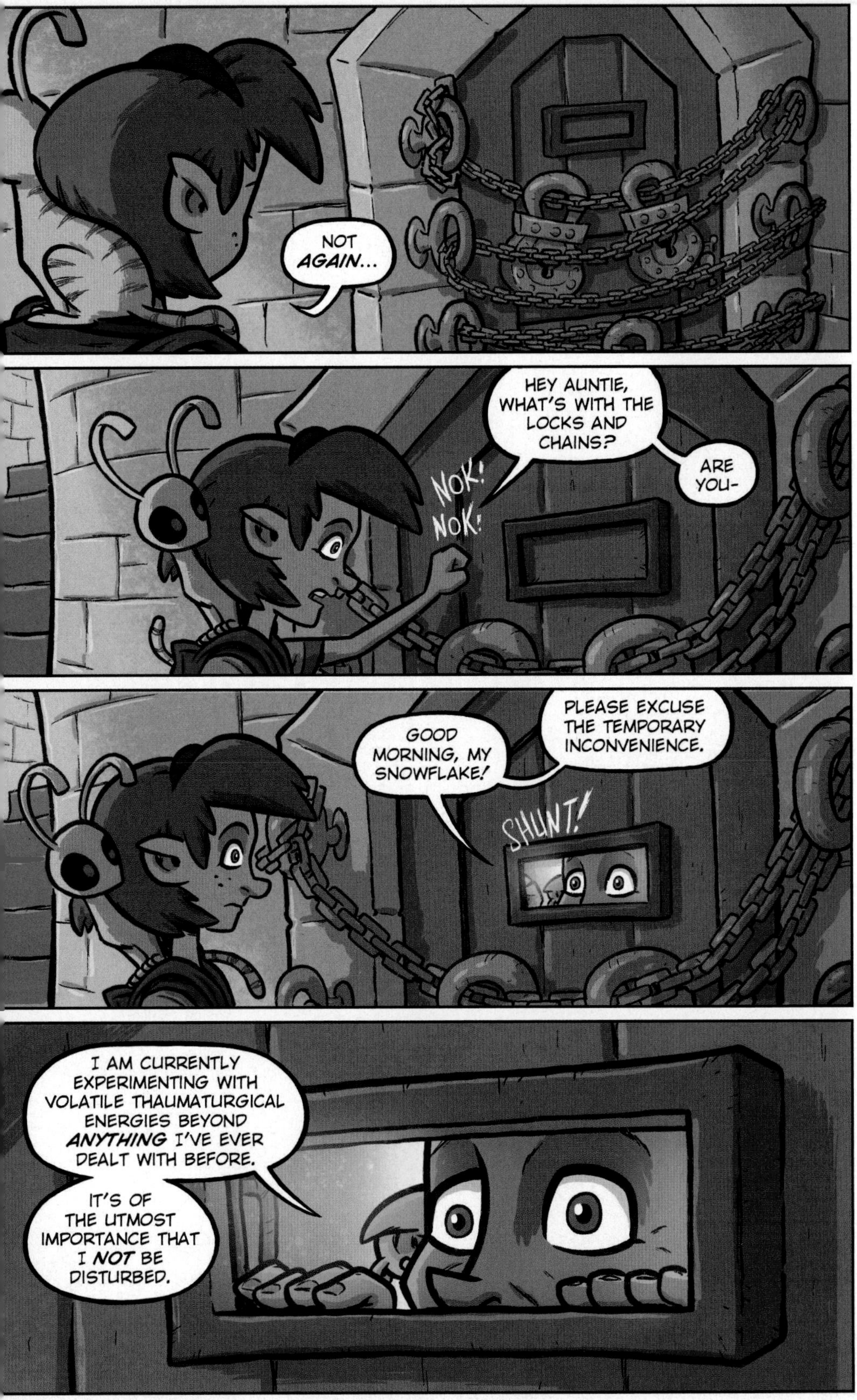
NOT *AGAIN*...
NOK! NOK!
HEY AUNTIE, WHAT'S WITH THE LOCKS AND CHAINS?
ARE YOU-
SHUNT!
GOOD MORNING, MY SNOWFLAKE!
PLEASE EXCUSE THE TEMPORARY INCONVENIENCE.
I AM CURRENTLY EXPERIMENTING WITH VOLATILE THAUMATURGICAL ENERGIES BEYOND *ANYTHING* I'VE EVER DEALT WITH BEFORE.
IT'S OF THE UTMOST IMPORTANCE THAT I *NOT* BE DISTURBED.

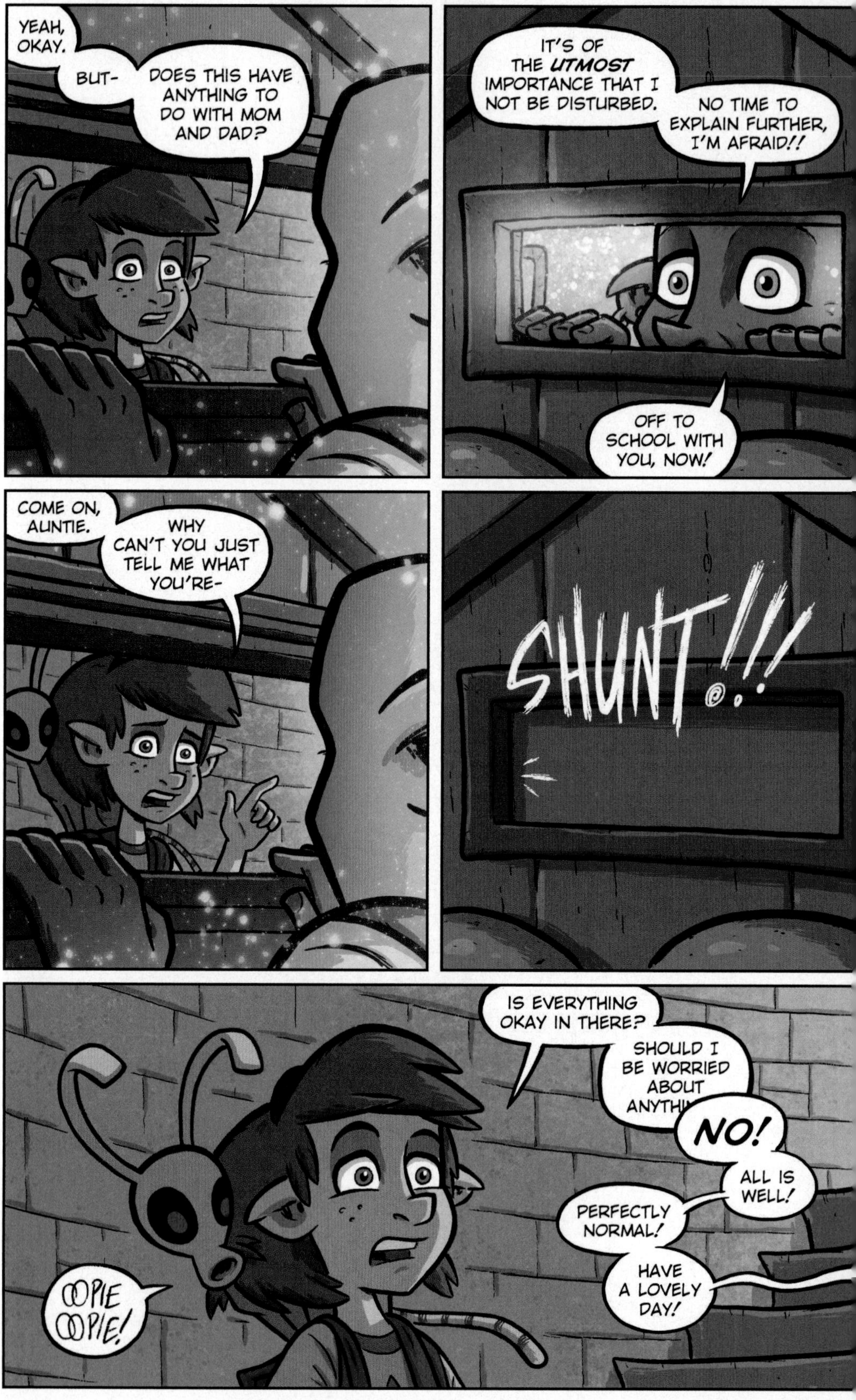
YEAH, OKAY.
BUT-
DOES THIS HAVE ANYTHING TO DO WITH MOM AND DAD?
IT'S OF THE *UTMOST* IMPORTANCE THAT I NOT BE DISTURBED.
NO TIME TO EXPLAIN FURTHER, I'M AFRAID!!
OFF TO SCHOOL WITH YOU, NOW!
COME ON, AUNTIE.
WHY CAN'T YOU JUST TELL ME WHAT YOU'RE-
SHUNT!!!
IS EVERYTHING OKAY IN THERE?
SHOULD I BE WORRIED ABOUT
NO!
ALL IS WELL!
PERFECTLY NORMAL!
HAVE A LOVELY DAY!
OOPIE OOPIE!

NORMAL.

THAT'S A LAUGH.

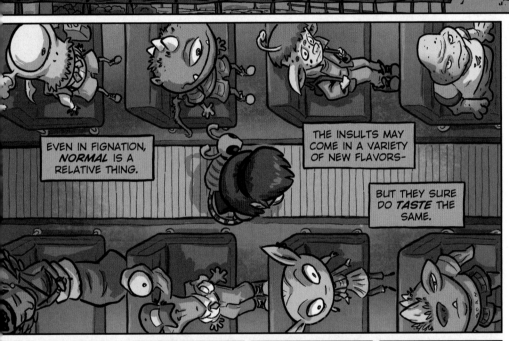

EVEN IN FIGNATION, *NORMAL* IS A RELATIVE THING.

THE INSULTS MAY COME IN A VARIETY OF NEW FLAVORS—

BUT THEY SURE DO *TASTE* THE SAME.

PISTACHIO NUT:

SHE'S WEIRD, I TELLS YA', *WEIRD!*

COOKIE DOUGH:

EARTHER SLAG.

EGG NOG:

BWAK!

HALF-BREED!

RIBBIT!

AND NEAPOLITAN:

FREAK.

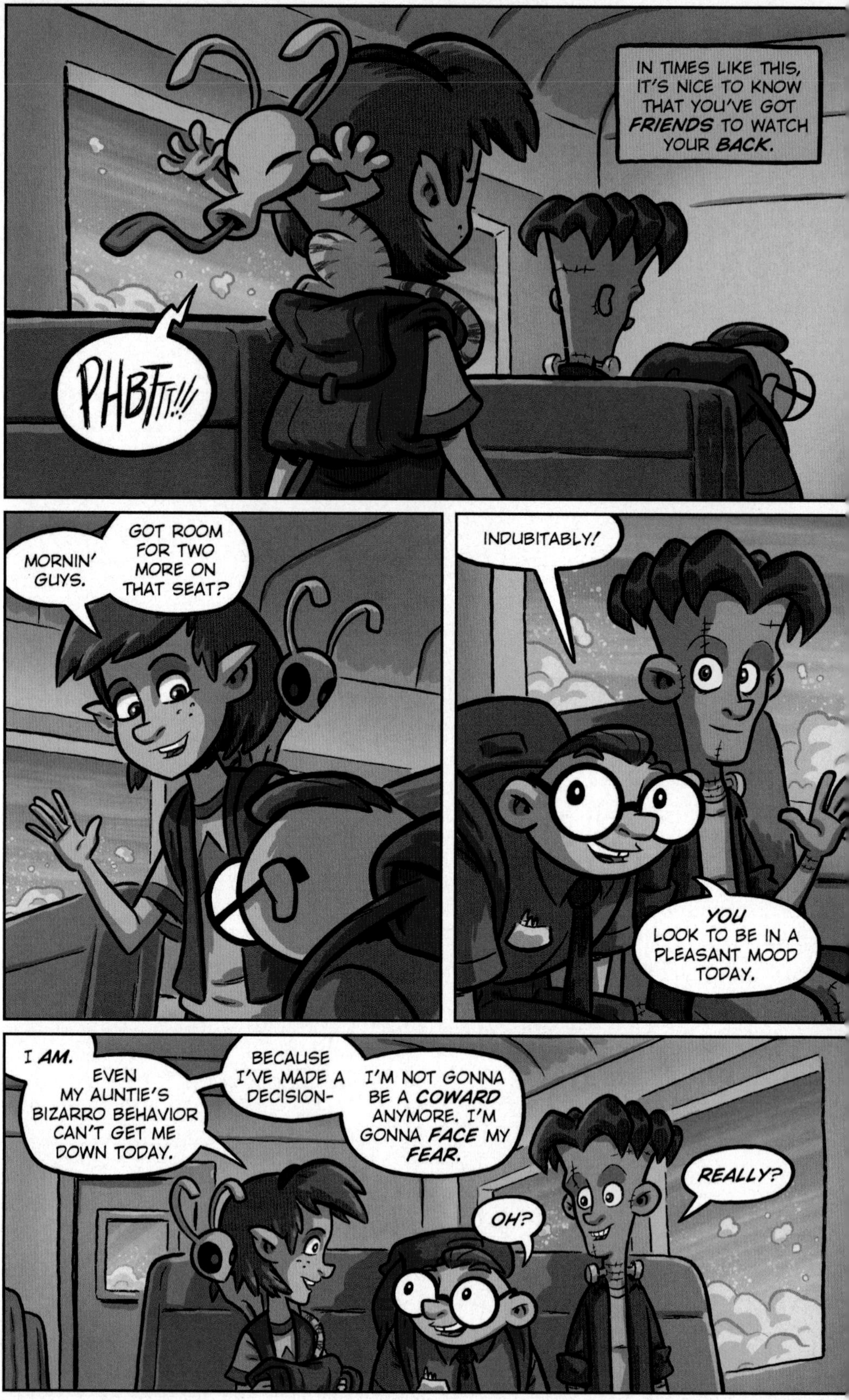
IN TIMES LIKE THIS, IT'S NICE TO KNOW THAT YOU'VE GOT FRIENDS TO WATCH YOUR BACK.
PHBFTT!!!
MORNIN' GUYS.
GOT ROOM FOR TWO MORE ON THAT SEAT?
INDUBITABLY!
YOU LOOK TO BE IN A PLEASANT MOOD TODAY.
I AM.
EVEN MY AUNTIE'S BIZARRO BEHAVIOR CAN'T GET ME DOWN TODAY.
BECAUSE I'VE MADE A DECISION-
I'M NOT GONNA BE A COWARD ANYMORE. I'M GONNA FACE MY FEAR.
OH?
REALLY?

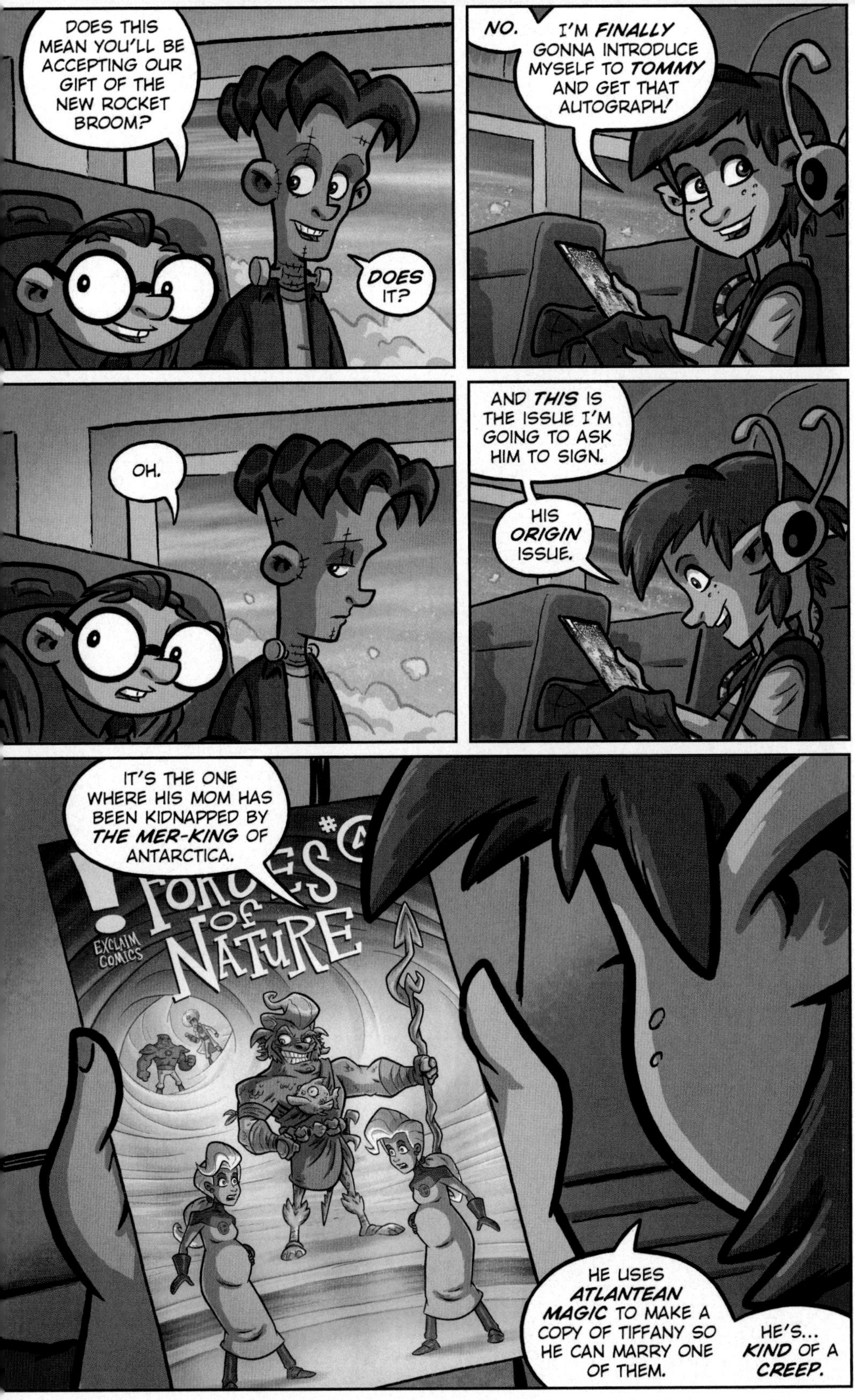
DOES THIS MEAN YOU'LL BE ACCEPTING OUR GIFT OF THE NEW ROCKET BROOM?
DOES IT?
NO.
I'M FINALLY GONNA INTRODUCE MYSELF TO TOMMY AND GET THAT AUTOGRAPH!
OH.
AND THIS IS THE ISSUE I'M GOING TO ASK HIM TO SIGN.
HIS ORIGIN ISSUE.
IT'S THE ONE WHERE HIS MOM HAS BEEN KIDNAPPED BY THE MER-KING OF ANTARCTICA.
FORCES OF NATURE
EXCLAIM COMICS
HE USES ATLANTEAN MAGIC TO MAKE A COPY OF TIFFANY SO HE CAN MARRY ONE OF THEM.
HE'S... KIND OF A CREEP.

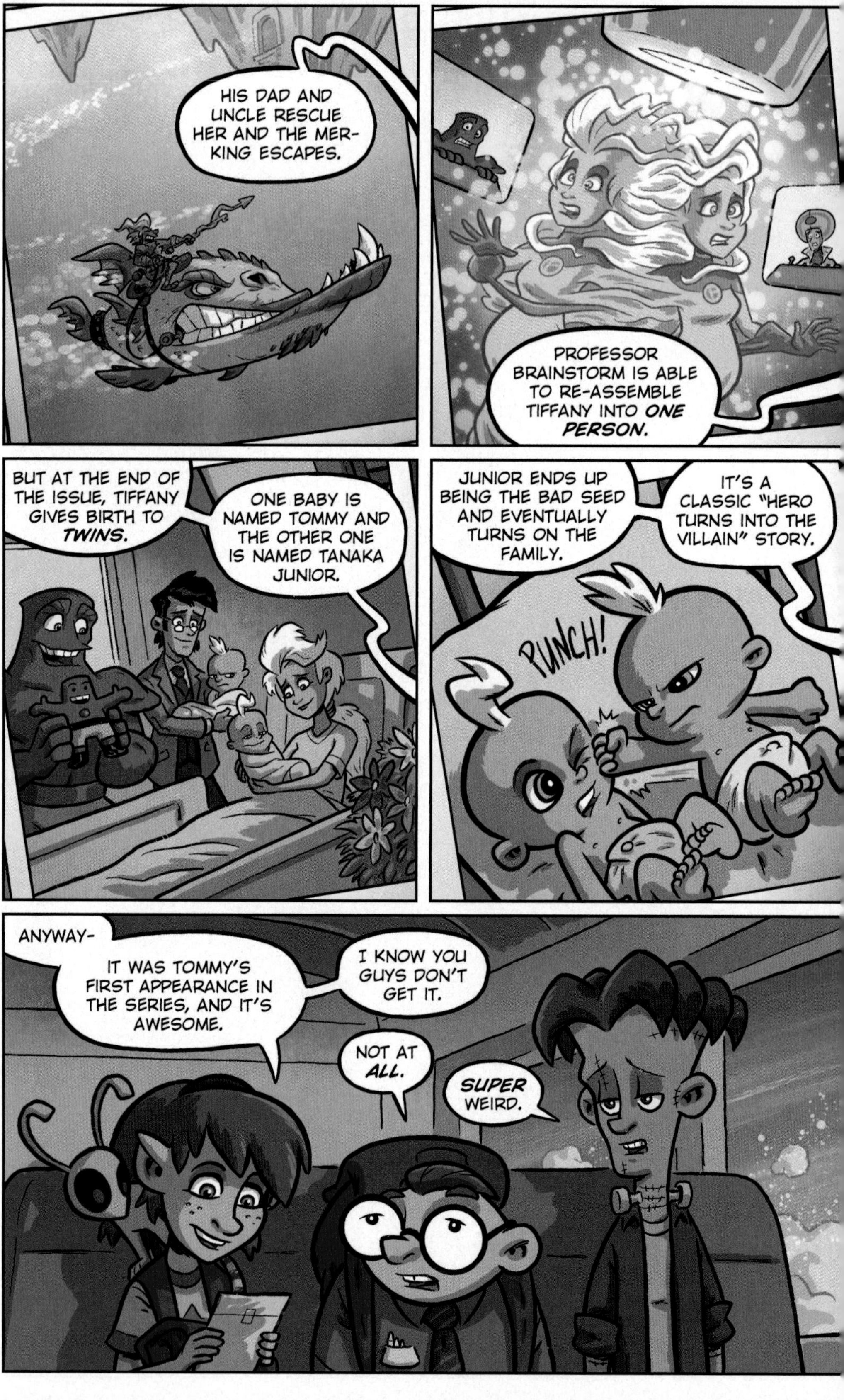
HIS DAD AND UNCLE RESCUE HER AND THE MER-KING ESCAPES.
PROFESSOR BRAINSTORM IS ABLE TO RE-ASSEMBLE TIFFANY INTO *ONE PERSON.*
BUT AT THE END OF THE ISSUE, TIFFANY GIVES BIRTH TO *TWINS.*
ONE BABY IS NAMED TOMMY AND THE OTHER ONE IS NAMED TANAKA JUNIOR.
JUNIOR ENDS UP BEING THE BAD SEED AND EVENTUALLY TURNS ON THE FAMILY.
IT'S A CLASSIC "HERO TURNS INTO THE VILLAIN" STORY.
PUNCH!
ANYWAY-
IT WAS TOMMY'S FIRST APPEARANCE IN THE SERIES, AND IT'S AWESOME.
I KNOW YOU GUYS DON'T GET IT.
NOT AT *ALL.*
SUPER WEIRD.

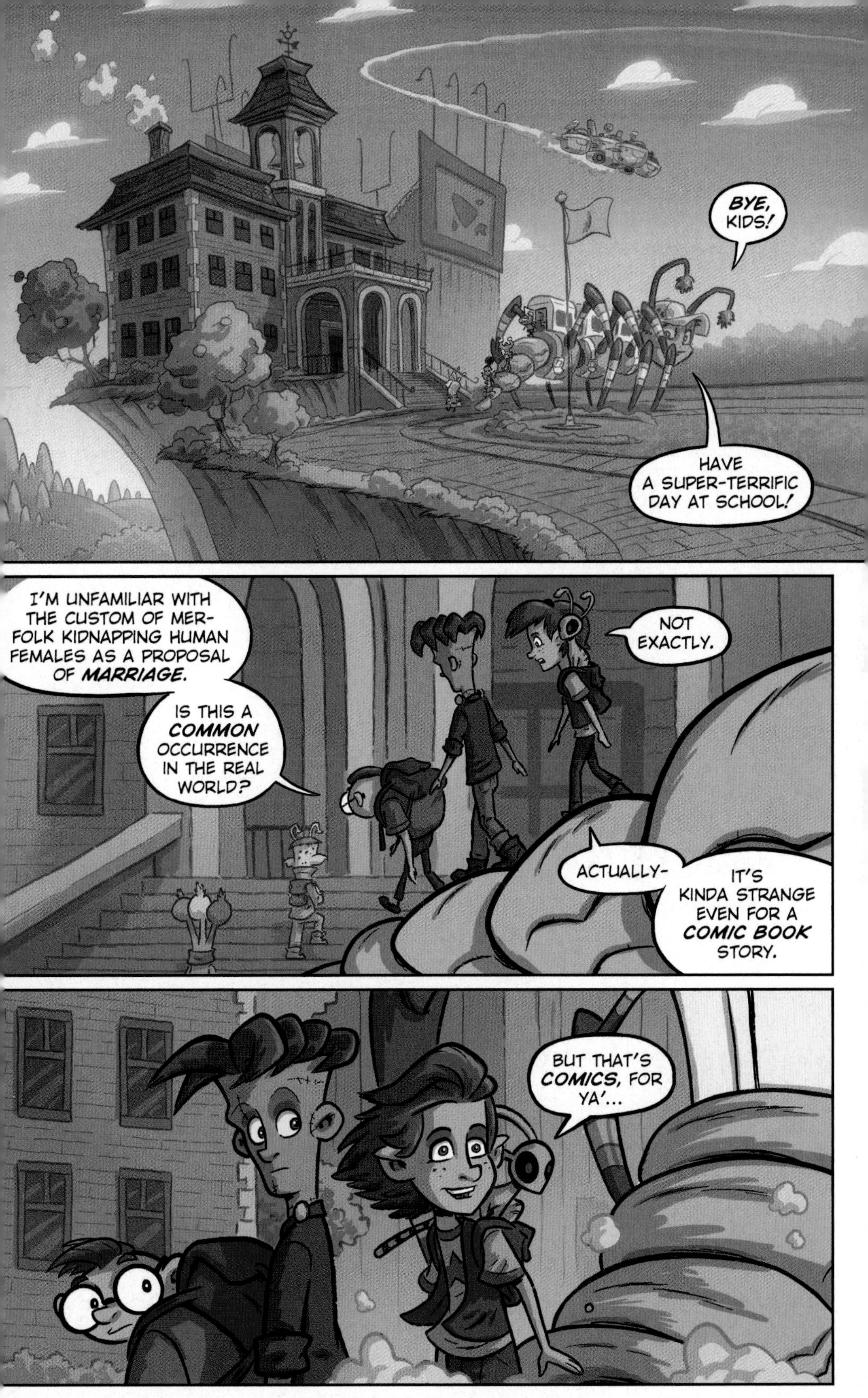
BYE, KIDS!
HAVE A SUPER-TERRIFIC DAY AT SCHOOL!
I'M UNFAMILIAR WITH THE CUSTOM OF MER-FOLK KIDNAPPING HUMAN FEMALES AS A PROPOSAL OF MARRIAGE.
IS THIS A COMMON OCCURRENCE IN THE REAL WORLD?
NOT EXACTLY.
ACTUALLY-
IT'S KINDA STRANGE EVEN FOR A COMIC BOOK STORY.
BUT THAT'S COMICS, FOR YA'...

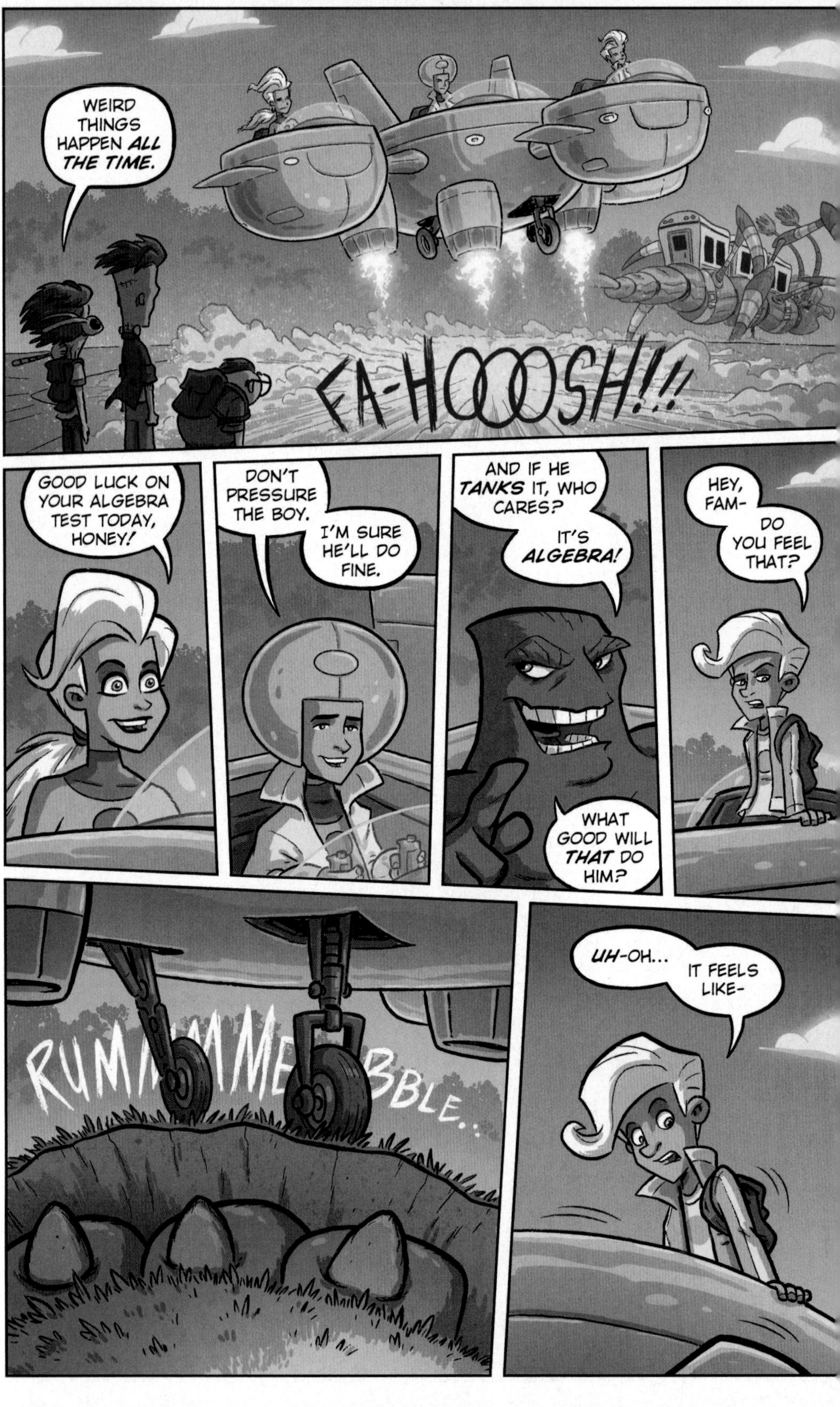

WEIRD THINGS HAPPEN ALL THE TIME.
FA-HOOOSH!!!
GOOD LUCK ON YOUR ALGEBRA TEST TODAY, HONEY!
DON'T PRESSURE THE BOY.
I'M SURE HE'LL DO FINE.
AND IF HE TANKS IT, WHO CARES?
IT'S ALGEBRA!
WHAT GOOD WILL THAT DO HIM?
HEY, FAM-
DO YOU FEEL THAT?
UH-OH...
IT FEELS LIKE-

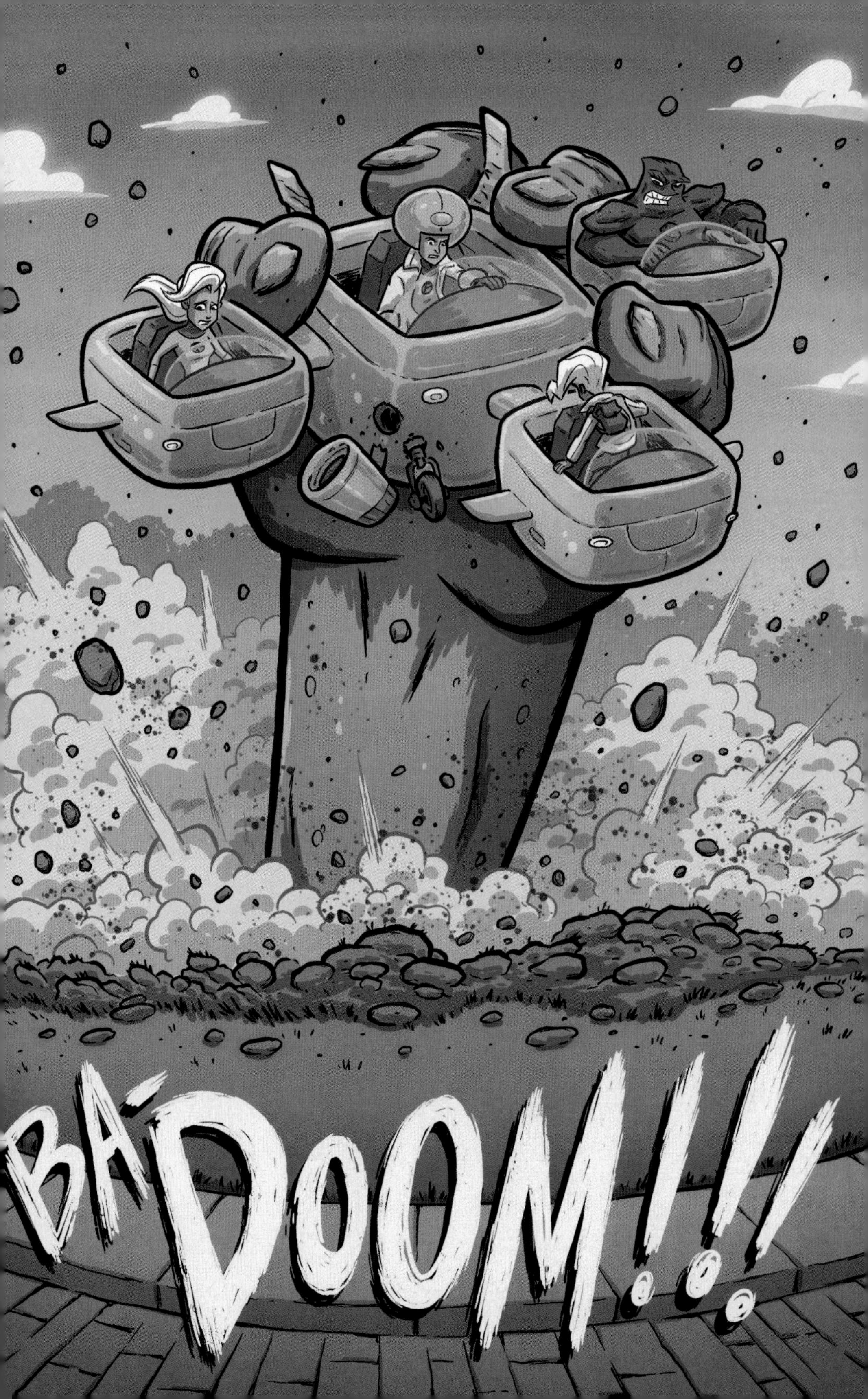
BA-DOOM!!!

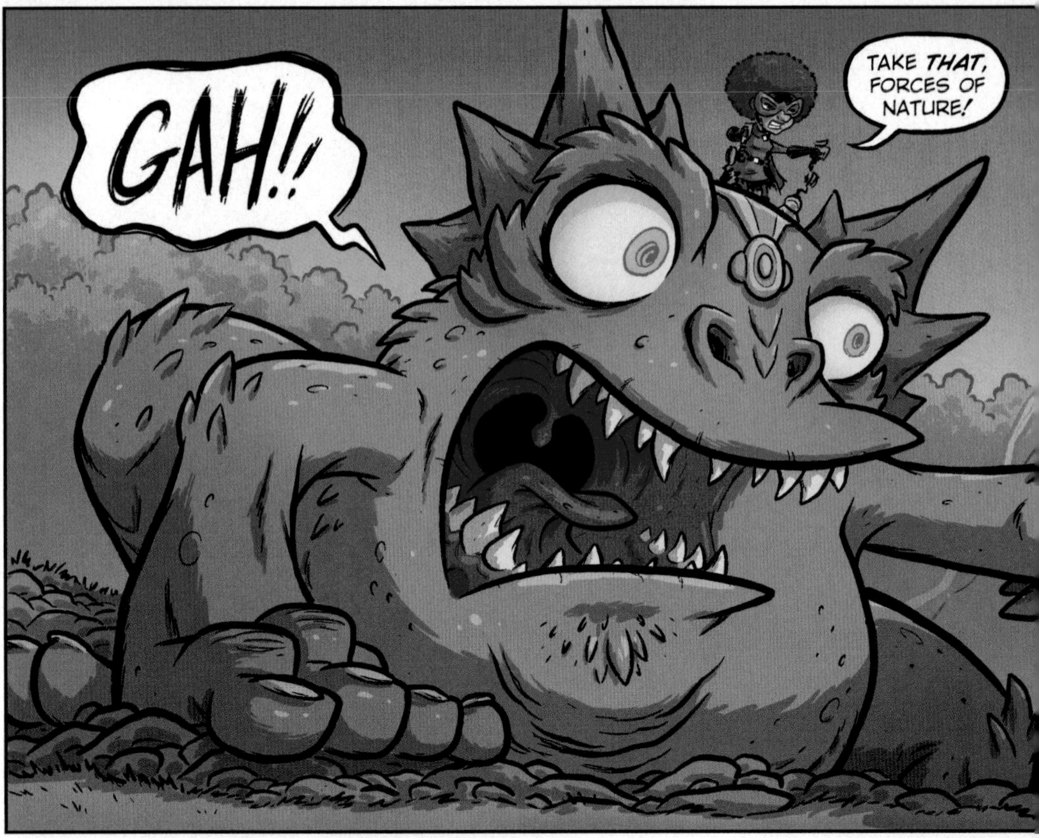
GAH!!
TAKE THAT, FORCES OF NATURE!

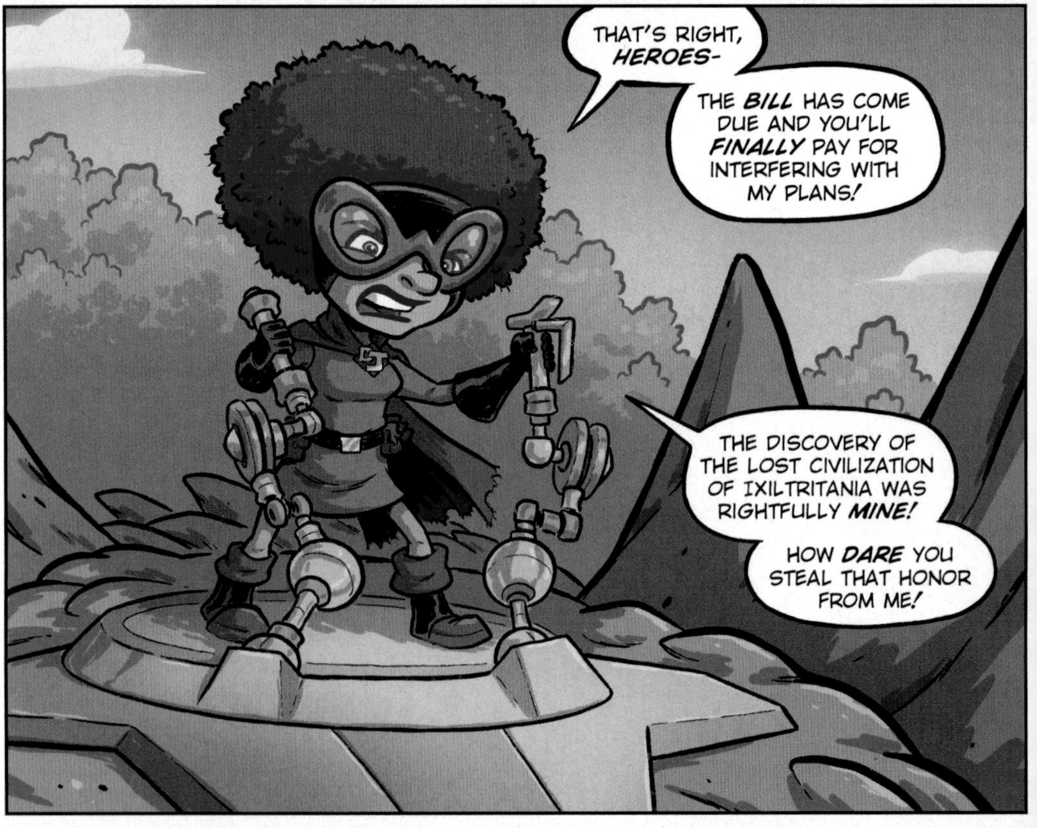
THAT'S RIGHT, HEROES-
THE BILL HAS COME DUE AND YOU'LL FINALLY PAY FOR INTERFERING WITH MY PLANS!
THE DISCOVERY OF THE LOST CIVILIZATION OF IXILTRITANIA WAS RIGHTFULLY MINE!
HOW DARE YOU STEAL THAT HONOR FROM ME!

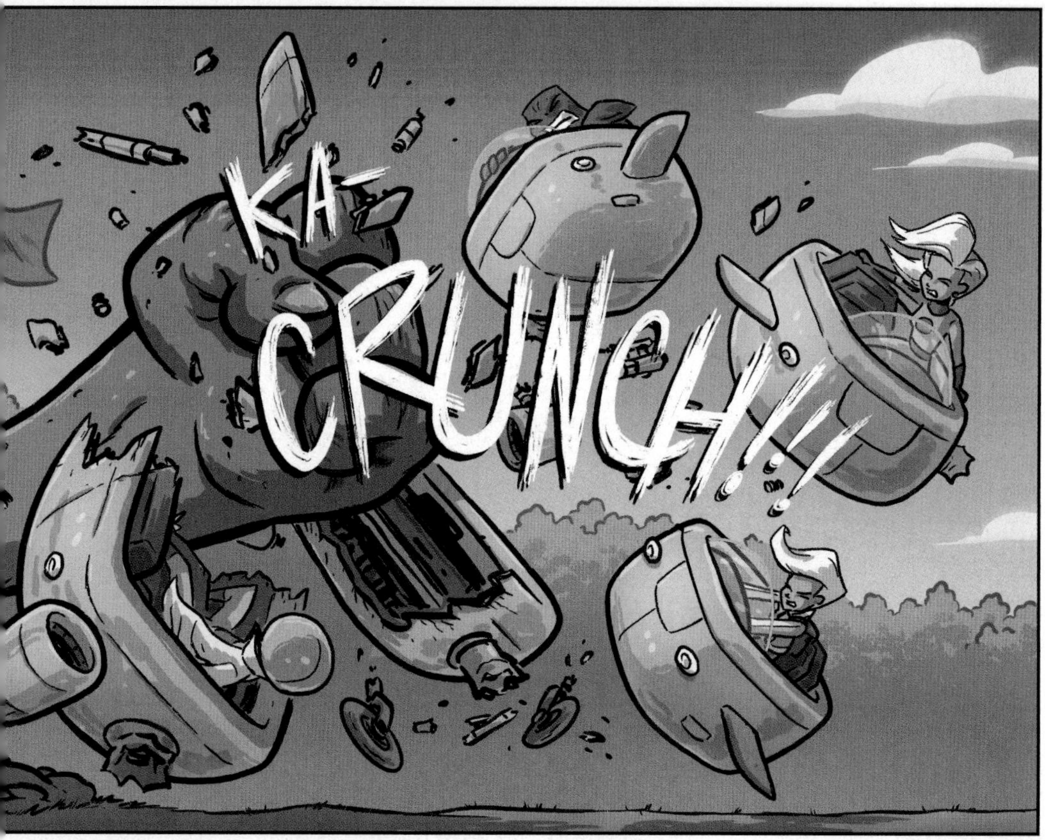
KA-CRUNCH!!!

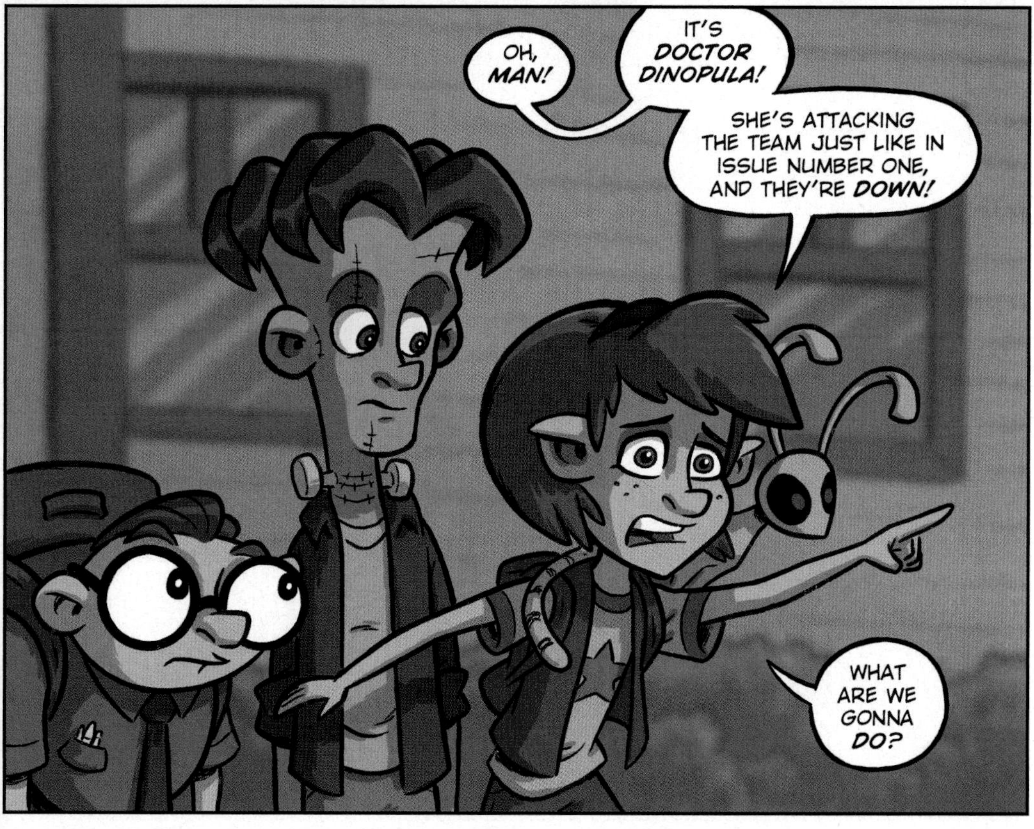
OH, *MAN!*
IT'S *DOCTOR DINOPULA!*
SHE'S ATTACKING THE TEAM JUST LIKE IN ISSUE NUMBER ONE, AND THEY'RE *DOWN!*
WHAT ARE WE GONNA *DO?*

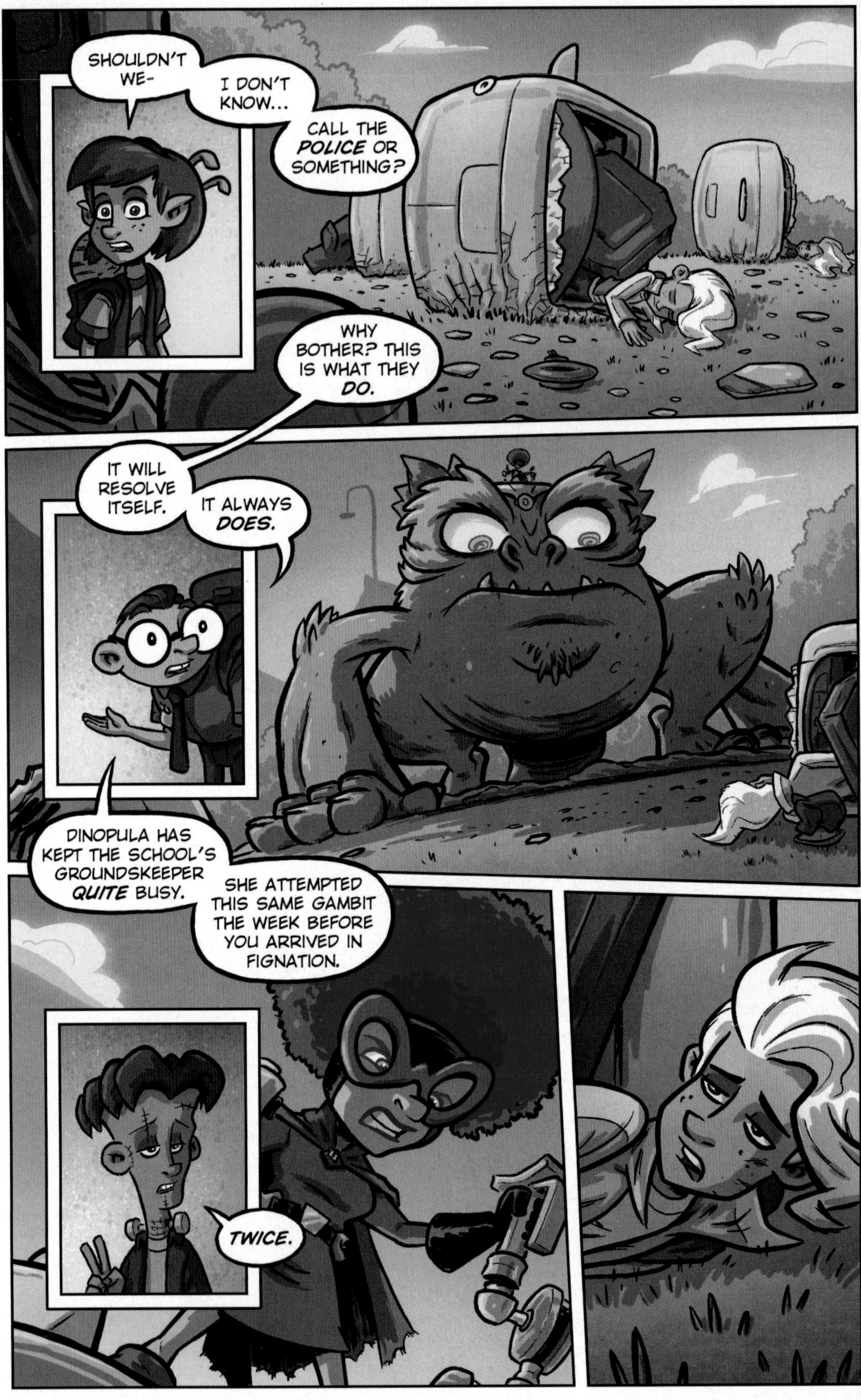
SHOULDN'T WE-
I DON'T KNOW...
CALL THE *POLICE* OR SOMETHING?
WHY BOTHER? THIS IS WHAT THEY *DO.*
IT WILL RESOLVE ITSELF.
IT ALWAYS *DOES.*
DINOPULA HAS KEPT THE SCHOOL'S GROUNDSKEEPER *QUITE* BUSY.
SHE ATTEMPTED THIS SAME GAMBIT THE WEEK BEFORE YOU ARRIVED IN FIGNATION.
TWICE.

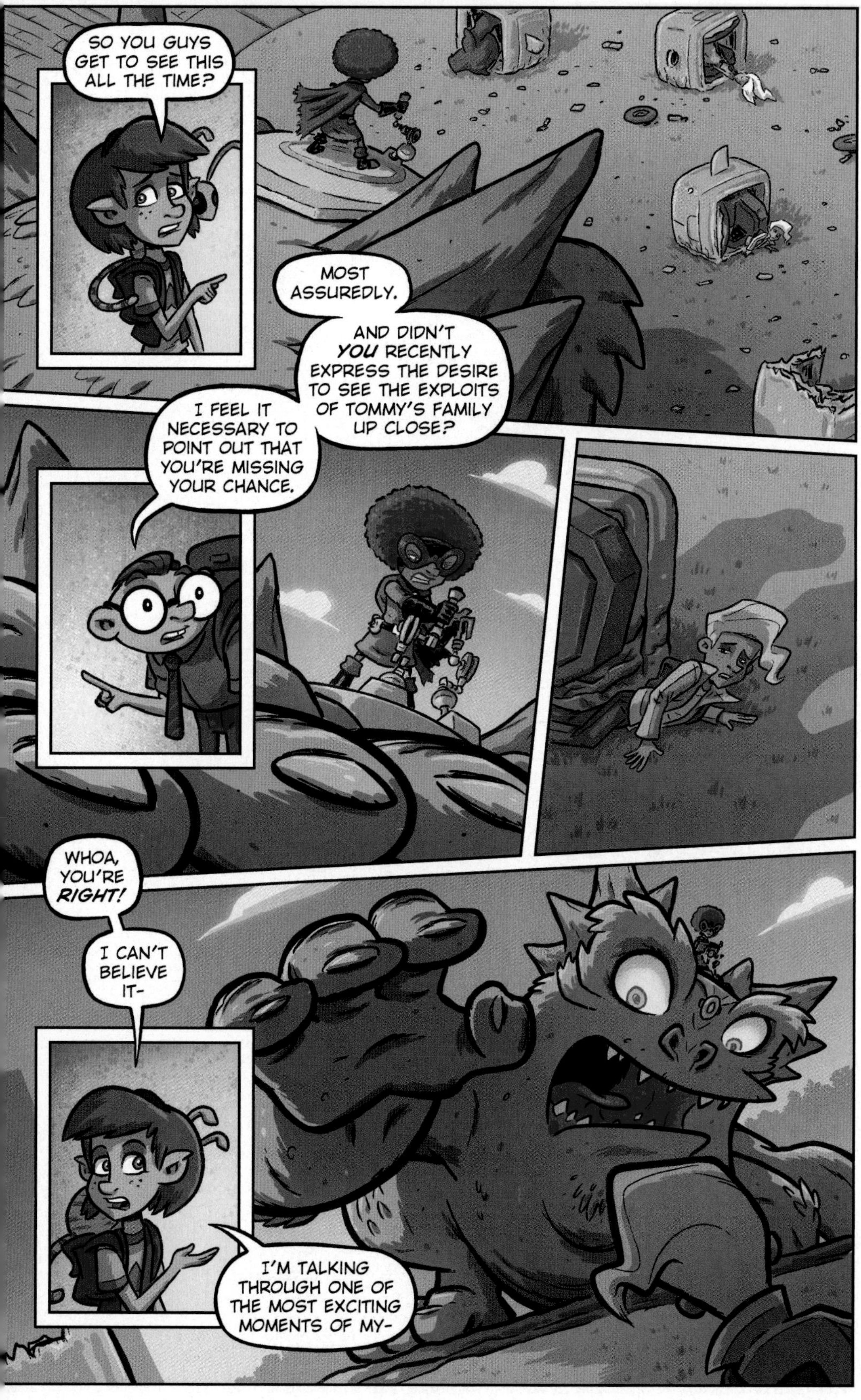
SO YOU GUYS GET TO SEE THIS ALL THE TIME?
MOST ASSUREDLY.
AND DIDN'T *YOU* RECENTLY EXPRESS THE DESIRE TO SEE THE EXPLOITS OF TOMMY'S FAMILY UP CLOSE?
I FEEL IT NECESSARY TO POINT OUT THAT YOU'RE MISSING YOUR CHANCE.
WHOA, YOU'RE ***RIGHT!***
I CAN'T BELIEVE IT-
I'M TALKING THROUGH ONE OF THE MOST EXCITING MOMENTS OF MY-

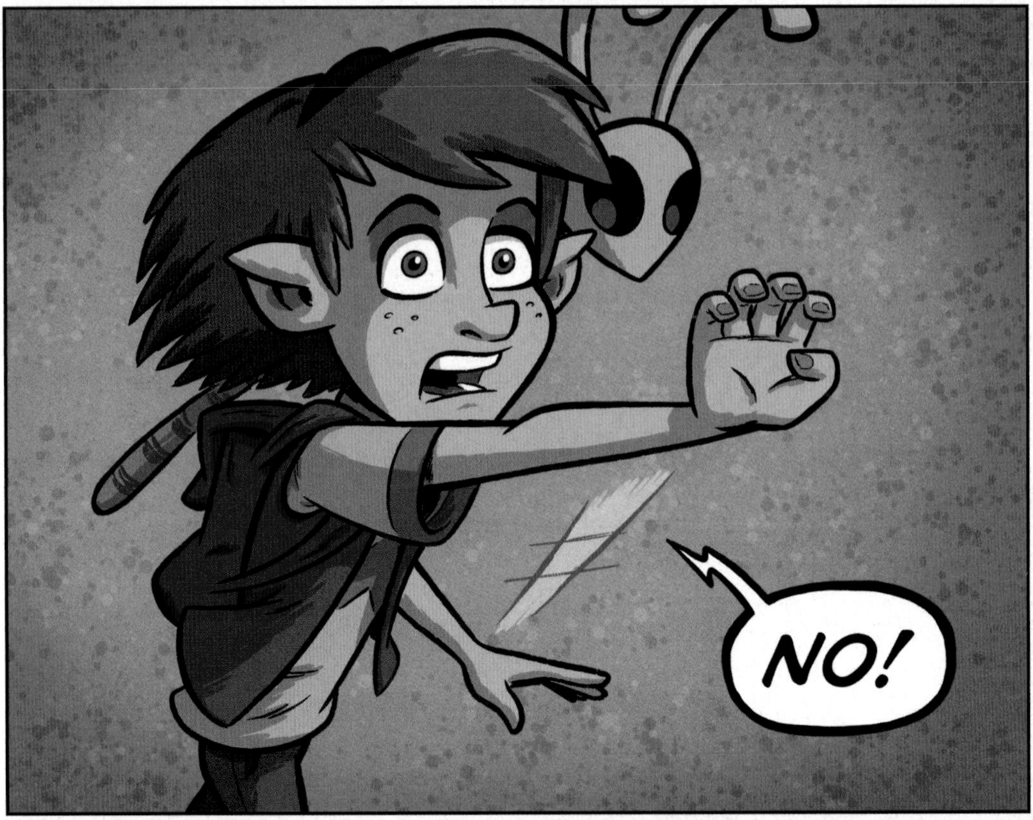
NO!

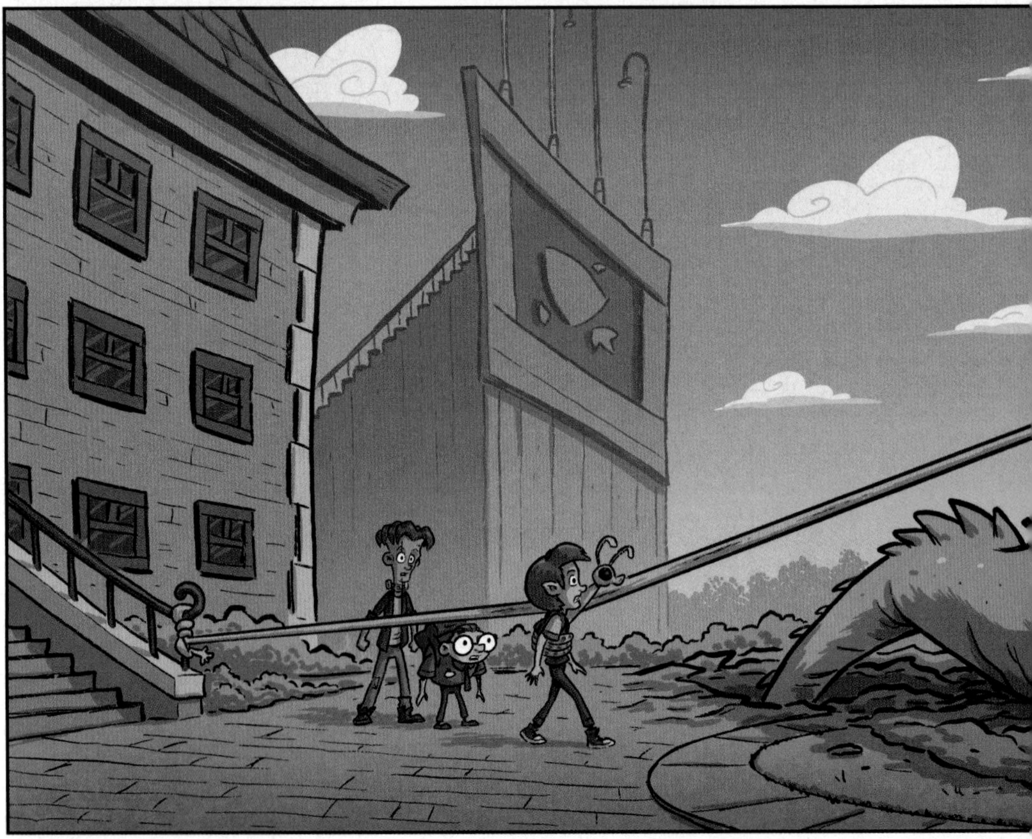

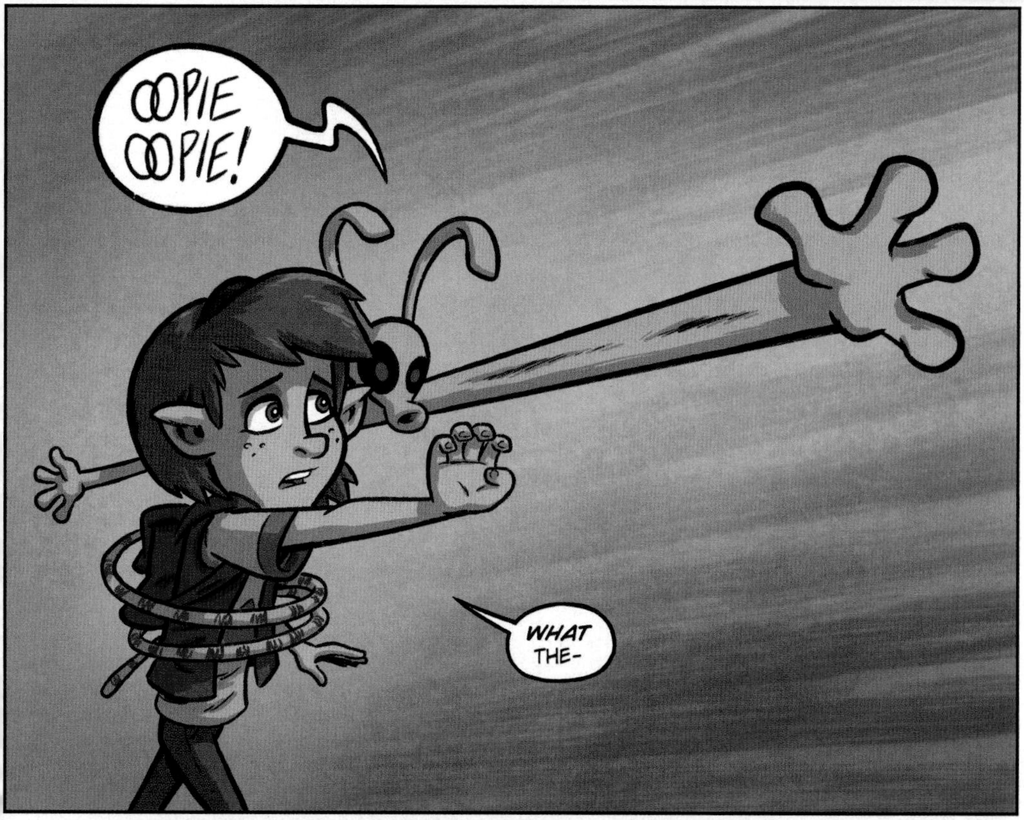
OOPIE OOPIE!
WHAT THE-

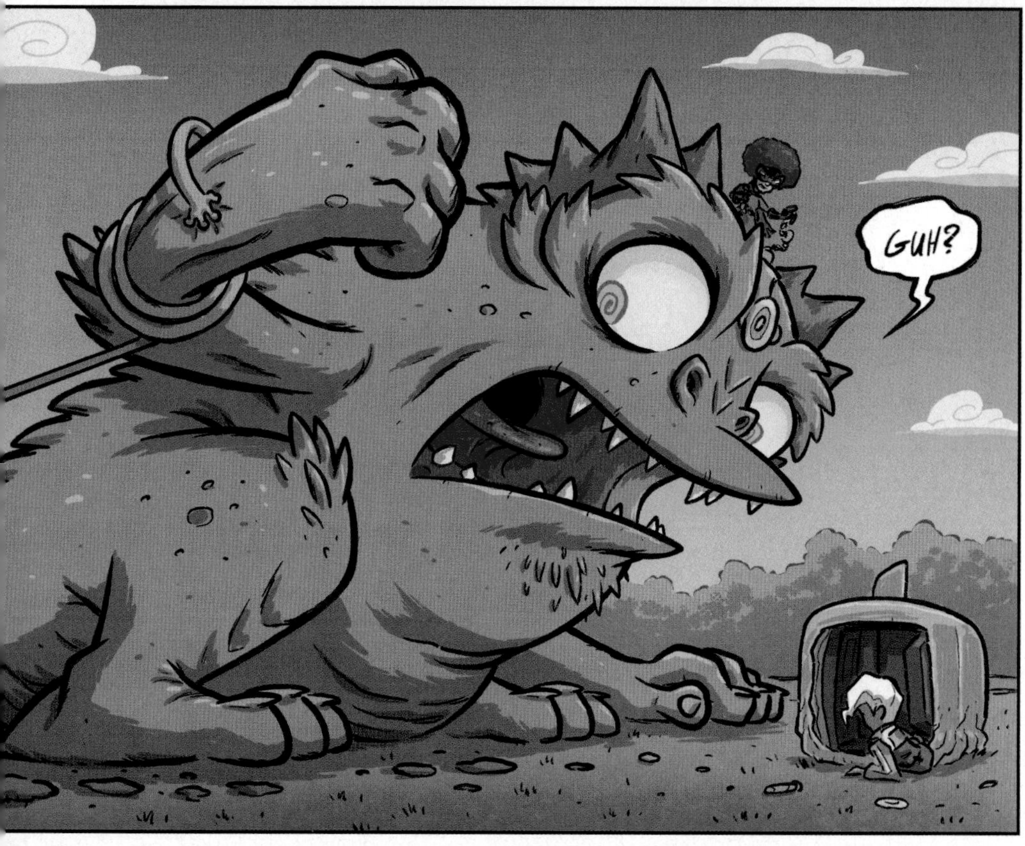
GUH?

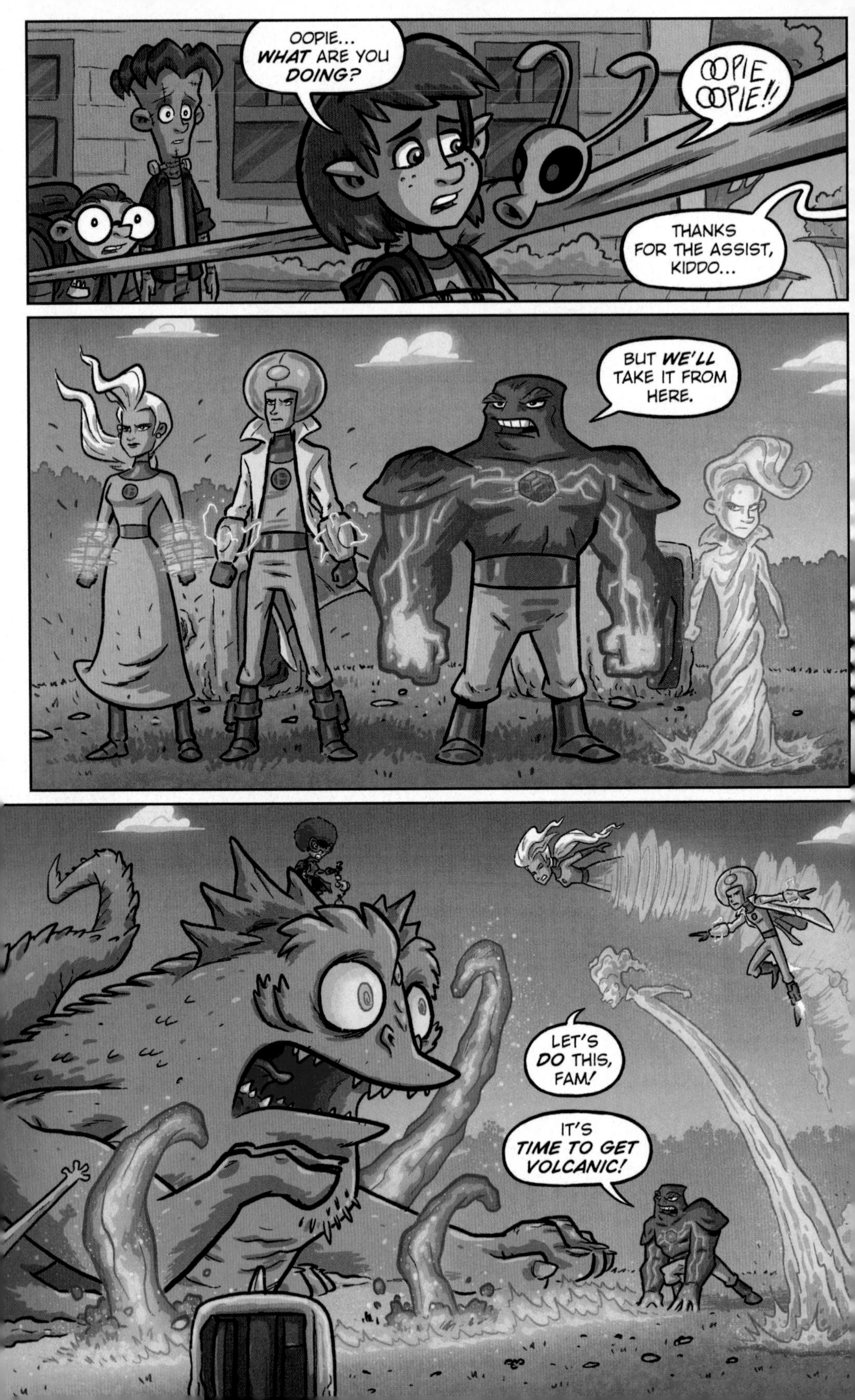
OOPIE... WHAT ARE YOU DOING?
OOPIE OOPIE!!
THANKS FOR THE ASSIST, KIDDO...
BUT WE'LL TAKE IT FROM HERE.
LET'S DO THIS, FAM!
IT'S TIME TO GET VOLCANIC!

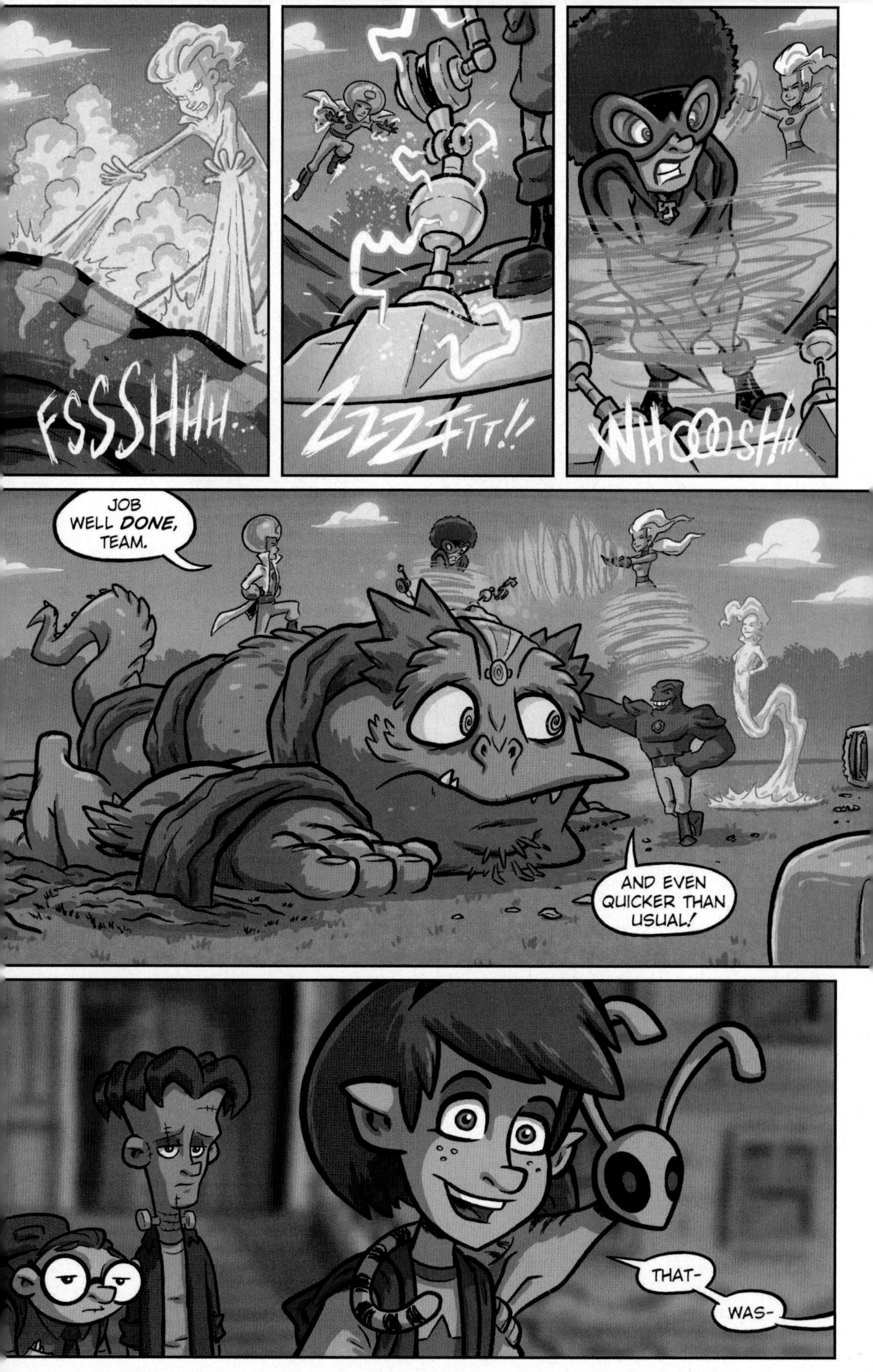
FSSSHHH...
ZZZFTT!!
WHOOOSH!!!
JOB WELL DONE, TEAM.
AND EVEN QUICKER THAN USUAL!
THAT-
WAS-

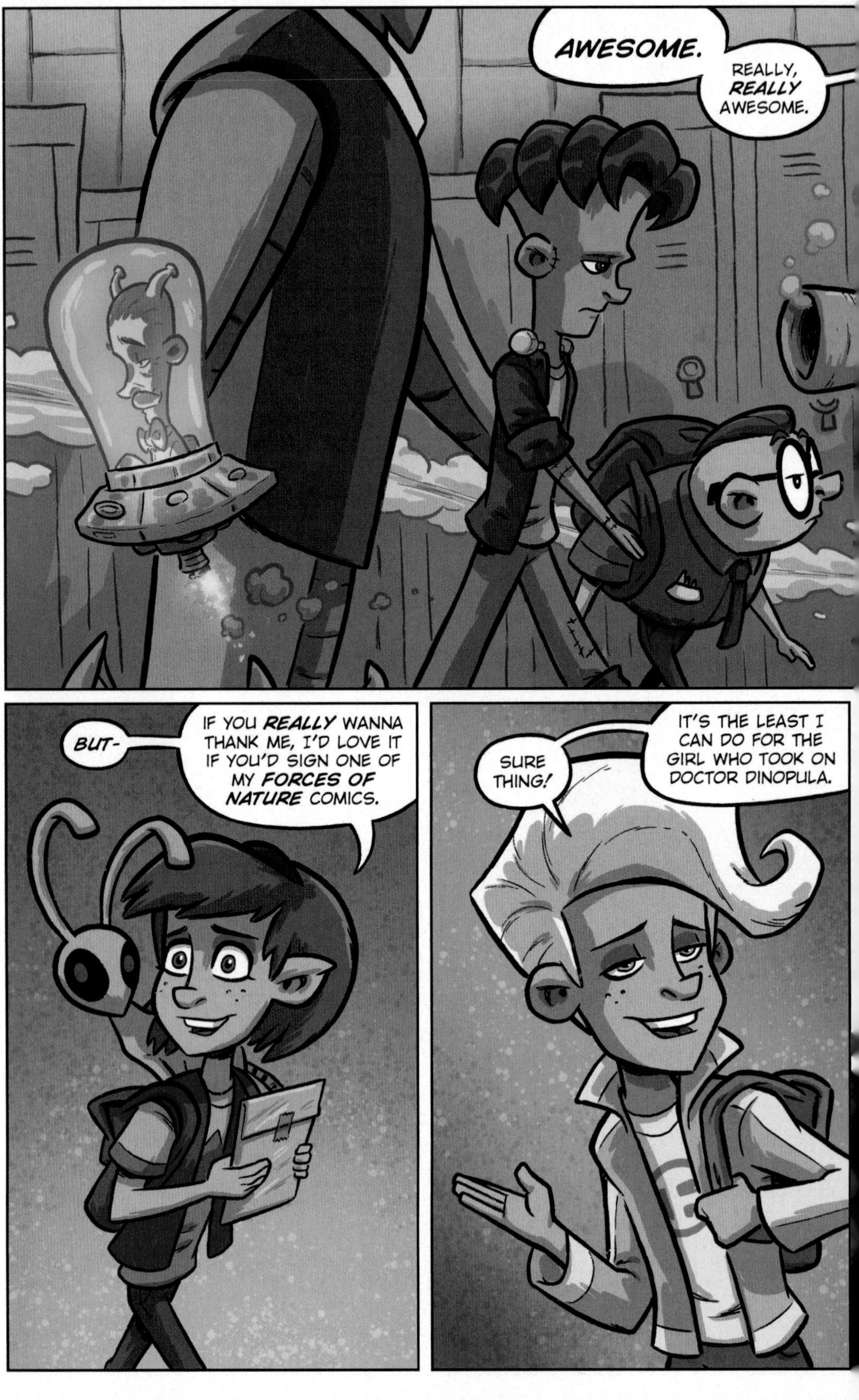
AWESOME.
REALLY, REALLY AWESOME.
BUT-
IF YOU REALLY WANNA THANK ME, I'D LOVE IT IF YOU'D SIGN ONE OF MY FORCES OF NATURE COMICS.
SURE THING!
IT'S THE LEAST I CAN DO FOR THE GIRL WHO TOOK ON DOCTOR DINOPULA.

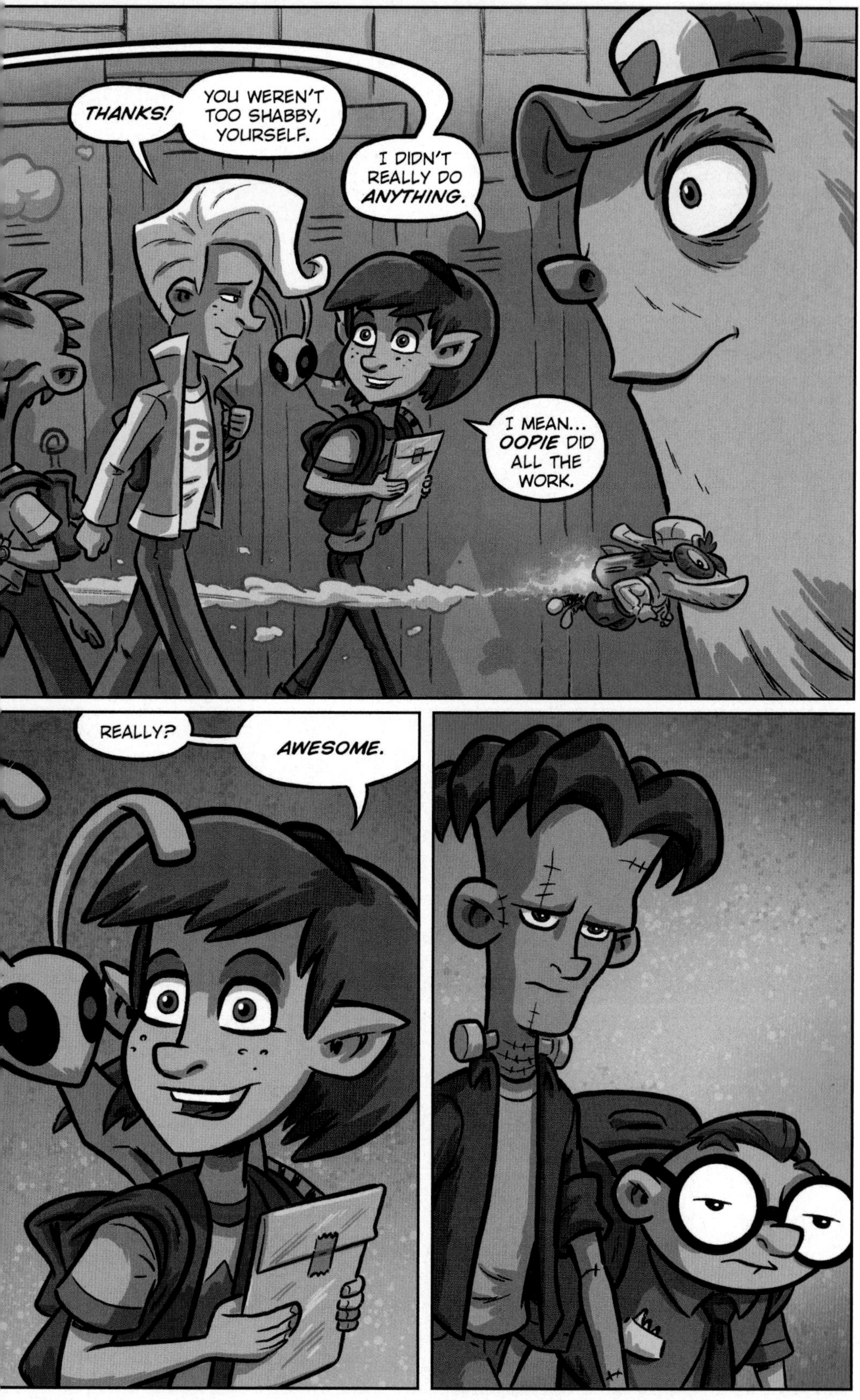
THANKS!
YOU WEREN'T TOO SHABBY, YOURSELF.
I DIDN'T REALLY DO ANYTHING.
I MEAN... OOPIE DID ALL THE WORK.
REALLY?
AWESOME.

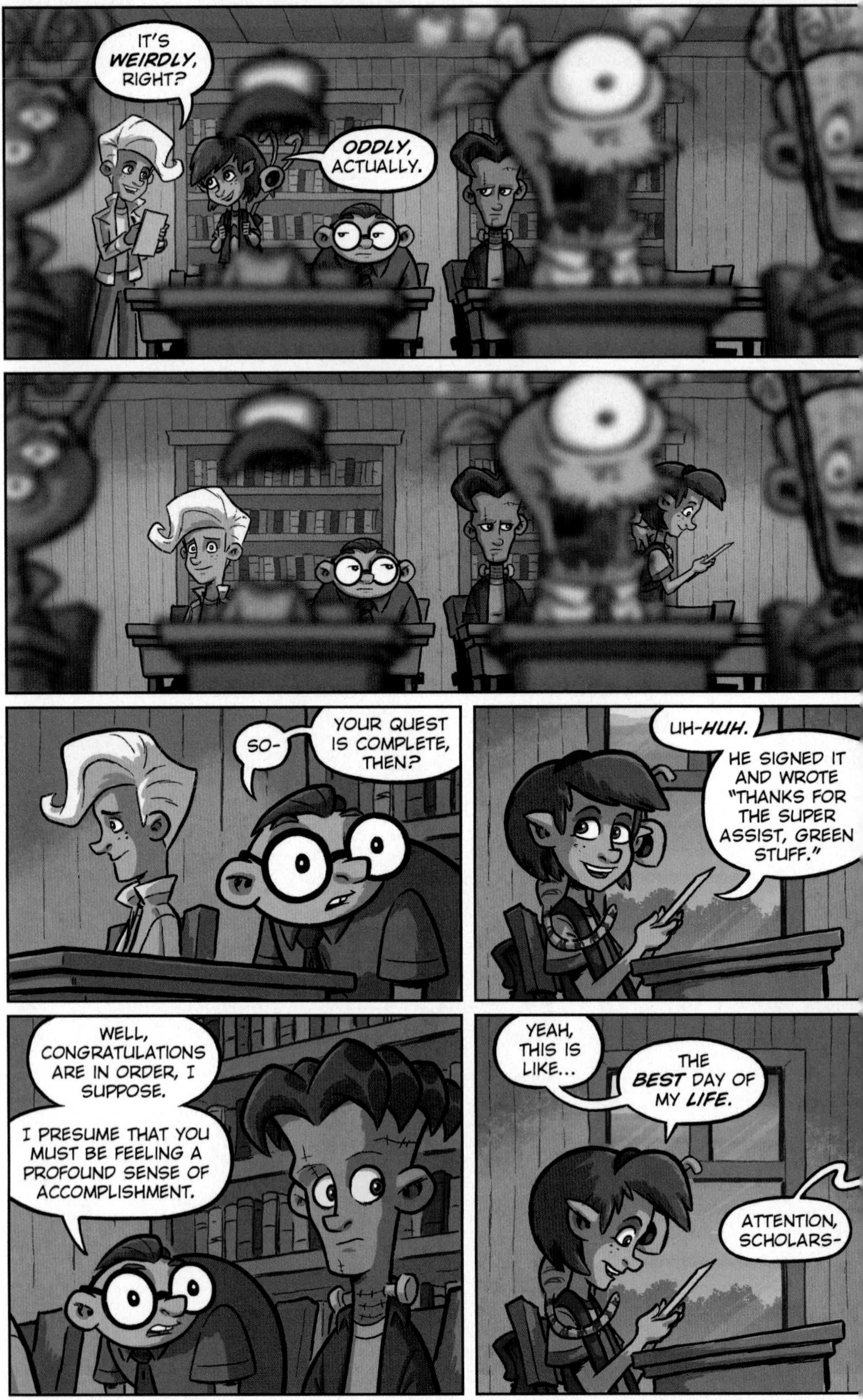
IT'S WEIRDLY, RIGHT?
ODDLY, ACTUALLY.
SO-
YOUR QUEST IS COMPLETE, THEN?
UH-HUH.
HE SIGNED IT AND WROTE "THANKS FOR THE SUPER ASSIST, GREEN STUFF."
WELL, CONGRATULATIONS ARE IN ORDER, I SUPPOSE.
I PRESUME THAT YOU MUST BE FEELING A PROFOUND SENSE OF ACCOMPLISHMENT.
YEAH, THIS IS LIKE...
THE BEST DAY OF MY LIFE.
ATTENTION, SCHOLARS-

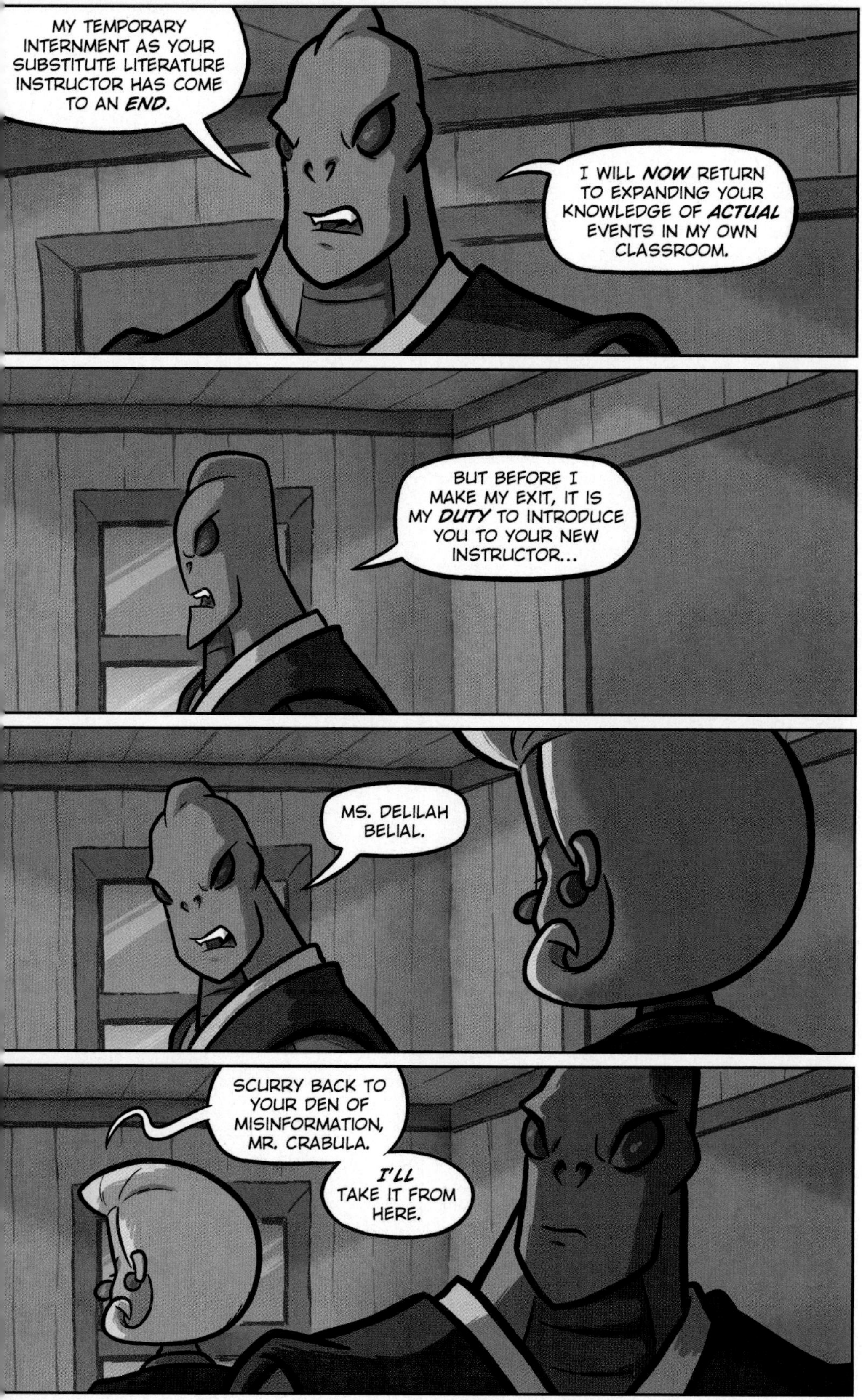
MY TEMPORARY INTERNMENT AS YOUR SUBSTITUTE LITERATURE INSTRUCTOR HAS COME TO AN END.
I WILL NOW RETURN TO EXPANDING YOUR KNOWLEDGE OF ACTUAL EVENTS IN MY OWN CLASSROOM.
BUT BEFORE I MAKE MY EXIT, IT IS MY DUTY TO INTRODUCE YOU TO YOUR NEW INSTRUCTOR...
MS. DELILAH BELIAL.
SCURRY BACK TO YOUR DEN OF MISINFORMATION, MR. CRABULA.
I'LL TAKE IT FROM HERE.

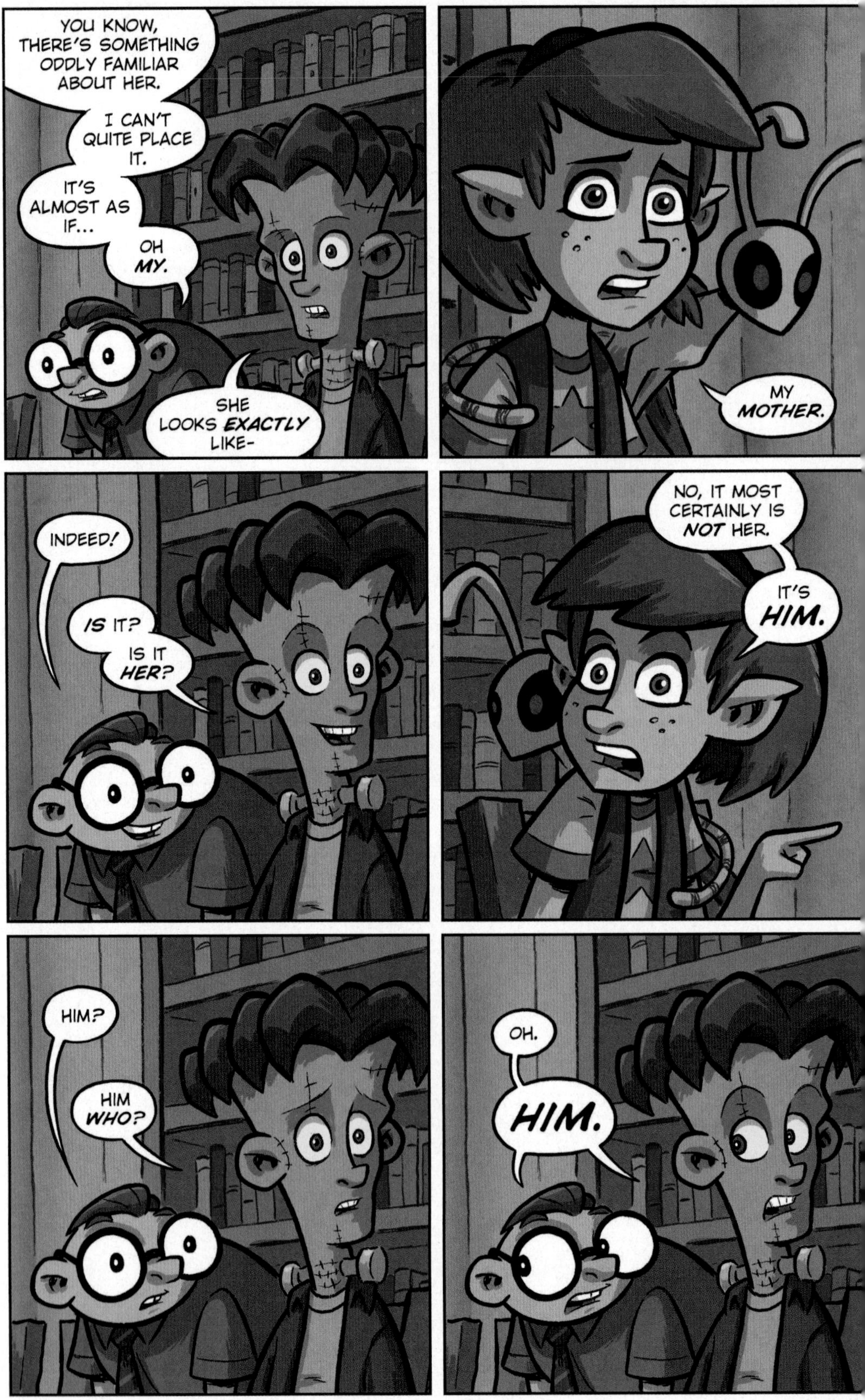
YOU KNOW, THERE'S SOMETHING ODDLY FAMILIAR ABOUT HER.
I CAN'T QUITE PLACE IT.
IT'S ALMOST AS IF...
OH *MY.*
SHE LOOKS *EXACTLY* LIKE-
MY *MOTHER.*
INDEED!
IS IT?
IS IT *HER?*
NO, IT MOST CERTAINLY IS *NOT* HER.
IT'S *HIM.*
HIM?
HIM *WHO?*
OH.
HIM.

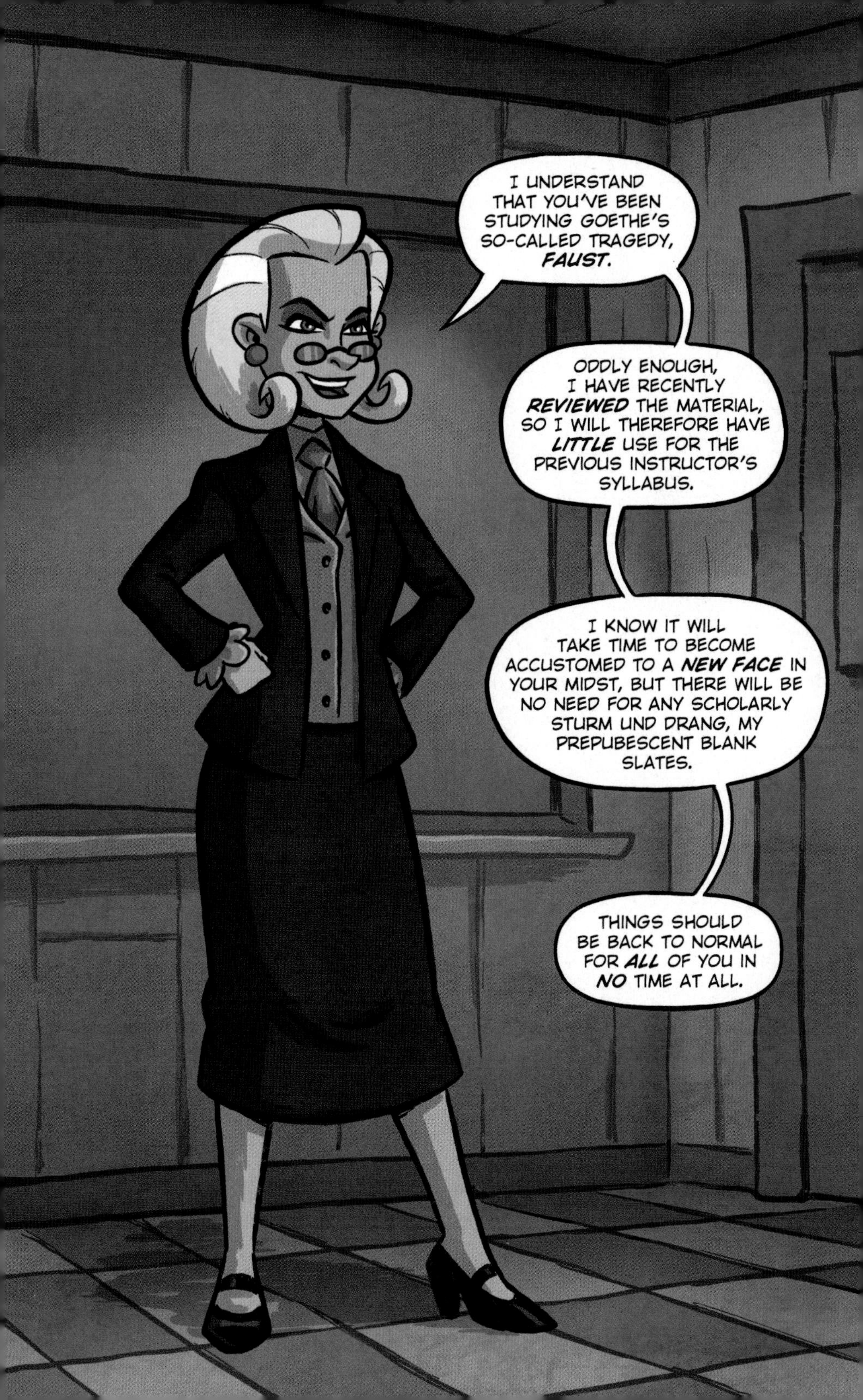
I UNDERSTAND THAT YOU'VE BEEN STUDYING GOETHE'S SO-CALLED TRAGEDY, FAUST.
ODDLY ENOUGH, I HAVE RECENTLY REVIEWED THE MATERIAL, SO I WILL THEREFORE HAVE LITTLE USE FOR THE PREVIOUS INSTRUCTOR'S SYLLABUS.
I KNOW IT WILL TAKE TIME TO BECOME ACCUSTOMED TO A NEW FACE IN YOUR MIDST, BUT THERE WILL BE NO NEED FOR ANY SCHOLARLY STURM UND DRANG, MY PREPUBESCENT BLANK SLATES.
THINGS SHOULD BE BACK TO NORMAL FOR ALL OF YOU IN NO TIME AT ALL.

Chapter 20

A New Game

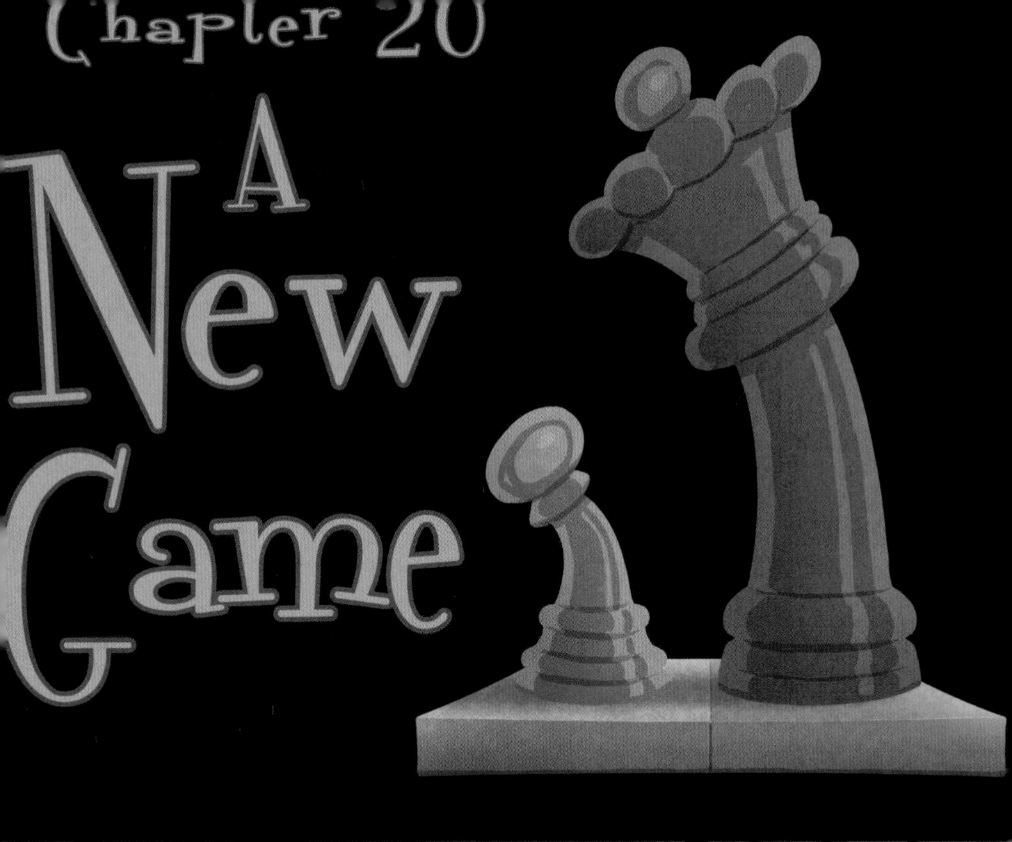

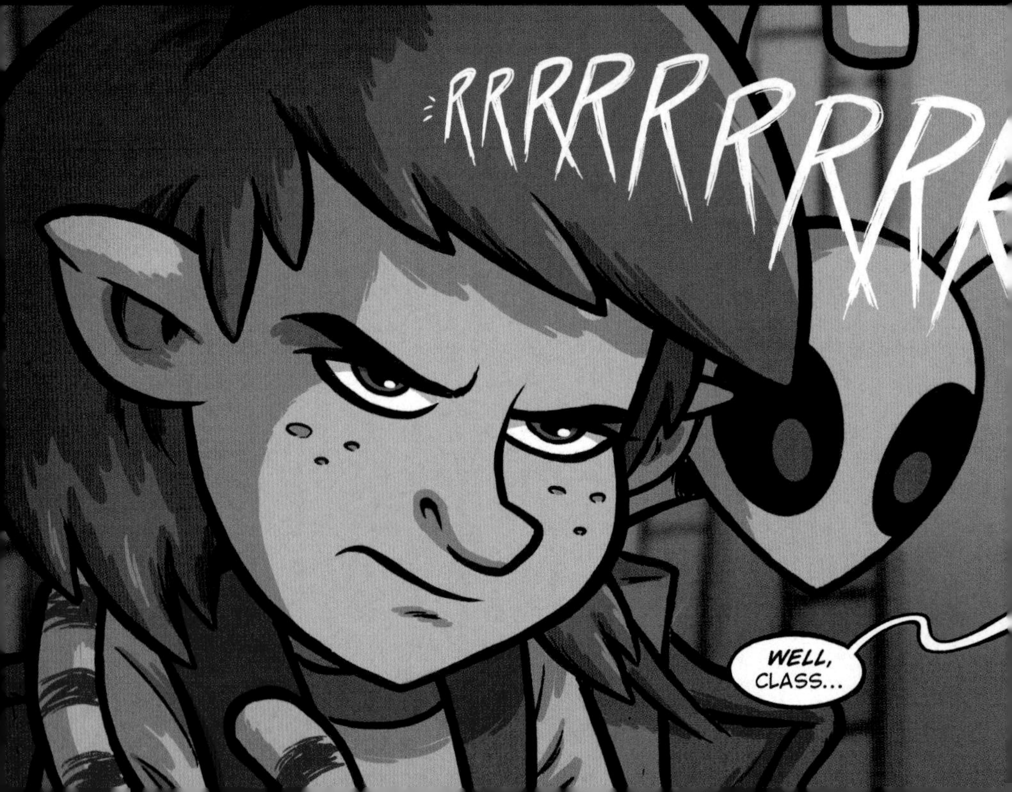
RRRRRRRRR
WELL, CLASS...

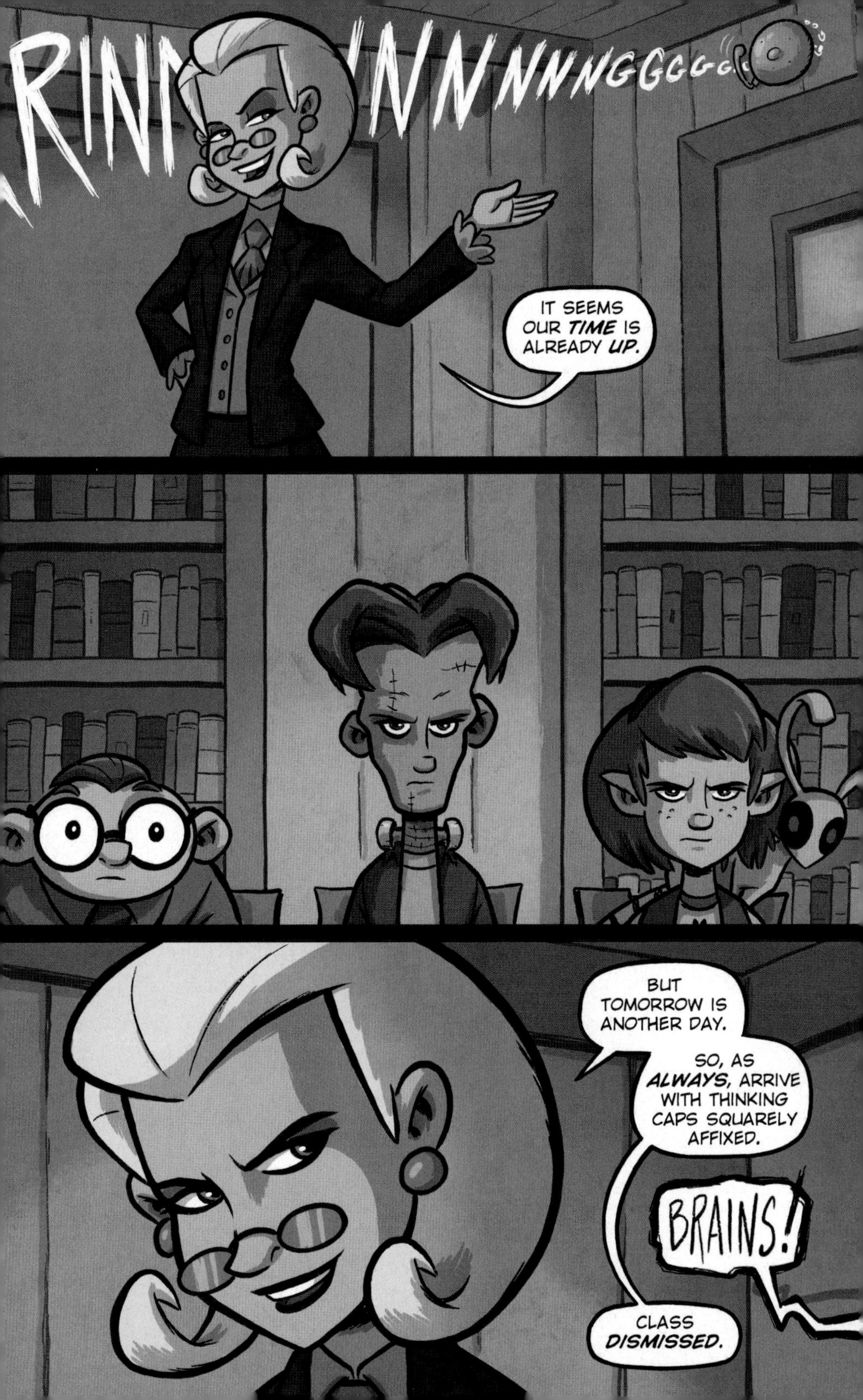
RINNNNNNNNNNGGGGG
IT SEEMS OUR TIME IS ALREADY UP.
BUT TOMORROW IS ANOTHER DAY.
SO, AS ALWAYS, ARRIVE WITH THINKING CAPS SQUARELY AFFIXED.
BRAINS!
CLASS DISMISSED.

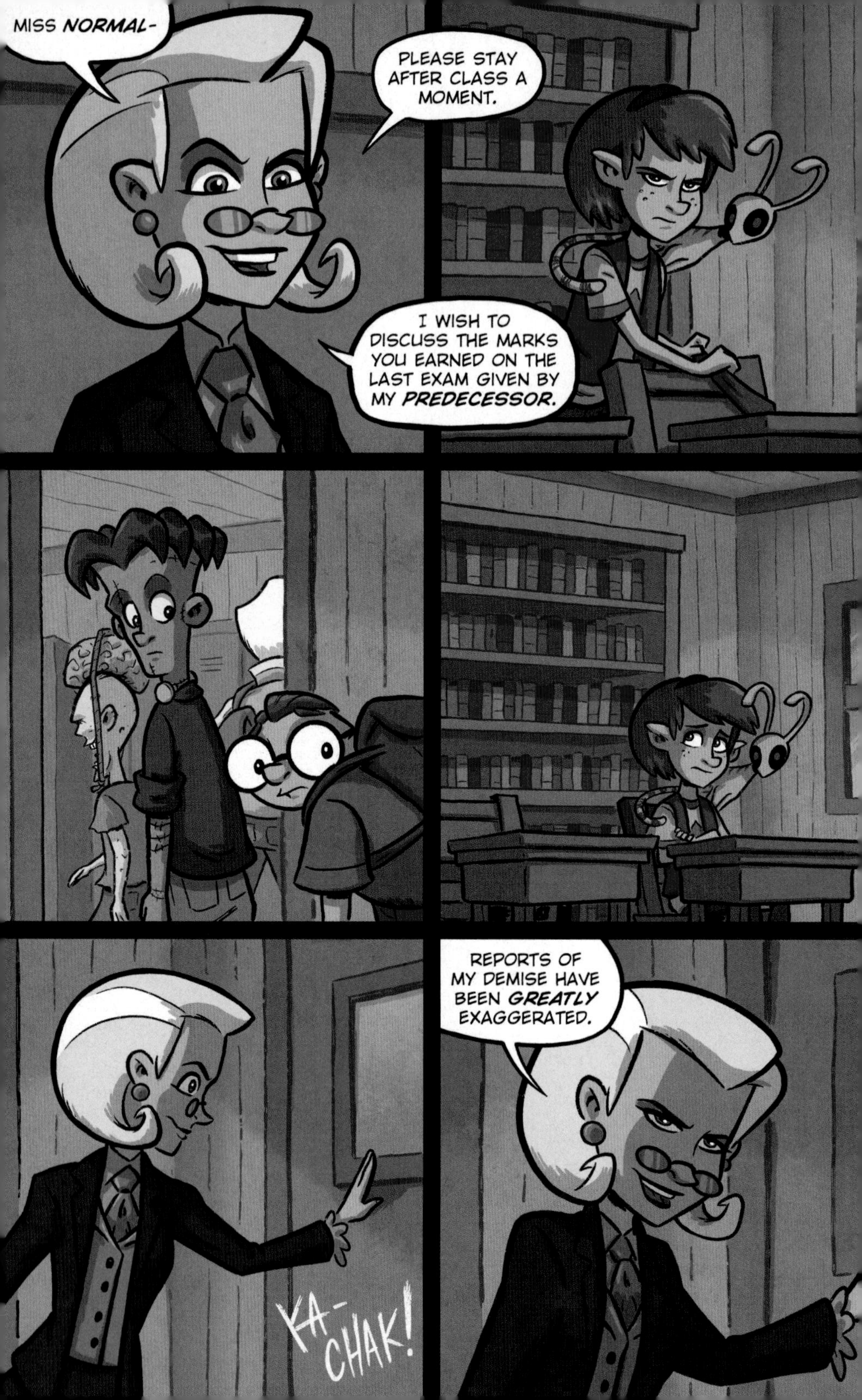
MISS NORMAL-
PLEASE STAY AFTER CLASS A MOMENT.
I WISH TO DISCUSS THE MARKS YOU EARNED ON THE LAST EXAM GIVEN BY MY PREDECESSOR.
KA-CHAK!
REPORTS OF MY DEMISE HAVE BEEN GREATLY EXAGGERATED.

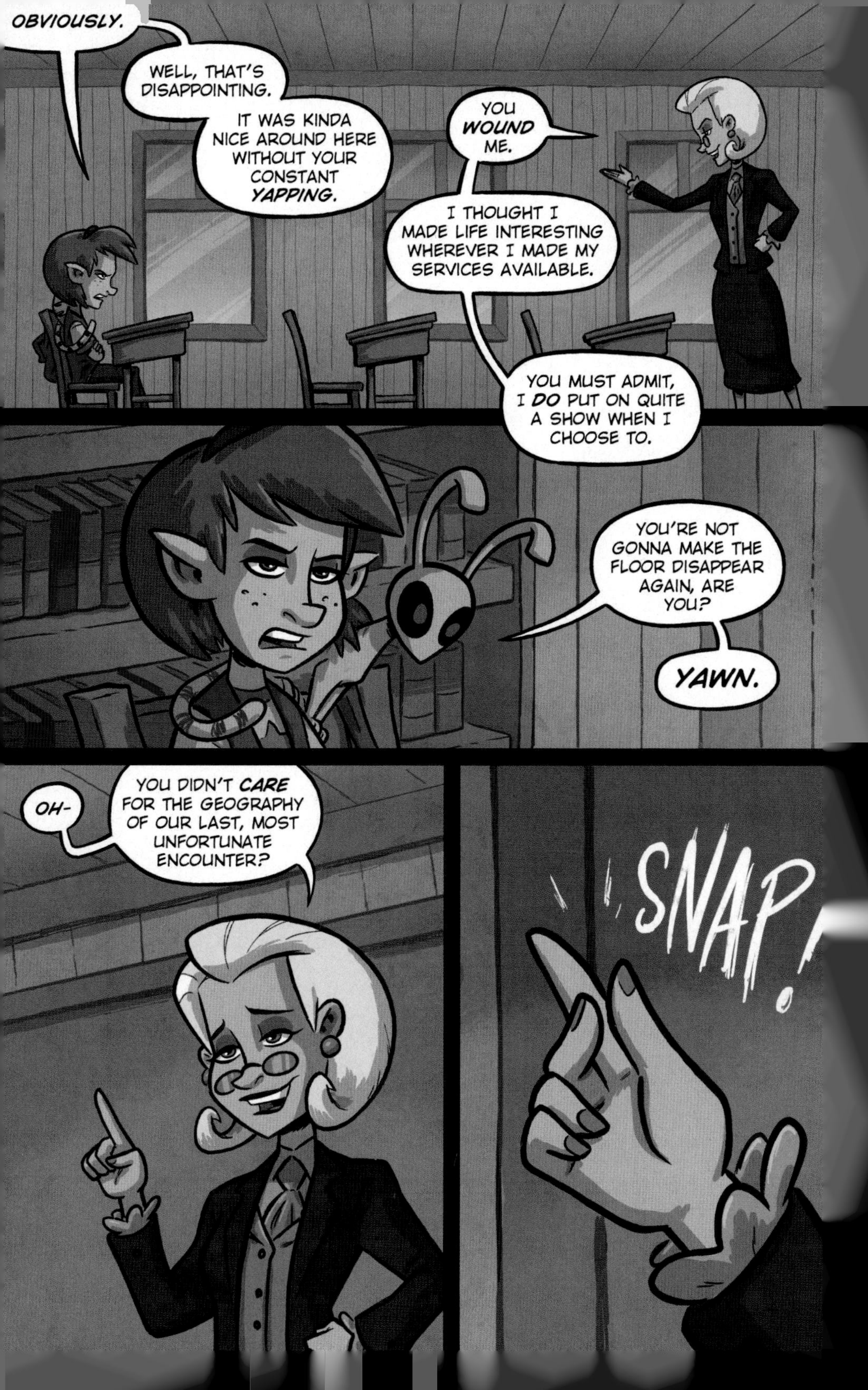
OBVIOUSLY.
WELL, THAT'S DISAPPOINTING.
IT WAS KINDA NICE AROUND HERE WITHOUT YOUR CONSTANT YAPPING.
YOU WOUND ME.
I THOUGHT I MADE LIFE INTERESTING WHEREVER I MADE MY SERVICES AVAILABLE.
YOU MUST ADMIT, I DO PUT ON QUITE A SHOW WHEN I CHOOSE TO.
YOU'RE NOT GONNA MAKE THE FLOOR DISAPPEAR AGAIN, ARE YOU?
YAWN.
OH-
YOU DIDN'T CARE FOR THE GEOGRAPHY OF OUR LAST, MOST UNFORTUNATE ENCOUNTER?
SNAP!

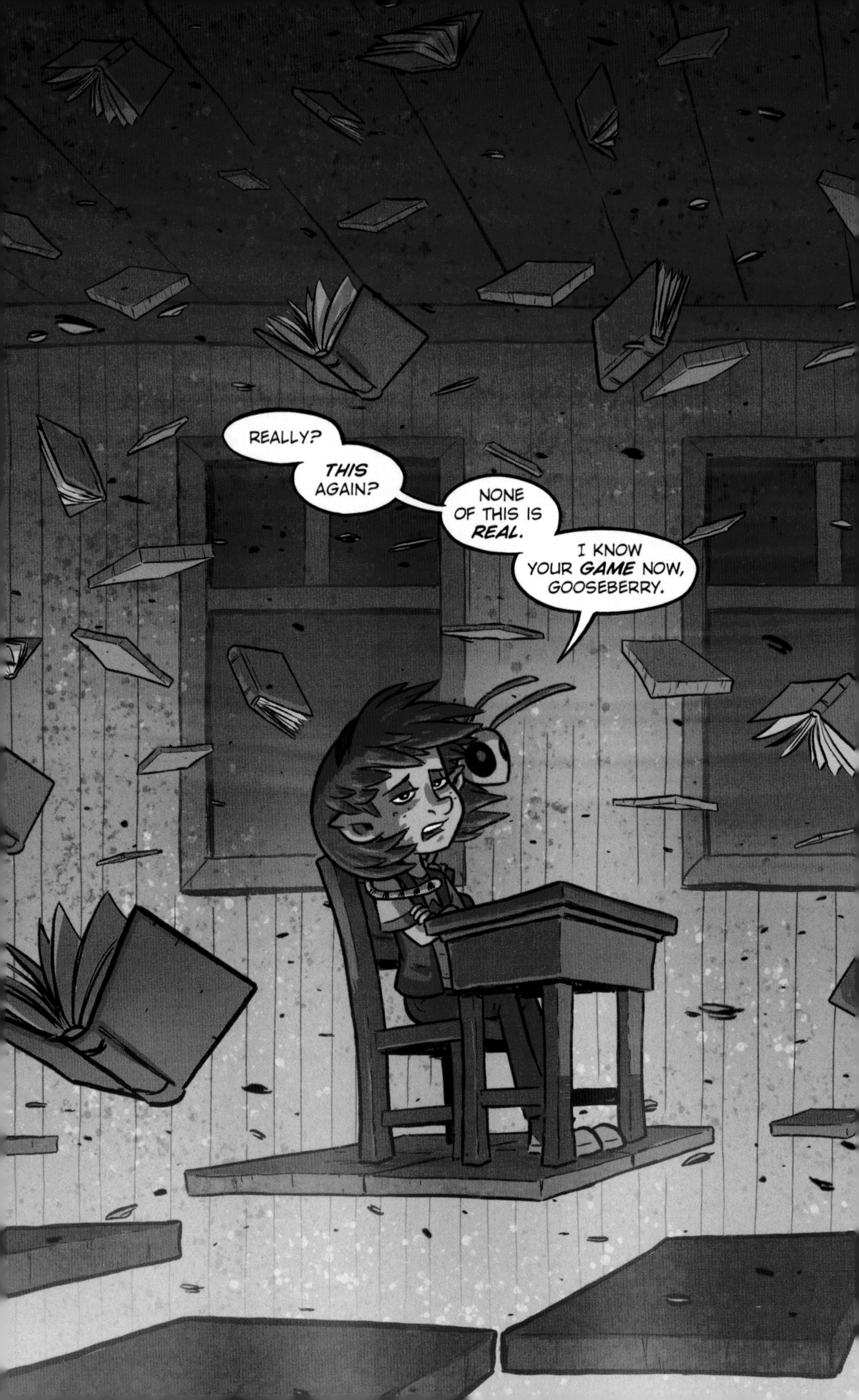
REALLY?
THIS AGAIN?
NONE OF THIS IS REAL.
I KNOW YOUR GAME NOW, GOOSEBERRY.

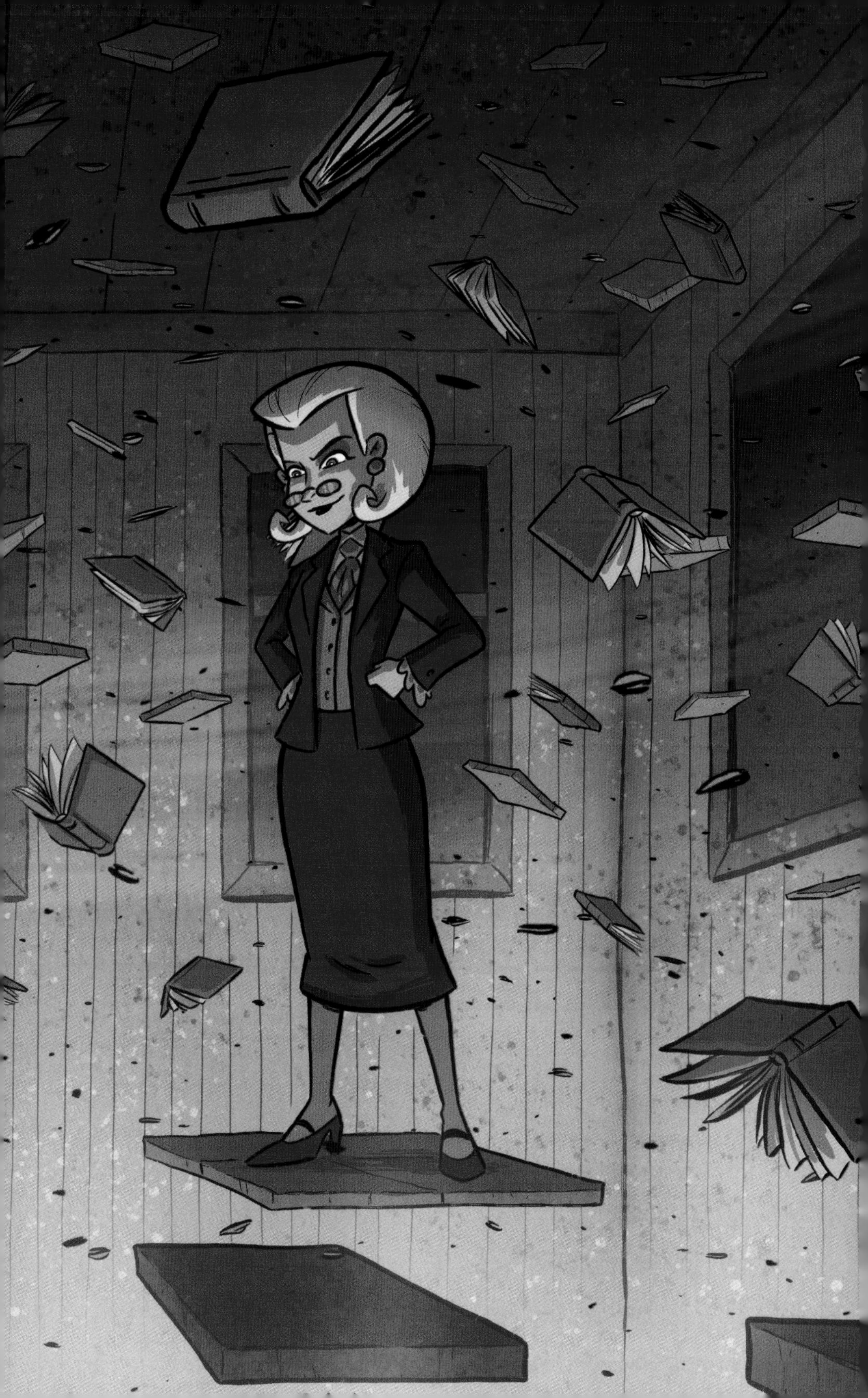

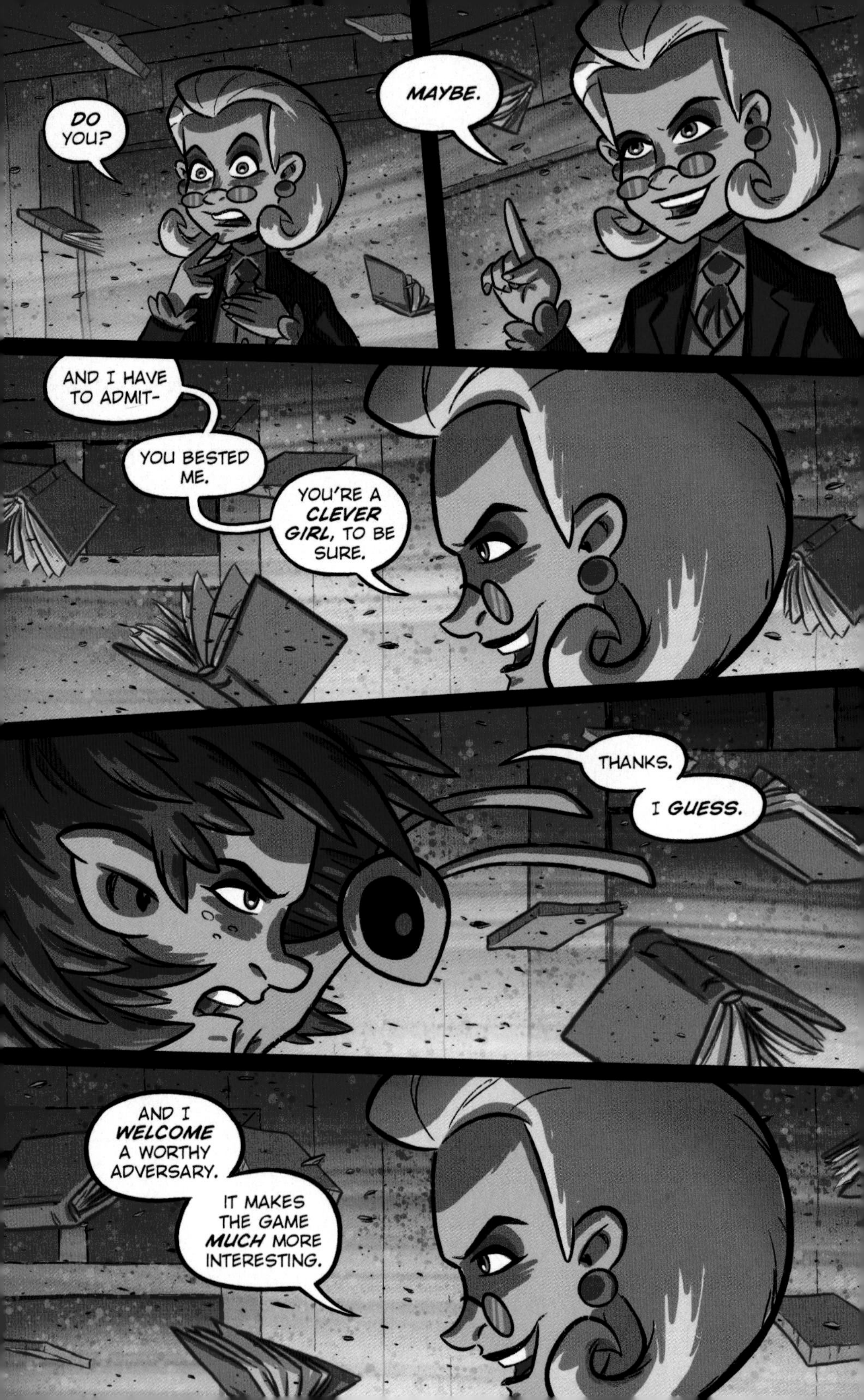
DO YOU?
MAYBE.
AND I HAVE TO ADMIT-
YOU BESTED ME.
YOU'RE A CLEVER GIRL, TO BE SURE.
THANKS.
I GUESS.
AND I WELCOME A WORTHY ADVERSARY.
IT MAKES THE GAME MUCH MORE INTERESTING.

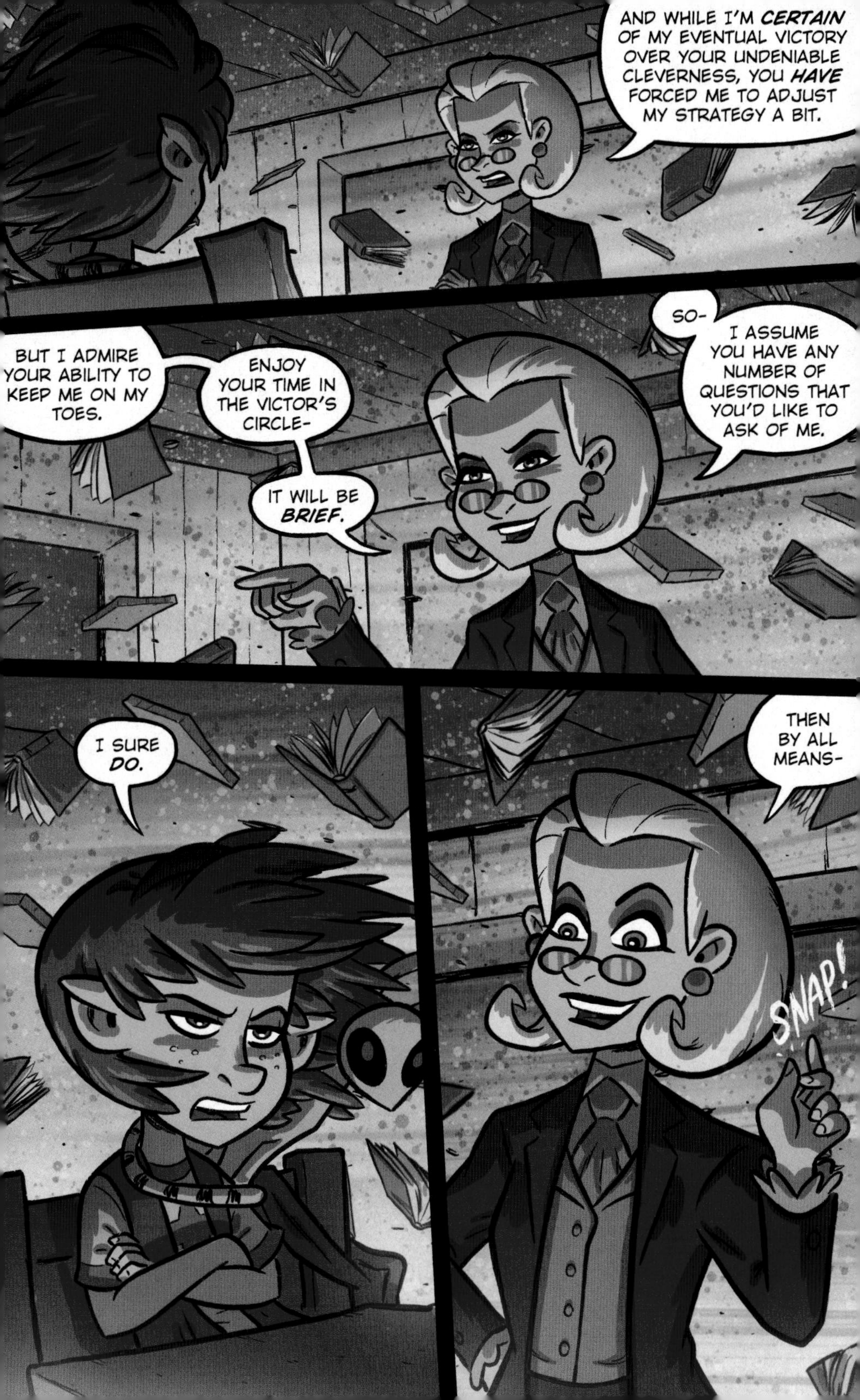
AND WHILE I'M *CERTAIN* OF MY EVENTUAL VICTORY OVER YOUR UNDENIABLE CLEVERNESS, YOU *HAVE* FORCED ME TO ADJUST MY STRATEGY A BIT.
BUT I ADMIRE YOUR ABILITY TO KEEP ME ON MY TOES.
ENJOY YOUR TIME IN THE VICTOR'S CIRCLE-
IT WILL BE *BRIEF*.
SO-
I ASSUME YOU HAVE ANY NUMBER OF QUESTIONS THAT YOU'D LIKE TO ASK OF ME.
I SURE *DO*.
THEN BY ALL MEANS-
SNAP!

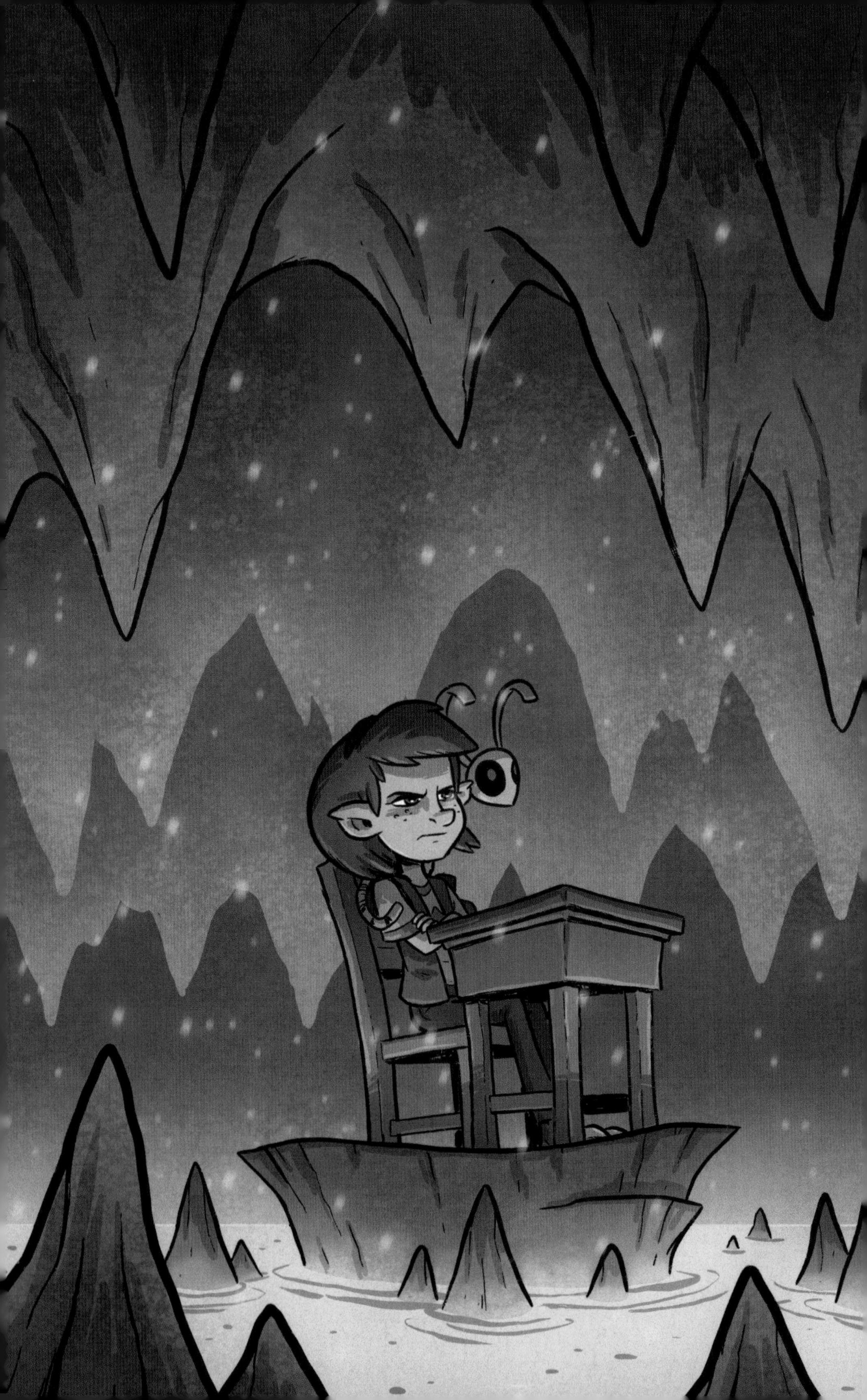

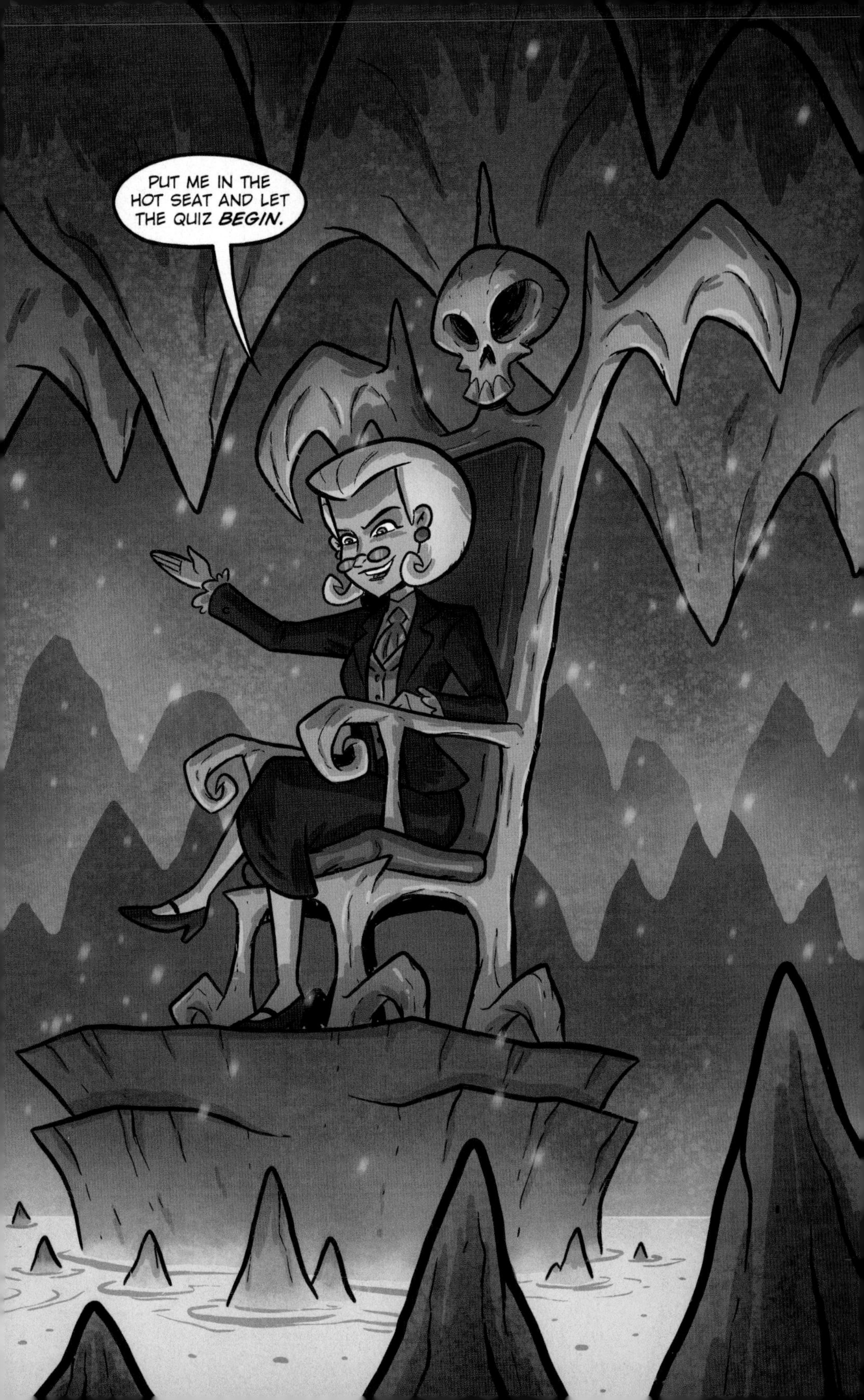
PUT ME IN THE HOT SEAT AND LET THE QUIZ *BEGIN.*

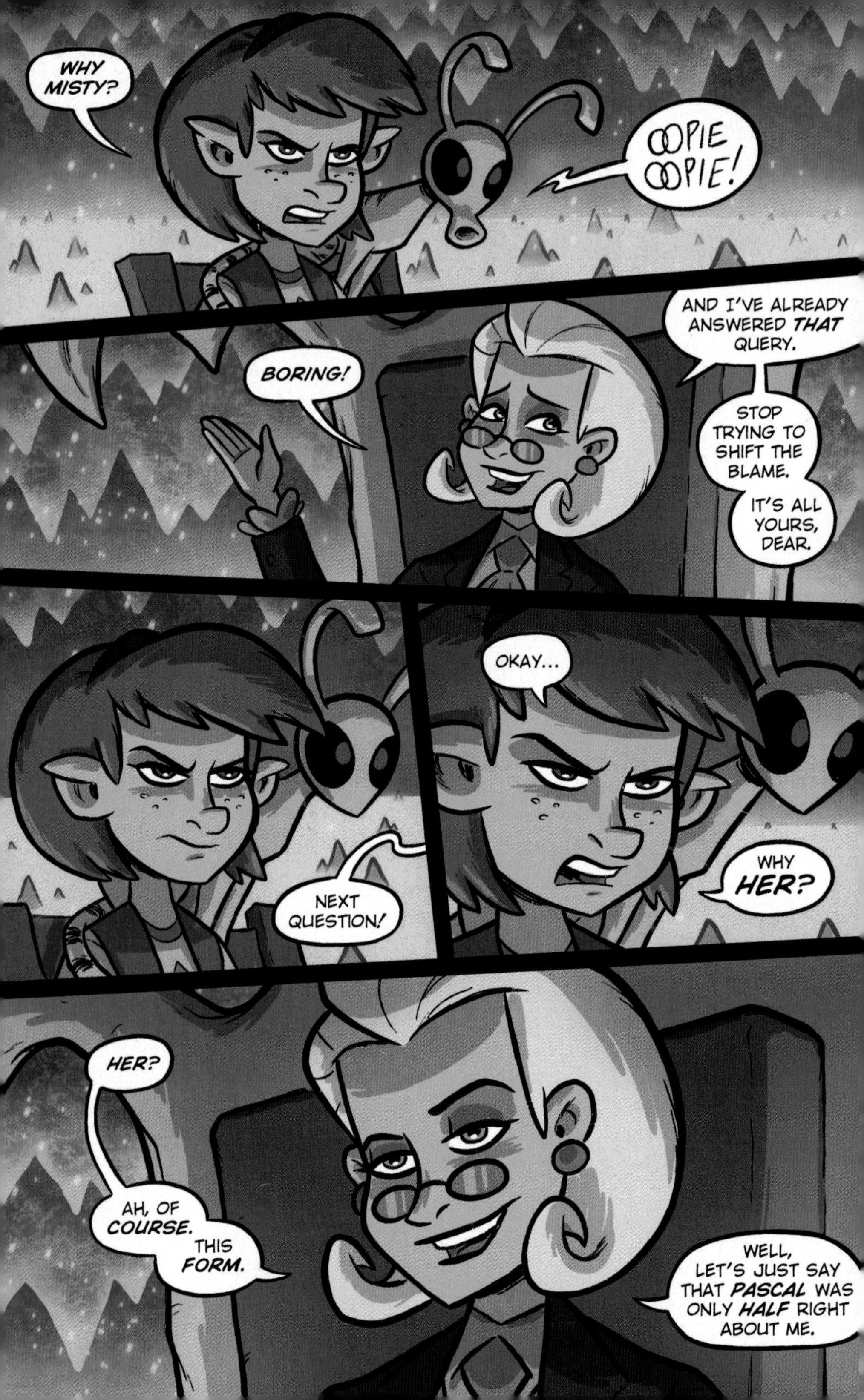
WHY MISTY?
OOPIE OOPIE!
AND I'VE ALREADY ANSWERED THAT QUERY.
BORING!
STOP TRYING TO SHIFT THE BLAME.
IT'S ALL YOURS, DEAR.
NEXT QUESTION!
OKAY...
WHY HER?
HER?
AH, OF COURSE. THIS FORM.
WELL, LET'S JUST SAY THAT PASCAL WAS ONLY HALF RIGHT ABOUT ME.

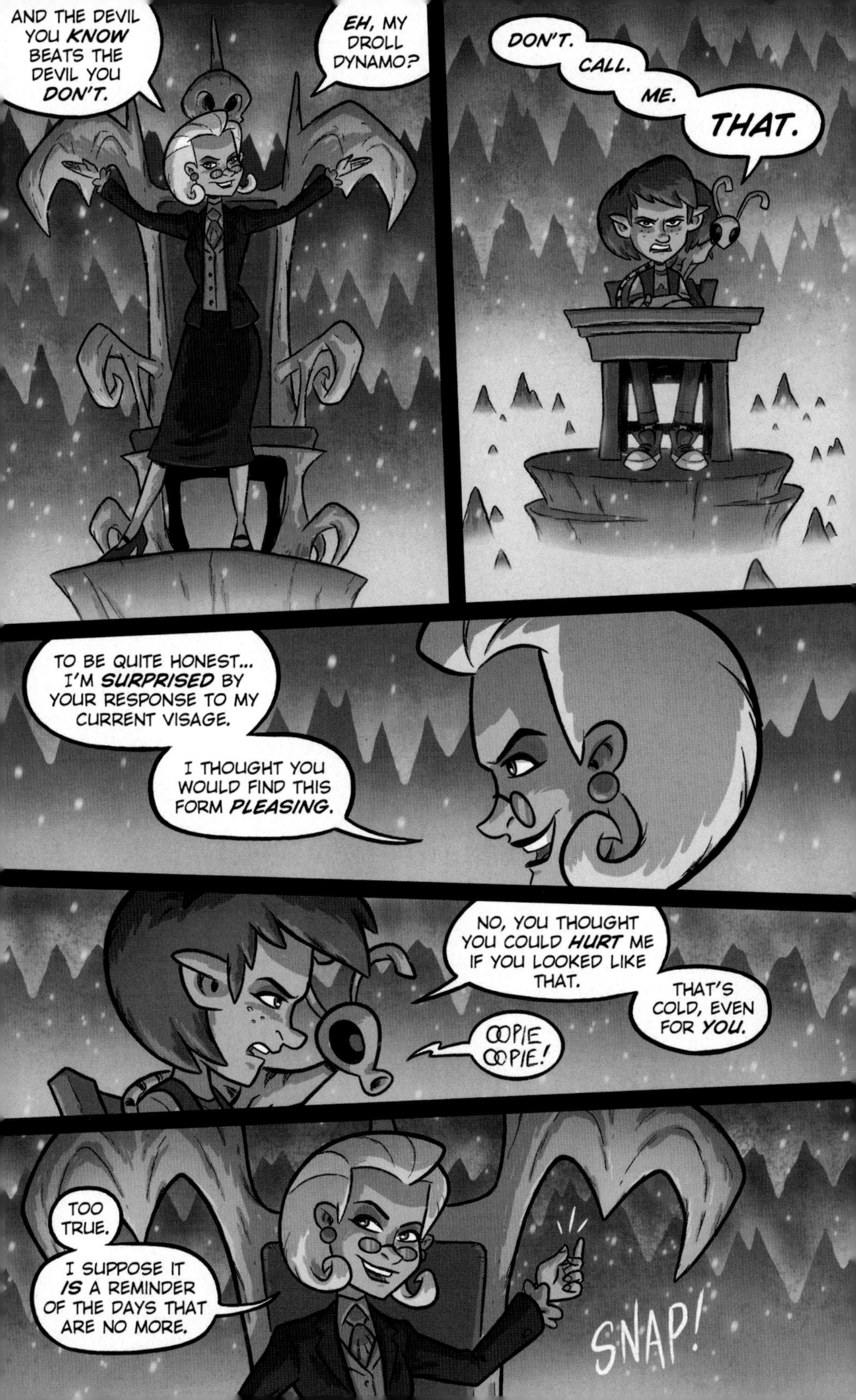
AND THE DEVIL YOU *KNOW* BEATS THE DEVIL YOU *DON'T.*
EH, MY DROLL DYNAMO?
DON'T.
CALL.
ME.
THAT.
TO BE QUITE HONEST... I'M *SURPRISED* BY YOUR RESPONSE TO MY CURRENT VISAGE.
I THOUGHT YOU WOULD FIND THIS FORM *PLEASING.*
NO, YOU THOUGHT YOU COULD *HURT* ME IF YOU LOOKED LIKE THAT.
THAT'S COLD, EVEN FOR *YOU.*
OOPIE OOPIE!
TOO TRUE.
I SUPPOSE IT *IS* A REMINDER OF THE DAYS THAT ARE NO MORE.
SNAP!

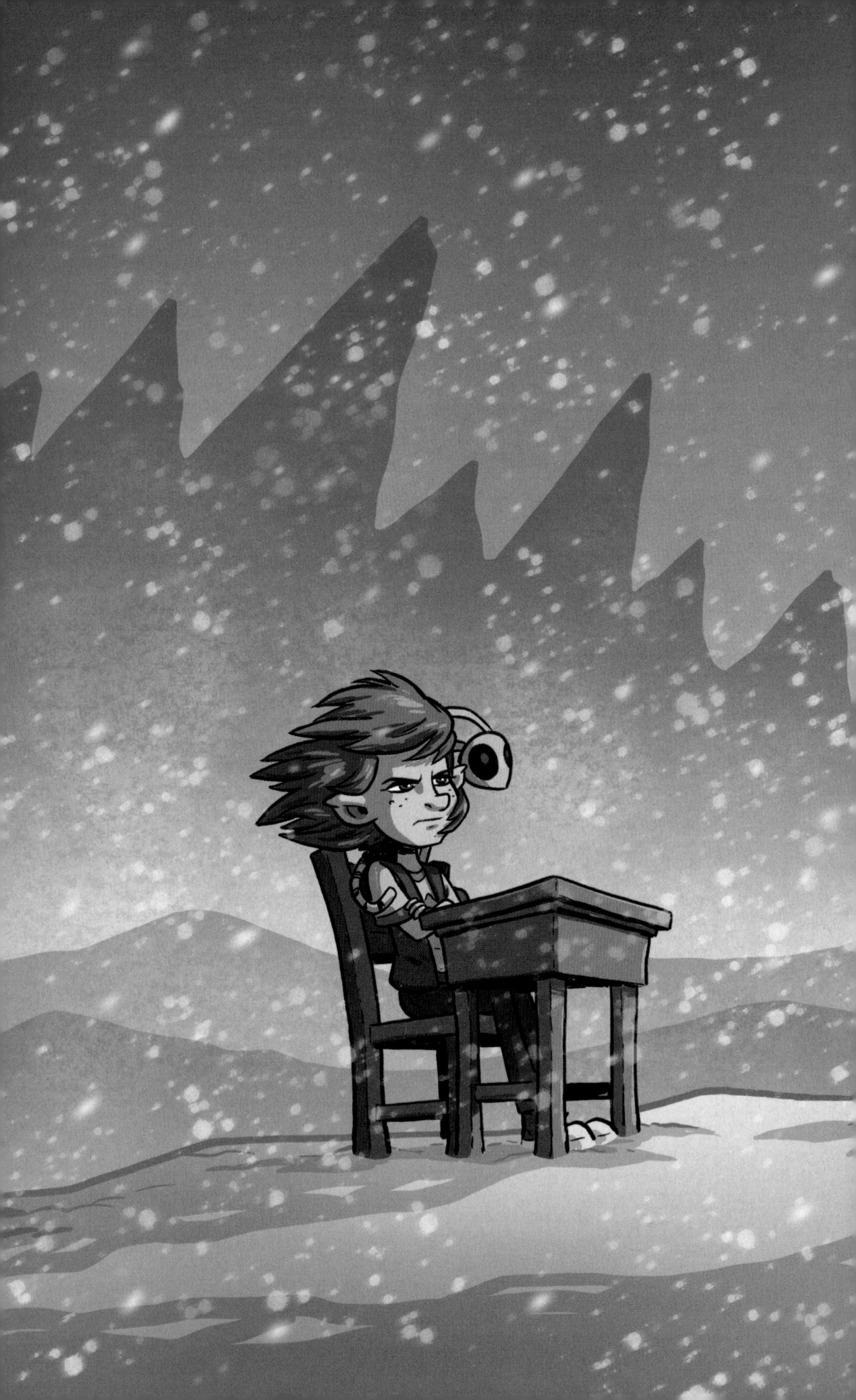

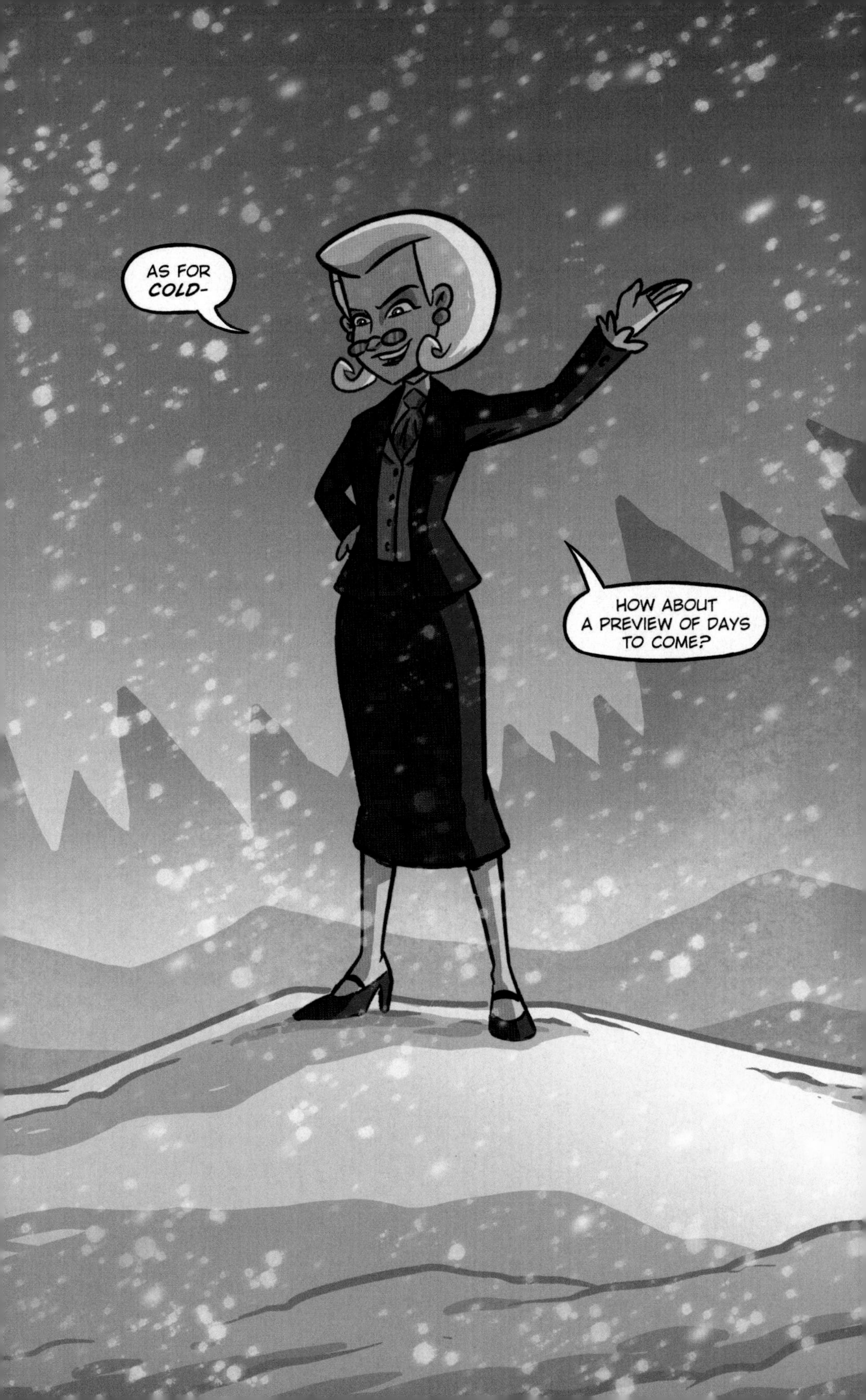
AS FOR COLD-
HOW ABOUT A PREVIEW OF DAYS TO COME?

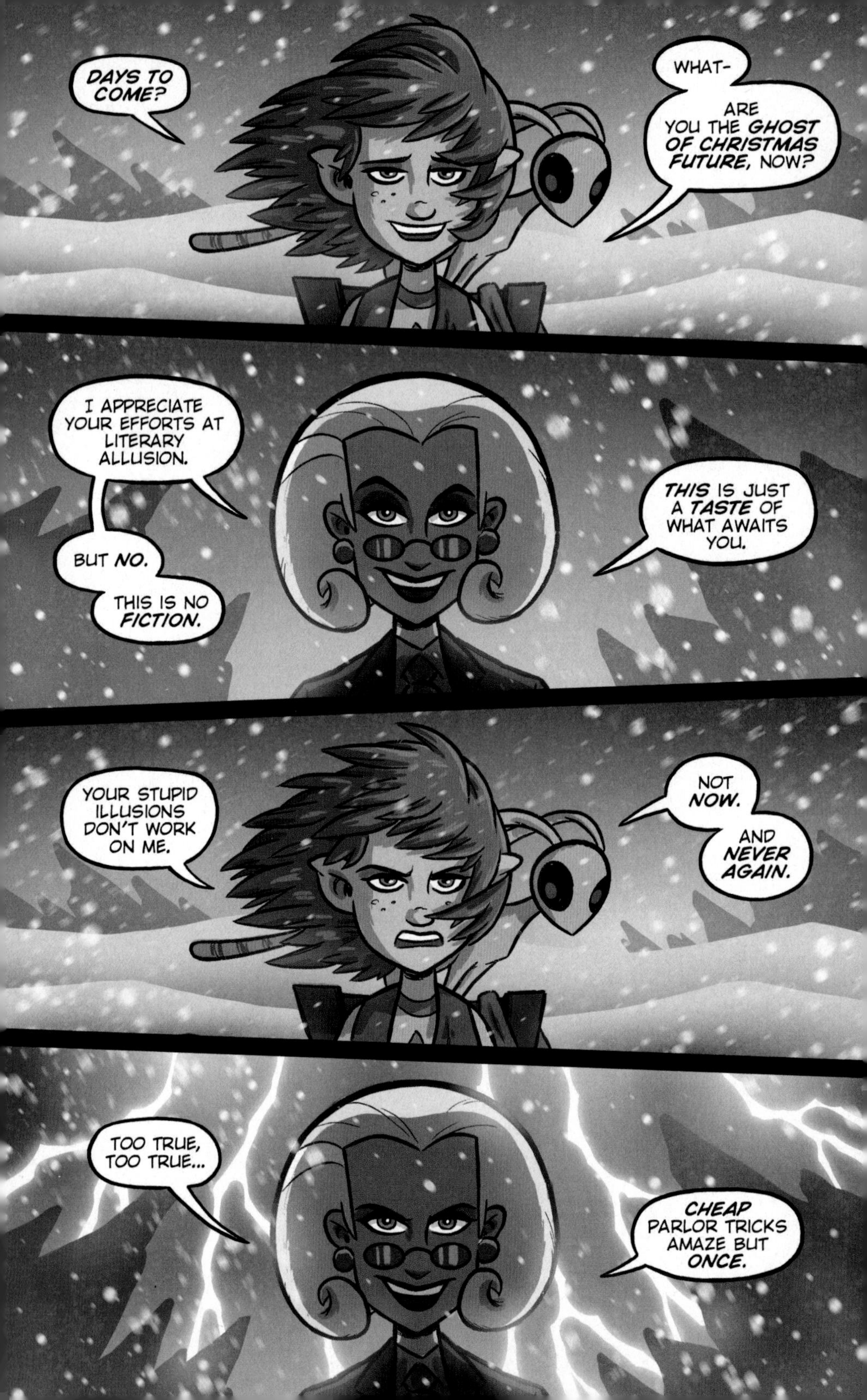
DAYS TO COME?
WHAT-
ARE YOU THE GHOST OF CHRISTMAS FUTURE, NOW?
I APPRECIATE YOUR EFFORTS AT LITERARY ALLUSION.
BUT NO.
THIS IS NO FICTION.
THIS IS JUST A TASTE OF WHAT AWAITS YOU.
YOUR STUPID ILLUSIONS DON'T WORK ON ME.
NOT NOW.
AND NEVER AGAIN.
TOO TRUE, TOO TRUE...
CHEAP PARLOR TRICKS AMAZE BUT ONCE.

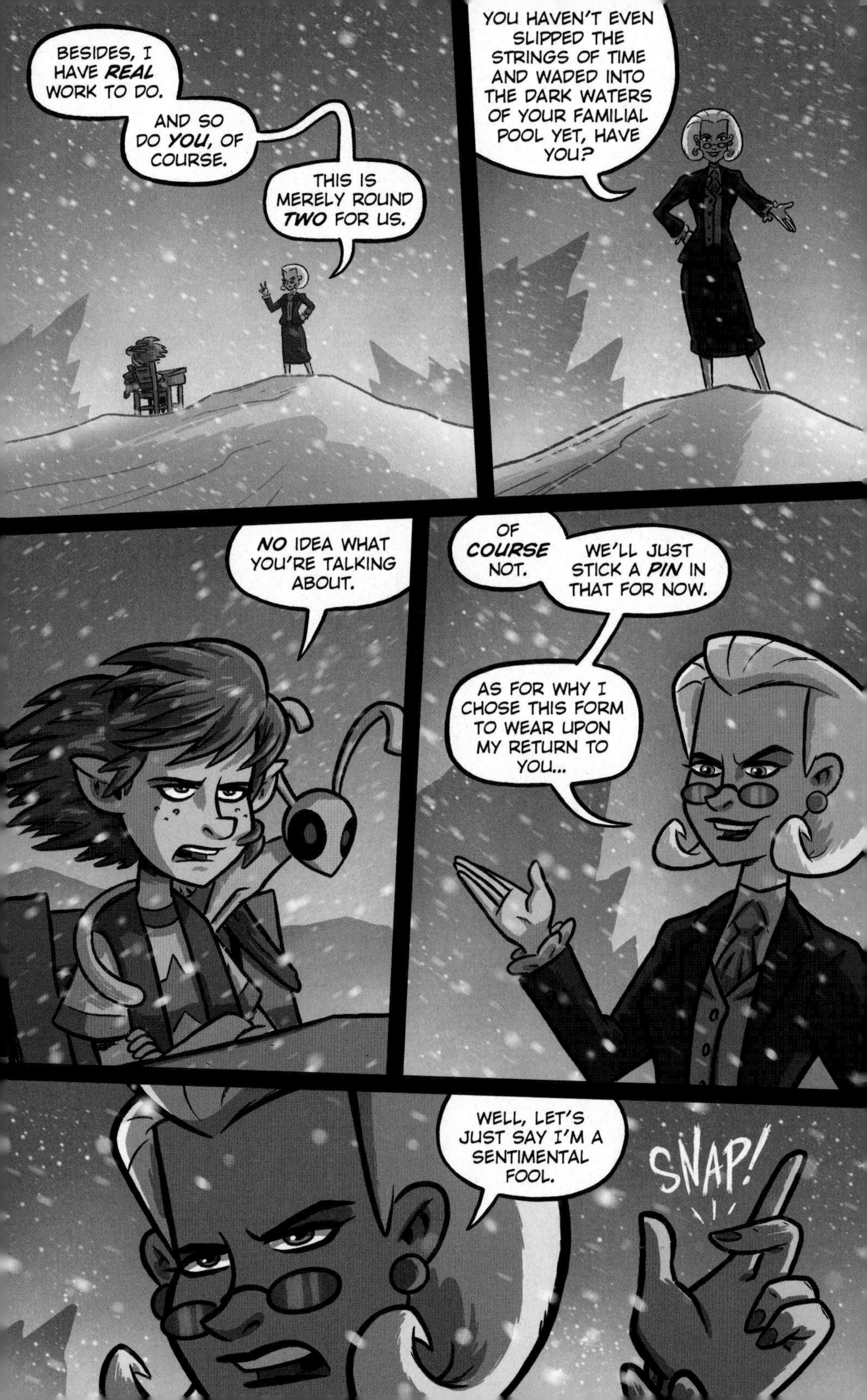
BESIDES, I HAVE REAL WORK TO DO.
AND SO DO YOU, OF COURSE.
THIS IS MERELY ROUND TWO FOR US.
YOU HAVEN'T EVEN SLIPPED THE STRINGS OF TIME AND WADED INTO THE DARK WATERS OF YOUR FAMILIAL POOL YET, HAVE YOU?
NO IDEA WHAT YOU'RE TALKING ABOUT.
OF COURSE NOT.
WE'LL JUST STICK A PIN IN THAT FOR NOW.
AS FOR WHY I CHOSE THIS FORM TO WEAR UPON MY RETURN TO YOU...
WELL, LET'S JUST SAY I'M A SENTIMENTAL FOOL.
SNAP!

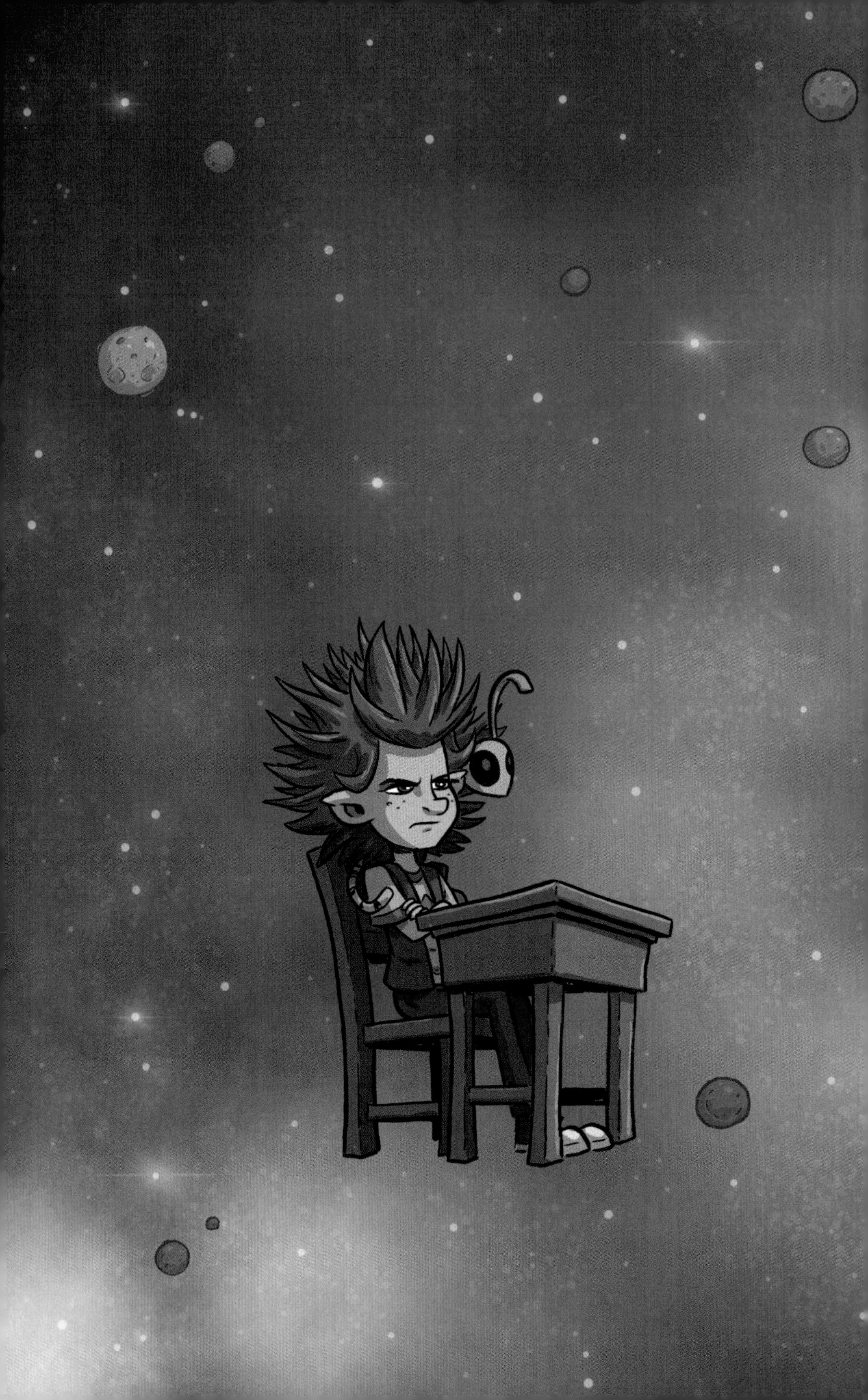

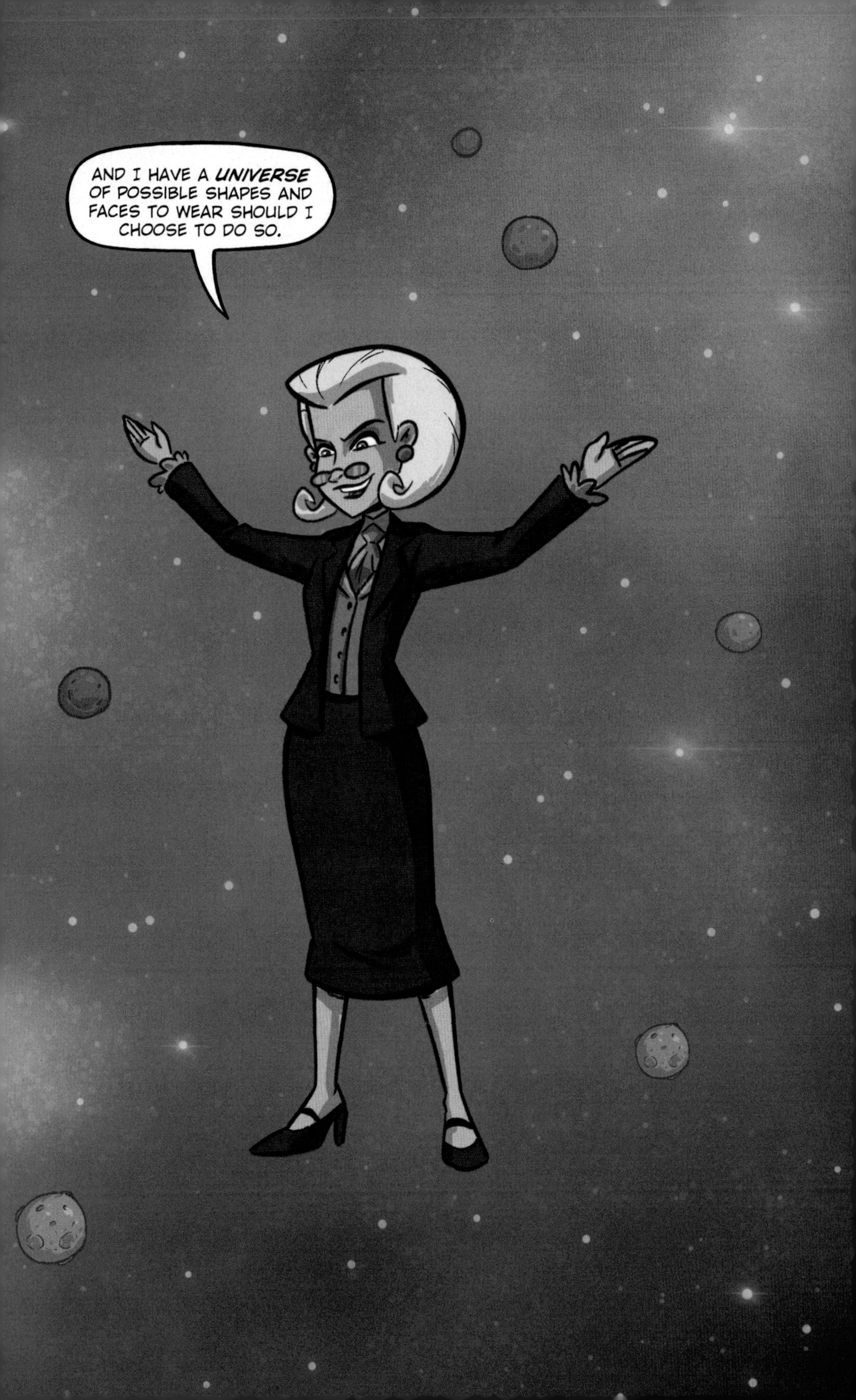
AND I HAVE A *UNIVERSE* OF POSSIBLE SHAPES AND FACES TO WEAR SHOULD I CHOOSE TO DO SO.

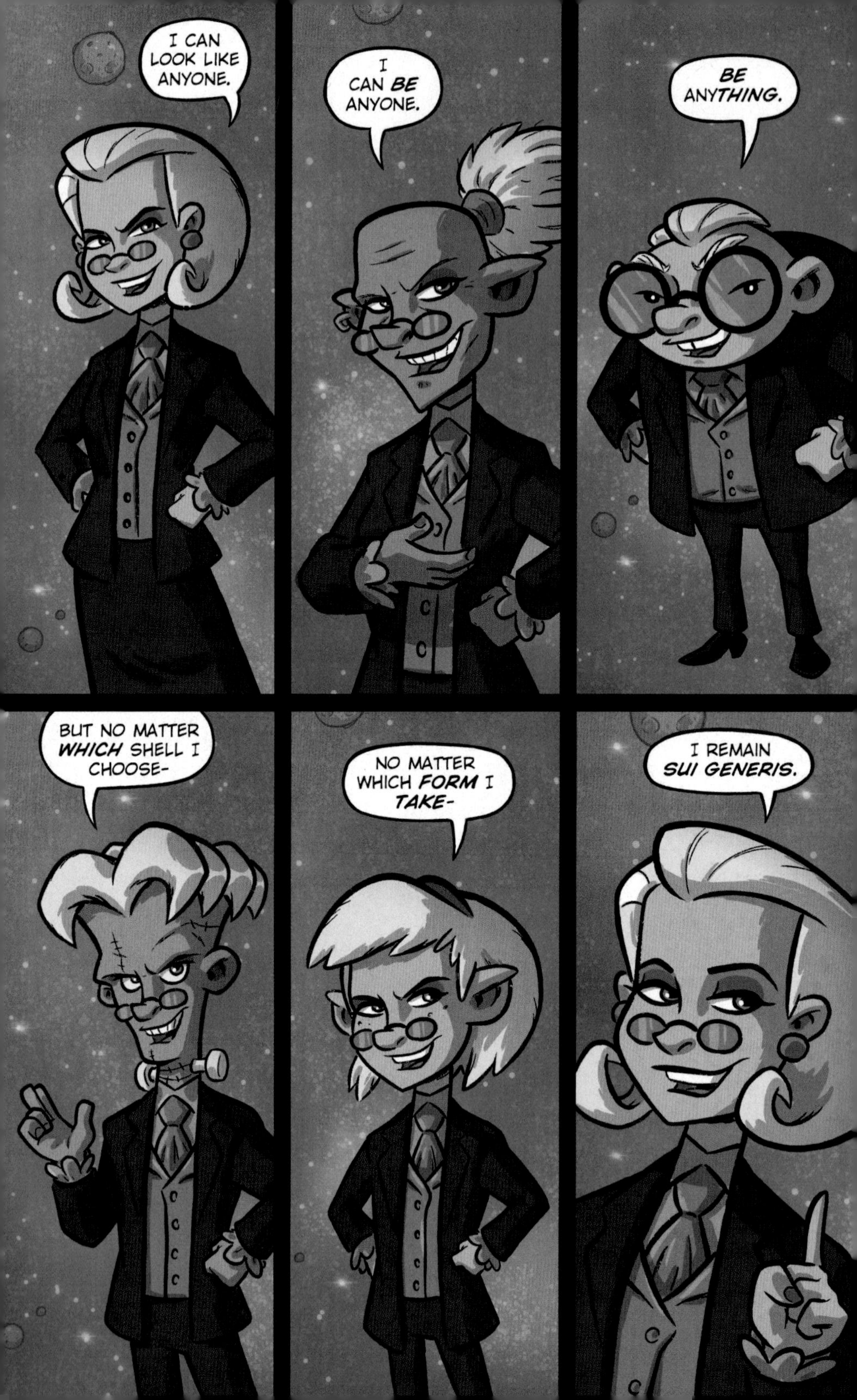
I CAN LOOK LIKE ANYONE.
I CAN *BE* ANYONE.
BE ANY*THING*.
BUT NO MATTER *WHICH* SHELL I CHOOSE-
NO MATTER WHICH *FORM* I *TAKE*-
I REMAIN *SUI GENERIS*.

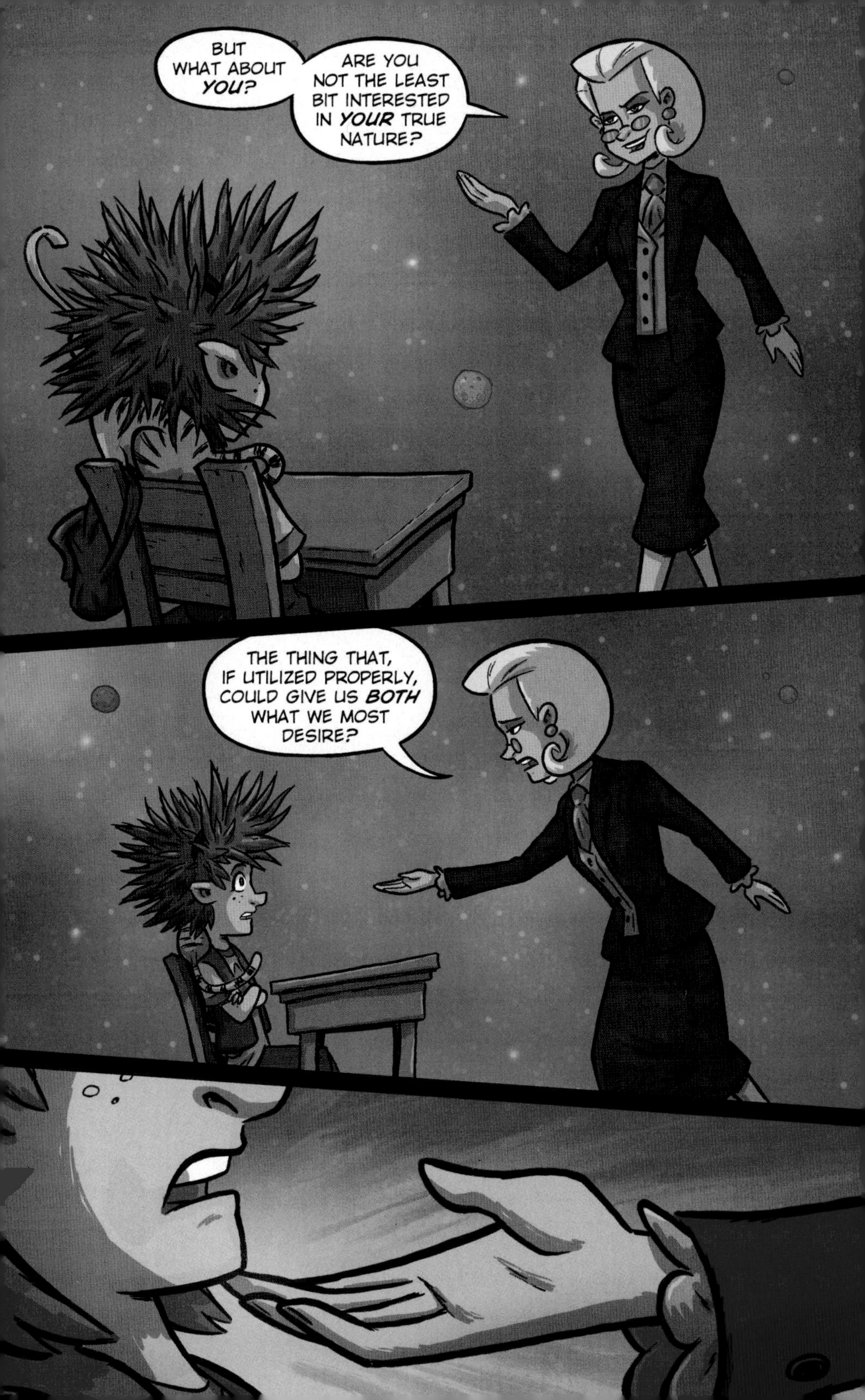
BUT WHAT ABOUT *YOU*?
ARE YOU NOT THE LEAST BIT INTERESTED IN *YOUR* TRUE NATURE?
THE THING THAT, IF UTILIZED PROPERLY, COULD GIVE US *BOTH* WHAT WE MOST DESIRE?

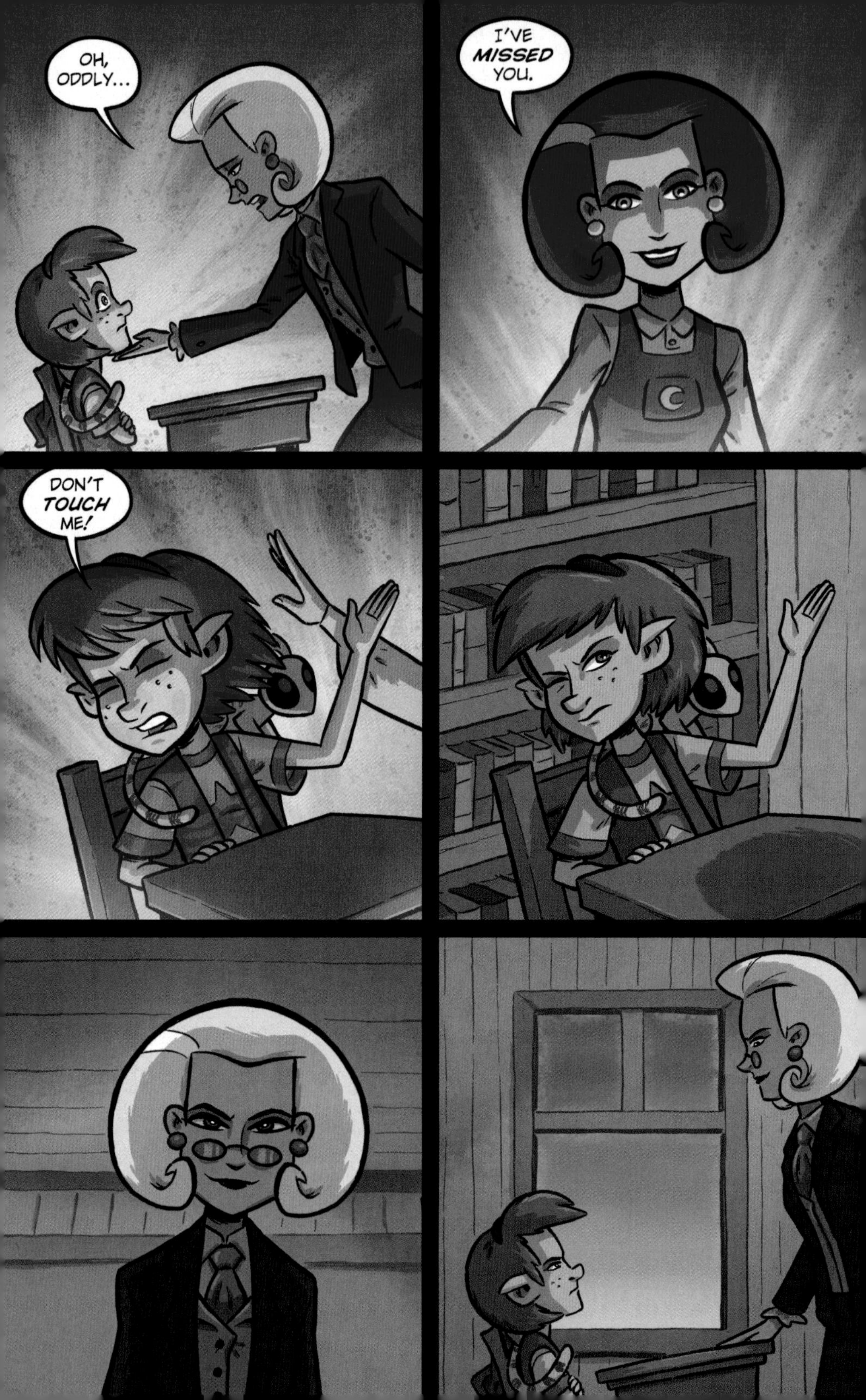
OH, ODDLY...
I'VE MISSED YOU.
DON'T TOUCH ME!

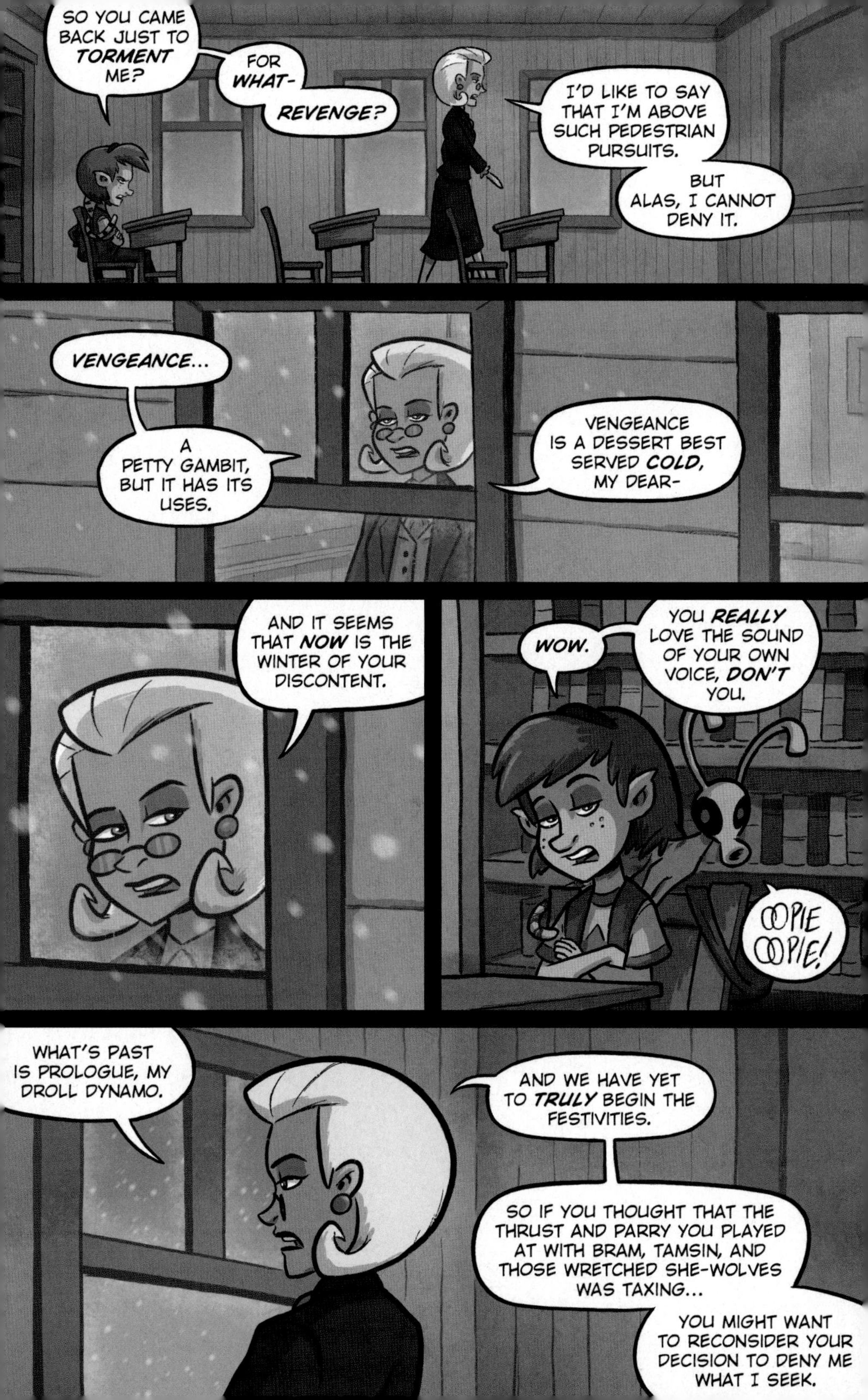

SO YOU CAME BACK JUST TO TORMENT ME?
FOR WHAT-
REVENGE?
I'D LIKE TO SAY THAT I'M ABOVE SUCH PEDESTRIAN PURSUITS.
BUT ALAS, I CANNOT DENY IT.
VENGEANCE...
A PETTY GAMBIT, BUT IT HAS ITS USES.
VENGEANCE IS A DESSERT BEST SERVED COLD, MY DEAR-
AND IT SEEMS THAT NOW IS THE WINTER OF YOUR DISCONTENT.
WOW.
YOU REALLY LOVE THE SOUND OF YOUR OWN VOICE, DON'T YOU.
OOPIE OOPIE!
WHAT'S PAST IS PROLOGUE, MY DROLL DYNAMO.
AND WE HAVE YET TO TRULY BEGIN THE FESTIVITIES.
SO IF YOU THOUGHT THAT THE THRUST AND PARRY YOU PLAYED AT WITH BRAM, TAMSIN, AND THOSE WRETCHED SHE-WOLVES WAS TAXING...
YOU MIGHT WANT TO RECONSIDER YOUR DECISION TO DENY ME WHAT I SEEK.

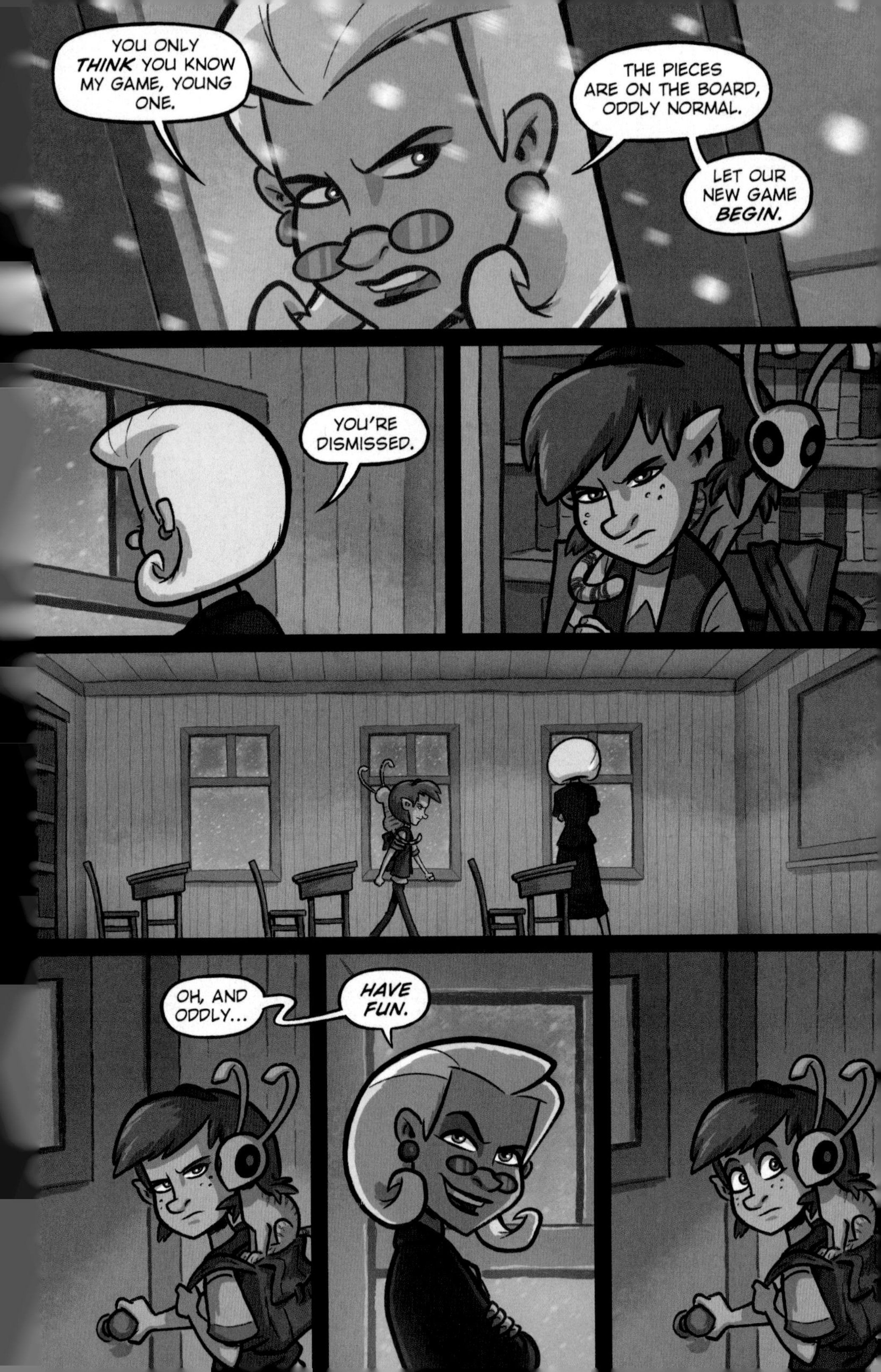
YOU ONLY THINK YOU KNOW MY GAME, YOUNG ONE.
THE PIECES ARE ON THE BOARD, ODDLY NORMAL.
LET OUR NEW GAME BEGIN.
YOU'RE DISMISSED.
OH, AND ODDLY...
HAVE FUN.

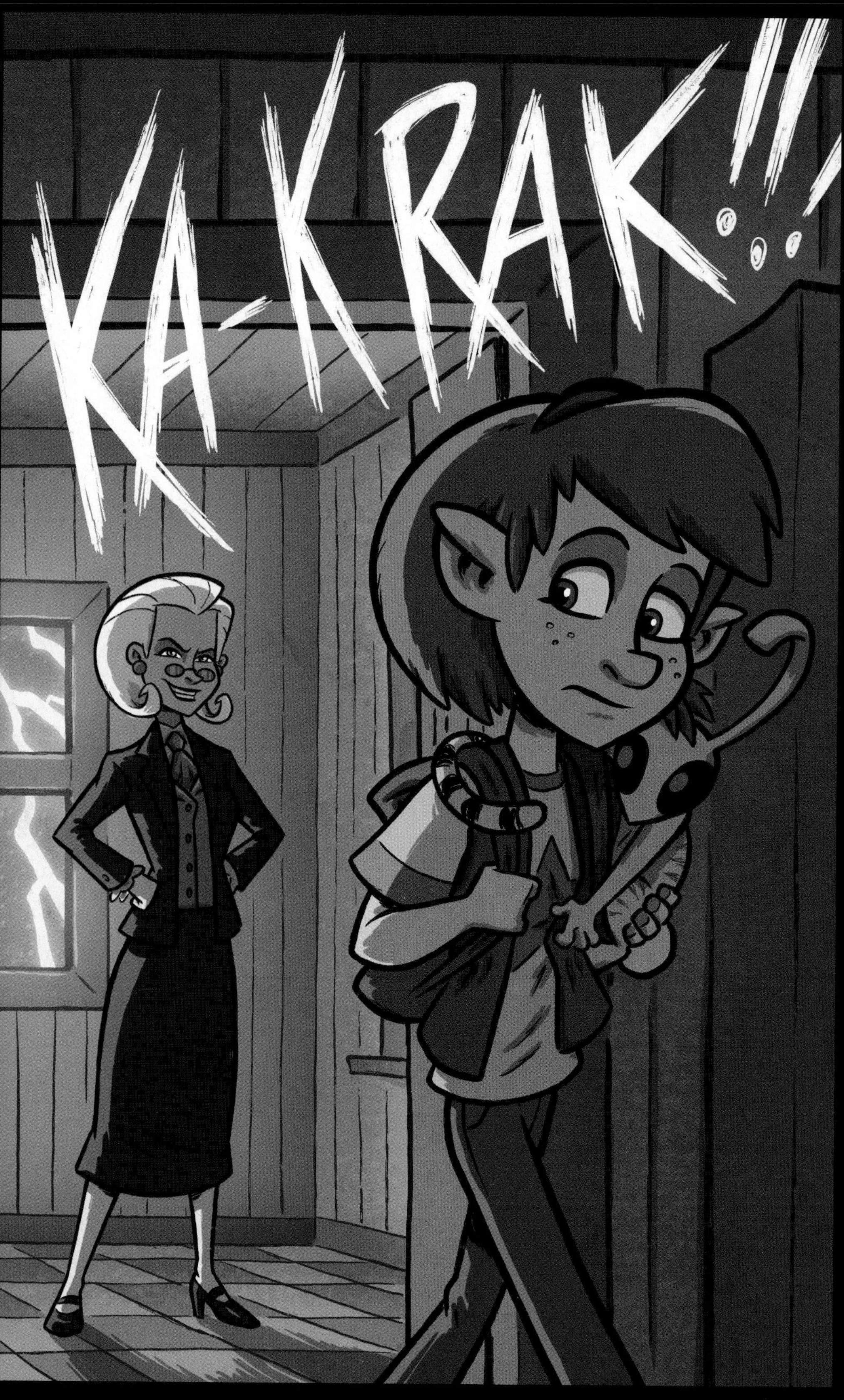
KA-KRAK!!!

Oddly ★ Normal

BOOK
4

WRITTEN, ILLUSTRATED, AND LETTERED
BY

OTIS FRAMPTON

COLOR FLATS BY
KATE FRAMPTON & OTIS FRAMPTON

ABOUT THE AUTHOR

Otis Frampton is a comic book writer/artist, freelance illustrator, and animator. He is the creator of the webcomic and animated series "ABCDEFGeek." He is also one of the artists on the popular animated web series "How It Should Have Ended."

You can visit Otis on the web at: www.otisframpton.com

COVER
GALLERY

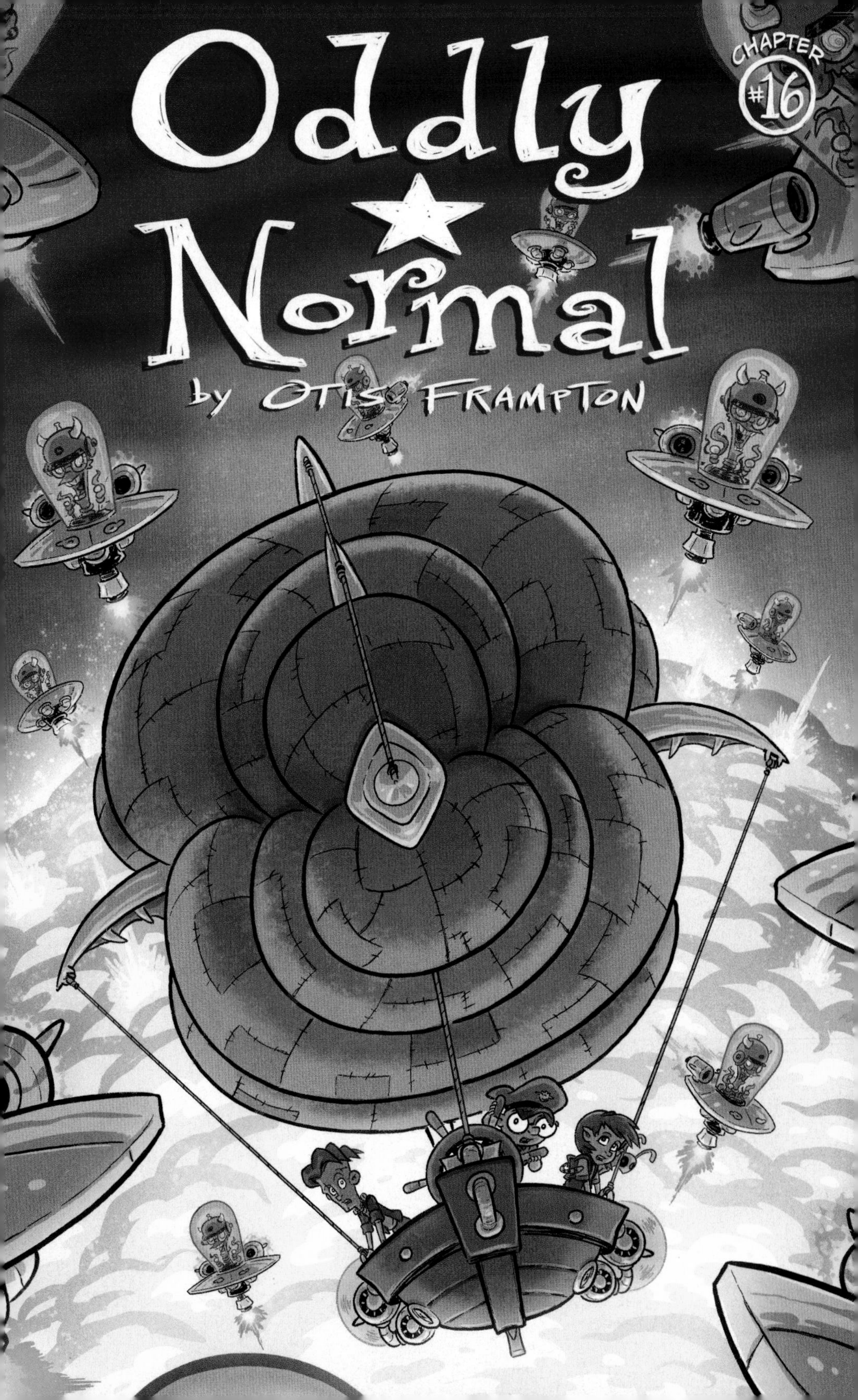
Oddly Normal
by OTIS FRAMPTON
CHAPTER #16

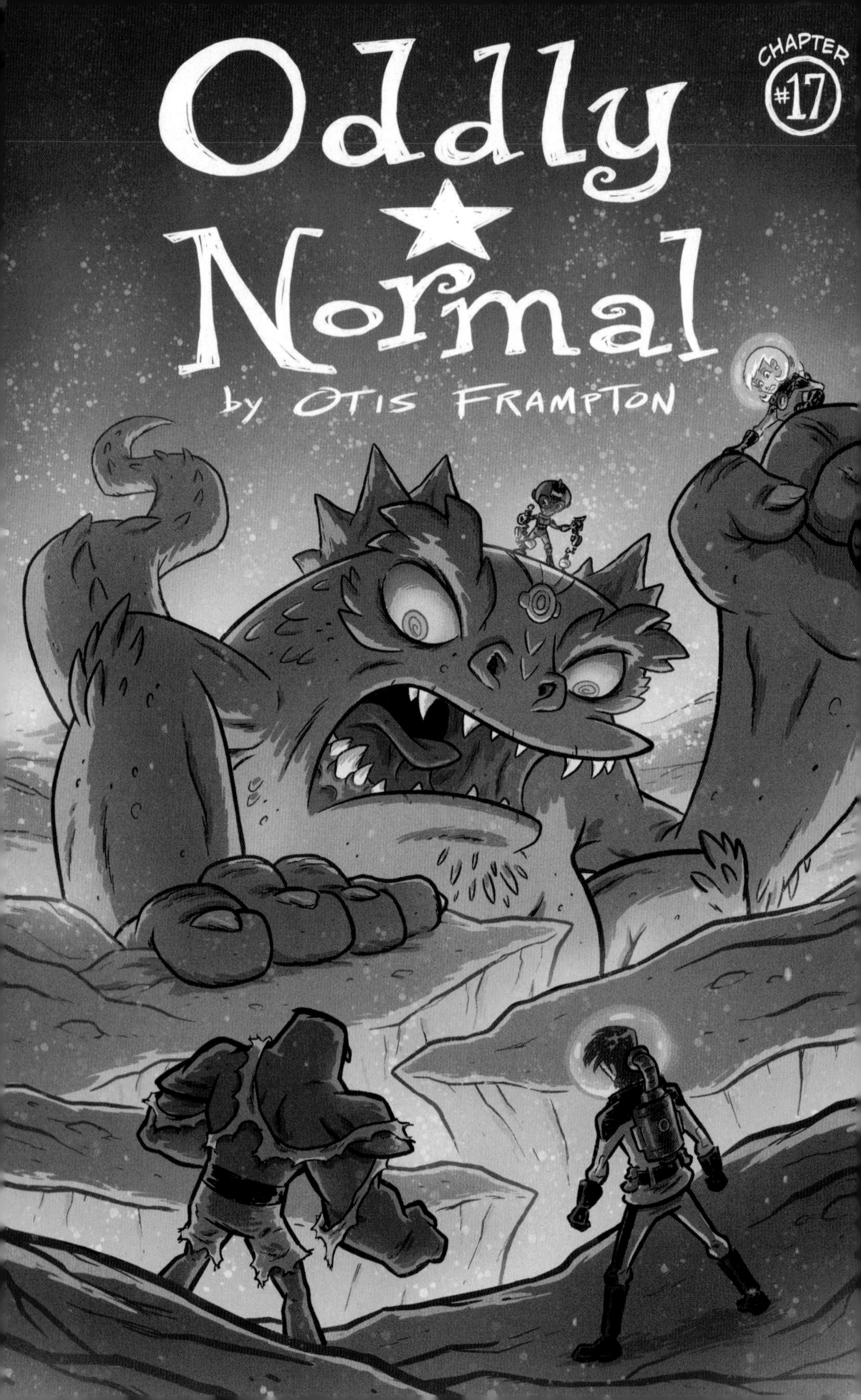
Oddly Normal
by OTIS FRAMPTON
CHAPTER
#17

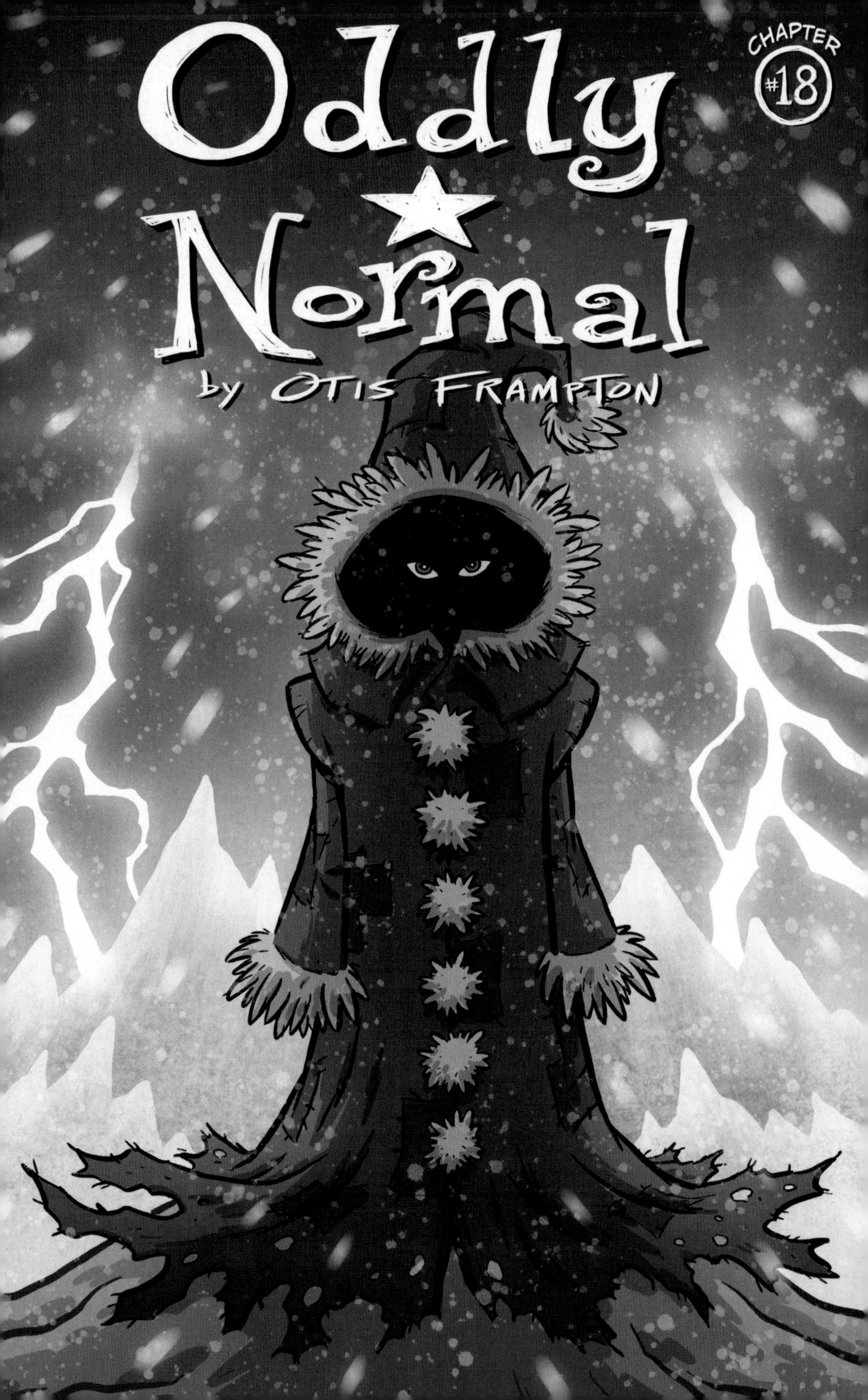
Oddly ★ Normal
CHAPTER #18
by OTIS FRAMPTON

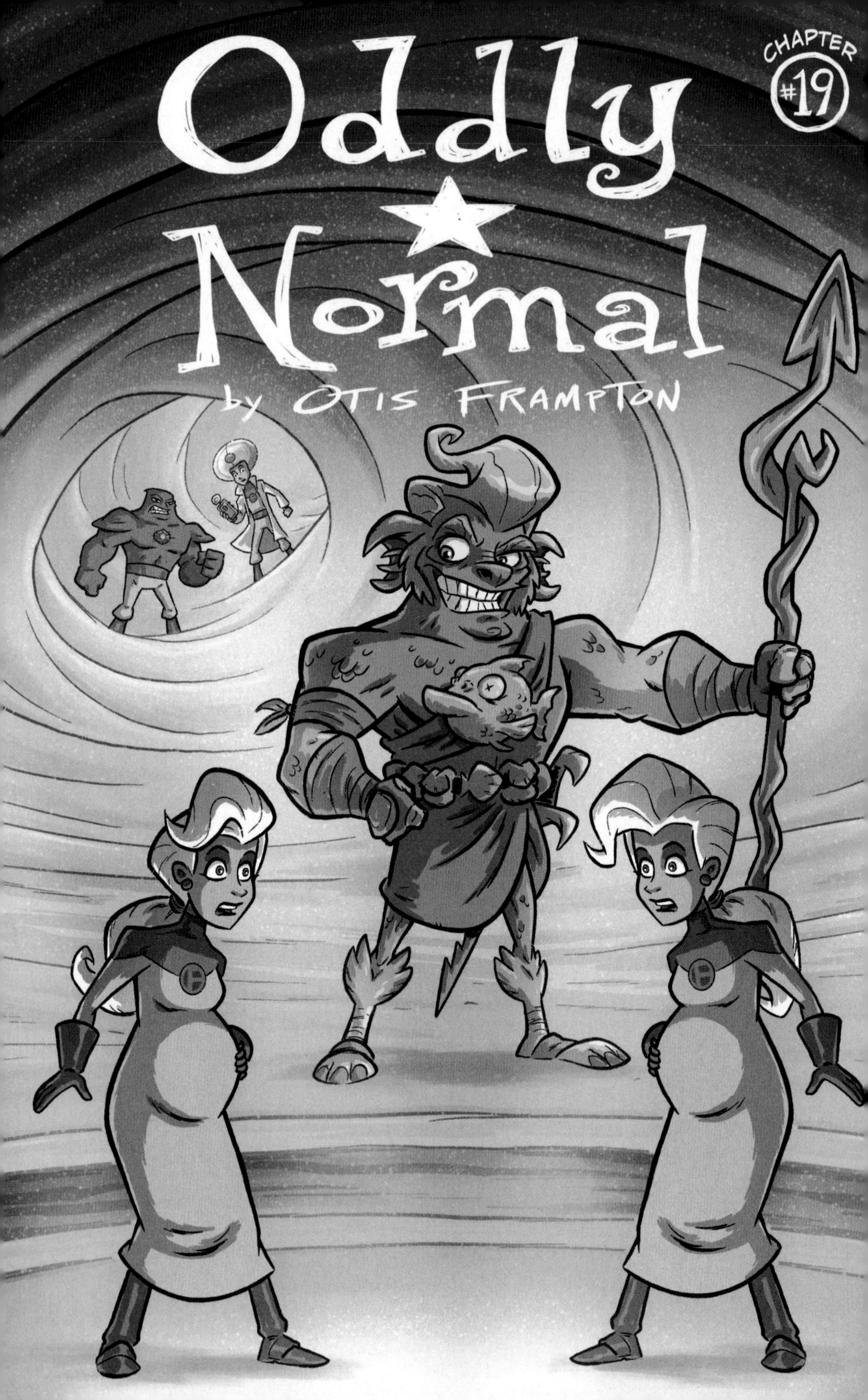
Oddly
Normal
by OTIS FRAMPTON
CHAPTER
#19

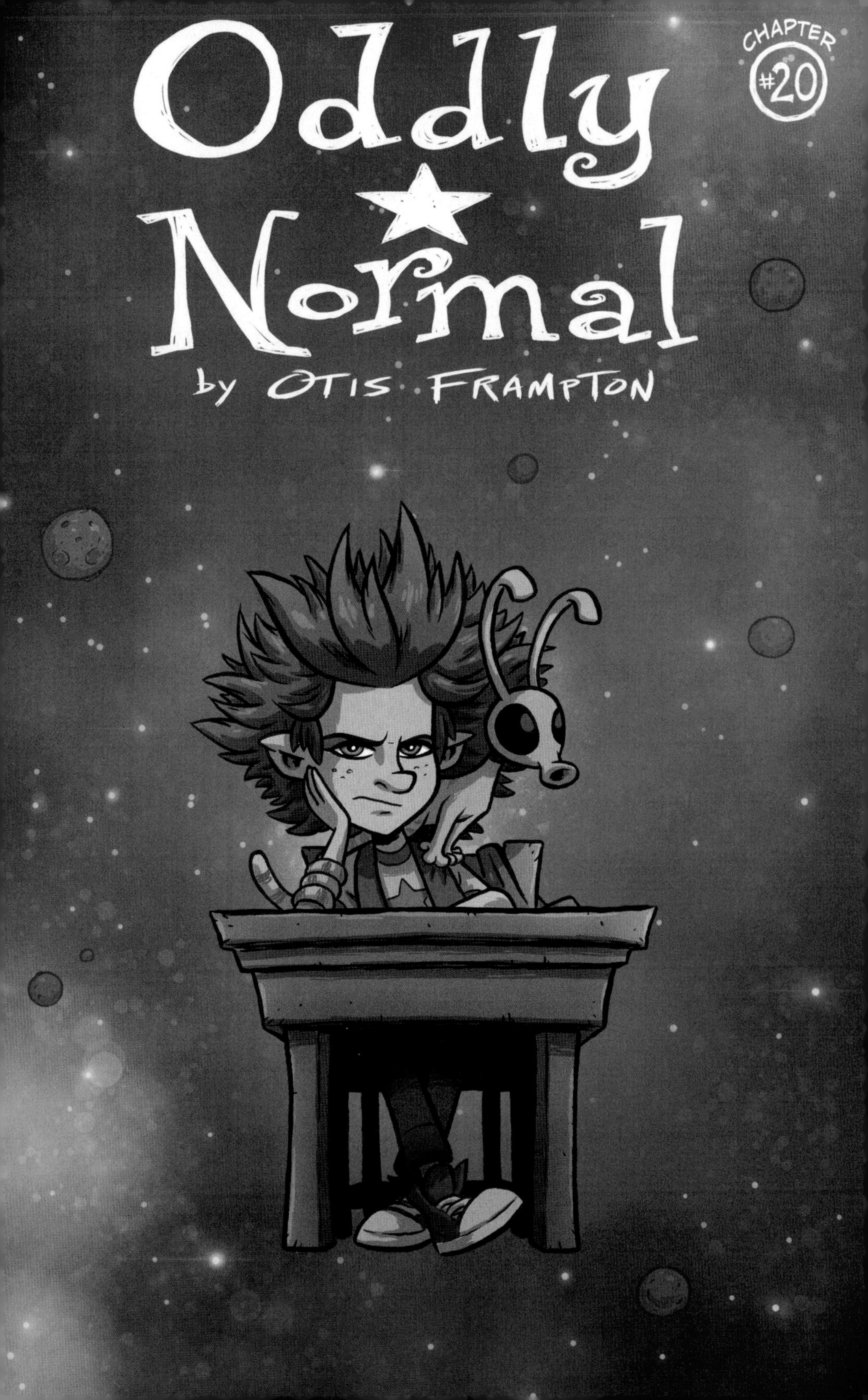
Oddly ★ Normal
CHAPTER #20
by OTIS FRAMPTON

ACKNOWLEDGMENTS

Thanks go out to everyone who helped make this book a reality!

First and foremost, thanks and love to my wonderful wife. Kate... this book wouldn't exist without you. You save my life every day.

Thanks and respect to Jeff Boison, Tricia Ramos, Eric Stephenson, and everyone at Image Comics for their patience and faith. This series has continued because they gave me the time I needed to make it happen.

Thanks also to the creative geniuses at Savage Interactive, the creators of the iPad app Procreate. Between books 3 and 4 of this series I started doing all of my drawing and painting in Procreate, and this book was created entirely in that app on the iPad Pro. Making comics in the comfort of my easy chair is wonderful!

I also want to say thanks to my readers for their patience. This book took longer to finish than I ever thought it would. So I hope you enjoy it and look forward to the next book, which (knock wood) will NOT take as long!

Thanks also to... Sergio Quijada, Carl Youngdahl, Leigh Lawhon Boone, Skottie Young, Hope Larson, Katie Cook, Michael Lovitz, Terri Lubaroff, Adam Cole, and (as always)...

My Mom.

ACKNOWLEDGMENTS

And many thanks to my wonderful Indiegogo supporters...

Charlie Aabø, Michael Adams, Greg Allen, Samuel G Alterio,
Cougar Andrews, Mark Arana, Luke Arthur, Alexi Balian,
Bryan Bean, Leigh Lawhon Boone, Stephanie Braman,
Karen Braman, Mitch & Elizabeth Breitweiser, Scott Brown,
Elliett Jonah Challans, Tababtha Pearl Challans,
Masson Patrick Challans, Christopher Cole, Shaun Colligan,
Janet Cotner, Kristy Golubiewski-Davis, demarts,
Molly deVries, DW, Mark Farris, Kevin Gault, Sam Gay,
Derek Gerlach, Matthew Gibson, HJ Gillham, Anya Glawe,
Philip Glover, Grant Gould, Maksim Grushin, Geoffrey Hartl,
Jessica Hausauer, Tony Hoaglund, Christina M Hughes,
Joseph Juvland, Sonja Kellen, Caleb Ketcherside,
Molly Kubiak, Rita Lanteri, Marcus Leab, Angela Lee,
Jeremy Lott, Terri Lubaroff, Rhoda Lucey, Brenna "Bee"
Lundquist, Leslie Lyles, Chris Magee, Kevin Marshall,
Michael May, Colleen McLaughlin, Sean McMillan,
Zack Meyman, Julie Mieseler, Timothy Morrell, Aaron Most,
Mark Nater, Rose Nelson, Michael Nguyen, Rob Noah,
Jo Otremba, Nate Pink, Tony Pirkl,, Debbie Pirkl, T.J. Pirkl,
rahnwestby, Luther Reid, Matthew Ries, Blair Rossi,
Neil Sambrook, Tim Scheidler, Leslee Sheu, Luke Thomas
Stebbing, Wendy Terry, Erik Thompson, Chris Tindale,
Peter Toman, Sarah Valair, Brian VanNierop, Jason Walker,
Brian Weissensee, Kyle Whitley, Michael Wright,
Carl Youngdahl, Angela Youngdahl, Scott Zirkel.

And lastly... a special thank you to:

Andrew S. Venteicher, MD, PhD, neurosurgeon with University of Minnesota Health

and

Matthew A. Tyler, MD, University of Minnesota-Department of Otolaryngology Head and Neck Surgery.

These two doctors also had a hand in making this book a reality by removing a tumor from my brain in May of 2020 that was, among other things, taking away my ability to see. My vision (and life) was restored by these two men, and I will forever be in their debt.

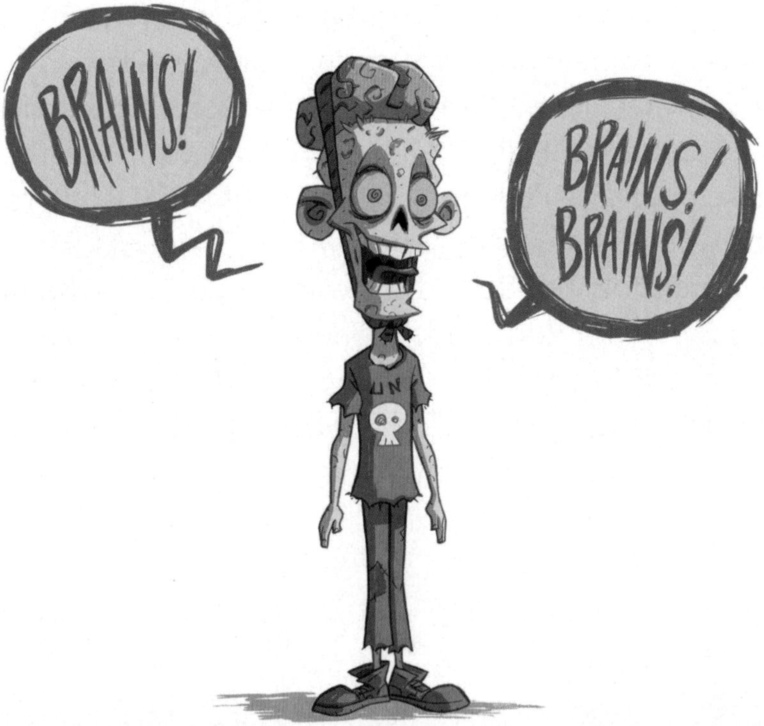
BRAINS!
BRAINS! BRAINS!

ALSO BY OTIS FRAMPTON

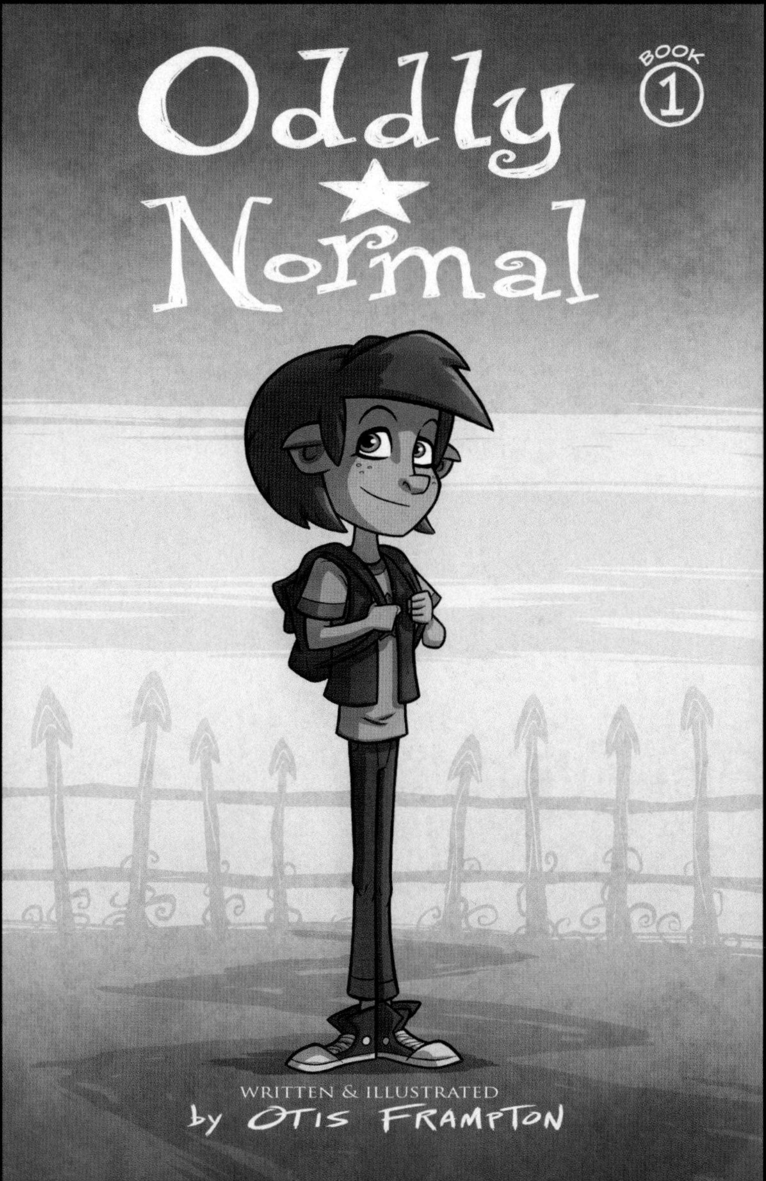
Oddly Normal
BOOK 1
WRITTEN & ILLUSTRATED
by OTIS FRAMPTON

ODDLY NORMAL BOOK 1

ALSO BY OTIS FRAMPTON

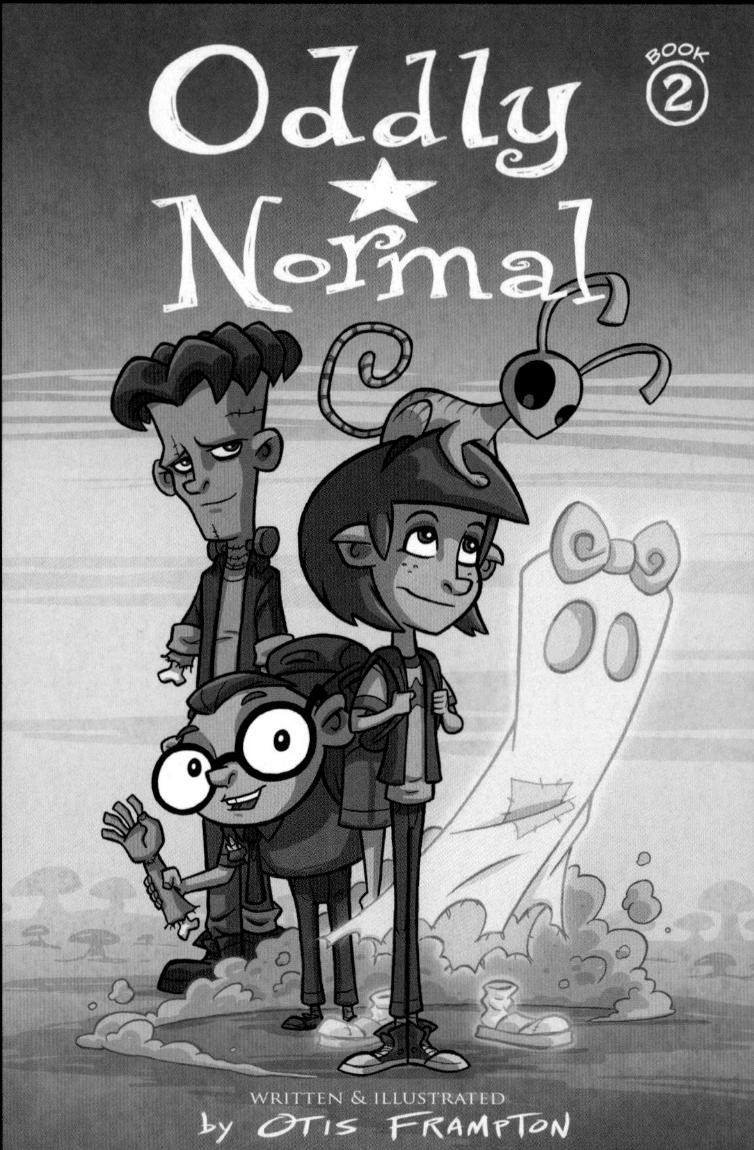
Oddly Normal
BOOK 2
WRITTEN & ILLUSTRATED
by OTIS FRAMPTON

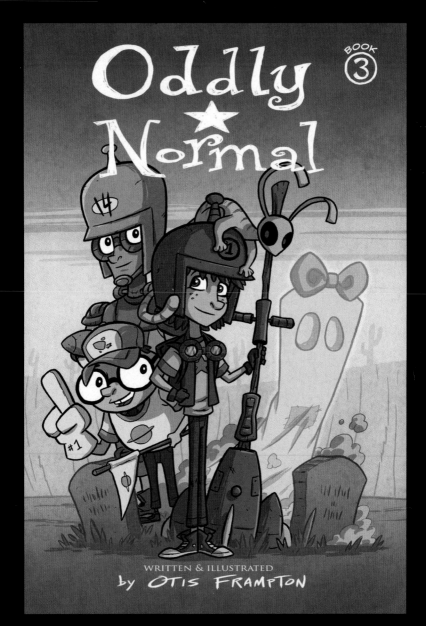

ODDLY NORMAL BOOK 3

Oddly ★ Normal

WILL RETURN IN

BOOK 5